About the Author

Born August 1969 in the north of England, fourth son to my Italian immigrant parents, I was raised until my teens in West Yorkshire before moving alone to Paignton in Devon. A few years later, I left Devon to return to Italy, travelling across the country, north and south. Eventually my journey took me to Corsica and then the south of France and later the south of Germany before I moved back to the south of France. My diverse travels, jobs and personal encounters allowed me to not only learn other languages but also meet an array of people from all walks of life. These encounters, along with friends, strangers and family, each of us, with our everyday daily challenges: joy, pain, happiness or heartache, have gifted me the joy of writing. Words and books have always shared their gifted energies, helping me grow. My wish is to spread this same energy through my words.

BUMP

Maurizio Biancardo

BUMP

Vanguard Press

VANGUARD PAPERBACK

© Copyright 2024
Maurizio Biancardo

The right of Maurizio Biancardo to be identified as author of
this work has been asserted by him in accordance with the
Copyright, Designs and Patents Act 1988.

All Rights Reserved

No reproduction, copy or transmission of this publication
may be made without written permission.
No paragraph of this publication may be reproduced,
copied or transmitted save with the written permission of the publisher, or in accordance
with the provisions
of the Copyright Act 1956 (as amended).

Any person who commits any unauthorised act in relation to
this publication may be liable to criminal
prosecution and civil claims for damages.

A CIP catalogue record for this title is
available from the British Library.

ISBN 978 1 80016 780 3

This is a work of fiction. Names, characters, businesses, places, events and incidents are
either the product of the author's imagination or used in a fictitious manner. Any
resemblance to actual persons, living or dead, or actual events is purely coincidental.

Vanguard Press is an imprint of
Pegasus Elliot Mackenzie Publishers Ltd.
www.pegasuspublishers.com

First Published in 2024

Vanguard Press
Sheraton House Castle Park
Cambridge England

Printed & Bound in Great Britain

Dedication

To all of you who walked by my side through the dark times, helping me reach the light. You know who you are. And what warms my heart is I do too.
A special thank you to ChrisChris, Mon Pote, Ma Princess et le beau gosse. Without forgetting "Lump" and you, you, you break my heart.

Acknowledgements

To all of you that loves our unique planet and its incredible animalia. You may often be working in the shadows but your silent, yet potent, actions are like the Earth's mightiest star on a foggy day. Little by little the sunlight comes breaking through. Lighting up the world.

A special thank you to all at Pegasus Productions. My old boss used to say. A great team is like an old grandfather clock. If you take out the big or small cogs it will just stop ticking. All your help, advice and presence during every step of the birth of my words into a book, show that all the cogs, big or small, are in the right places. The grandfather clock's tick tock of time making our dreams come true. Thank you.

CHAPTER ONE

CATCHING A FALLING LEAF

A strange presence hung in the atmosphere, as though young Marco was being secretly observed by an otherworldly entity. The air was filled with a bizarre energy, as though a storm was without doubt due to begin.

"Figlio di puttana. (Son of a bitch)," said Marco in a whispering chant under his breath his teeth grinding together, as though he was trying to squeeze the amplifying loathing out from himself. His angry silent outburst followed instantly by a calmer.

"Mi scusi, Mamma. (Sorry, mum)," said Marco. Thinking for a second of his attentive mother and her exceptional forgiving aura. Marco's thoughts divided in two. Forgiveness or vengeance? An angry rage surging once again upon his calm. It seemed as though even his mother's merciful nature's influence, seemingly not strong enough to calm down her son's anger this time. Marco's mind working overtime. Flashing thoughts of vengeful acts overpowering his emotions, amalgamated with wishful desires to have the power to be better, wiser, stronger and more intelligent. His soul, silently screaming only to be perceived by himself and his faithful gods.

"One day I'll be better, wiser, stronger and more intelligent and what's more. More powerful than any of them," said Marco, referring to his tyrannical supervisor and working colleagues, together with every other insensible, heartless, callous, cruel, evil individual who'd ever crossed his and his devoted mother's path. Even if his pardon was sincere before his mother and her dominating faith. Something inside of him was yearning for more. Something inside of him would even seemingly sacrifice his very soul to change his life and that of those he loved and cherished the most.

"Orrrrrr, ye going home to mummy now?" said an arrogant voice, mockingly blurting out between burst of swaggering laughter in a strong northern English accent. Marco gazing across from where he was sitting. His stare, like a hawk's glare upon its prey. The rage seething from his stomach, like an erupting volcano. His palms clenched around the steering wheel of his 1982 cerise Ford Fiesta as though he was trying to strangle it. The sheer force of his gesture causing the plastic to warp under his grip. The sardonic voice continuing to bedevil Marco, teasing his very poor broken English and strong Italian accent.

"Don'ta forgeta to tello the mama to maka the spaghetti," said the snorting, guffawing bursts of roaring sniggers chillingly echoing into the atmosphere, like pigs being slaughtered. Bill and his three fellow local colleagues persisting with their insults and offensive hand gestures. Holding their clutches out in front of their faces, the back of their hands facing Marco, thumbs pressed against their index fingers trying to mimic an Italian speaking with kinesics. At the same time blurting out, like relentless parrot's vulgar racial obscenities.

"Fucking I-Tie, Spic, Spaghetti-Slurper, Salami face, Geep, Grease Ball."

"Fuck off back to your own country and take your mother with you, slimy foreign piece of shit," said Bill and his fellow colleagues. Tears arising within Marco's eyes, like somebody having just poked him in the heaviness of hearts. Using all his force to fight his sob, not wanting Bill or his bullying colleagues to see him and profit even more from his hurt. Gritting his teeth as though he was about to receive a severe punch, Marco raising his head, catching a glimpse of his fury in the rear-view mirror, it was as though he could see the hateful vengeful thoughts that were overpowering his mind seeping out of him, like he'd been possessed by some diabolic force. His abhor enlarging, his right hand moving, like a controlled robot from the steering wheel to the door handle. In his young nineteen-year-old head, Marco was thinking how he could fight the four men. Maybe he wouldn't win, maybe he'd be seriously hurt, but he knew his rage would bring brutal injuries to his adversaries. A lightning intuition flashed in his mind. He'd start with Bill. Bill a ginger, spotty six foot two and as broad as a grizzly bear obnoxious bully. Although twice the size of Marco. He was as agile and as fast as a tortoise. Marco contemplating his plan of attack in his brain.

"If I bring Bill down maybe the others will flee, like scared rats?" said Marco. The others, half the size as Bill, and half as broad.

"Si andro per Bill che il grasso, allampanato, bullismo stronzo merita di essere partato giu un passo o due." (Yeah I'll go for Bill that fat, lanky, bullying arsehole deserves to be brought down a step or two), said Marco, under his breath. The car door clicking open, causing a sudden gush of cold air to enter the auto, like an angel's whisper against Marco's heinous caprice. Marco gazing again in the rear-view mirror. A chimera apparition of his father appearing in the back seat, causing Marco to relive the scene of his father's last gestures and his final devoted words to his loving only son. Although he did not know at the time, theses lovingly spoken words from his dad, would be the last he would ever hear him pronounce.

"Siamo fieri di te." (We are proud of you).

"Sono stato donato da Dio per avere un figlio come te.(I've been gifted by God to have a son like you)."

"Un giorno sarai l'uomo della casa." (One day you'll be the man of the house).

"Proteggere sempre tua madre." (Always protect your mother).

"Ti amo (I love you)," said Marco's father before leaving one cool spring morning for work as normal, only the evening he would never return. The doting smile and affectionate words of his father's once expressive emotions, ingrained in Marco's very essence for eternity, especially.

"Always protect your mother," said Marco's father. Bill disappearing through the factory's large, long, thick plastic strips, hanging down over the spacious door area allowing easy access for delivery trucks as well as permitting the forklift to manoeuvre freely, but also stopping the cool autumn air from entering the workshop area. His malicious working colleagues having followed him back into the printer's factory, like sheep following their shepherd. Each having disrespectfully thrown their cigarette butt ends onto the floor, not even taking the care to extinguish them. Marco now alone letting his emotions go. Tears rolling down his face, as though his earlier protecting force having been mysteriously taken, each unstoppable oozing drop, carrying months of pain and torture.

If only Bill and his sheep following unintelligible colleagues could have seen or endured an ounce of Marco's and his family's misfortune. Would they really be so unkind to him? said Marco in his mind, at the same time wiping his weep, taking a deep breath, like a knight preparing to go into battle. Glaring a long moment at his reflection in the rear-view mirror, secretly wishing to see the phantasmal vision of his dad again. He'd inherited the handsome features of his father, his thick curly long black hair and piercing green eyes, combined with the soft caring smile of his mother and her elegant allure. Now integrated into a five-foot nine sportive physique. Marco's reserved timid character turning many a young girls stare. But his only devotion was to his mother. Never in the seven months which had now passed from his father's last breath, had he forgotten his promise to always protect his mother and that he was now the man of the house. Turning the key in the ignition. The car started after the second attempt, a thick burst of black smoke coughing out of the exhaust pipe, the car was the oldest and the less technologized as well as the rustiest vehicle parked in the factory's car park. But Marco didn't mind. It had been bought from the last of his father's savings. His father, Arnaldo, never forgetting his promise before leaving their small Italian village in the South of Italy only nine months earlier, to buy his son a car. As he drove across the busying streets. Shops and cafes seemed to be filled with pensioners all looking for a bargain or a familiar friendly face to have a chat with. School having just finished and busloads of over excited kids quickly filled the town, each staring more at their mobile phones then as too where they were walking. The mass of pensioners all expressing the same guise.

"Kids today."

All seemingly having past an era where their memories reminded them of their once modernising youth. Marco having finished his agonising morning shift, already apprehending the six-a.m. clocking in time of the following day. Only Thursday and Friday to go then his much-needed weekend far from Bill and the others.

"What he wouldn't give to never step inside that factory again," said Marco. This very thought whirring in his mind as he parked the car, walked up the seven flights of steps to his council estate flat, turned the key in the cold unwelcoming wooden door and slumped himself on the couch, as though all his force having now been drained from him. 'Pasta' the dog lifted his head then turned over in his basket as if to say.

"Oh, it's only Marco."

This was the welcoming Pasta gave Marco every day, he would only become extra companionable around six p.m. where and when he knew Marco would take him for a long walk and when they were back home, Anna, Marco's mother would be home too. And a bowl full of food would be waiting. Pasta was a cross between a Jack Russel and a Westie, his fur was brown and white, one brown ear one white ear, his face was that of a Westie with a constant expression, except when Anna was home, of.

'Look at my sad face my life is so hard'.

He was a little bigger than a Jack Russel but bared the distinguished tail of one. In all fairness maybe Pasta had, had a hard life. He'd followed Anna home one night, strayed lost and as skinny as a rake. For some unknown reason he'd fled every other person who'd tried to approach him. But not Anna. Maybe his sixth sense knew Arnaldo and Marco would soon not be there. Maybe even with his scraggy undernourished heartbreaking façade, Pasta already knew he would be Anna's force and comfort throughout the upcoming anguishing months and clairvoyant events to come. Marco stretched his lethargic arm over to the remote control. With a click, bright images filled the bleakly furnished front room, the sudden light and babbling voices, not disturbing Pasta nor the more, still happily snoring in his basket. Marco flicking through the channels, various programmes and repetitive soap operas seemingly all expressing the same story line. Not really understanding the dialect vocabulary. Marco's English still very week, he settled for a cookery programme, following more the actions then the linguistic expressions. It didn't matter he only understood two words out of every ten. Cooking he knew a lot about, taught by his father, mother, Zia Maria (Aunt Maria), and Zio Antonio, (Uncle Antonio). Cooking he could understand. The tittle of the dish being cooked, appearing in written text at the bottom of the TV Set.

"Toad in the hole."

(Rospo nel buco).

Marco inquiringly looking up each word in his English dictionary which represented this typical English dish. Having translated every lexical. Screaming out in disgust.

"Madonna cosa c'é di sbagliato con queste inglese?"

(Madonna what's wrong with these English?).said Marco. Nauseated thinking real toads were being cooked, he quickly flicked off the TV and walked over to the balcony to get some much needed fresh air. As he ogled at the people below, like an active miniature world animating before his stare. The autumn wind, whistling through the sky carrying the air of winter and its changing climate. The firmament filled with dotted clouds representing different shapes and sizes. Every now and again the sun breaking through causing an effulgent luminous rayon to emphasize the resplendent metamorphosing pigmentation of the tumbling seasonal herbage. In the near distance the distinctive coastal line of the sandy beach, with the rippling froths of the North sea's waves washing upon the arenicolous shores. A gust of wind pervaded under the balcony's corroded metal barrier, swirling up the last of the fallen leaves from the Clematis. Which now looked more an abandoned bird's nest. Drooping twigs and lifeless manifestation. The Clematis once bravura periwinkle blossoms now as distant as the summer's warmth. The last two dried out khaki foliage twirling in the air for a second, before spiralling down to the old sod below, like pirouetting Maple leaves waning out of sight. Marco watching the fading leaves being carried safely to another place.

"If only humankind could have the same power and knowledge to displace themselves with such ease." said Marco. This very poignant thought persistent in his mind as he re-entered the living room. Gazing around at the under furnished accommodation, which consisted of a small non modern kitchen adorned with an electric cooker and oven, a stainless-steel sink encompassed by a two door cabinet. To the left side of the basin a small pantry opening, covered by dangling curtain beads. Opposite the sink another set of three cabinets with a laminated work surface. Above three more kitchenette cabinets the same length. The old fridge rattling, like a clangourous monster in the far corner. The rectangular window allowing only the minimum of light to infiltrate the area. The window dominated by the passing corridors which accessed the other apartment residence.

Opposite the kitchen was Anna's room. A big double bed. A large crucifix poised over the bed head. Two small wood effect bedside cabinets, each missing the draw handle. A five-draw chest with the same wood affect impression, standing across from the bed, decorated with a photo of Jesus on one side and Marco's father Arnaldo on the other. In the middle a large three-way mirror, reflecting the images of Christ and Marco's dad around the room. Thick brown curtains hanging, like hanged monk's tunics covering the large square windows, blocking most of the sunlight from breaking through. At the end of the corridor Marco's bedroom, a single bed, a large wardrobe, a bedside cabinet with a night lamp and an old wooden chair. A few posters of his homeland, Italy, blue tacked against the woodchip wallpaper. Next to the entrance a small bathroom, consisting of a small bath. Simple square white tiles seven tiles high around the bath area. At the tap end of the bathtub a small, glazed glass window, overlooking the same corridor as the kitchen pane. To the baths left, a chipped white sink with only the cold water working. Above a sliding two mirrored door cabinet. Behind the door, the toilet. Next to the lavatory a plastic clothes basket for dirty clothes. Anna worked in a laundrette, mostly washing and ironing other people's clothes, but she would stay over some times and finish hers and Marco's laundry. The front room, the largest in the flat, consisted of a three-seater old couch and a single armchair. Their tattered textile covered by Anna's knitted square blankets, bringing a touch of warmth and colour to the bare living room area. In the far corner opposite the balcony a circular table with four wooden chairs, the fifth chair in Marco's room. Behind the 90s TV set, which poised upon a small wooden table. A glass cabinet filled with a cherished, porcelain ornament of the Madonna inside. Above a picture of Our Lady and a simple photograph of Anna, Arnaldo and Marco, taken the day before they'd left Italy for England. Every room without exception was decorated with magnolia painted woodchip wallpaper. As Marco stared around at the bleak surroundings, he was far from knowing the paranormal events which were awaiting him within the forthcoming hours, would take him far away from this forlorn ambiance. But even worse far away from his devoted promise to his father.

"Proteggere sempre tua madre." (Always protect your mother).

The light of day was slowing drifting away. Pasta as if some inner seasonal alarm clock having just rang with him, jumping out of his basket and began welcoming Marco. Wiggling his little body in a zigzag. Marco knew it was time for his walk and without hesitating grabbing his coat, Pasta's lead and the battery illuminating dog collar, along with the pocket size torch. Before leaving the flat, clicking on the dining room light so that his mother, due home within the next hour wouldn't have to enter a gloomy obscure apartment. Little loving gestures of this sort, Marco and Anna always deeded for one another. Closing the door behind him Pasta, already running down the steps his lackadaisical attitude now as distant within him as his once troublesome times. He waited excitedly in the hallway entrance obediently staying put until Marco having caught up to him. A distant neighbour entering the digit data security code and a second later pushing open the apartment blocks hallways glass doors, acknowledging Marco with a polite.

"Good evening," said the neighbour. Marco returning the respectful gesture with also a good evening. Before exiting the building clicking Pasta's swivel hook lead into the collars secured ring. Pasta was a very placid dog, but from some reason he disliked to a very aggressive degree black dogs. Small, fat, large or small, he would growl at them in a very defensive manner and should they dare to fight with him. Then fight he would. Marco and Anna putting this disesteem hostility to something from Pasta's past and they'd just try to eschew any black dogs whilst walking him. Once outside Pasta relieved his natural urge and peed on the nearest bush. The brightest star beginning to dusk in the near but far distance, bestowing the earth's atmosphere with a magnificent crepuscular crimson ruddiness. Marco and Pasta persisted heading towards the seashores, walking through the large public park, dominated by a magnanimous quantity of sublime saplings, bushes, shrubs, flowers, herbs, plants and trees. *Alder, Ash, Beech, Birch, Blackthorn, Cherry, Crab, Dogwood, Elder, Elm, Hawthorn, Hazel, Holly, Hornbeam, Juniper, Lime, Maple, Oak, Rowan, Spindle, Whitebeam, Willow and Yew.* All huddled near and far, like harmonising energies. Each in their own specific naturel graceful manner, metamorphosing their resplendent splendiferous coloration from the sun's iridescence aura, as well as preparing their plantae essence for the cyclical transition. Marco watching Pasta ruffle through the diversified perishing foliage's, reminiscing about his father's lost presence and devoted love. As another bunch of tumbling leaves glided in different directions and sped towards the ground. Marco reliving a joyful moment back in the south of Italy with his dad only two years earlier. Again, the autumn wind was passing fast, like a quick visiting relative, presenting the gracious splendour of the seasonal transition. Arnaldo loved autumn more than any other season, for him it represented not only a festival of contrasting glorious colours. But harmonization, as though Mother Nature and Father Time were in perfect balance. Resting together, like a midsummer siesta, recuperating some much-needed force and energies before the harsh winter months and the challenging spring's workload. This love for autumn and nature having been transmitted into Marco, like some chromosome genetic code. Visualising his father in his revering state, running under the trees, kicking the dense pile of tumbled leaves, like an excited child at Christmas running through the snow, trying at the same time to catch a falling leaf. Something very difficult to do. His father with his superstitious family inherited beliefs telling Marco.

"If you manage to catch a falling leaf, you can make a wish and maybe your wish will come true," said Arnaldo. A fall two years earlier Arnaldo having achieved for the very first time in his life, to catch a falling leaf. He'd wished to come and bring his family to England. Wanting to flee the Mafia run district and poverty of his native village and land. Give his adored son and wife a chance to live in a place a country, where freedom of speech and expression were as respected as God himself. An aspiration fulfilled ten months later but with heart-breaking consequences. Arnaldo having been killed only six months after his arrival in England. Hit by a lorry while simply crossing a road. He'd stopped to buy himself and his fellow workers some fish and chips, wanting for the first time to relish in the great British tradition. Happy and content, running gladdened back to the building site where he'd found a job. His manual constructive knowledge and skills, along with his peaceful caring character, very much needed, appreciated and honoured by his co-working colleagues. In his joyful state he'd forgotten in England people drive on the left-hand side. Having seen his right side clear, he'd naively, foolishly stepped in front of a camion. Hit on a busy road at 50mph. Arnaldo having died instantly his head having smashed against the tarmac, like an egg. Anna and Marco having stayed in England to pursue Arnaldo's dream. Something which proved harder for Marco and he secretively knew, although they never talked about it, like an avoided subject. Difficult for Anna too. Another leaf tumbled gliding past Marco's right shoulder as though to tease him. He contemplated for a moment about his father's superstition credence.

"If just by catching a leaf you could grant yourself a wish," said Marco in an optimistic tone to himself. If he had an aspiration, firstly it would be for his father to be back by their sides. But Marco, like his mother had been taught to except death as part of life, even though painful. Arnaldo a great fan and amateur philosophe had often throughout his life quoted his admired philosophers. Platon, Aristote, Thomas Jefferson, Socrate and so forth. When he talked about death, having seen and witnessed his family and many friends' part long before him. Arnaldo would simply quote Socrates philosophy.

"Death maybe the greatest of all human blessings," said Arnaldo. This educative way of rationalising life was very present in Marco's intellect. Another few leaves floated in a zigzagging manner before Marco, as though to goad him. It worked seconds later, Marco found himself running under the Maples trees trying to catch a drifting tumbling leaf. His wish clear in his mind.

"I wish I could speak fluent English."

"That way I'll find myself a better job and look after Mia Madre, (My mother), better," said Marco. He optimistically to himself. Pasta now off his lead, wandering a little further away, ignoring Marco as though embarrassed to be seen alongside a crazed grown man, trying desperately to catch falling leaves. More leaves fell and whizzed past Marco, like miniature descending fighter jets. The dusking sun was shimmering its last shafts of light onto the golden foliage bestowing a magnificent magical aura. Two leaves affixed together spiralled, like a miniature helicopter landing to the left side of Marco's shoulder. Another larger leaf elegantly drifted almost in slow motion towards him. Marco's palms held out facing upward as though he was about to pray. The leaf heading right for his open hands, but at the last second, like a kite in a gusting wind, it whirled to his right. Marco changing position blaming his incapacity to catch a simple leaf, from the surrounding bushes growing under the bulky tree trunks. Standing in silence, a quick stare to make sure Pasta hadn't strayed too far and no black dogs were in a threatening vicinity. All was OK concerning Pasta. Gawking up into the trees, many of their branches, already denuded from their once dominating greenery. Waiting patiently. Nothing happened, it was as though the leaves had supernaturally communicated with one another, depriving Marco for some strange unknown reason any chance of catching a leaf and grant his self- desire. Marco time lagging a little more. Not a single leaf tumbling. The air as still as concrete, not even the remotest of breezes. Marco losing his patients turning, heading towards Pasta who was happily continuing his promenade towards the beach, only a stone throw away from the park.

"Pasta, vieni qui." (Pasta, come here), said Marco in an authoritative voice. Pasta just turning giving an inquisitive glare and carrying disobediently on his way. Marco yelling again only louder repeating his command in English, only his Italian accent dominating his intonation.

"Pasta, comé here, Pasta comé here," said Marco. Pasta obeying Marco's order as much as a naughty child would do as he was told in a toy store, advancing happy and go lucky on his own. Marco a little annoyed raising his voice another decibel.

"Pasta, Pasta, *Pasta*!" said Marco. A young couple strolling through the park hands held together in a lovers embrace, witnessing Marco almost screaming *Pasta*. Not having noticed his dog. Pasta, already heading across the hill side and down the meadow's embankment towards the coastal shores in the now near distant. The young local man acknowledging Marco in a friendly but curious manner.

"Listen mate, if you want Pasta, there's a fast-food shop on the main street that sells pizza, I'm sure they'll do you some *Pasta* or *Spaghetti*, or something of that sort, or right mate," said the young man, causing the young girl to burst into a juvenile laugh. Marco not having understood all of what the man had said, just politely smiling. His wish to be able to speak fluent English, even more dominant in his mind, alongside his embarrassment, wishing his mother had chosen a different name for Pasta. Just before leaving the park, the sun was rippling its flaming semblance across the seawater, transforming the green sluggish appearance of the North Sea, into undulating twinkle of phosphorescent light. Even the tips of the bulging waves having metamorphosed into alabaster holy glow, as though every drop of Adams ale was transporting angel's wings ashore. From nowhere a sudden zephyr causing a mass of leaves to float past Marco, like plummeting stones, causing him to turn and face this strange unexpected phenome. To his great surprise the heavenly breeze having detached a multitude of differential foliage from different trees, all gliding at a deviating pace and height towards him. Marco ceasing his chance to grasp a leaf, but even with this unpredicted swarm the leaves were whizzing, twirling, flying, spinning, and floating past him. It seemed almost a taunting and even cruel display of chance, as the earlier clusters of foliage, rapidly diminishing. When all of a sudden, Marco's right hand clasped a small Maple leaf, about four centimetres wide and five centimetres long. The fragile blistered leaf didn't crumple or break from his grip. Opening his hand and staring a little moment at the flimsy object. He could distinctively still see the three translucent stem forms. One stretching in the middle the other to its left and right, like an arrow etching pointing downwards. There were still traces of its once dark green pigment, now manifested in small dark dots, like freckles. Certainly, for most people it would have merely meant another perished autumn leaf. But to Marco, it was a chance of a wish. An inner warmth of achievement along with a conquered quest, dominated his footsteps as he heads towards the beach. Whispering again to himself his personal desire.

"I wish I could speak fluent English," said Marco.

CHAPTER TWO

A STORM BREWING

The suns flaming effulgence gradually waning in the vastness. Its almighty force soothingly immersing into the Oceans liquid, like a majestic superior heavenly force easing into a soothing bath. The rippling waves carrying a harmonious resonance as they softly washed upon the sabulous oceanfront. The last of the twilight afterglow transforming the beaches sandy hue into a sumptuous saffron luminosity, causing the small fragments of quartz crystals to coruscate, like miniature stars. Marco walking along side Pasta. Pasta having re-acknowledge him as his so-called master. The air mild and still. Marco taking off his shoes and socks, rolling up the bottom off his jeans a few notches and promenading across the sands. His feet squishing into the sodden earthen, bequeathing him with a strange sensation. As he approached the oceans tide line, the seas ebb quite some distance from the main shores. The wild blue yonder having metamorphosed into a sumptuous azure. There wasn't a cloud or star in the sky, not even the North Stellar visible, only the waxing beginning of a new moon in the far radius.

Marco and Pasta alone, not another soul to be seen or heard for what seemed miles around. Far behind him the distant street, shops and house lights of his now hometown having illuminated. Bestowing him a reassurance that he hadn't wandered too far. The calm waves washing gently over his feet, the first few seemed ice cold, but Marco's naturel body heat adapting, like a chameleon to this changing atmospheric temperature. Pasta splashing through the water, like a happy child on a summer's beach. A mass of migrating geese breaking the oceans harmonious melody, chattering in a loud honk, like nagging old men and ladies. Marco wondered.

Where were they heading?

Which lands and cultures would they cross throughout their journey? What would they see?

Would all of them make it? said Marco. His questioning daydreaming thoughts distracted by a large piece of drifting wood, resembling something from a wooden case with something written in small white paint upon it. The driftwood drawing nearer to Marco, only to be swept back by the ebb, repeating this teasing gesture several times. Marco intrigued to see what was written upon the piece of timber waiting patiently by the seas ebb. Not before long he was holding the driftwood in his hands, having lost his patients and waded further into the sea to grab it. The length of lumber, rough to touch, untreated and rectangular, around two-feet-long and ten inches wide. Written athwart was New Zealand.

"New Zealand," said Marco reading the inscription to himself, at the same time wondering where this piece of wood had come from.

Had it been part of a large case? Fallen from a shipwrecked vessel?

Had it been carried to the English shores all the way from New Zealand?

Maybe there was treasure to be found? said Marco. A multitude of questions swarming his brain as he softly caressed his right hand over the voyaging object in his grasp, wiping away the granules of sand. Abruptly a scintillating light in the far distance caught Marco's attention. Blinking his eyes, a couple of times to adapt better to the darkening nightfall. It happened again, a distinct gleam.

"Tesoro." (Treasure), said Marco, his heart racing twice as fast, a burst of adrenalin having shot through his whole body, like a puissant electrical charge, running towards the glittering unknown object. Pasta excitedly sprinting by his side not questioning where his master was heading and why his was scuttling. In the vastness where the brightest star having earlier dusked an accumulation of rumbling clouds, began uprising in the atmosphere, forming an image of a mountainous panorama. The magnitude of manifesting nebulosi seemed to be rising from the ocean rather than forming in the earth's atmosphere. Not before long excited, curious and a little out of breath, Marco and Pasta reached the area from where the scintillating light was coming. Marco expecting to find a treasure chest filled with gold and other precious, valuable jewels. But instead, he was greeted by an enormous spherical object, resembling a giant boulder, only a few feet away from the tides line, but a good distance from the shores. Shining his powerful flashlight against it. It looked grey-coloured and at closer view seemed to be composed of mud, sand or clay.

"Moeraki Massi." (Moeraki boulders), said Marco in an excited yell. He'd read about them curiously only a few weeks earlier at the local library, Marco always having been interested and fascinated in the earths unexplained occurrences. These unusual large mudstone spherical boulders, found between Moeraki and Hampden in New Zealand, with various unexplained myths and legends concerning the strange phenomenon of the boulder's happenings.

"But New Zealand was in the Pacific Ocean, over eleven thousand miles from Great Britain."

"How in God's name did one of them arrive on the north English coast?" said Marco befuddled. Without warning where the clouds having magnitude, now resembling a frothing gigantic monster from another world, immense flashes of light, illuminated the obscurity of the hours of darkness. Another powerful flash. Pasta looking at Marco as if to say.

Oh, can't you see there's a storm brewing let's get out of here, said Pasta's stare. Another almighty shimmer, followed by a horrifying rumble and a powerful gigantic crack. Marco looking at Pasta and acknowledge his anxious questioning cute glare with a gesture from his head, moving from his right to his left, as if to say.

You're right Pasta, let's go, said Marco's head gesture. Then it came again the glittering light having intrigued Marco and caused him to run so far out from the shores. At the bottom of the strange sphere-shaped boulder, a smaller object twinkled again in the lightening's flashes. Marco approached eagerly.

"Tesoro." (Treasure), said Marco in a soft whisper to himself, at the same time directing his flashlight at the unknown entity. As he got nearer, kneeling, like a worshiping follower before his master. The shaft of light from his torch directed onto what seemed to be nothing more than a large pebble. But as he raised the curious oval shaped mineral now in his grasp, around seven by five inches in size closer to his view. Firstly, noticing it was a magnificent olive green. Extremely smooth to touch and the whole pebble form thing, covered with peculiar hieroglyphics in a sublime sapphire tint, which appeared to be encapsulated within the weird stone.

Marco ogling closer examining the mysterious matter. In the middle of the strange mass, a smaller decagon shape with what seemed a miniature brain characteristic embedded. Diminutive electrical discharges, like fulgurations were supernaturally surging from the alien shaped form. Marco so captivated by his find not noticing the storm having now surrounded him. A gigantic mass of Undulatus Asperatus clouds having moulded above him, hoovering, like a menacing presence. Multitudes of lightning flashes fulgurated from all around him, causing the electrical shimmering's to expulse from the encapsulated cerebrum. The flares so bright, causing Marco to squint, liked he'd just stared directly at the sun. Without warning a deafening vociferous crackling fulminated from the heavens. The thunderous roar so loud, Pasta, scared, began running in a yelping panic back towards the shores. Marco also shaken by this clamorous admonition, rapidly placing the stone object in his left jean pocket, stuffing his socks into his right jean pocket, and swiftly placing his sneakers over his bare feet. In the centre of the Undulatus Asperatus clouds, a Fall streak Hole, having mystifyingly appeared directly over where Marco was stood. In his panic to place his sneakers on, Marco losing his balance causing him to fall onto the dewy sand. Now laid on his back staring up at the petrifying yet majestic sight. As the Fall streak Hole seemed to widen, revealing the celestial sphere. A travers the opening he could see a multitude of stars glittering their supreme galactic aura, as though another world was levitating above that of which Marco and the rest of mankind lived. Marco feeling a sudden warm sensation from his left pocket, reaching his left hand to pull out his weird and wonderful discovered object, as his touch came into contact with the smooth rock like substance. Without warning a single bolt of lightning struck Marco at his forehead, his arms flopping to his side in a motionless state. Darkness and silence were now his world.

CHAPTER THREE

A MOTHER'S STRENGTH

Anna had been at home a little over half an hour ago. She'd smiled whilst hanging her coat on the hook in the hallway entrance, because of Marco's loving gesture having left the light on for her. Entering the front room, she gazed at Pasta's empty basket and then directed her regard to the photo of her, Arnaldo and Marco. A half-hearted expression overpowering her emotions. Tears overwhelmingly mounting in her eyes, one dripped uncontrollably from her right eye. Anna taking a big sigh as though to fill her lungs with oxygen, having twisted her stare to her precious porcelain Madonna ornament. A courageous force as only women truly have surged within her, as she secretly whispered in her mind, her mouth as still as a ventriloquist.

Thank you for Marco, said Anna, at the same time letting out her held respiration seconds after her merciful thought. Without any further hast pushing aside her wondering thoughts, entered the kitchenette, proceeding with her chores, firstly preparing Pasta's food. Then making herself a nice warm cup of tea, having adapted to this British custom almost as though she was a native. Clicking on the TV, sitting, relaxingly in the armchair. As she sipped at her hot tea, she was pondering what she would make to eat for her and Marco. The storm having intensified, the deluge thrashing against the windows almost horizontally. A thunderous crack followed forthwith by a powerful flash of lightning illuminating the wild blue yonder as well as the living room, like an otherworldly firework display. The lights flickering as though some poltergeist having possessed apartment. The widows vibrated and clattered as though a gigantic monster having grasped the building and was shaking at it, as if to bring it to a tumbling rubble. The howling gale encircling the whole town. The ceilings light, lightbulb erupted from its socket and bounced off the couch tumbling onto the carpeted floor without breaking. Anna instinctively picking it up. The bulb was red hot. She let out a scream and let the fragile glass object fall from her grasp, this time it shattered on the floor. A terrifying intuitional feeling arose within Anna, taking the recent events as a pre-warning omen.

"Marco."

"Something has happened to him," said Anna. Her powerful motherly sixth sense hollering inside of her. Anna running to the widow, staring panicky outside, hoping to see Marco running home with Pasta. As she gazed scrutinizing every inch of the area below. Apart from the winds thrashing the tree branches in every direction, like a ship sails in a hurricane, from the violent storms force. The powerful current of water streaming through the streets covering the tarmac substances and the pavements with a gush of fast flowing water, transporting fallen leaves, broken branches along with the populations abandoned rubbish bits along with its current. The streets were bare, not a living human soul or animal could be seen. Water grates, bubbling as though a frothing energy was uprising from beneath the earth. Anna's motherly intuition trying to reassure herself. Her thoughts more rationally saying, maybe Marco had taken cover somewhere. When suddenly her comforting reflection, destroyed instantly by fear, as she horrifyingly witnessed little Pasta, fighting to stay afloat in the powerful flooding current.

"Mio Dio. Mio Dio." (My God. My God), said Anna, raising her hand over her mouth, in a horror-struck state, a second later, sprinting down the stairs, like a juvenile young girl, leaping two three steps at a time. Repeating to herself.

"Mio Dio. Mio Dio. Mio Dio…" said Anna in a repetitive chant, slamming open the apartment blocks front entrance door, like a police raiding officer looking for a criminal. Cold water rushed around her legs, almost knee level. With an unforeseen force wadding through the torrential flooding undercurrent. Pasta still fighting for his life, his little legs paddling in all directions. Anna too far to grab him. As Pasta approached, she leaped in a lifesaving dive across the water, the powerful waters flow transporting her instantly as though she was as weightless as a leaf. Parked cars began twisting from their neatly stationed positioned. One car, its rear end turning out, Anna thwacking against it with her back and shoulders. The force of the impact almost winding her, but her inner strength immersed and with another heroic pulsating thrust, lunging herself de novo into the inundating water. The strong current hauling her once again, only this time she'd managed to grasp Pasta, who was now shivering, scared and panicked in her loving grasp, licking at her face in an overwrought manner. Anna with Pasta now secure within her grip, allowing herself to be transported by the current. Deviating objects as though her body was a canoe. Shortly after the torrential rain calmed, along with the flooding deluge. Anna and Pasta coming to a slowing halt.

"Pasta Dove é Marco? (Pasta, where is Marco?)," said Anna. Pasta still quivering looking up at Anna with his saddened lost expression, simply answered by re-mercifully licking Anna's face hysterically once again.

"Tutto apposto, Tutto apposto." (All right, all right), said Anna replying in a reassuring manner, whilst at the same time stroking her hands over Pasta's head to calm and comfort him. Raising to her feet, drenched to the bone, her clothes sticking to her, like some sort of glued material. Walking calmly back towards her apartment building, carrying Pasta like a small child. Gazing at the surrounding aftermath of the storm and the odd victim coming out of their protected hiding places, acknowledging Anna with a simple nod as if to say.

Thank God, it's over, said the expressive stares. But Anna wasn't thinking of God, or others. Not even herself and the dripping blood from her grazed and bruised body. She was thinking of her only son and where he was and if he was safe. Walking wearied up the flights of steps in her apartment block. Pasta still clutched in her arms now a little calmer, the front door still partially open. A rush of faithful adrenaline possessing her physique thinking Marco was home. Anna having forgotten she hadn't taken the time to close the door behind her, after her life saving sprint to save Pasta. Pushing the door open wider with her foot, calling out in an optimistic voice.

"Marco," said Anna, only to be greeted by a terrifying silence. Placing Pasta on the floor. Pasta running directly to his basket, ignoring his full bowl of food, curling himself up like a scared animal. Anna going directly to Marco's bedroom, tapping politely on the door and entering. The lightly furnished room occupied only by an unwelcoming faint carroty glow from the neighbouring apartment's lucent and streetlights. Anna gazing at the map of Italy pinned on the wall, her shadow projected over it, like some ghostly form. Letting out a worrisome sigh, her inner faith of love being secretly tested to its maximum, asking her tormented mind once again.

'Where her son was?' said Anna. Continuing with her concerned inquisitive thoughts.

'Surely she and her family had suffered enough?'

'Surely God wouldn't, couldn't punish her any more, after so much recent immense misfortune?' said Anna. This interrogative reasoning probing her mind, as she dried and saw to the pasta then, nursed and changed herself into dry clothes. A faint tap resounded from the front door. Anna sat on her bed extending her neck, like a Giraffe and approaching her ear towards the hallway entrance, unsure if she'd distinctively heard the knock. And if so, was it coming from her door or that of her neighbours. The thump intensified, causing Pasta to sit up in his basket and bark in a pre-warning manner. Anna leaping to her feet, thinking maybe Marco had forgotten or lost his keys. Opening the front door hastily, expecting to find her son drenched, cold and hungry, but safe behind the entrance. Instead, she was greeted by two very tall middle aged police officers, standing hard-faced and concerned. Each one standing plumb with their characteristic yellow luminous jackets, their blue and white chequered strip band on the left hand side and blue and white inscription 'Police' athwart integrated. Both officers having tucked under their left arm, their Custodian Helmets. Each officer neatly presented, with a black tie and white shirt. Their black trousers immaculately ironed and black shoes polished, like an army officer, strangely not even the slightest drop of water on them. Both policemen uniformed identically like twins, even their belts with their distinguishing truncheons, portable phones and walkie talkies, were placed identically into each individual cincture. The officer to Anna's left side spoke first.

"Mrs Rosalinni?" said the first officer, in a quiet inquisitive voice, his North English accent caterwauling the musical pronunciation of Anna's married name.

"Si errr, yes," said Anna, in a worried and stuttering way.

"Mrs Rosalinni, we have some good and bad news for you, may we come in?" said the first officer.

"Naturalmente, Certo," (Certainly, of course), said Anna replying in an anxious panic, forgetting her English. Seconds later the two well-built men were squeezed, inside Anna's narrow hallway. Pasta letting out a warning growl, but returned in a silent cowardice manner, having unsuccessfully aroused the remotest of fear within any of the two officers. Without further hast the Policeman continued with his explanations revealing calmly the Good and Bad news to Anna.

"Mrs Rosalinni, we've found your son, Marco," said the first officer. An amalgamated emotion of joy and fear hurtled into Anna's core, her knees weakening and her stomach turning as if she was suffering from sea sickness, but a faithful hope was pounding with every beat of her heart.

The officer continued. "I say we've found your son, actually it was a young couple walking home through the park, having seen Marco earlier. They were caught in the storm and took shelter under the bridge leading to the beach's shores. When the storm eventually calmed. They ventured back home, they were a little shocked, but quick to react when they discovered your son Marco floating in the sea," said the first officer, his words causing Anna to place her hands over her mouth as though she'd just witnessed a terrifying accident, simply.

"Oh Mio Dio. Mio Dio." (Oh My God. My God), said Anna.

"Urrrrh, sorry Mam I don't speak Italian. What did you say?" said the first officer.

Anna not taking the time to translate, only replying with a straightforward question.

"Is my son, OK?" said Anna. The police officer sighing and then looking at his colleague, as if to say. "You'd better help me with this question mate," said the first officer's stare. The second officer seemingly having telepathically understood the distraught expression coming from his co-worker continued explaining to Anna where his fellow partner having stopped.

"As my partner said, Mrs Rosalinni. The young couple were a little shocked, but quick to react when they discovered your son Marco floating in the sea. At first, they thought he was dead, but after pulling him safely ashore the young man, who's a nurse at the local hospital, detected a weak pulse. Without hast he called his fellow workers. He probably saved your son's life. At the moment Marco is in the intensive care unit of the Royal Duchess Hospital. He's in a coma. I won't lie to you, he's in a critical way, having been in the cold North Sea for some considerably time. And doctors believe he's received a severe shock, may even have been struck by lightning. But he's alive and fighting," said the second officer, Anna's force leaving her body as though an unforeseen energy having depleted her incredible feminine might, falling to her knees with the horrifying information. The first officer quick to react, grabbing Anna and helping her slowly to her feet, proceeding into the front room where he gently aided her to sit on the couch. The second officer having rushed into the kitchen to pour a glass of water. Pasta jumping up on the settee placing his head reassuringly upon Anna's left thigh.

"Are you OK, mam?" said the second officer warm hearteningly, at the same time passing Anna the glass of water.

"Si, Si." (Yes. Yes), said Anna, taking a couple of sips from the glass. Her motherly potency rapidly charging within her physique. Handing the officer back the glass of water followed by a considerate Thank you. Anna standing puissant, taking a big sigh, rubbing her face and her closed eye lids with her hands, letting out her exhalation, before kindly asked the two policemen in a more defiant tone.

"Can you take me to see my son?" said Anna. Moments later after having settled Pasta down and having grabbed her coat. Anna was whizzing through the lanes in the back of a police car, sirens blazing. Familiar streets, shops and architectural edifices flashing rapidly past her eyes as though she was in some strange time machine. The police vehicle racing through thoroughfares in a life and death threatening situation. Not an obstacle or red light standing in its way. Only moments later, Anna was steeping out of the car and proceeding towards the brightly illuminated entrance of the Royal Duchess Hospital. Pacing at the heels of the first officer, the second having stayed in the car. Once inside a few authorising words from the officer, explaining who Anna was. Within seconds she was diverted from the busy, bustling lobby of the infirmary, towards the 7th floor unswervingly to the intensive care unit where laid her son Marco between earth and the heavens. Anna entering the room alone, the officer respectfully waiting outside, having soothingly placed his right hand upon Anna's left shoulder as if to say.

"You're not alone," said the officer's gesture. But at this precise moment. Arnaldo gone, Marco in a comatose state, her family, homeland and friends thousands of miles away. Never had Anna felt so lonely. Once inside the hospital room, Anna's incredible motherly and womanly strength hit, like a tsunami upon her hopeful, loving, faith. Only the force of her angels seemingly keeping her from fainting. Before her eyes laid her son bare chested, a crumpled Linteum bed sheet covering his lower body to the waist. A mass of tubes intravenous syringes penetrating different areas of his torso. Another bigger pipette inside his mouth and strange cap covering his crown seemingly hiding his long dark curly hair. Cables connected to various electronical medical devices blurting out terrifying clatters and tinkles, monitoring every organ of Marco's comatose state body and mind before being transferred to unreadable pathological charts. A nurse around Anna's age dressed in her light blue uniform, with a darker blue mask covering her mouth and nose and a hood the same colour covering her hair. As she injected another of Marco's vein, she gazed up at Anna and smiled with her eyes. Anna half-heartedly smiling back, taking a step closer towards her son, as she drew nearer, she saw Marco's chest reassuringly inhaling and exhaling with his respiration, his somnolence appearance bestowing his handsome visage with a peaceful calm. Anna noticed his hair had been shaven and a magnitude of smaller cables connected to a strange bonnet. The electroencephalogram wiring leading to a strange machine. She went to place her left hand upon Marco's left hand, wanting to gently caress the top of her sons touch with her thumb. The door opened and two doctors in their late 50s penetrated the room not really acknowledging Anna, a picayune rapid glance from both of them. The nurse mumbled from under her mask.

"The E.E.G. (electroencephalogram), readings are the same professor," said the nurse. One doctor replying in English but with a strong Indian accent.

"Thank you, Wendy, we'll take over from here," said the doctor. With that statement Nurse Wendy as written on her badge, left the room, acknowledging Anna de novo with a friendly smile from her eyes. The two doctors excitedly looking over the E.E.G readings once more. Anna listening in to their mumbling whispers.

"It's crazy, it's not possible, have you ever seen anything like it?"

"I know, I know, he should be dead or even frizzled, like an egg with such a puissant shock," said the first Doctor, adding.

"Are you certain the E.E.G is working normally?" said the second doctor.

"Yes, yes 100% this is the third time I've done this analyst. These data readings are without doubt accurate. That's why I called you and our Colleague Professor White. He was so befuddled by what I sent him and showed him via video conference he's already left the states to come here to England," said the first doctor.

"Unbelievable," said the second doctor, before turning to Anna acknowledging her name in a polite well-spoken queens English.

"Mrs Rosalinni?" said the second doctor. Anna nodding courteously, whilst lovingly caressing her son's sleeping face.

CHAPTER FOUR

UNEXPLAINABLE BRAIN ACTIVITY.

"Mrs Rosalinni, I'm Professor Joseph Cloud and this is my colleague, Professor Abi Rama, we are specialists in brain trauma and coma victims," said Professor Cloud. Anna listening attentively to the following information as Professor Cloud carried on with his explanations, of who he was. What had happened to Marco? What they understood and were doing for him. What would follow? And more disturbing. What they didn't know, and what they couldn't do.

"Mrs Rosalinni, your son Marco has received a very severe shock of some kind. We believe it was a lightning strike, but never have we ever seen someone survive, from such massive electrical shock intake. Marco's body has plunged itself into a coma. A coma comes from the Greek word 'Koma' meaning deep sleep. And that's exactly what Marco is doing. What is curious here, is a person in a coma cannot be awakened and fails to respond normally to light, sound and painful stimuli. A patient suffering from a comatose state exhibits a complete absence of wakefulness and is unable to hear, feel or speak," said Professor Cloud looking at Anna and then at his fellow colleague. Professor Rama, acknowledging professor Cloud's cue accompanying his fellow Doctor. Continuing the unhelpful explanations to Anna.

"Mrs Rosalinni, for a patient to maintain consciousness, two important functions must be active. First the cerebral cortex, the grey matter that forms the outer lawyer of the brain if you like. The second is the brain stem, medically called 'Reticular activating system' or (RAS), for ourselves," said Professor Rama. Anna looking at both Doctors with a befuddled expression, all she wanted to know is if her son would be ok and when would he come out of this coma. Medical whys and wherefores were about as useful and helpful to her as a life vest in the middle of the dessert. Professor Cloud stepping in again.

"What my dear colleague and I are trying to explain, Mrs Rosalinni, is that injury to both or either one of these components in the skull is sufficient enough to cause a person to fall into a coma. What we must do and are trying to do now, is to diagnose and treat the underlying reasons. Depending on the gravity of the coma, your son may also require resuscitative measures. But the E.E.G, sorry electroencephalogram, I apologies once again, the strange bonnet with all those wires interconnected to it on Marco's head. These readings from Marco's mind are abnormal. And when I say abnormal, I mean it in a strange and positive way. Marco's brain is sending data readings a thousand times more precise and active than any other data we have ever seen. Not only for ourselves here in England but to our fellow members across the globe. The data analyses are so uncharacteristic, that the top specialist from New York (Professor Jonathan White), has already left the States and will be here tomorrow. Your son's mind and the extraordinary data and the reaction it's given is simply alien to us. Marco is somewhere between this world and a world no one has ever explored," said Professor Cloud, like an over excited medical student who'd just been given straight As for a project.

Anna gently rubbing her son's left cheek with the back of her right hand, transmitting her love and desire for him to pull through. She softly whispered after hearing the strange half reassuring but demi perturbing whys and wherefores of both professors.

"Tornare a casa Marco, mamma ha bisogno di te." (Come home Marco, Mamma needs you)," said Anna. Professor Cloud having identified Anna's worrying unease, changing his discourse into a more human and conscientious one. A father of two adolescents himself.

"Mrs Rosalinni, we take these readings as a very confident sign that Marco will get better and come out of this somnolence. What we'd like to do with your permission, is a series of minor tests to understand what's happening within Marco's brain. It is essential we focus or bringing Marco back safely, it may be that he will be a little disoriented, confused. He may even pronounce inappropriate and incomprehensible words. His motor response and obey commands maybe slower, and he may have abnormal flexion posturing and extensor posturing," said Professor Cloud in a more soothing. Howbeit the changing of Professor Cloud's discourse was still medical irrelevant rambling for Anna. Her only need was to comprehend with a straightforward *yes* or *no*, if her son would be OK. Asking this very question in a more firm and assertive voice this very, to both professors, who simply looked at each other in a flummoxed manner. Doctor Rama sighing looking at his colleague perplexed, all their joint years of experience and knowledge and exceptional IQs were as stumped in replying to Anna's lucid question, as if she'd ask them to prove the existence of Angels. Professor Rama replying to Anna in a softer tone.

"We simply don't know. I'll be honest with you Mrs Rosalinni, Marco should be dead, his brain should be as inactive as a day-old corpse with the puissant shock he received. He was bare footed on a wet surface, so his entire body absorbed the massive energy of an electrocution. But all his bodily functions are working perfectly normal, like you and I. But his medulla oblongata. Sorry. Mind. Is sending extraordinary unexplainable data readings. Marco's brain is expressing an intelligent life form that I, my dear colleague and the whole planet have never seen. Your son's cerebellum records are extra-terrestrial to us. With the output information already analysed from Marco's encephalon. My apologies again. Intelligence. His grey matter readings are a thousand times more powerful than any other living creature we know," said Professor Rama. Anna not expressing the same fervour for extra-terrestrial brain data readings. But she signed the documents allowing the professors to continue their minor tests. Anything that would bring Marco back from his wondering universe. Back to Anna's world and life. Over the following week's Professor Cloud and Rama leaded by Professor Jonathan white. Having arrived the following day tired but eager to meet Marco, wanting to see first-hand the unexplainable E.E.G data readings. Weeks turned to months and Anna having adapted a routine. She'd helped the nurse's bed wash her son, preventing bedsores and any infections which could be deadly such as Pneumonia. She slept at the hospital by Marco's side. The hospital having kindly placed a second bed in Marco's room. The least they good do after Anna's authorising signature for further tests upon her son. Anna not knowing how to drive. She got up two hours earlier every day, caught the first bus home, walked Pasta and then caught her bus to work. She then proceeded with the same rite only late evening. Walking Pasta again once back home from work. Then catch the two buses to the hospital, where she would stay until the morning. Pasta's sixth animal sense understanding the troubles of his adored master and even though lonely he expressed no self-centeredness. He gave all his love and devotion to Anna and dutifully accepted this saddened change in their lives. Sleeping respectfully on Anna's bed cushion and inundating her with loving licks, and a doting welcome every time she came home. The harsh winter months were fading, but still snow and ice coated the sidewalks, tree branches and certain rooftops, bequeathing her everyday surroundings with a picture postcard panorama. Christmas had been extremely hard and lonely Anna's prayers never having been so distraught. Marco's unopened present still perched on the dining room table. His bedroom sombre and absent of life. Anna having neatly poised his favourite jeans and T-shirt and jumper on the end of Marco's bed. The same habiliments he'd worn the night of his terrible unexplainable accident. Having emptied his jean pockets of their contents before washing them. A one pound, Fifty and twenty pence coin. A dried small Maple leaf and a magnificent olive-green pebble, extremely smooth to touch, the whole stone form covered with peculiar encapsulated foreign matter scintillating, like a constellation of minuscule interstellar. A smaller decagon obscure taint in its centre. She hadn't given any further curious observation of what she considers to be a simple worldly pebble. Anna having kept it with her as an amulet, along with the maple leaf and the unused coins. Her superstitions beliefs safeguarding, like a priceless treasure all that was close to Marco the night he'd so closely spoken to death. Dawns and dusks later bringing Anna's 46th birthday. Friday the 13th of February 2015 arriving, bestowing Anna more of a painful reminder of the minutes, hours, weeks and months Marco having laid unresponsive. Anna, exhausted after her months of demanding devotion and ritual chores. She'd fallen asleep, sat in the chair beside Marco's hospital bed, her head poised on his mattress, and her long greying hair, rippled over Marco's left-hand fingers. A faint soft sweet whisper floating, like a magical fairy's enchantment into her auricle.

"Mamma," said the whispering voice. Anna's eye lids flickering as though she was profound within a beguiling dream that was screening in her mind. In her dreamful state she felt a tender touch of what felt like fingertips upon her crown. Turning her head drowsily from her left to her right. The caress of fingers on her crown turning into a gentle stroke of a hand, followed by a louder croaky cry.

"Mamma."

Mama said the croaky voice. Anna exciting her somnolent state and abandoning her mesmerizing fantasize, as though a bucket of ice-cold water having just been thrown upon her. Lifting her head excited as a young child before Christmas presents. Greeted by the groggy awakening of her son. Marco still weak and muzzy, greeted by an inundation of kisses on his brow and cheeks by Anna.

"Mamma."

"Dove sono"? (Where am I?), said Marco in a more audible voice, whilst rapidly and horrifyingly enlivening. His vision engrossing the strange machines and surroundings circumambient-ting him.

"Sei in ospedale, tutto va bene adesso tesoro."

(You are in hospital, all is OK now my treasure love). said Anna. Marco hearing his mother call him Tesoro, transporting his reminiscent mind back to the beach, the Moeraki Boulders and the strange pebble. He was just about to ask his mother some further questions when the hospital room door swung firmly open. Three tall, emaciated men wearing a white doctor's blouse and a stethoscope thwarter their shoulders, followed by a rotund auburn coloured hair nurse in a light blue uniform, emerging hastily in his room. One doctor went straight to the data pathological charts. The other observing the

E.E.G. The nurse accompanying the last doctor who sat to Marco's right side and without saying a word, gently lifting Marco's right forearm from where it was resting on the bed. Pressing his right hands index finger and middle finger upon Marco's wrist to monitor his pulse. A minute's silence as though a remembrance ceremony was being honoured, not an utter heard, even the sourdine machines having seemingly muted the annoying din. The sixty seconds pulse taking reticence now over. Doctor Rama standing looking at the data pathological charts.

"The E.E.G biofeedback indicates higher readings from the dorsolateral prefrontal, orbital frontal and ventrolateral cortex. There are also superiors' analyses 'from the hypothalamus, the nucleus accumbens, the amygdala and olfactory bulb. But much more diminutive of what we've witnessed over the last few weeks. His readings seem to be stabilizing," said professor Rama in an analytical manner. Professor Cloud whilst triple checking there were no defects with E.E.G, acknowledging his dear colleague's findings, with a slow nodding of the head along with a straightforward unemotional.

"I confirm," said Professor Cloud. Professor Jonathan white having taken Marco's pulse. Now listening to Marco's heartbeat through his stethoscope, nurse Wendy busy checking on Marco's adrenalin drip after having ruffled Marco's pillow acknowledging him with a gentle smile. Marco trying to understand all the commotion around him, staring worrisome at his mother, his frightened expressing eyes as large as tarsier. Not only could he not understand the medical jargon. But the English vocabulary too.

CHAPTER FIVE

THE 'BUMP' ALGORITHM

"Welcome back, Marco," said Professor White in a warm-hearted manner, placing his big left hand upon Marco's left shoulder, expressing his compassion by a gentle tender squeezing of his fingers and thumb, whilst at the same time slipping his right hand into Marco's right palm in a hospitable handshake. The instant Marco's hand coming into contact with Professor Whites grip. Marco sensing a strange tingling from his toes to his fingertips, conglomerating at his phalange as though his palmar crease were sensing minor electrical intake. These weird pins and needles and charging energetic force. Amalgamated with a peculiar humming in Marco's auricles, like a faint whale's cry, simultaneously with a powerful throbbing in his brains Motor sensory Cortex. As though a potent pulsation buttressing with every passing second throbbing in the centre of his crown. Thirty seconds later the strange tingling from his toes to his fingertips, along with the minor electrical intake conglomerating at his phalanges palmar crease. The peculiar whale's humming cry in his auricles, simultaneously with the potent pulsation from the inside of his cranium. Abruptly vanished. Professor White releasing Marco's grasp having himself sensed no strange abnormalities from their intermingled handclasp asking Marco in a more professional modus a series of questions.

"How are you feeling, Marco?"

"Any pains or strange sensations?"

"Do you remember anything about your accident?"

"Do you remember anything about your dreams over these past months?" said Professor White. Anna having listened attentively to Doctor Whites questions, naturally began, as always to translate in her mind the English demands in Italian. Comprehending and wanting to aid her son due to his very poor understanding of the English language. Anna opening her mouth slowly, beginning to express the interpreted questions to Marco. Anna suddenly stunned, like she herself having just received some unexplainable electrical shock by the incomprehensibly auscultating reply to all four of Professor White's reservations in a perfect English with even a slight American intonation from Marco.

"I feel fine, Doctor."

"Nope, no pains or strange sensations."

"The only thing I remember about the accident, was walking on the beach and the crackling thunder and lightning around me."

"As for my dreams, nope can't say I had any," said Marco. The three professor's and Nurse Wendy having never heard Marco speak, thinking nothing more to his English stated responses. But Anna, like Marco knew some inhuman paranormal phenomena had occurred. Marco by some extra-terrestrial, psych with the synchronous physically gesture to shake Professors Whites hand. He'd bumped by an otherworldly energy the data within Doctor Whites mind. The transfer of all Dr Whites knowledge now pairing inside Marco's brain. Marco turning his regard to his mother, without expressing vocabulary. From his glare Anna knew she was to say nothing. Marco's mind having absorbed not only Dr Whites intelligence, as Marco understanding, like he'd studied, graduated and even excelled in the medical profession, comprehending with great ease, every medical expression and term being fluctuated around his hospital room. As well as Dr White's memories. Present and past. He knew he'd married his high school sweetheart, had twin girls, had studied at Harvard, excelled in medicine, achieved his MBBS, MD, and even his PhD. Marco also knew Dr White was a faithful husband, devoted to his family and work, that his parents were still alive and relatively healthy for their age, that he'd an older sister and a younger brother. That his younger sister had died of an unexplainable brain disorder. This suffering memory and traumatising period of his younger life motivating Dr White to become a great neurosurgeon. Personal, sad, happy, present and old knowledge. Like Dr White having a great passion for skiing, achieving many medals within his earlier younger years of the alpine sport. Marco along with every other of Dr Whites known recognition also, knowing Dr White's secret memories too. All now absorbed into Marco's brain as though he'd lived them too. Dr White exiting the room somewhat shadily, leaving his fellow colleagues and Nurse Wendy to attend to Marco and Anna. His stare caught by Marco's eye. Marco understanding immediately, Dr White had discovered something his fellow co-workers had ignored. On Marco's medical sheet Anna having clearly stated, just in case Marco should ever awake from his comatose state and if she wasn't there, that Marco spoke and understood very, very little English. Yet he'd replied and expressed everything asked of him in English.

"How had he learnt to speak and comprehend the English language and vocabulary whilst having been in a coma for nearly four months?" said Professor White to himself before leaving the room. Marco knew with his new paranormal intellect, having bumped and cloned Dr White's intelligence that Dr White was going to make a call to his old companion, Dr Martin Hausbeck, a fellow MD and PhD who'd studied at Harvard alongside Dr White and now worked with NASA as a psychiatrist or so that's what he told his entourage. Marco also perceiving the strange sixth sense in Dr White, that his old colleague couldn't been 100% trusted. But even so the strange and unexplainable phenomena concerning Marco's accident and his miraculous recovery pushing Dr White to question his own knowledge and seek that of others.

It was eight p.m. in England. Two p.m. in Washington. Dr White scrolling down his iPhone searching for Martin Hausbeck contact.

"Hausbeck cell," said Dr White whispering to himself, sighing as though hesitating, then doubting himself no more he whispered again.

"I gotta know, this is too strange," said Dr White, his right-hand index finger touching his phones screen, a few seconds later he could hear the dialling tone. Sighing again at the same time raising his iPhone towards his left ear. No sooner had he approached the phone to his lobe. Hearing a familiar loud dominating voice on the other end.

"Hey Johnny boy, is that you?"

"Long-time no hear, buddy, I heard from a little bird that you was over in England, drinking afternoon tea and eating scones with the queen and all. Talking about queens, how's that beautiful wife of yours? Now she's a real queen." said Hausbeck. Dr White stuttering he wasn't prepaid for Hausbeck to answer so quickly. Knocking him a little of balance.

"Errrrrh, hi Martin, Emma is fine, busy with our two daughters, the house, her roses and her cooking club, far too busy to miss me, you know

Emma, never a dull moment in her life." said Dr White. Hausbeck replying in his typically sarcastic manner.

"Maybe she got another man, got tired of you always gallivanting to other countries and leaving her at home," said Hausbeck. Dr White laughing a few seconds calmly agreeing.

"Yeah, maybe you're right she never seems to reply when I call," said Dr White, smiling to himself, for never he doubted Emma's love and devotion and vice a versa, their relationship, friendship, marriage and adoration was as strong and as deeply rooted as the oldest of the earth's oak trees. No personal storm or jealous malicious innuendoes could ever weaken or harm this powerful trust and bond. Causing many, especially Martin Hausbeck to be green with envy. Hausbeck a three-time divorcee having tried his luck with Emma a few years earlier at an award ceremony. His handsome posture and witty charm, making it all the way to nowhere concerning Emma. Hausbeck just couldn't understand what Professor

White had physically more than him, with his little pot belly, grey receding hair, half-moon glasses and scruffy beard, he couldn't comprehend, Emma looked to the heart, not the physical features. Dr White's heart was as pure and precious as crystal. Far from the evil heart of Hausbeck, with his I'll step on anyone and anything to get where I want to be. But even with this dangerous awareness about Hausbeck. Dr White intuition needed to know more and access files from NASA. Something only Hausbeck could do. An awkward silence lingered over the phone, broken by a less arrogant and acrimonious Hausbeck.

"So, Martin, to what do I owe the pleasure? You calling me on a beautiful spring afternoon here in Washington." said Hausbeck.

"Where are you anyway?" said Hausbeck. Dr White answering serenely, having already disregarded Hausbeck's mocking.

"I'm still in the North of England, I've been studying and surveying a particular patient with a very unique case file." said Dr White. Hausbeck's curiosity aroused, he knew Dr White was probably one of the most, intellectual minds in medicine, and for him to call upon Hausbeck meant only one thing. He was on to something big.

"So where do I come in? This cloak and dagger stuff, doesn't seem like you, Johnny boy. Have you been watching too many Sherlock Holmes or Agatha Christie movies?" said Hausbeck.

"No, no I've not been watching movies, to tell you the truth I've not been out of the hospital since I came back in the new year. Spent the holidays with Emma and the girls, but have not been home since," said Dr White. Still not getting to the point.

"So, Johnny, are you going to keep talking small talk, or get to the point" said Hausbeck, his arrogant attitude bouncing back into action, causing Dr White to politely excuse himself.

"Yes, yes Martin, sorry of course, you're right, I'll get to the point. I was called over to England last October, here at the Royal Duchess Hospital. A young nineteen-year-old Italian man was rushed here after receiving a severe shock of some sort. We believe it was lightening, but here's the weird part. Marco, the young patient was standing on a wet beach bare footed and washed up upon the shores after spending we believe, nearly an hour in the cold sea. If he hadn't died from the electrical intake his body absorbed. The black cicatrices which stemmed across his occipitofrontal (forehead), indicated that's where he received his electrocution. He'd have died from hyperthermia or drowned. I've been racking my brains along with my fellow colleagues, Dr Rama and Professor Cloud. How he lived? The E.E.G readings from Marco's mind were also abnormal. And when I say abnormal, I mean in a strange and positive way. Marco's brain was sending data readings a thousand times more precise and active than any other data we have ever seen. But all his bodily function is working perfectly normal. His medulla oblongata was sending extraordinary unexplainable data analyses, expressing an intelligent life form that I and my dear colleagues have never seen. His cerebellum records were extra-terrestrial to us. With the output information already analysed from Marco's encephalon. His grey matter readings were a thousand times more powerful than any other living creature I know. Until this morning when he came out of his nearly four-month coma. At first his readings were once again inexplicable, but after coming out of his coma, apart from his cerebral cortex data, his readings are back to normal. We've used three different electroencephalograms all without exception indicated the exact same data. The other strange phenomena, is Marco's occipitofrontal cicatrices has completely vanished and his oculus dexter (right eye), has a cerulean pigment his oculus sinister (left eye), an olive green. What's more?"

"My God there's more," cried Hausbeck.

"Yes, yes. He speaks fluent English," responded Dr White excitedly.

"What's so special and abnormal about that, millions of intellectual beings speak fluent English? said Hausbeck in a more befuddled manner.

"Yes, I know that. But how many people do you know who before going into a coma, couldn't speak a word of English, or very, very few. And four months later he's speaking like a native, with the same accent I have?" said Dr White, almost shouting this information down the phone.

"Are you sure?" said Hausbeck, intrigued by this revelation, he knew Dr White was not one to make up stories or invent fictional fantasies.

"I checked and double checked. Marco's mother, Mrs Rosalinni, specifically indicated on her son's medical form, that he spoke no English, and if he should awake in her absence, she was to be notified immediately. What's more when I asked him a series of questions about the night of his accident, Mrs Rosalinni began to translate. But she was stopped and stunned to hear her son replying in a language he didn't speak or understand before his near fatal accident. The others didn't notice, but I noticed the shock and bewilderment upon Mrs Rosalinni's visage," said Dr White. Hausbeck replying in an analysing tone.

"OK, so what you're saying is Marco, right," said Hausbeck.

"Yes, yes Marco," said Dr White, rapidly acknowledging Hausbeck. Hausbeck grateful for the confirmation, but he wasn't questioning, more thinking out loud continuing with his analyse.

"Marco. To survive a lightning strike and unexplainable accidents, that's rare, but not unheard of. His scare has totally vanished too, that's nothing unheard of in the medical profession. His eye pigments have changed and each Oculus, have now a different colour. That's not so uncommon in today's world. Maybe an effect of such a powerful electrical intake? But to learn a foreign language whilst in a coma, now that's something I've never heard of before, maybe his brain was over active and taking in data whilst he was in a comatose state, maybe his electrocution instead of damaging his neurons it activated them to a greater level and that's why the readings were abnormal and, as you said a thousand times more puissant. It's possible while his body was sleeping his mind was absorbing information. That could explain why he spoke with a similar accent as you. His temporal lobe and entorhinal cortex were absorbing your words and knowledge. Strange but logical, after all we've heard of coma patients after years of lying in a vegetable state. Acknowledging and remembering conversations and events witnessed from their hospital bed throughout the years," said Hausbeck.

"Yes, I see your reasoning, but there's something more, my gut feeling is telling me." said Dr White in an unconvinced and unaccepting response to Hausbeck's philosophical rationalising. "Arrrrrrh that famous gut feeling, no medical science or technology can or could ever explain," said Hausbeck, adding two questions.

"So, what's your gut feeling telling you?"

"And where do I come into this? said Hausbeck. Dr white pausing a long moment, before coughing as if to clear his throat, then coming out with his reason for calling Hausbeck along with his whys and wherefores concerning his gut tangibility.

"What can you tell me about the O.W.I.Q. project?" said Dr White.

"Hey, how the hell do you know about the O.W.I.Q. project? That's NASA's and the government's top-secret stuff?" said Hausbeck, his voice raising a tone.

"You know, Martin, in today's world nothing is really *Top Secret*, it doesn't matter how I know. But that I know," said Dr White in a hastily response. Hausbeck, caught off guard, insisting with his interrogation.

"You been talking to Snowden, or another one of our country's traitors?" said Hausbeck.

"He's no traitor, Hausbeck, and you know it, people have a right to know what our governments and world leaders are doing to us and our planet," said Dr White defending Snowden and his actions.

"Look Martin, we could talk politics all day, all week, for Christ's sake all year, you and I know we'll never agree. But science, we do agree on and I have a powerful feeling Marco has been affected by some extra-terrestrial intelligence. So again, what can you tell me about the O.W.I.Q. project?" said Dr White. Another awkward silence lingering across the line, broken this time by Hausbeck coughing and after a long sigh replying.

"Look, Johnny boy, let's just say hypothetically if such a project existed, I'm not saying it does, but in a make-believe fantasy world such things did," said Hausbeck, pausing as if sensing some sort of fear, then added in a more coded formal manner.

"You know Johnny, it's been years since I've been back to England, and I've never been to the North. Maybe we could meet up and talk about old times," said Hausbeck. Dr White reading between the lines understanding, Hausbeck didn't feel safe talking about such *Top Secret* issue over the phone, simply adding.

"Be great to see you, Martin, that way you could meet Marco too, you'll find me at the Royal Duchess Hospital, I'll mail you the address," said Dr White.

"No need, Johnny, I'll find you," said Hausbeck, quickly. Seemed he was more experienced in cloak and dagger scenarios than Dr White.

Dr White replying with a simple. "Seventh floor," said Dr White. But was answered only by a hanging up hum, from Hausbeck's phone. No goodbyes or see you laters. He wondered if he'd done the right thing. His gut feeling split between yes, he had, and no, he hadn't, but it was too late. His gut feeling knowing with certitude Hausbeck would be there very soon. Anna now alone with her son. Dr Rama, Professor Cloud and Nurse Wendy all having left the room together a few seconds earlier. Anna in English with her Italian intonation, whispering as though she believed the room was bugged or something.

"Marco sinca when do you speaka sucha good Inglese?" (English), said Anna. Marco replying in his perfect English, with his slightly blended American accent. A trifling smirk emerging across his face.

"Since this morning, mamma, I was just as surprised as you to hear myself speaking fluent English, it just came out of my mouth as though it was my mother tongue," said Marco. Anna making a cross sign from her forehead to each shoulder with her right hand. "The Father the son and the Holy Spirit," whispering.

"Caro Dio io spero che questo non e un cattivo presagio."

(Dear God, I hope this is not a bad omen), said Anna.

"No mamma, don't think things like that, it's a good omen, I'll be able to find a better job, we'll be able to find a nicer place to live and things can only get better now," said Marco. Anna replying to her son's positivity, with a loving smile at the same time caressing Marco's face with both hands.

"Things now already better, you be here with me. I don't care where you went to or where you have to go too, you're safe well and come home now," said Anna. Marco unable to stop himself correcting his mother's grammatical sentences.

"I don't care where you were or where you've been, you're safe and well and will be coming home soon," said Marco.

"Don't get cheeky with your mamma," snapped Anna, her emotions mixed between, happiness, pride, incomprehension and an uncertain presentiment.

"Sorry, Mamma, I can't help myself. Before shaking Dr White's hand, I couldn't understand anything that was being said around me, but as soon as my palm connected with Dr Whites palm, I felt a strange tingling in my toes and my fingertips, conglomerating at my phalange as though my palmar crease was sensing a minor electrical intake. These weird pins and needles and charging energetic force, were amalgamated with a peculiar humming in my auricles like a faint whale's cry, along with a simultaneously powerful throbbing in my brains motor sensory cortex. As though a potent pulsation buttressing with every passing second in the centre of my crown. A few seconds later the strange tingling in my toes and fingertips, along with the minor electrical intake conglomerating my phalanges palmar crease, including the peculiar whale's humming cry in my auricles, simultaneously with the potent pulsation from inside my cranium, just vanished. And then all seemed clear, what's more mamma I can even understand all this medical technology around us and the significances of these pathological data charts. I feel like I'm a doctor," said Marco.

"Mio Dio, Mio Dio." (My God, My God), said Anna, once again making another cross insignia. She hadn't understood half of what her son had just explained to her. Her English was good, but Marco was talking, like he'd swallowed an English medical dictionary.

"Conglomerating, phalange, palmar crease, amalgamated, auricles, motor sensory cortex, potent pulsation buttressing."

For Anna, Marco could have as well been talking in Japanese.

"There's something else, Mamma, too" said Marco without giving his mother the time to absorb the unexplainably phenomena which had emanated in her son.

"I also know Dr White's memories. Present and past. I know he married his high school sweetheart, Emma. That they have twin girls that he studied at Harvard, excelled in medicine, achieving his MBBS, MD, and even his PhD. I know Dr White is a faithful husband, devoted to his family and work, that his parents are still alive and relatively healthy for their age, that he has an older sister and a younger brother. That his younger sister died of an unexplainable brain disorder. This suffering memory and traumatising period of Dr White's younger life motivating him to become a great neurosurgeon. I know, Dr White, has a great passion for skiing, achieving many medals in his earlier years, he could have even become a world champion. But medicine was and still is his true passion. It's as if his memories are now mine too. I also know he's suspicious about me now knowing how to speak English. He knows, because of what you noted on my medical files, that before my accident and comatose state, I couldn't speak any or very limited English. And I know with this paranormal intellect, having bumped and cloned Dr White's intelligence. I know that Dr White went to make a call to his old companion, Dr Martin Hausbeck, a fellow MD and PhD who he'd studied at Harvard with, and now works with NASA as a psychiatrist. And I perceived the strange sixth sense in Dr White, that his old colleague Dr Martin Hausbeck couldn't be a 100% trusted. What's more he'll be here in England very, very shortly." said Marco.

Anna's eyes as wide open as an owl during the night scrutinizing her world for food and potential danger, her hands poised and still on Marco's hospital bed. She wanted to take his hand, she wanted to tell him what had happened was great, a magical gift, even a sacred blessing of some sort. She wanted also to understand. But her womanly force was screaming inside her telling her this offering given to her son from beyond, was going to take him on a destiny, a trail, a voyage she would never be able to follow. A tear drop forming in the corner of her right eye. Anna turning her head gently and with her inner strength as life had so many times forced her to do. Fighting back her heart-breaking emotions and smiling. Hiding her fears, her pains, her worries and her inner sadness once again. Marco sensing something was not quite right, stretching out his fingertips towards his mother's hand.

"Mamma, take my hand, let's see if it happens again. If I can bump and absorb the intelligence and memories of those who shake my hand, then I'll be able to tell you things from your past I didn't know, souvenirs and long-ago events only known to you, I'll even be able to help you knit," said Marco smiling with enthusiasm and excitement extending further his right hand. Anna placing both her hands palm down firmly on her knees, hiding her palms.

"No Marco, no," said Anna in a quiet soft voice. She didn't want her son to know her past or present souvenirs, she didn't want her son to bump and absorb her intelligence and memories. She didn't want her son to know what she knew.

Every woman has the right to have a secret garden, especially a mother, said Anna, whispering in her head. Their conversation broken by Dr White re-entering the room. Reading one of Marco's medical charts held in his left hand, at the same time rubbing his forehead with his right hand as though questioning his mind about something. Glancing at the chart, then again at Marco, at the chart, then again at Marco, at the chart, then again at Marco. Almost as though he was scrutinizing a wanted picture and double, even triple checking that Marco was the same guy as on the poster. Dr White reticent not even acknowledging Anna or Marco with a facial expression, walking directly over to the E.E.G checking its data output. Silence prevailed causing Anna and Marco to glance at each other, both frowning with curiosity.

"Your E.E.G algorithm, seems to have attenuated at the cortical processes, maybe we should take a closer look into the latencies and amplitudes of the peaks in the ERP (event related potential), waveforms at certain electrode locations, what do you think, Marco," said Dr White, now staring directly at Marco.

"Should we not simply compromise or do some simple t-tests. You seem to be forgetting the *ANOVAs*." (Analysis of Variance), said Marco. Anna staring at her son, her eyes almost popping out of her head, her neck and face stretched forward, as though she was trying to undo a muscle strain. Her stare was one of disbelief, not because her son had replied once again, like he too had studied medicine at Harvard. That shock Anna had already grasped and come to terms with. No, her disbelief was how naïve Marco had just been, walking into Dr Whites suspicious trap, like a wild animal stripped of its senses and extraordinary survival instinct. Marco may have been given the gift to bump and absorb anybody's knowledge by simply connecting his hand to theirs for thirty seconds. But wisdom was far from his new otherworldly intellect. Even with Marco's ethereal, transcendental yet terrifying supernatural puissant ability to osmose knowledge. Wisdom so it seemed, still had to be lived. Dr White scurrying out of the room, like a mouse trying not to be seen by a cat.

"Marco what do you do and say, you talk like you are a medicine man, you must be more saggio, (wiser), you must be intelligente. (Clever). What do you thinka these men and women do too you when they know you have this power, I tell you, I know, I tell you because I am your mamma. They put you in a cage, like an animale, (animal), a mouse or a maiale, (pig), and they torture you with strange machine, like those Nazi do in the war. They hurt you, stab you, drain you, and look inside your head, look inside in places not even light can go.

"You must be more intelligente, Marco. I am scared now; no I am terrified. I nearly lose you one time. Please don'ta make me you lose you again, per piacere." (Please), said Anna, with her broken English, replacing certain words in Italian. Her fretful state of mind causing her to forget the English equivalent.

"OK, Mamma, I will be wiser, I promise you. Don't worry, don't fret, things will be OK. OK," said Marco, at the same time reassuring himself. He hadn't thought that his gift could bring upon him danger. Hurt, stab, drain and looking inside his head in places not even light can reach. As his mother having so poignantly and rightly pointed out. The door opening again, the first to enter the room was Dr Rama, followed by Professor Cloud and Dr White, behind them Nurse Wendy. Each holding strange objects and medical equipment. Marco's eyes now as wide opened as an owl. Flashes of torturing scenes from old war and horror movies his mind having subconsciously preserved, all coming rushing back and crashing into Marco's hippocampus (memory), like an old steam train colliding with a TGV. These past visions reinforced by Anna's recent warning.

My God, they going to torture me now, cut me up, open my mind and poke around. Hurt, stab and drain me, said Marco's in his mind and vivid imagination working overtime, at the same time he was trying to think of a plan to escape, get out of there. He couldn't jump he was on the seventh floor, he could attack one of the doctors and steal his clothes, but the others would raise the alarm. He'd have to attack all of them, even Nurse Wendy. But what about his mum, maybe she could be, would be hurt in the scuffle.

If he wasn't fast enough maybe she'd be taken hostage, even worse, what if they tortured Anna instead. Hurt, stabbed and drained her. Marco's agitation and panicking state being felt and eased by his mother, as secret and tender as a loving puff open a grazed child's knee. An understanding and sensitivity already existent before Marco's other worldly unexplainable powers. That umbilical affection between mother and son that maybe sometimes be, hidden, stolen, displaced or even abandoned but never lost. Anna's invisible bond and instinct calming Marco's panicking emotions with a simple tender caress upon her son's forearm. Anna not having forgotten what her son had explained to her concerning the power of his touch to bump and absorb the intelligence and memories of others. Avoiding delicately and discreetly any contact to Marco's hand. Her tenderness reassuring her son instantly, her soothing presence allowing Marco to not have made a panicking fool of himself. As the three doctors along with Nurse Wendy simply replacing certain medical equipment with their equivalent exchangeable part, like replacing used bed sheets from old used ones. It was clear to Marco and Anna, even though unsure Why. Dr Whites' suspicions, having been kept to himself, except of course for Hausbeck, who was already at 20,000 feet and climbing to cruise altitude. First class to London with Virgin, it was only a question of hours before he and Marco would be maybe shaking hands.

CHAPTER SIX

A CURIOUS HANDSHAKE

"How you feeling, Marco?" asked Dr Cloud. Marco just about to answer, when Anna stepped in, not wanting her son to blurt out another unexplainable medical response, with words only fellow doctors could understand.

"He's tired, he wants to sleep now," said Anna. Marco not protesting, he was tired and did want to sleep. But more than anything, he wanted to go home. Anna as though having by some clairvoyant energy perceiving her sons want to go home asked just that.

"When can I take my son home? He needs to come home now, and I need him to be home," said Anna.

"Shortly," said Dr White in a lightening response to Anna's question. Dr White, not even allowing any of his fellow co-workers to intervene.

"Very shortly, just a few more days of observation, we mustn't forget the great shock and near death experience your son encountered. For his sake its better he stays here until we are 100% sure your son has recovered completely. Don't worry he's in safe hands," said Professor Cloud, having stared at his fellow co-worker professor White, as though his expressive state was telling him to be more sincere. Anna replying with a half-hearted smile. Marco having already drifted into his dreams. The three doctors leaving the room together, only Nurse Wendy still pottering around, arranging medical equipment and checking Marco's intravenous bag. Nurse Wendy smiling at Anna.

"Your son is as strong as you. You need not to worry no more, he's out of danger and will be home very soon," said Nurse Wendy. It was the first time in all the past months Nurse Wendy's having spoken. Not even at Christmas or the New Year, had she addressed Anna. Her comforting words flowed directly into Anna's heart, she detected alongside Nurse Wendy's slight east European accent, a hint of sadness, like she'd lost someone close, maybe her own son. It was almost as though her tender words to Anna were saying.

"Why couldn't I have had the same luck as you?"

Nurse Wendy leaving the room as she passed Anna, without looking at her she gently squeezed her shoulder as though to say from women to women.

"Stay strong. Women always have to stay strong."

The door silently closing behind her. Anna staring at her beloved son sleeping peacefully, before leaving him to attend her daily duties and obligations, one being Pasta. She left the hospital ward for the first time in months with the sensation and knowledge, Marco would not only reawaken from his current snooze but that very, very shortly he'd be home.

Hausbeck's 747 flight landed twenty minutes before schedule, the jet stream and rear winds helping advance the mechanical giant. As the 580-tonne mass touched down on the east runway as elegantly as an eagle flowing onto a branch. An explosive round of applause from a group of Italian students broke the powerful sound of the air brakes robotically bursting into action. Certain passengers were already disrespectfully dethatching their seatbelts as the majestically mechanical wonder taxied to its parking position. Agitated passengers disregarding the hostesses and captains announce with their various useful information to some, unnecessary to others about weather and authorising documentation required. Hausbeck having watched the nostalgic aerial view grow bigger and bigger, sitting patiently and considerately in his seat until the aircraft coming to a complete stop. The ping of the seatbelt sign 'off' causing a commotion of movement, passengers frenziedly reaching for their overhead lockers as though they could access the terminal by jumping directly out of the aircraft's windows. After a few minutes Hausbeck dethatching his belt, collecting his overhead luggage, smiling politely at the pretty hostesses, descending from the plane, like a VIP passenger. Only he was on no official business, no state car or neatly costumed chauffeur holding out a card with his name printed across. Hausbeck having been greeted in foreign lands in such a mannerism so many times before. This time he was incognito, as incognito an official American government agent could be. Formalities were passed with ease, Hausbeck entering her majesty's soil almost as easy as a native Londoner. A suspicious sentiment stirred within him, doubting maybe he'd been followed, so from time-to-time Hausbeck pausing at certain areas where the reflection of the view behind him would be revealed without him having to turn is head and look behind him, like a befuddling unprofessional. A sunglass stand, a shops vitrine, a reflecting metal surface, even a show rooms car mirror. Hausbeck knew them all. Nothing no one in near sight his incognito mingled and lost within the thousands of faces passing through the world's busiest terminal. What he couldn't see that his movements were being discreetly monitored by Stanford. Hausbeck's boss, from the hidden NASA's own central intelligence base Stanford having created back in Cleveland Ohio. A sister Langley for NASA's personnel not even Hausbeck knew of. Even though tired. Hausbeck driving directly Northbound. He could have got a connecting flight even the train, but he enjoyed driving it helped him to think. And thinking was what was overpowering his mind as he staidly pursued his journey to the North of England. His hired cars GPS easing his need to plan his route, a simple address and then just listen to the voice and follow the arrows. His journey long and tedious,

Hausbeck's intelligence having not anticipated for the constant road works upon British motorways and its relentless speed cameras which'd seemed to cause the GPS warning, to bleep every few minutes.

"No chance of dozing off at the wheel, with such a racket blaring out," said Hausbeck, listening to the GPS blurt out warning noises once again. The only good side of things Hausbeck telling himself. It was exactly 2.53 a.m. when he finally turned into the private car park of the Royal Duchess Hospital. With flight time, driving time, the five hours difference between England and Washington he'd been almost awake and on the move for over twenty-four hours, luckily, he'd recuperated a little much needed rest on the plane bestowing him with that little extra force to drive. The car park lights were dim, various windows of the hospital façade glimmering, like cat's eyes in the night accompanied by the powerful gleam of the emergency sign. A few shadows marking the presence of human activity silhouetted across the building's walls and car parks tarmac, like ghostly figures. Hausbeck too tired to notice if it was staff or patients, probably a combination of both. Parking his car and staring for a few instances at the Hospital, wondering in his mind which window was Marco's room.

Counting the windows to the seventh floor, at the same time pulling the seat handle to readjust his sitting position to recline.

"Tomorrow, or actually today I'll know which room he's in," said Hausbeck, murmuring to himself. No sooner having closed his eyes, falling into a profound slumber, his dreams agitated by Dr White's earlier comments and revelations.

"What can you tell me about the O.W.I.Q. project?"

Marco having been awake for over three hours. He'd slept right through the hospital visit. Anna Having watched her son peacefully sleeping, a harmonious sentiment overpowering her heart from the first time in so many months, weeks, hours, and minutes. An emotion every loving parent longs to have and know. That special feeling which tells you.

"Your children are safe and well."

This wonderful happiness Anna having toted home with her. And for the first time since Marco's accident, having slept in her own bed with her ever loving, devoted, understanding and extremely overjoyed Pasta by her side. Well actually above her head Pasta having acclaimed Anna's pillow for his own, weather her head was laid upon it or not. Marco staring at the Tupperware containing fresh meat balls. The green plastic tub and its unmistakable contents marking clearly the presence of his mother's visit. He turned wondering why she hadn't woken him at the same instant glaring at the cold unwelcoming white tiled celling. There was what seemed like a coffee stain in the centre, he'd wondered how it had got there. What strange incident or events had caused such a blemish so high and out of anybody's hand reach. Things like this wouldn't have normally taken any time or space within his mind before his accident, but since his unexplainable bumping, the intellect and memories of Dr White. Marco's own mind having become more inquisitive and analytical.

"I'm bored," said Marco, gliding out of his hospital bed, feeling instantly the cold draft wafting against his bare arse hanging out of his hospital gown. Placing his feet inside his slippers at the same time, like an instant reaction to cover his bare buttocks, grabbing his dressing gown. Left arm slipped in nicely. The rest of the gown wrapped across his chest and tied together at the front with its belt, like a kung fu outfit. The intravenous syringe plunged into his right arm, hindering Marco from correctly dressing himself. Pulling the intravenous stand towards him, one of its small black pivoting wheels broken, another squeaking like a trapped mouse. The last three pivoting wheels seemed to be working, accept the stand always pulling to the left like a possessed shopping trolley. Disregarding this minor obstacle Marco leaving his hospital room for the very first time. The uniformed cold corridor seemed bare from any activities, unsurprisingly as it was 3.33 a.m. The same white tiled ceiling stretching as far as the eye could see. The light grey durable, resilient and easy to clean Linoleum floor as unwelcoming as its neighbouring plafond. Circular lights suspended incrusted in a white metal surrounding, placed precisely in the centre of the ceiling and uniformly spaced apart. Not all were lit, those which were dispensing a dim projection of their force, reminding Marco of the circular lights in the 'Star Ship Enterprise'.

In a juvenile sentence almost laughing out loud. "Beam me up Scotty," said Marco, still grinning like a car salesman who'd just sold a wreck to an innocent naive trusting punter. His eyes continuing his visit. Resting his left hand on the wooden rails which stuck out a few inches, waist high from every wall to his left. The ligneous rectangular lengths installed to protect the fragile plastered walls from the constant, but unwanted banging collisions of the hospital beds. Wheeled day in and day out through the bleak corridors into individual chambers, with individual patients, some possessing luck, others accompanied by the unforeseen Grim Reaper, not even the exceptionally qualified doctors and nurses could see. Powerless to this invisible omen. Sometimes patients, like Marco having entered a room with such severe injuries, certain medical staff having said to themselves in that all personally unheard, silent thought. But with that all powerful gleaming stare to a fellow co-worker.

"This one's a goner, no way he or she can survive such injuries."

And there were times that certain wounds having seemingly seemed so banal, nonchalant almost blasé. Doctors and nurses un-stressfully looking at one another as if to say.

"She or he, will be out by tomorrow."

Angels and *Death* like, luck and curses. All mankind possessing both. Only fate individualistic. Marco placing his right hand against his plain brown laminated hospital room's door. Waited an instant to see if any reaction penetrated his senses, like a spiritual guide, a powerful clairvoyant, possessing the gift and curse to foresee what had once taken place. Maybe he'd discover the true incident of the coffee stain. Nothing, no tingling or strange sensation from his physical contact or in his mind. thirty seconds had longed passed but still zilch. Caressing his fingers over the sliver-coloured plastic numbers upon his door 715. Counted separately.

"7.1.5, adds to thirteen, is that a good or bad omen?" said Marco in his mind, almost as though he was talking to the possessing spirit his sixth sense telling him that was now seemingly sharing his body. Walking a little further down the corridor, an abandon wheelchair sat destitute next to the radiator. Marco placing his right hand upon its folding black leather seat. Still nothing, he moved his touch onto the metal spoke wheels. No otherworldly unforeseen reaction there too. Persisting with his eagerness to understand and obtain the same strange phenomena having occurred as his hand having physically embraced in a reassuring, welcoming and calming handshake that of Dr White. Eager to absorb even more intellect. Marco becoming, like an uncontrolled junky wanting more and more and more. More of the drug which would ease the unfamiliar craving, scratching and desire to learn in his mind. His hands gentle stroking over the green foam padded chair a few feet away from the wheelchair. Foundling the cold metal legs, like a carpenters embrace upon his latest sculpture. Once again, no physical or mental reaction consequent. Marco sighing feeling almost as destitute as the empty wheelchair. Gazing a moment out of the corridor's windows, at the shadowing movements of life below, without knowing his eyes having even hovered across Hausbecks car.

Downstairs seems to be more active, on the ground floor, the lobby, entrance, reception desk even the emergency area there are people, of whom I can touch. Place my hand in theirs and see if it happens again, said Marco. His mind in a pirouetting search to find a solution. A hesitant thought scrambling in his thoughts like a warning, dominant, supreme master.

"If I have the power to bump people's intellect along with their memories by my physical touch upon their hand. Will I also absorb their illnesses too? After all a hospital is not exactly full of holiday makers searching for sea, sun and sex."

"My God, I hope Dr White is not seriously ill," said Marco, his mind working overtime, like the inside of a hornet's nest.

"Don't be so panicky, you know everything about Dr White and you know the only thing he's suffering from illness wise is an Acromioclavicular joint strained." (Strained shoulder muscle). said Marco, telling and calming himself in a reassuring voice. Clasping his chin with his left hand, his thumb pressing against the bottom as though to hold his mouth closed, his index finger rubbing the corner of his mouth and the side of his right cheek, up and down, like a philosopher thinking of a solution to a riddle. Staring down the corridor his regard halting at the next light brown wicket door which lead to the adjacent room.

"There inside would be another patient. Man, woman, or child, any age. There I could come into physical contact with another human being. There I could see if it happens again," said Marco. At the same time a conscious respectful voice, as though a spiritual caring whisper from his mother, overpowering and ending his drug needy want to enter the room of a perfect stranger. Penetrate his or her intimacy, disregard their suffering and physical state. Hinder even maybe their healing status. Only to crave his instinct to bump another soul's intellect and reminiscence. Marco turning, walking slowly back to his room, telling himself the humble whisper of his mother echoing from within, was right. He had no moral right to invade the intimacy and privacy of a total stranger. No matter what his scratching, aching mind was niggling at him to carry out. As he pushed open his room's door. His mind set on going back to bed. His head forced to turn because of the creaking noise coming from the far distance. There, a few meters away to his right approaching a hospital intern, his turquoise attire in contrast against the dull pigment of the passageway's décor.

The creaking coming from the corridors swing door hinges, springing back into place. Pushing the door to close automatically behind the young intern as he passed pushing an empty hospital bed. The young nurse surprised to see Marco stood in the corridor with his wool velvet dressing gown half draping from his left shoulder like a lord. As he approached Marco, his handsome young adolescent face becoming clearer. Marco staring a moment at the young man's piercing blue eyes and almost feminine features the nurse's appearance ravishing. His hair think black parted with a crease to his left, then brushed backwards. The right side of his pleat longer hanging over his right ear. The young man's eyebrows were neat and clipped, and the only facial hair visible upon his visage. Marco thinking.

"He looks more like a male model then a nurse, maybe he was and just filling in to pay the bills before he hit it big time," said Marco. The handsome interne acknowledging Marco, his voice as feminine as his allure.

"Now young man, what are you doing wondering around these creeping unfriendly corridors at such an hour?" said the intern. Marco replying with his instant explanation.

"Couldn't sleep," said Marco.

"*Ahhh*, couldn't sleep," said the intern, his eyebrows rising as if analysing the two-word response.

"What you need young man is a nice cup of cocoa and a mind full of little dreams," said the interne.

Marco smiled but not replying.

"Oh, is this your room 715, or you're that Mr Marco Soffione Rosalinni, the one who was struck by lightning," said the interne. Marco's eyes raising out of surprise and curiosity, he wanted to ask some questions, but no need Nurse Brian. As he was about to learn. Bursting out into conversation carrying on with his informative babbling.

"By the way I'm Nurse Brain, I normally work in the other building block, but Susan and Racheal are both ill. I think they've gone away together, but who am I to gossip *ehh*?" said Nurse Brain, whilst at the same time looking around him, as if to make sure nobody else could hear is accusations.

"Do you know they call you the miracle boy around here, *orr* yes, you're very, very lucky to be alive, normally with the powerful intake of electricity your body absorbed you should be in a world beyond. Gone forever, burnt to cinders, like a flimsy piece of paper in a blazing inferno. But no, you're here dressed like somebody out of a Shakespeare play, believe me I know all too well the dress wear I'm and actor, and I love Shakespeare. 'My hero'. Just doing this job until Broadway or Hollywood calls me. Anyway, yes, you're alive and well and all those intellectual minds running around here, like mad scientists don't have a clue how. We all had a bet on you to see if you'd come out of your coma, most of us, I'm sorry to be so harsh and frank, myself included thought you'd be brain dead.

A useless vegetable laid there hopelessly staring into and unknown abyss. But no, no, no. you're alive like 'Frankenstein'. He's alive I tell you *alive*. Sorry, don't be upset it's the actor in me, can't help myself," said nurse Brain. Marco giving a half-hearted smile. He couldn't figure out if nurse Brain was crazy, unfriendly, both, or just simply innocent, his words not meaning to harm. After all, if everybody on the planet told the truth. Told people, strangers, neighbours, and friends, family and loved ones the truth, the honest plain innocent truth. Who wouldn't be offended? A flash blitzed in his mind.

"I could shake Nurse Brain's hand. Bump his intellect and consciousness. One, I'll see if it happens again. Two, I'll know more about my situation and the hospital gossip. Three, if none of the others I'll learn about Shakespeare," said Marco in his curious mind. Interrupting Nurse Brain politely, his plan already analysed and perfected in his mind.

"Sorry to interrupt you, Brain, you said something about a hot Cocoa, would you be…" said Marco, not needing to finish his sentence, Nurse Brain jumping into his planned strategy, like a debutant chest player lured into the strategic game plan of a master.

"But of course, now you get yourself into bed, I'll be there in a jiffy to tuck you in, along with a fresh hot nice cup of Cocoa, OK," said Nurse Brain in a gleeful yelp. "Thank you," said Marco.

"*Orrr*. No need to thank me young man, it's a pleasure. Especially after all you've been through," said Nurse Brian.

"At least let me shake your hand. Where I come from, we thankfully shake the hand of those of whom we are deeply grateful for, would you mind," said Marco. Nurse Brain without questioning Marco, having already extended his left hand, like a robotic gestural response to Marco's right hand stretched out before him in a welcoming and thank fulling manner. Seconds later their palms connected, drawn to one another, like the North and South Pole of a magnet sticking together. The seconds began to tick, like a chronometer inside Marco's mind. He smiled gracefully, Nurse Brain enchanted by Marco's allure and tender gesture having no desire to disconnect their palms embrace. Ten seconds having passed, Marco still grinning, Nurse Brain believing it was because of some sort of physical attraction to him. In a certain sort of way, it was. But Marco's contentment was more because it was happening again. He was sensing the strange tingling from his toes to his fingertips, conglomerating at his phalange. His palmar crease sensing de novo the minor electrical intake. The sensation of pins and needles and charging energetic force, amalgamated with a peculiar humming in his auricles like a faint whale's cry, simultaneously with the powerful throbbing in his brains motor sensory cortex. Thirty seconds later once again the strange tingling from his toes to his fingertips, along with the minor electrical intake conglomerating at his phalanges palmar crease. The peculiar whale's humming cry in his auricles, simultaneously with the potent pulsation from the inside of his cranium. As with Dr White abruptly vanishing. Marco opening his clasp, Nurse Brain a little saddened. He'd enjoyed more the personal corporal handclasp than Marco.

"May I ask you a personal question?" said Marco, a secure feeling of trustworthiness towards Nurse Brain.

Brain replying, his heart pounding, like a young maiden seeing her prince gallop over the hill tops, racing towards her. A powerful attraction towards Marco had installed.

"To be or not to be, that is the question."

"The earth has music for those who listen," said Nurse Brian, quoting Shakespeare. Marco having bumped the intellect and intimate souvenirs of nurse Brain, understood without any further explanations his Shakespearian passion and constant use of certain phrases. It was now axiomatic for Marco who Nurse Brain really was. A lonely young man who'd found shelter, protection and even love inside the theatre and through his acting. A boy whose stigmata had been carved for eternity inside his heart. Cast aside by his mother and Father because of his homosexuality.

Tortured, teased, bullied, physically and emotionally all his young adult life. Pushed to the limit because of the surrounding incomprehension around him. That he was no different from another. Despite the fact that his love, passion dreams and goals similar to that of thousands, millions. His suicide attempt having miraculously failed. Life and those he'd encountered at the hospital, guiding, helping, reaching out to Brain. The zephyr of expectance. The aspiration of wanting to live life to its fullest, overcome the barriers people, bad people had put before him and except the man he was. Forget the monster those of whom he'd screeched out for their love and understanding had made him out to be. The hospital and theatre having reunited Brain with his soul. He was Nurse Brain through the night shift at the Royal Duchess Hospital. There for others, with a sincere care, a unique tenderness and the patient of the saint. Through his acting he was anybody he wanted to be. A thief, a cook, a crook, a priest. He was everybody, adapting to each role like a chameleon to his changing environment. He was great and destined for greatness. Brains heart felt no abhor towards his tyrannisers only a desire for peace and forgiveness. The certitude that he was not weak but those without understanding were deeper lost in the labyrinth of hate then he would ever be. Marco feeling and acknowledging everything having absorbed the lost demons and rising saints of Brain. Comprehended almost everything, his own intellect and body having once again otherworldly acquired. But one thing he didn't know.

Had Nurse Brain also felt anything? said Marco, in a silent whispering thought. As their hands had physically embraced and the strange phenome having possessed Marco's psyche and minds energy once again. Had Nurse Brain felt what Marco had felt?

"So, what's your question young man don't be shy, spit it out. Be free. Free!" said Nurse Brian in an exalted voice, flinging his arms to his side, like Rose on the Titanic.

"Did you feel anything?" said Marco. Brain looking befuddled, what a question he thought, bursting out into his acting status even though what he was expressing was true. Brains right hand limp, like a dog's paw asking his master for a treat, his left hand placed upon his chest, fingers spread widely, like a French actress expressing the simple emotion and question, response.

"Moi."

"*Orrr* Chou, Chou I can't say that I felt nothing. There was a little flutter in my heart, but nothing like what I felt with Jonny Johnson, *ohhh*, I can still feel him now, if you know what I mean." said Nurse Brian. Marco feeling a certain unfamiliar sensation in his arse. He didn't want to say that.

Yes, he did know what Brain meant.

A little embarrassed by the new sensation, but Marco quickly understanding, by Nurse Brain's vague response to his question. He hadn't felt the same sensations, pins and needles, tingling's, electrical intake, whales humming and throbbing mind. His question answered. Only himself could feel and procure this alien force.

What in God's name has happened to me? said Marco, the question echoing in his mind.

"You look tired. Get yourself back into bed and I'll bring you that hot Cocoa I promised, OK," said Nurse Brain. His nurse's tenderness leaping back in the centre stage, like a tiger. Marco did feel tired, exhausted. Seemed this was one of the downsides of bumping the intellect and emotional memories of another being. Pushing the door open, placing his dressing gown on the end of his bed, slipping back under the sheets. Next thing he was woken by a familiar, and an unfamiliar voice chattering rather loudly. His eyes adjusting to the light and his ears tuning in on the conversation. He wondered for an instant if he'd dreamt about his encounter with Nurse Brain. But the cold cup of Cocoa by his bed side, placed delicately upon a small, pleated piece of paper reassuring Marco it wasn't a dream.

CHAPTER SEVEN

THIRTY SECONDS TO SHAKE A HAND

"*Arr*. You're awake, hope we didn't wake you?" said the familiar voice of Dr White. Marco sitting up, yawning, rubbing his eyes with his index fingers knuckles. Replying a little groggy.

"No, no you didn't wake me. What time is it?" said Marco. The unfamiliar voice answering, "Ten fifty-seven hours precisely," said Hausbeck, his dominant presence now only inches away from Marco. Marco coming around slowly from his profound sleep not replying to Hausbecks military response. Instead, delicately pulling from under the full mug of cold Cocoa Nurse Brains folded note.

'You were sleeping like a baby, didn't want to wake your blissful moment. Off for three days, then back to my normal building block. Great to meet you. Even greater to see you up and well. He's my number, call me when your home. Xxx. Brain',said the note. Marco smiling cheekily to himself. Thinking of Brian's passion for Jonny Johnson. His new special intellect knowing exactly what Brian was wishing for. Folding back the pleats of his intimate little note, placing it inside his bedside top draw.

"Marco this is an old fellow colleague and close acquaintance, Dr Martin Daniel Hausbeck. He is currently working with NASA, and is very interested, like ourselves to understand what happened to you the night of your accident. Don't worry we're not talking about little green men here. That fact is only very few, well actually none. No other human being has survived an electrocution your body and mind received. Maybe you didn't know but NASA is one of the leading investigators into new world changing health healing technology and your case files has got many of us white blouse intellects befuddled. But as also given us new unthought-of opportunities and possibilities. Your case and E.E.G data reading has opened up a Pandora's Box and presented us with visions, channels, directions we never even dreamed of," said Dr White. Marco glaring at the ceiling, his eyes fixed upon the coffee stain. His mind having registered Dr White's recent words. But his new all-powerful intellect reliving the incident of the coffee blemish. Again, it was as clear as a vivid dream, the souvenirs of Nurse Brain now that of Marco's too.

It was the 2nd of June 2014. Nurse Brain along with his two co-workers Nurse Susan and Racheal had been sent to clean and prepare room 715. They'd been informed seventy-nine-year-old, Mr Jenkins. Who'd been admitted three weeks earlier because of a stroke which had paralysed the totality of Mr Jenkins left side. The information given was that poor old Mr Jenkins had succumbed to his attack. Nurse Brain along with Susan and Racheal, once again heavy heartedly carry out their dutiful tasks. Brain and Susan disposing of the old bed sheets. Racheal clearing away the remains of Mr Jenkins last meal. It was 5.42 a.m. the chambers door wedged open for easy access to new material, fresh linen and cleaning products. The sun blazing through the hospital corridors windows, projecting a divine glimmer, like an angelic halo into the bed chambers. When all of a sudden Mr Jenkins gently ambled from the bathroom, his feet sliding at a slow pace across the floor, like he was walking on ice. He was wearing white pyjamas. The dominant effulgence of the sun ricocheting from the bathrooms mirror reflecting a holy white aura, projected directly behind Mr Jenkins. Standing himself in astonishment why his room was being cleared. The suns force and archangelic glow, bestowing Mr Jenkins with that of a ghost. Brain had screamed like never before. Susan and screamed even louder. Racheal had thrown the remains of Mr Jenkins supper into the air. Plate, saucer, cup, knife and fork all projected towards the platform, like out of controlled flying crafts. The coffee cup with its residue contents having been the only article to ricochet of the ceiling, leaving for many years to come the presence of Mr Jenkins passage. The wrong information having been given to the young internes. They were supposed to clean room 751 where a Mrs Bailey was due to be admitted within the forthcoming hours. Nobody understood, how or where such an error of misguiding messages had been wrongly filtered. Mr Jenkins nearly completely healed from his attack, finding his role as a ghost, rather amusing. A story he tells all those who he encounters. For Nurse Brain, Susan and Racheal a moment of horrific fear, rapidly transformed into joyful laughter and unique brotherhood and sisterhood, like a special bond, whenever they're asked about the coffee stain in room 715.

Marco smiling to himself. He liked knowing these curious little things. He was beginning to see more and more unlimited possibilities of his alien telepathist offering. It was with this very calm and satisfactory simper. Knowing he already knew more than many and could learn endlessly, that he greeted Hausbecks cold, closed arm folded allure. Hausbeck taking over from Dr White, his arms still folded as though somehow, he sensed he should not come into physical contact with Marco, his voice robotic and cold.

"As Dr White just said, NASA are one of the major leading investigators into future technology, we thrive on knew opportunities and unique incidents which in return could help millions amongst us. For example, Marco, in your case we could understand more about coma patients, accessing a way to reach into their minds and bring them back from the black hole of solitude themselves and families live through. You've lived through. You've survived an unaccountable amount of energy from a major force. An electrically conducting plasma. Lightning strikes often result in a cardiac arrest or even worse. Those few who have ever been resuscitated sufferer irreversible brain damage, with various degrees of disability. Those few who do survive are never the same again. Those who have obtained an intake similar to yours have never survived. You are the first, a unique being living, walking, and talking, unscarred and uninjured. Here to tell the tale. To put it another way, more scientific if you like. Lightning travels through the atmosphere around 434.52289 kilometres per hour or about

"120.7008 kilometres a second and typically lasts for one 10,000th of a second, during its brief existence it burns at 30,000°C or six times hotter than the earths brightest star. Sun to simplify things. Those who stand it its path. Well, I've already said, in simple terms. They lose. You Marco are the David who has overpowered Goliath," said Hausbeck. Silence prevailed, like the instant hush before a president makes his or her speech.

"David and Goliath," said Marco, his voice silent, like a whisper. Marco sensing a sure uncertainty about Hausbeck but at the same time he was curious to understand more about his four months lost memory. Repeating Hausbeck's words in his head.

"For example, Marco, in your case we could understand more about coma patients, access a way to reach into their minds and bring them back from the black hole of solitude themselves and families live through. You've lived through," said Marco. With these words a reminiscing vision emerged in Marco's mind. Laid on his back staring up at the majestic sight, of the Fallstreak nebulous hole widening, revealing the heavens, and through the opening the multitude of Stella's twinkling their supreme galactic force, as though another universe was levitating beyond. Along with the recalling vision of his left hand reaching his into his left pocket to pull out his weird and wonderful discovered object.

"My God, the weird pebble I found. Has somebody taken it?" said Marco, His mind puzzled looking over at his bed side cabinet.

"It wasn't in the top draw; I would have seen it when I put Nurse Brains note inside," said Marco mumbling the thought in his mind.

Staring at the wardrobe.

"Maybe it's still in my jeans?" said Marco. The thoughts in his mind reassuringly answering his wondering frets. At that instant the door opening. Anna walking inside Marco's hospital room, her face radiant accompanied by a light touch of make-up, like she was going on a first date. She'd slept like a kitten in the bosom of her mother for the first time in months. Anna smiling politely at Hausbeck, seeing him for the first time, gently stroking the left arm of Dr White at his triceps, continuing directly to Marco's bed side, placing her handbag upon his bedsit cabinet, leaning over her son, lovingly kissing him upon his left cheek.

"Buongiorno mia amore." (Morning my love), said Anna. Her voice full of glee.

Dr White turning to Hausbeck as if to say I told you so, as they both stared upon mother and son, rapidly babbling away to each other in their home tongue, like two lonely housewives who'd suddenly been given the grace of God to speak.

"Sorry to interrupt you both," said Hausbeck, seconds later coughing, as though clearing his throat from phlegm.

"You speak English Marco, right?" said Hausbeck. The way of asking his questioned seemed bizarre, the slight smug smirk upon his face as though he knew some inside information cautioning Marco's acceptance of his baiting strategies.

"Off course he speak the English, he is clever boy and learn your words to help his mother and his father." said Anna. The instinctive nature of a mother to protect her own outpouring from Anna's semblance and ricocheting from every angle in the hospital room. Anna at the same time gesturing the sign of the cross thinking of her beloved Arnaldo. Nurse Wendy having just entered the room before Hausbecks questioning, gazing at Anna. Their eyes for a split second united in a feminine understanding only women have.

"I apologise, Mrs Rosalinni, I didn't mean to offend you or Marco," said Hausbeck, his voice seemingly expressing an authentic sorry.

"It's OK, we are just now a little tired and I want Marco to come home now. It's been long now he sleep away from me and Pasta," said Anna. Hausbeck smiling warmly at Anna. Her beauty, loyalty and sensual Italian accent with her cute grammatical errors, seemingly having charmed his earlier hard-faced military scowl.

"I understand. We all understand what you've both been through these last few months. But I was just explaining to Marco moments before you arrived. His unique situation and miracle healing if you like, have led me and many of my colleagues down a different road. A road which none of us could have possibly imagined. Marco could be the key to unlock many doors for many, many people. So, it is why we would like to do a series of new tests on Marco. But not hear in England. Back at our NASA's Glenn Research Centre in Cleveland USA," said Hausbeck, his words causing a pin drop silence to fall upon the room so intense it was though the world had annihilated sound. Not even human respiration could be heard. Anna gazing at her son for an instant, their eyes telepathically entranced in a mutual compassion. Even though his outstanding muscular physique and ever growing, developing manly features staring back at her. All she could see within his stare was her little boy, lost, scared and frightened. Anna replying short, firm and assertive.

"I am very sorry for the road and keys you and your colleagues want too going on and turn. But my son go only on one road. That is home to me and Pasta. Here in our town, not the millions of miles you talk about. And he come home today," said Anna.

"But Mrs Rosalinni!" said Dr White in a childish stuttering manner. Anna replying with a look as powerful as the Medusa that would have turned the devil himself into stone. Followed by four cold and assertive words.

"Marco comes home today!" said Anna. Nurse Wendy grinning secretly in an enormous admiration for Anna. As if to say.

"Good for you girl."

Then raising her eyes staring at Hausbeck and Dr White expressing a cautioning glare, as if to say.

"Don't even think of getting of the wrong side of a women. Even more so a mother, for no mercy upon earth or beyond will save you," said Nurse Wendy's glare. At that moment Professors Cloud and Rama, entering Marco's hospital room. Their heads faced down scrutinizing the individual medical charts. The tension and discharging ambience hitting them both, as though they'd just walked straight into a brick wall.

"Is everything OK?" said Professor Rama, in a cautious slow mummer.

"Everything is just fine. Mrs Rosalinni was just telling us that she is taking Marco home today," said Nurse Wendy. Anna smiling gratefully woman to woman. The four men staring at each other befuddled, as though realising their male intellect had no way of understanding a female's mind. Marco could hardly keep his excitement. Home after all these months, weeks, days, hours. His gloomy, poorly decorated bedroom seemed as exhilarating to him now as if he'd just been told he had won a voyage into outer space. Marco gazing at the intravenous drip its needle still implanted in his right arm. Nurse Wendy as though having read his mind, instantly attended to disposing of the now unneeded medical aide. She gazed across at Hausbeck, Dr

White and Professor Cloud and Rama. None of which hindered or tried to stop her actions. Seconds later Nurse Wendy said. Her voice soft and tender.

"There, Marco, your free. Free to move around and dress yourself with no obstacles getting in your way. Free to go home with your mum," said Nurse Wendy. Mother and son embraced in a tear-jerking moment. Home together after all Anna's hardship and worries. Finally, the moment she'd begged and prayed for so intensely to God and every saint she knew. At long last a beam of promising hope illuminated her world and Marco's too.

"Look, Mrs Rosalinni, all I ask if you come back sometime next week. A time which is convenient for yourself and Marco. So, we can monitor

Marco's progress and make sure everything is OK. Will? Can, you do that for us?" said Hausbeck. Having rapidly realised if he was to get any way closer to Marco and extract any information. He needed to be as cautious as a photographer approaching a wild animal for the ultimate unique photo. Anna turning her eyes towards Nurse Wendy. Nurse Wendy acknowledging her with a slight bowing of the head, her eyes closed for an instant, like someone in pray, as if to say.

"It'll be OK, when you come back I'll be here too. And it's better to be safe than sorry concerning any side effects concerning Marco. You can trust us," said Nurse Wendy's mannerism gesture. Anna replying with her own silent nod. The minor clairvoyant bodily gestures exchanged with a gigantic comprehension, as powerful as witnessing the suns orb, silently dusking acknowledging to all around nightfall was approaching their doorstep.

"Thank you, Anna," said Hausbeck, having interpreted the exchange of bodily gestures between the two women adding.

"You can make all the arrangements necessary with Nurse Wendy, she'll inform me of the time and day, which will be appropriate for the both of you," said Hausbeck shaking Anna's hand, but only tapping Marco rapidly upon his left shoulder before leaving the room. Marco a little frustrated, he wanted to shake Hausbeck's hand. Bump his memories and intellect, discover what he knew and what his true actions was. An interrogating question arising within Marco's mind, like a scientist having thought of another way to an unsolved solution.

Why had Hausbeck not wanted to shake Marco's hand? said Marco, to himself in a silent whispering thought.

"We'll leave you to get dressed and prepare your things ok Marco. And we'll see you sometime next week OK," said Professor Cloud, having now made some understanding of the earlier tensioned atmosphere.

"OK," said Marco, at the same time gently caressing his right forearm with his left hand at the spot the intervenors needle had lived for nearly four months, now replaced by some cotton wool and a plaster.

"Wait," said Marco almost in a shout, having seen Professor Cloud and Rama approaching the door to leave his room. "Aren't you at least going to shake my hand to say goodbye, is it not an English custom?" said Marco.

"Yes, of course," said Professor Cloud, at the same time turning to walk towards Marco. His right hand stretched out in a welcoming manner.

Professor Rama standing behind his colleague in a patient statue, waiting his turn to express a handshaking goodbye. No sooner had Marco's right hand come into contact with Professors Clouds right hand. He was sensing the strange tingling from his toes to his fingertips, conglomerating at his phalange. But before he had time to count the thirty second stop watch in his head, until his paranormal powers had bumped and absorbed all of Professor Cloud's wisdom and knowledge. Professor Cloud pulling away his hand only a few seconds after their palms having embraced. Marco only having downloaded a fraction of Clouds reminiscence and savoir faire.

"See you next week, Marco, and take care of that wonderful mother of yours, she's been through more than you can imagine. Oh and stay away from storms. We don't want to see you back here in the same state you arrived last year OK," said Professor Cloud, before finishing his little speech with a stern pat upon Marco's left shoulder as if to say.

"Stay out of trouble."

Marco more concentrating on how he'd lost contact with his otherworldly handshaking embrace. The question jumping into his mind for the first time like a revelation.

"To hold or shake a stranger's hand for thirty seconds wasn't going to be that easy," said Marco, in a curious mind analysing manner. Quickly improvising before grasping the extended gestured hand, stretched out before him of Professor Rama.

"Thirty seconds, thirty seconds," said Marco, slowing gliding his palm into that of Professor Rama, but once their hands clasped together tightening his grip, like a noose around an animal's neck. Instantly the sensation of pins and needles and charging energetic force, amalgamated with a peculiar humming in his auricles like a faint whale's cry, simultaneously with the powerful throbbing in his brains motor sensory cortex charging once more into Marco's physique. Professor Rama after a few seconds gesturing to pull his hand free. But Marco smiling not realising his firm grasp in a bizarre modus, like some deranged fool. Professor Rama trying to loosen his palms grip from Marcos. Marco feeling his reaction. Clasping over the top of Professors Rama's right hand with his left. Only fifteen seconds having gone by and the bewildered expressing upon Rama's face followed by Marco's reluctance to release his grasp, causing even Nurse Wendy and Professor Cloud to question Marco's out of the ordinary action. Only Anna secretly knowing what he was doing. Coming quickly to her son's aide her words instantly calming the dumbfounded countenance of Nurse Wendy, Professor Cloud and a more concerned Professor Rama.

"In our culture we shake a hand for long time, it's our way of showing more gratitude," said Anna. It was a lie. Anna didn't like to lie; she was as truthful and honest as the Virgin Mary. But she was certain God would forgive this minor sin, if it helped her son. After all, they'd been through so much. Her tall tale words, so convincing Professor Cloud looking all the more shocked for having pulled his hand away so quickly. As though profoundly concerned he'd disrespected Anna's and Marco's cultured traditions. Thirty seconds later the strange tingling from his toes to his fingertips, along with the minor electrical intake conglomerating at his phalanges palmar crease. The peculiar whale's humming cry in his auricles, simultaneously with the potent pulsation from the inside of his cranium. Stopped. Marco unclasping Professor Rama's hand. Now knowing everything about him. Explaining it to his mother as they sat on the bus together for the first time in over four months, direction home.

CHAPTER EIGHT

LIFE ALMOST BACK TO NORMAL

"He comes from Andhra Pradesh the only son from a family of eight, he's the youngest. His parents both died years ago and one sister. The other six sisters still live in India. He's been in England nineteen years seven months and three days. And he lives with his two teenage sons and nine-year-old daughter on Town's lane avenue. Number twenty-four. His wife, Hayi, is his village sweetheart and she came to join him in England five years after him, when he'd saved enough money to provide for her. She waited five years for him. He left two months after their marriage. And…" said Marco, in a rapid chant.

"It's OK, Marco, you don't need to tell me all. This is private life of this man and personal memories," said Anna. Her voice worried and almost whispering. Glancing around the top deck of the bus to make sure the three other passengers were out of ear shot. Her words making Marco gaze out of the window. The bustling streets whizzing past his almost hypnotic state, like past memories. His eyes more fixed on the rain drops shimmering down the bus's windows from the vehicle's vibrations, like transparent creatures spiralling down the glass surface.

"Marco," said Anna in a gentle voice. "Marco!" said Anna with a stronger intonation in her voice. Marco seemingly to be in an open-eyed coma, as if he'd entered a world no other being, not even his own mother could follow him too. Marco thinking of all he'd recently learnt about Professor Rama. He was even thinking in Telugu. The Indian language spoken in Andhra Pradesh.

This new language I've learnt could become quite useful, especially when going to the local Indian restaurant, said Marco. Opportunities, dreams, situations, scenarios, chances, options and a whole load of silent whirl winding ideas humming inside his mind.

"Marco, look at me." said Anna once again. Marco seemingly unreachable.

"Marco Guarda me per favour!" (Marco look at me please), said Anna. The tearful pain-stricken voice of his mother finally penetrating Marco's entranced mood. Turning staring at his mother, the tears in her eyes causing his heart and soul to silently scream out in hurt.

"What is it, Mama? What's wrong?" said Marco. Anna sighing, her exhaling cry so intense it was almost as though her spirit had physically left her body. A ghostly mist seemed to discharge from her mouth, enter the atmosphere then recrudesce within her.

"What is it, Mama? Tell me what's wrong," said Marco. Anna opening her mouth to express her sentiments, but her words seemed to be locked within her, staring at her son then down at her wedding ring. Her hands delicately poised on her knees, like a queen. Caressing her matrimonial halo with her left thumb, her tender touch upon the ring, causing a flood of memories to pour into her mind, heart and soul. She needed no others reminiscence, only hers. Her exhaling breath discharging another mist of air, only this time words followed.

"Mia amore. I don't know if this thing which happen to you is great gift or great curse. But I am wise to know, to understand if you don't use this as great gift, it will become to be great curse. You have been given, chosen these special powers for something. But what other people don't have, other people always want. What people don't understand, these people do anything to discover. You can learn anything from anybody, their memories, their knowledge, their way of speak, their skills, their intellect, even their secrets. But this unique power will leave you alone. To be able learn and absorb absolutely anything from anybody. Only God know where this take you. And me. You are mio figlio (my son), and I always be there for you, I always carry you in my heart. But I sadly know, the more you learn, the more you understand, and the more you *Bump*. Like how you put it. Then further from me you will going. I am scaring for you Marco. I am scaring for tomorrow," said Anna. Marco staring at his mother in great silence, both now alone on the bus, the other passengers having descended from the bus at the last stop. Marco reaching out his right hand in a loving gesture going to place it onto his mother's hand. Anna instantly moving her hand away, like he was carrying some sort of disease. Their eyes fixed to one another both in secrets thoughts. Marco impuissant to what was being said in his mother's mind. The silence broken by the bus coming to another stop and a chattering group of young school kinds, loudly making their way to the top deck. Amongst them two Indian girls. One staring at Marco for a moment before saying to her friend in their dialect tongue and language, giggling in a girl like manner.

"Look at him, he's well fit," said the young girl in her Indian language. Marco smiling quietly to himself, having understand word for word the juvenile adolescent's confessions. But he was thinking more of his mother's warning.

"A gift or a curse," said Marco. These very words still humming in his head, as he anxiously walked from the bus stop, across the streets and then up their apartment buildings staircase. The front door creaking open before Anna. Marco's absence not having changed the gloomy apartment. But Pasta was ecstatic to see him. Leaping from his basket in a juvenile frenzy, jumping up at Marco, like a crazed fan seeing his or her idol up close.

"It's OK, its OK little man. I'm sorry I should have listened to you when you barked at me to go home that night, I'm sorry, I'm sorry," said Marco. Realizing maybe if he'd have listen to Pasta and his warning barks that famous November night. Then he wouldn't have been struck by lightning or have brought some much heartache upon those he loved and cherished the most. Pasta still leaping up at Marco and bursting out joyful yelps, even though Marco having kneeled down to his height.

"He's missed you, he feels bad, responsible. Feels he's to blame for what happened to you. He told me time and time again" said Anna.

Marco baffled.

How did his mother know what Pasta felt?" *"Could she talk to animals?* said Marco, whispering these silent questions in his head, before his lightning bolt idea.

I could discover what Pasta is thinking after all if my ability to bump information works on humans maybe it would work on animals too? said Marco, in a silent thought. Anna having hooked her jacket neatly on the coat hook, entering the kitchen, starting to make herself and Marco a cup of tea and something to eat.

"Are you hungry Marco?" said Anna in a loud voice from behind the door, Marco could see the light from the fridge exposing her shadow along the floor, like a ghostly presence.

"Affamato." (Starving), said Marco. Listening to the bustling of pans and the slicing of something, probably tomatoes knowing his mother. Seizing his opportunity like a thief, knowing his victim was out for the night. Marco approaching Pasta's paw. Pasta letting out a little anxious yelp, as though his six senses having perceived something in Marco which made him uneasy. It was if his fragile little body and mind was torn between seeing the Angel he knew, followed by a demon's presence. Marco grasping Pasta's front paw with both hands, like he was cupping a butterfly inside his palms. Instantly he sensed the strange tingling from his toes to his fingertips, amalgamated with the minor electrical intake, along with the sensation of pins and needles, and the peculiar humming in his auricles like a faint whale's cry. Pasta tried many times during the thirty second transfer to pull away his paw. But Marco only releasing his grasp when his otherworldly strange bodily perceptions having stopped. It had happened again, even with an animal Marco could bump the knowledge and reminiscence of their soul. Pasta staring at him, as though he'd been saddened, like the hurtful glare of deception from somebody who trusted you with all their spirit only to discover their faith in that person had been abused. This very stare outpouring from Pasta's eyes as he glared at Marco from his basket to where he'd retreated. Marco witnessing the wounded face of Pasta comprehending more and more his mother's warning about his new extra-terrestrial powers becoming a curse. He'd learned Pasta's traumatising tyranny and even why he carried so much abhor for black dogs. He'd seen the torturing nightmares of Pasta's first master. Kicking him, starving him, even burning his skin with cigarette ends. He'd seen the visions of Pasta traumatic earlier life, snipped at and often attacked by his old masters second dog, a black mongrel bastard a mix between a Bulldog and a Jack Russel turned into a demon because of the unlawful sadistic education of its owner. One of earths creatures sadly falling into the hands of an evil soul, with only a thinning hope to be saved by a loving master. Marco understanding now where so many scares, internal and external having come from. He'd also seen Pasta's horrendous street life, after finally, one cold winter's afternoon slipping free from his chains, his weak malnourished body sliding out of the manacles, climbing the dark bleak cellar steps and escaping unnoticed out of the half opened back door, across the rubble garden and into the rear streets, whilst his tyrannising master lay in a half drunken slumbering state. Pasta living for months scavenging through dustbins for a little food, until one evening he'd followed Anna home. Her Angelic aura and pietistic spirit recognised by his sixth sense.

Marco having also learnt that the great understanding that his mother had of Pasta was not by some otherworldly energetic force. Not by absorbing or Bumping Pasta's secret possessions. But because of the most powerful force in the universe.

"Love."

Marco feeling guilty and bad like he'd taken something he shouldn't have. Seized a precious object and he'd been caught, exposed. Wishing he could take back his actions. But it was too late. What was done was done. Like the presence of peoples acts and choices be those good or bad. Not even his new gift or curse gave him the powers to turn back the clock. Pasta turning in his basket turning his back to Marco like a sulking child. Marco rising to his feet displeased with himself, entering his bedroom. His single bed, large wardrobe, bedside cabinet with his night lamp, his old wooden chair. All standing like waiting spectres for Marco's presence to return. Staring a moment at the posters of his homeland Italy. His regard turned towards the five objects neatly placed on his bedside cabinet. A one pound, Fifty and twenty pence coin. A dried small Maple leaf and a magnificent olive-green pebble.

"Tesoro." (Treasure), said Marco, reliving the flash back images of the moment he'd found the strange stone. Placing his bag at the end of his bed, sitting down on the opposite side of his bed next to the pebble, staring at it for a long instant. He could still make out the curious oval shaped minerals magnificent, peculiar hieroglyphics in a sublime sapphire tint, encapsulated within the weird stone. But it was no longer olive green. Now more of a lime green.

In the middle of the strange mass, the smaller decagon shape, only there was no miniature brain characteristic embedded, no diminutive electrical discharges, like fulguration supernaturally surging from the alien form. Stretching out his hand, then hesitating like he was approaching fire. The last reminiscing flash of lightning before his comatose black out, hurtling back into his mind. Pulling his hand away in an unsure gesture. But then noticing the closer his presence toward the pebble. Small shimmers of light, like tiny sparks appeared from with the decagon form. Plucking up all his courage, grasping the pebble within his left palm, the silky-smooth texture mollifying instantly Marco's earlier apprehensions. Sensing a weird and wonderful tingling in his fingertips, like something was being extracted from him. He thought maybe the information he'd bumped was being somehow transferred into the alien object, like a computer download. But even though he didn't want his recently accumulated intellect to be taken from him. Marco feeling powerless to this mysterious sensation, almost as though he was paralysed. Suddenly his bedroom door abruptly swung open. An exasperated Anna standing arms folded.

"Marco, I call you seven times now. Your dinner going to get cold," said Anna. The startling appearance of his displeased mother causing Marco to leap out of his trance state and drop the pebble on the floor. The pebble rolling into the corner like a giant marble.

"Sorry mama, I'm coming," said Marco. Anna ruffling his short rapidly growing back hair, in a pardoning gesture.

"Vieni, Vieni." (Come, come), said Anna, Marco raising to his feet, taking one last stare at the pebble then ruffling his right hand through his shortened hair. He suddenly realised, since his awakening he hadn't even looked at his appearance. The mirror in the hospital room had been taken out, the reflection from the busses widows blurred by the rain drops and he couldn't remember seeing or having any other chance to stare upon his reflection. An enormous urge to gaze upon his new mirror image and see what everybody else could see, penetrating his mind, like a young maiden having just had her hair done in a new style. Exiting his bedroom only a stone throw away from the bathroom and its looking glass. Marco's urge soothed seeing his mother sat at the dining table patiently waiting for her son. Having seen him enter the room, Anna having already started dishing out heaps of spaghetti onto his plate. Marco discerning, just how many times his mother must have sat at that dining table alone. Just how many meals she'd shared with silence and emptiness. And just how long she must have been praying for this very moment, to sit with her only son and share a tender moment together. At first the only noise between them was the cluttering of cutlery and the munching of mouths. But after a short while

Anna bursting out into conversation explaining to Marco all that had been said to her, from neighbours, working colleagues and family members. Making excuses for hers and Arnaldo's family for not having displaced themselves to help Anna or see if Marco was ok. Instead, she explained about the little piece of blessed cloth, attached to her chain adding.

"All the family wore a piece of blessed cloth around a chain. It had to touch your skin at all times. It worked your home. Back from darkness into the light. Back with Mama," said Anna. Marco caressing his mother's visage replying.

"It's good to be home, Mama, and it's good to eat your home cooked spaghetti again," said Marco. A small silence prevailing, each in their own tender thoughts, but each very happy.

"I'll wash up and clear away the table mama, you go sit down and rest your feet," said Marco.

"No, no let me wash and clear away, you must rest, you been in opsedale (hospital), you rest mia amore," said Anna in an insistent voice.

Marco starting to clear away the plates from the table, but Anna's desire for him to rest was very persuasive. Not feeling tired at all, Marco turning the situation offering to walk Pasta. Presenting himself convincing arguments that the fresh air, after being cooped up in that hospital so long would do him good. And that there was no storm in sight for Anna to worry about lightning strikes. Adding he'd terribly missed walking Pasta. They agreed and Pasta wagging his tail in an eccentric joy agreeing also. It seemed even he'd already pardon Marco for penetrating into his secret memories. Like he'd had a long yearning to finally tell somebody about his tyrannising passed. Marco before walking Pasta, entering the bathroom and taking a long hard stare at himself. His appearance insight, to his great relief hadn't change too drastically, he was a little thinner, his hair was shorter, but it gave him a certain charm. At the front seemed to be growing some whitening strikes. But again, this in itself didn't give him cause for alarm. His scar stretching from the centre of his forehead towards the right, just above his eye. Having vanished. What shocked Marco the most was the differing eye pigment his right eye cerulean and his left eye a beautiful olive green. Blinking a few times to make sure he'd correctly identified the different colouring within his optics. Thinking to himself if this truly bothered him, he could always wear contact lenses with a unified colour.

But all in all, he was presently and happily surprised that these were the only apparent physical changed characteristics from his near-death ordeal. Moments later, Marco venturing down the stairs, followed by an over excited Pasta crossing two of his distant neighbours chattering away to each other in their northern dialect. It was strange. Marco for the first time could understand ninety percent of their English expressions. Only a few local terminologies and typical Yorkshire sayings seemed to be still uncomprehensive to him. But never had he imagined four months earlier on that cool November evening, with the remembrance of how he'd struggled to understand the English language. Never in his wildest dreams had he envisaged he would have such an understanding of this foreign linguistic. Once outside Pasta relieving his natural urge, peeing on the nearest bush. It was like a flashbacking image from that famous November evening. The cool late afternoons cloud filled sky, hiding the presence of the earth's brightest star. Marco and Pasta persisted de novo, heading towards the seashores, walking through the large public park, dominated by a magnanimous quantity of sublime saplings, bushes, shrubs, flowers, herbs, plants and trees.

Alder, ash, beech, birch, blackthorn, cherry, crab, dogwood, elder, elm, hawthorn, hazel, holly, hornbeam, juniper, lime, maple, oak, rowan, spindle, whitebeam, willow and yew. Still all huddled near and far, like harmonising energies. Each in their own specific natural graceful manner, metamorphosing their resplendent splendiferous even in the misty gloom. Apparitions of new buds, sprouts, shoots, outgrowths, nuclei, germs and florets slowing presenting their audacious reviving aura preparing their plantae essence for another cyclical transition. Exposing the denominating power of Mother Nature and her message that she waits for no man, woman or child nor their individual's trials of life to move forward upon earth. Marco walking through the park, Pasta scrupulously marking his territory in selected areas. Marco thinking to himself.

"Just how much pee, does a little dog like Pasta have?" said Marco, having counted in his head the eleventh pee from Pasta. It seemed this information was not downloaded from his recent bumping of Pasta's knowledge. Marco staring at the few dried withered crumpled foliage. The reminiscing vision of his leaf catching wish to be able to speak fluent English taunting his mind. His desire having been fulfilled, the superstitious beliefs of his father about catching a falling leaf and then making a wish apparently true.

If only I'd have wished for my father to be alive. If only I hadn't doubted this superstition. Maybe today dad would be here. Here with us, said Marco. These tormenting echoing thoughts and wishes piercing Marco's mind. A sickening feeling of regret and lost chance, bombarding his heart. It would be months before the leaves would fall from the trees again.

Maybe I could go to another part of the world, where the autumn season has just begun. But then I'd have to leave mama again, said Marco. These arguments and scenarios whizzing through his mind as he reached the end of the park. Heading for the first time in months across the hill side and down the meadow's embankment towards the coastal shores. The tide was in. The ash grey and green waves splashing against the promenades rock face barriers, causing spits of water to splatter, like a firework display in different directions. The moved-up ebb hiding the presence of the gravelled sandy shores. Marco staring out across that vast cold ocean wondering, where he had once seen Moeraki Boulders and discovered his alien pebble. Allowing his lungs to inhale the pungent oceanic breezing atmosphere. The twilight duskiness swiftly approaching the hours of darkness. The earlier glooming veiling mist having majestically faded, allowing the meniscus appearance of the terra's neighbouring planetoid to expose its awesome allurement. Even with only the demi presence of the moon, its powerful luminescence effulging the murky waters aura. Causing the crashing waves to glimmer like mounds of sparkling diamonds tumbling from a treasure chest. Marco's shadow caused by the celestial body's shaft of light upon him. Outstretching in front of him like a gigantic underworld presence. He stared long and hard at the half moon peering its almighty force down at him like an opened eye. Talking to the moon as though he was talking to a fellow human, he asked.

"Is it from your world where this strange pebble has come from, or from another of the universes planetoid worlds?" said Marco. His words as firm and serious and his posture. Eagerly and expectantly waiting for some sort of response. Marco greeted only by silence, like the unanswered prayers of a worshiper. Walking home in a sluggish pensive pace, still questioning where the pebble was from and why this gift or curse had been offered to him. Pasta running up the stairs before him. Anxious to get into the apartment, see Anna and collect his evening treat. Followed by a lethargic evening in his basket. The flat was dim only the small lamp and the flickering images of the television giving some diminutive light. Even the half-moon seemed to have displaced itself to another part of the firmament. Pasta running too Anna. Anna slumped in her armchair her right arm draping towards the floor, her left hand placed upon her thigh covering a mound of letters. Pasta laying devotedly and silently at her feet, not even manifesting his desire for his treat. Anna breathing heavily. Marco watching the respirations of his mother's torso exhaling and inhaling, her closed eyelids, twitching in a spasmodic manner, like she was captivated in a bad dream. Marco observing one of the letters bright red stamped warning. Thwart in the centre of the white A4 sized type written letter.

"Final demand."

Sliding the clump of menacing papers as delicately as approaching a butterfly from under Anna's fingers. Not wanting to disturb the much-needed slumber of his mother. Threat after threat, after threat. The big fat profitable giants sending out their vulture letters. Stabbing, biting, clawing intimidating the weak and vulnerable. Not one suggestion of help, understanding or sympathy. Not one comprehending advising solution. Not one caring gesture from one human being to another. Greed and demanding aggressive hunger of total strangers having added masses of worries to Anna's already traumatised situation. Marco's hospitalisation and the absence of his income, due to his temporary working contract at the printing firm. Having psychotically created a serious hostile portending status quo. The echoing words of his beloved father penetrating Marco's heart like a reminding omen that he'd failed his dutiful mission.

"Proteggere sempre tua madre." (Always protect your mother).

Marco placing the knitted cover from the couch over his mother, then tenderly stroking her face, he stared down at her right hand hanging over the armchair, a split second idea entering his mind.

"I could take mama's hand and use my new telepathy extrasensory perception to bump her memories and dreams. That way I'd know what would make her happy," said Marco. Approaching his hand closer to his mother's exposed slumbered palm. Suddenly the flashing image of Pasta's deceptive regard staring back at him, along with his mother's words concerning his earlier offer to take her hand and discover her knowledge.

"No, Marco. No," said Anna reminiscing words. Marco retreating his hand turning his attention to the threatening bundle of 'final demands' sitting himself down at the cleaned and uncluttered dining table. Adding up exactly just how much money he would have to find.

"One thousand, two hundred and ninety-three pounds and sixty-four pence. One thousand, two hundred and ninety-three pounds and sixty-four pence." said Marco in a repetitive voice. Marco whispering once again the sum in his mind before tumbling himself into a deep sleep. His dreams and preoccupied bethinking teeming with ideas of how he could quickly acquire such a sum. To certain upon the planet this amount of money would be peanuts. A new pair of shoes, or a bag. Or in some cases an extravagant meal accompanied with a luxurious bottle of wine. But to Marco and Anna this quantity of debt was like a peasant being told he owed millions.

"I could shake the bank manager or manageress's hand and discover the codes to the vault. Or the passwords to transfer money from one account to another. I could shake the hand of a rich man or woman and obtain the secret code to their credit cards. I could shake the hand of a star and bump their abilities to sing, act or dance," said Marco. A Shakespearian quote hopping into his plotting dreams. Thanks to his handshaking bumped gift from Nurse Brain.

"*Who would not wish to be from wealth exempt*? Since riches point to misery and contempt?" said Marco. His synopsis scenarios all forgetting the hallowed purity of his mother. Anna's contempt knowing her son had bequeathed money through illegal and unfaithful practise would only bring more misery to hers and Marco's lives. No, if he was to gather such a sum of money, he must find an uncompromising legal way.

CHAPTER NINE

NAPLES LOVE

The suns stream of light breaking through Marco's half open shutters projecting a sanctified beam upon him, as though the heavens having approved his moralistic praiseworthy decision to use his other worldly powers righteously. As Marco aroused noticing a pigeon sitting on the paint flaking balcony's metal barrier.

"I wonder if I could bump the intellect of a pigeon, after all I've always wondered what goes on in their minds," said Marco rubbing his awakening eyes with his emerging energy. The pigeon staring at Marco through the glass, its head twitching in different directs like a chicken plucking at corn. Marco opening his bedrooms glass door leading to the balcony, as delicately and slowly as a teenager sneaking back home after staying out, much later then the agreed and allowed time of his or her parents. The bird didn't move, only letting out harmonious cooing, its head still twitching like a plucking hen. Marco moving a little bit closer, placing his footsteps as though he was treading on thin ice. His hands stretched out, like Frankenstein's only inches away from the fowl. Swiftly the bird leaping into flight, flapping its wings only a couple of times, but enough to fly out of reach from Marco's grasp. Before turning in flight landing at the far end of the metal rail, staring at Marco letting out a cooing cry as if to say.

"What do you take me for a pigeon?"

Before plunging in flight and landing down onto the grass below.

"I've seriously got to get a grip of myself, use this ability that I have acquired on something or someone with information useful to my needs. After all what if I only have a limited amount of capacity? What if my mind is like a computer and the quantity of data intake will only be able to amplify a certain magnitude? My God, I wonder how much space and storage I've used already. Maybe animals use up less volume?" said Marco thinking of the strange paralysing hypnotic sensation he'd felt, after having held the pebble within his palm. Like something was being extracted from his being. Turning to stare at the weird stone, still lodged where it had rolled the evening before, between the bedside cabinet and the wall. A cluttering of crockery coming from the kitchen turning his regard from the unknown object.

"Shit, the letters, I left them on the table, shit mama will be angry with me for having pried," said Marco, already dressed having slumbered in his clothes, making his way hastily towards the kitchen. The dining table already set for breakfast and no signs of the buddle of threatening 'Final demands'.

"Buongiorno mia amore. Avete dormito bene? (Morning sweetheart. Did you sleep well?), said Anna.

"Caffè?" said Anna holding out the percolator, in a serving proposing manner.

"Yeah, slept great. And yeah, would love some coffee," said Marco, answering both of his mother's questions.

"I ring the hospital this morning, and I make arrangement we go Tuesday afternoon at two p.m. I cannot the Monday. I work double shift now your home for Pasta. But Tuesday I work only morning, so you come to meet me at work and we go. Va bene," said Anna, not giving her son a chance to reply continuing with her recently organised planning.

"I want make sure all is good with you. I tell that nice Nurse Wendy and Professor White on phone, I call you nearly seven times yesterday but you not answer me until I nearly shout. Professor White want, like me to make sure nothing is wrong inside your head."

Marco understanding his mother's concerns and that her poor English vocabulary saying.

"Nothing wrong in your head."

Didn't mean she thought he was crazy, but simply that she wanted to make sure, he was one hundred percent out of any danger or any unknown worrying side effects.

"Va bene, Mama," said Marco agreeing without any opposition to his mother's whys and wherefores.

"I go to work in a few hours, can you get bit of milk and bread and some biscuits for Pasta," said Anna extending a twenty-pound note, offering it to Marco.

"Talking about work, Mama. I thought about going to see Mr Richmond today. See if I could get my old job back at the printing firm," said Marco. Anna glancing at her son, nothing had been said or implied about the pile of menacing bills, she knew he knew. But she'd cleaned away the evidence and swept away the incident silently under the carpet. Her stare was a combined expression of devoted pride witnessing her son's desire to work and help. Mingled with that of shame. Her unspoken recent revealed secret highlighting that she was powerless to such vultures, and that her son would have to find work so soon after his hospitalisations home coming.

"First, I want to see all is OK with you. And you have none of these side effecting things the doctor say to me this morning, OK," said Anna. Sipping her coffee, holding her cup within both hands, like she was warming her palms.

"Yes but there's no harm in asking. And if everything is OK, which it will be. Then I can go back to work. It will do me good to see some other faces, and now that my English is better, then things won't be so hard there like before. Maybe I could even find work in the offices," said Marco. His positive reasoning bringing a half-hearted smile to his mother's face. Anna abruptly changing the subject.

"Oh, I forget, you have dentist appointment in afternoon at three. I don't change it, because it take forever in this country to get dentist appointment. And also I know deep inside, you come home to me," said Anna.

"Three! This afternoon?" said Marco, like he'd been told a bus load of distant relatives would be arriving within the next few hours and he would have to make food for them all.

"Yes, three, I write down here. You look, you see. Why what is the matter, you can go either before you go see Mr Richmond or after no?" said Anna still pointing to the scribbled note she'd written in Italian, in the calendar. Marco puzzled even himself by his sudden questioning outburst. After all he had nothing urgent planned. Before doing anything, he walked Pasta, making his way down the stairs of his apartment building. Pasta's lead in one hand twenty pounds in the other.

"Listen, Stevie mate, it's a sure winner, you know Andy Butchers the painter from North Street, always goes in the Fox and Hounds. You know everybody calls him Bubba, cause he looks and talks like Bubba from 'Forrest Gump'," said an unknown voice.

"Or yeah, yeah I know who you mean, drives that old Nissan pickup," said another voice.

"Well Bubba's uncle owns two greyhounds, and spends a lot of time at the races, he gave Bubba a sure bet 200/1 on a horse he and another bloke have shares in called '*Naple's love*' racing at 'Cheltenham' five thirty today. Can you imagine a two hundred to one shot, if you place just twenty quid, you'll win four grand, mate. Listen Stevie mum's the word. We gotta keep this between us, if Bubba founds out we discovered his tip then we'll be in big trouble. So, what we'll do is put down a cock and henner (ten-pound) between us and split the winnings," said the first voice.

"How did you find out Bubba's tip?" said the second voice.

"Some things better not said Stevie lad, some things better not said." said the first voice.

"Fuck, there's that kid from number seventy-seven," said Stevie. His eyes wide open in a panicking manner, freighted that their money-making scheme had been obviously overheard by a stranger.

"Na mate, don't worry about him, he's that I-Tie. He speaks and understands about as much English as that Paki in Delhi's fast food shit hole, where we got those dodgy Kebabs last Saturday night," said the first voice.

"Fuck me, you were well pissed, Ryan," said Stevie.

"Not as pissed as I'll be when we win, Stevie lad," replied the first voice. Coming from Ryan Archer one of the apartment blocks antagonistic neighbours. Even more so when it came to anyone outside of Yorkshire not to mention from another country. Ryan a seven pint a night, fast food every day and piss taking unsociable character. This aggressive temperament, strangely reassuring Marco on his recently discovered information. This unkind man wouldn't even help his grandmother, never mind a total stranger. And a Foreigner too. The only reason he was sharing is cunning money-making plot with Stevie is because he needed twenty pounds. Marco over hearing Stevie slip Ryan a twenty-pound note with the false promise from Ryan that he would exchange it for two 'cock and henners'.

"200/1 'Naples Love' racing at 'Cheltenham' five-thirty today." said Marco smiling at both of them in a dim-witted manner, slipping his mother's twenty pounds inside his left jeans pocket. Whispering in his head.

"The milk, bread and Pasta's biscuits can wait," said Marco. Placing the lead around Pasta, hearing Ryan say stridently to Stevie.

"Told you mate that spic doesn't speak English. Fucking immigrants," said Ryan. Certainly, thanks to Nurse Brian's acting skills and adeptness to diversify facial grimaces. Marco's dim-witted countenance working a charm. Ryan and Stevie's pretentious arrogance, believing Marco hadn't understood a word they'd exchanged to one another. After his dedicated affectionate walk with Pasta. Marco's first considered mundane lackadaisical day, having suddenly become a tight scheduled planned afternoon. Rendezvous with Mr Richmond including, travelling to the Printers firm. Dentist appointment at three. The dentist situated at the other side of town, and 'Chatham' at five-thirty. Which wasn't too bad the betting office being only around the corner from the dental surgery. Marco's father Arnaldo would sometimes place a small bet with or for his old working colleagues, being the only worker to live at the other end of the town and pass the betting shop on his way home. The reviving memory of Marco and his mother which would sometimes meet his father in the town and share an ice-cream whilst walking home hand in hand. Causing Marco to feel sad. Shortly after Marco arriving back home. Anna having cleaned and tided the breakfast cutlery she'd even pre-prepared some lunch for her son and Pasta's bowl also prepared. A little note scribbled in English. His mother's efforts to write in the foreign language subconsciously transmitting a message to Marco about his recently attained linguistic knowledge.

"I go work now, all clean and I make some minestrone, don't forget dentist at three. Love Mama." said the note. The bike ride to his old work in the beginning seemed pleasant. Anna having had to sell his ford Fiesta to pay some of the early vulture's bill. Marco pedalling through the streets, the winter months rapidly fading into the shadows and the brightening hope of spring projecting an orchestra of singing birds combined with the new blooming resplendent pigments of budding flowers. Moments later Marco speeding along the canal's dirt path, approaching the last meters of the factory's yard. Not even the harmonising vernal equinox along with Mother Nature's magnificent Fauna, which he'd encountered along his journey, through the nearby forest, down across the river and over the canal banks. The fox, the squirrel, the hawk, the robins and swallows, the swan, otter, ducks and ducklings combined with an outburst of diverse insects. All seemingly wanting to greet and salute Marco in some sort of ironic manner and welcome him back. But none of these enchanting encounters being able to erase the pulsating tantalising fear arising within him. That of seeing Bill and his bullies again. But the worrying concerns of those 'Final demands' together with his unconditional love assimilated with his parents' force and faith to always face your demons and overcome your fears motivating Marco. Like a warrior facing his enemy across a battlefield, Marco taking the final steps and enter the lion's den. There where his traumatising urge to be able to speak better English and become someone better, sparking the igniting flames of his selfish desire. A wish which almost cost him his life. Atypically the very person Marco dreaded most to come across was the first person he saw.

"Flippin eck, if it ain't old 'Spaghetti-Slurper' we eard ye'd been wacked by lightning is that reight? Mi'sen at first din't believe it like. Appen it were true," said Bill. Marco only understanding a fraction of Bills Yorkshire intonations, but he'd made out that they'd learned of his lightning strike accident.

"Yes, Bill, it's true I did get stuck by lightning. I've been in hospital for these last few months, but to be honest with you, I don't remember much about it," said Marco.

"Nar'n look at ye speaking English. What thee done swallowed a dictionary," said Bill whilst exerting a haunting laugh. His facial appearance mixed. His mouth smirking in an insulting manner, but his eyebrows raised in a mystified state. As if his personality was fighting between his unfriendly aggressive bullying forces, against the side of him which was constantly trying to understand the difference of others around him.

"Look, Bill, I don't want any trouble, all I want, is to see if Mr Richmond's got any work for me. Maybe we could shake hands and let bygones be bygones, as you say in English," said Marco. Bill eyes as wide opened as a cat seeing a mouse in the obscurity of night.

"Eck ye speak, like one of those intellect folk, like are kid's father-in-law, he's a doctor. How thee bloody hell ye learnt to speak so proper like?"

said Bill. Strange as it were, this very being having tyrannised Marco's life for over so many weeks and months. Bill on his own without an expectant audience to please, seemed more like a little lost sheep wondering the hills and valleys. His complete baffled regard concerning Marco's ability to speak so good English bestowing Bill the look of a child who'd just witnessed a mystical magic trick. Marco approaching Bill. His right hand extended in a friendly let bygones be bygones way. His own visage expressing a slight incomprehension why he'd let this lonely little sheep domineer so much of his life. seconds later their hands united in a clan embracing style. Instantly Marco's otherworldly supraliminal sensations began generating throughout his body. Even with this once, considered enemy, the thirty seconds hand clutching exchange, was over within a flash. Never in a thousand years had Marco believed one day and so soon, that he'd be stood in the very courtyard. There where his rising hate for Bill and his three colleagues having been planted and fed over the passing weeks and months. There was Marco having endured so many insults, mockery, aggressive regards and racist cruelty. But as he stared upon Bill having now bumped his intellect and reminiscence. Marco saw the lonely little boy he really was. Battered and abused by an alcoholic father. Abandoned by an uncaring mother who'd blamed Bill for years upon years for all her misery. Deserted by his older brother, who'd escaped the everyday oppressive ambiance of unloving parents, to face his parentage persecuting abuse all alone. Bills bullying towards others. More a cry for help. His tall corpulent body and own personal shame, making Bill's wrenching desire to scream out his pain and yell to the heavens and beyond.

'Please help me!'

Practically impossible.

Marco and Bill staring at each other in an unfamiliar way. As if both just realising the full impact of their thirty seconds coupling. Small the gesture may had seemed too many. It was like the East vs West cold war having been instantly pardoned to allow the refulgent incandescence of peace to shine upon both of them.

"Wang us ye cigs Bill." (Throw to me your cigarettes Bill,. said a familiar voice. Followed by.

"Well, well if it ain't 'Spaghetti-Slurper' wot ye doing here?" said the voice. Marco opening his mouth to reply, disregarding like he'd done with

Bill earlier the racial insult. But the beginning of his phrase overpowered by the loud dominating voice of Bill.

"Leave him be, he's all right is this lad. And his name's Marco," said Bill, addressing a very puzzled Robert Dunn, at the same time wang-ing a packet of cigs to him. Robert still looking at Bill befuddled. But thanking him for the cigarettes and quickly apologising to Marco.

"Ta, Bill. Soz Marco, only kidding," said Robert.

"Aie ye better had bin kidding, otherwise ye'll see the back of mi hand lad," said Bill at the same time winking and smiling at Marco in a warmly manner, adding.

"Gaffers in his office, hurry up and get it sorted we got friggin loads of work on," said Bill. It was not only as if Marco having exchanged an understanding of Bill. An understanding he'd have never believed, along with his Yorkshire expressions and pronunciations. Ecstatic to finally comprehend words like 'Wang' meaning to throw or 'Mi'sen' meaning myself or 'Appen' meaning perhaps even 'Gaffa', the boss. But it was also as if Bill had collected a surcharge of information about Marco and though from British blood he may not be. The young man he was, was simply trying to respect the devoted desire of his lost father.

"Proteggere sempre tua madre." (Always protect your mother).

A bond having been fortuitously united between the two young men only a few years apart from age. Marco making his way to Mr Richmond's office with an amplifying feeling, that at last everything would be OK. Co-sided with the growing urge to return quickly to work. His meeting with Mr Richmond went even better than expected. No handshake exchanged only a welcoming pat on the shoulder Mr Richmond demonstrating his happiness to see Marco up and well combined with a comforting admiration, that Marco wanting to return to work there. Mr Richmond hadn't taken to much notice of Marco's ability to speak so good English. Most of the interviews and demands concerning staff were dealt by his wife, who was absent. Mr Richmond simply assuring Marco that there was plenty of work and when his hospitals tests that were due the following Tuesday were over, and he had the all clear. He could even start as early as Wednesday morning. Marco leaving the Printers factory in seventh heaven the brightening hope of spring projecting an orchestra of singing birds combined with the new blooming resplendent pigments of budding flowers bursting from his aura.

Picking up his bike ride time still in good stead to make it to the dentist surgery on time. Greeted once again by a very friendly wave from Bill and caring goodbye.

"Tarra Marco see thee when thee's back T'werk. Tek care on ye bike, looks like it's going to silin down later," said Bill.

Unbelievable thought Marco easily translating Bill's Yorkshire in his mind ('Tarra' goodbye. 'Thee' you. 'T'werk' at work. 'Silin' heavy rain). At the same time presenting his own goodbyes.

"Tarra Bill, see thee next week," said Marco. Unbelievable thought Bill.

"Lad even speaks Yorkshire now," said Bill. Marco just about to exit the printing firm's yard, when a very beautiful dark haired, Bambi face, brown eyed Rebecca Brant Jones, stood in front of him. Causing Marco to skid upon the gravel and nearly fall of his bicycle. Pulling himself and his bike straight staring at a sweet-faced Rebecca, her long curls rippling with the light breeze, like a Sahara's plain, her smile timidly cheeky, her lips of natural rose, her eyelashes curled towards the heavens. Marco's stare, actually more like a gawking fool. Rebecca's vestments revealing the form of her slim body accentuating her curves and bumps all in the right form and all in the right places.

"So, after all these months of being away, you were just going to leave again without saying hello," said a bolder Rebecca.

"Err, err sorry Rebecca, I didn't mean to offend you, if that's what I've done," said a nervous stuttering, Marco. A small pause hovering between them. Rebecca taking a moment to admire the handsome young man in front of her. His different coloured eyes, and grey streak at the front of his short hair adding a mysterious allure to his already existing charming features. Her eyes moving towards his strong young hands, making her way to his thick forearms and bulging biceps and triceps. Continuing her fantasising journey down from his rounded shoulders to his large torso. Hovering a moment, watching the powerful respiration of this young stud. Her regard swaying down to his slim waist and then to his bulging thighs, stopping embarrassingly, only a fraction of a second on his bulge, enough to imagine what his sex would be like. Rebecca was two years older than Marco, and even though her Bambi timid feminine features made her come across as sweet and innocent. Her powerful charm could even seduce the holiest of men. Few knew that she was a very assertive young woman, knowing exactly what she wanted in life, work and love.

"Well, I'll only be offended if you don't take me out on Friday night, I'll meet you in JB's in town at eight, OK," said Rebecca with a confident affirmation.

"OK, eight Friday at JB's," said Marco, somewhat surprised and happily bemused, by his continuing strokes of luck. Marco having fancied Rebecca since the very moment he'd seen her. But his reserved shying nature along with his inability to speak English having chased the remotest of hope, chance or desire of such a fantasied instant.

"By the way, I don't remember your English being so good," said Rebecca.

"I've been studying and I'm a fast learner," said Marco, adding, "See you Friday," said Marco, having noticed the time.

Rebecca shouting after him. "See you Friday and don't be late!"

"By the way, the short hair suites you," said Rebecca. Marco not answering, having realised the time, and if he didn't hurry, he would be late for his dentist appointment. Anna would be upset, not angry but upset, after all she'd never cancelled this appointment. The physiological significance more important than the actual check-up. That very reminder jointly with the desire not to let his mother down, motivating every pushing energetic force upon the pedals, as Marco raced across the canal banks, side roads and eventually the main streets, like a weekend off road biker. His efforts rewarding, arriving in good time. Moments later sitting patiently in the surgeries waiting room, apart from a young mum with her little boy, who was playing with the provided toys they were alone. The young mum raising her eyes only briefly from her mobile phone to acknowledge or more, see who'd just walked in. Marco greeted with a rapid smile. The young mum returning quickly to her portable phone, not even taking the time to glance upon her son, now nosily throwing toys around. Most certainly in a desperate attempt to obtain his mother's attention. Marco wondering just how many times and ways, Bill had tried to obtain his parents attention and more so their love. Something Marco had never been denied. His parents love. His thoughts, quickly turning to his enchanting rencontre with Rebecca, and her curvy anatomy. Wondering what he would wear Friday.

"Mr Rosalinni," said the young assistant calling out his name at the same time looking around the waiting room to see who would answer. Marco finding the young assistant's method bizarre. After all, he was the only Mr there. Marco standing following the mademoiselle. The young mum giving him an angered look. Most probably riled he'd arrived after her but gone through to the dentists first. Her son threw a hardback book at Marco, the young assistant just rolling her eyes and the young mum, turning in silence back to her phone.

"Mr Marco Rosalinni," said the gravelled voice of Dr Denise Dent. Dr Dent was not only a dentist but a qualified Orthodontics surgeon. Obtaining with great pride and honour the statue of a doctor.

"Now... I... read... that... you'd... been... struck... by... lightning," said Dr Dent talking to Marco very slowly, with long pauses. Articulating every word with great precision as people often do when addressing a child, or in Marco's case someone with very little knowledge of the spoken tongue.

"Yeah, I did, or should I say I was, but I'm OK. Don't really remember much about it," said Marco.

"Well now, your English is perfect. Whatever that lightning strike did. It did your English a world of good," said Dr Dent. Marco fixing his mind on the word 'World'. Thinking again which, or what world had his alien stone come from. His mind daydreaming suddenly brought to a harsh reality. Sensing the strange tingling from his toes to his fingertips, conglomerating at his phalange. His palmar crease sensing once again the minor electrical intake, combined with the sensation of pins and needles charging energetic force, amalgamated with a peculiar humming in his auricles, like a faint whale's cry. In his lost in thought reverie. Marco not noticing until it was too late, Dr Denise Dent having grabbed his hand with a congratulating acknowledgment for his fantastic progress with her native language. Marco feeling the otherworldly supraliminal sensations generating throughout his body. Trying to pull his hand free from that of Dr Dents. Something's he didn't want to know. Obtaining the intellect of a dentist and his or her savoir faire, along with the clairvoyant images of their past and present lived events of Dr Dent was something Marco wasn't yearning for. Especially if, as he'd convincingly began to believe. His abilities and otherworldly seer energies were limited to a certain capacity of intellectual intake. He could think of many other ways and professions he'd rather require then that of a dentist. This time it was Marco trying to pull is hand free. But Dr Dent having clasped his hand, like a trapped animal, gripping Marco's hands with both her palms, with almost a crazed expressive grin upon her face repeating like a parrot, over and over again.

"Well done, Marco, Bravo. Well done, Marco, Bravo," said Dr Dent. The otherworldly supraliminal sensations generating throughout Marco's body coming to a sudden stop. It was too late, Dr Dent's intelligence and memories were now bumped and paired with that of Marco. The first time he'd not wanted to bump someone else's semblance. But he knew not how to stop the extra-terrestrial phenomena or erase undesired data. This unwished-for brainpower amplified as Marco laid upon the dental chair. A sadistic selection of torturing instruments. Dental scaler, probe, tweezers the rotary instruments (Airotor), with its burs and stones. A convey of filling materials with their rounded ends, for shaping, sculpting, brushing, presented before him. All neatly uniformed like medieval punishing appliances.

Even the plain and magnifying mouth mirrors seemed terrifying. What was worse as Marco laid his mouth open, like a young chick with its beak ajar waiting for worms to be dropped inside by its parents, he now also understood what every instrument was for, including the exchanging phrases of dental Jargon, between Dr Bent and her two young assistants.

"Lateral and central incisor, scaling, unilateral, cavity (Cuspid), canine. Porcelain. Some stomatitis. Diastema second and first Premolar (Bicuspid)," said Dr Dent, in a mumbled voice from under a white face mask. Marco thinking to himself, his eyes closed like he was waiting for the nightmare to end.

"I don't want to know. I don't want to know," said Marco, desperately trying to erase the images from his mind. But as the burrowing sound of the burs drilled into his Cuspid. It was like he was picturing the horrific scene in 3D, with digital sound, amplifying the taste of his own blood, along with the urge to swallow, rinse his mouth, and close his mouth.

"What I wouldn't give for it all to be over," said Marco in his tortured mind seeing the anaesthetic needle plunging into his inner gum, as if he was witnessing the scene live. Marco trying to focus on the other information he'd attained from Dr Dent. Her horse-riding skills and passion, her great love and interest in crosswords, her culinary knowledge. But even with these compensating thoughts and knowledge, he too could now do. Concerning theses passions and skills. These compensatory acquired data having very little effect from diverting Marco's mind from the magnified images in his brain. Eventually his ordeal coming to its end. Marco patted on the shoulder for his bravery and calm. Dr Dent patronising repetitiously saying.

"Bravo, bravo," said Dr Dent. Marco, more frozen with fright, then brave and calm. Choosing not to divulge this enlightenment with Dr Dent. Instead, he happily shook her hand goodbye. Strange as nothing happened. No weird sensations or otherworldly exchanges. A curious thought arose in Marco's mind, like a demi revelation. He'd only shook people's right hand every time the strange feeling dominating his body. But if he shook somebodies' hand with his left hand. Would he reverse the processes? With this revealing flash, he quickly changed hands with Dr Dent, in the hope to return her intellect and free his mind from this unwanted data, and at the same time recuperate some much-desired capacity in his mind. Marco still convinced that his data storage was limited. But as he switched hands from right to left, nothing occurred.

"I'm going have to try to collect enough intelligence to understand the maximum information concerning extra-terrestrial activities. And chose my bumping, Johns and Janes, with a precise goal in mind," said Marco, with the churning disappointed sensation inside his stomach, that he'd wasted some much-needed data space capacity within his extra-terrestrial mind.

Maybe I could wear gloves, but in summer that might seem a bit pretentious. I could tell people I'm a chauffeur. Chauffeurs wear gloves all the time, said Marco. These mind puzzling scenarios occupying his mind whilst he more than happily distanced himself from the dental surgery. No need to return before six months. Making his way to the betting office. Twenty pounds in his left jean pocket. His earlier obtained tip in his butterflied stomach.

"Naples love, Cheltenham, five-thirty."

Arriving in the town Marco turning his head to the town's clock tower, it chimed at 17.15. Perfect timing. Pushing the door of the betting office open at a snail's pace at the same time haltingly peering behind the door into the building in search of Ryan Archer or his mate Stevie Fisher. To his great relief they were nowhere to be seen. Apart from two retired locales who didn't even take their engulfed faces away from the TV screens opposite them, and another middle-aged man sitting sipping a coffee from a plastic vending machine cup. At the same time slipping a bundle of fifty pence coins into the flashing fruit machine. The only other people in the establishment were the two young employees sat facing each other discussing the weeks earlier football match between Norwich and Manchester City. Marco having no idea what to do quietly whispered to the two men.

"I'd like to place twenty pounds to win on 'Naples Love' racing at five thirty Cheltenham today," said Marco.

"Just write it down on one of those slips, twenty pounds one way to win, 'Naples Love' five-thirty, Cheltenham. You can use one of those little blue pens, mate," said one of the employees from behind his glass protected confined office. Pointed to the little doubled up rectangular paper slips around the size and width of an adult's palm. And a plastic tub containing an overloading mass of little blue pens the length of an adult's thumb and the thickness of a standard pencil. Marco scribbling the information given to him.

'Twenty pounds'.

'Win'.

'Naples Love'.

'Cheltenham five-thirty', wrote Marco. No sooner had he passed his small piece of paper through the rectangular letter box glass slot, accompanied with his mother's twenty pounds. His papery information was slipped through a machine and a carbon copy piece given back to him. Seven minutes to go. Marco's nerves causing his fingertips to tremble, his heart, beating so fast and hard he could feel it pumping in his mouth. His stomach felt like a candidate facing his or her judges on a talent show. Four and a half minutes to go, the two older men, ripping up pieces of paper from the earlier race and letting the fragments twirl untidily to the floor.

"Cheltenham."

The horses lined up 'Naples Love' number thirteen, Anna's lucky number.

"And they're off," said the televisions commentator rambling out names and numbers so fast, not even seemingly taking gulps of air between his accelerated vocabularies.

"Naples Love, in position seven," said the commentator, causing Marco's heart to sink, like an anchor inside him. Thinking to himself. "Position seven that's way behind," said Marco, under his breath.

"Naples Love, squeezing through the gap with five furlongs to go, Naples Love position four," said the commentator, blurting out the information as though his life depended on how fast he could speak. Marco having no idea what a furlong was or how far and long, Naples Love, would have to run. The commentator still screaming information like his life depended on the rapidity of his words. The last furlongs two names were being repeated more than any others.

"Naples Love, running alongside Daisy Maze. Daisy Maze still a head length away, but Naples Love not letting anything go," said the commentator. As the last furlong approached. Both horses, Naples Love and Daisy Maze, were neck and neck. The old man to the right suddenly jumping to his feet, like he'd received a shock from a defibrillator. Screaming with all his might, at the same time repeatedly slapping his right buttock with his right hand, like a jockey tapping a horse with his or her whip.

"Come on, Daisy Maze. Come on, Daisy Maze. Come on, you beauty. Don't let me down," said the old man in a frantic high-pitched voice.

The commentator in a frenzy shouting.

"Now, it's Daisy Maze. Now, its Naples Love. Now, Daisy Maze. Now, Naples Love," said the commentator. The last words Marco heard was.

"Naples Love," said the commentator, his voice having returned to a slower speaking pace. Marco at first not realising what had just happened, only until the reaction of the older man crumpling his piece paper in an angered contesting aggression. The name and odds of Naples Love. Screened across the monitor accompanied with the commentator's calmer spoken comments.

"Outsider, Naples Love, wins first race at Cheltenham 200/1. An absolute shock result, a total bowl over. Naples Love," said the commentator. Marco couldn't believe it. He'd just won 4,000 pounds. Slowly repeating the number in his head.

Four. Thousand. Pound,. said Marco. This meaning the wolves at the door could be fed. His mother's mound of 'final demands' could now be paid. And even more so to Marco. The promise and devoted desire of his beloved father realised. The cognizance and full importance of this responsibility submerging Marco's entire body, soul and mind.

"Proteggere sempre tua madre." (Always protect your mother).

Moments later collecting the totality of his win as well as his waging twenty pounds. Counted out meticulously before him by the second young employee. A bulging pile of dosh combined of old and new fifty, twenty, ten and five pound notes, tallied up and bundled together. Every bank note expressing the same statement.

"The end of money worries for his mother."

"There you go, mate. Four thousand and twenty quid. Must be your lucky day. Don't spend it all at once," said the young assistant. Marco carefully placing the wad of money inside his zipped top, tucking the bottom of his hooded clothing inside the top of his jeans, pulling his belt tight to secure even more, nothing would fall out. Exiting the bookmakers slowly but filled with an overwhelming desire to get home quickly, and explain to his mother what had happened, inpatient to see the reaction upon her face. As the door closed behind him, he overheard the two older men say at exactly the same time to each other.

"Lucky bastard," said the two older men. Bastard, he was not. But Marco had to agree, he was lucky. Different scenarios of how his mother would react seeing the pile of money he'd won, like a child bringing home a found kitten. Most parent's reaction to a cute find would be.

Where did you get that from?

Marco knowing he'd also have to explain about using Anna's valuable twenty pounds, on a very risky tip. But also, he would be able to prove to his mother he'd obtained the money without using his otherworldly powers in an unlawful or sinful manner. Marco back home, carrying his bike up the seven flights of stairs, his body full of adrenalin. Turning the key slowly and as silent as he could in the door. The apartment was silent only the tick toking of the old clock, and a shuffling groan from Pasta as he changed from sleeping on his side onto his back welcoming Marco. Strangely enough the gloomy bleak furnished apartment never seeming so radiant. Marco's joy multiplied as he collected the pile of letters slipped through the letter box which had tumbled onto the floor behind the door. Recognizing two of the envelopes from Anna's pile of vultures 'Final demand'. Placing them onto the dining table, alongside the change from the twenty pounds. Marco's required chores accomplished.

Milk, bread and Pasta's biscuits.

Arranging the shopping items in their respective cupboards and fridge. Placing the bundle of money under his mattress. After a daydreaming walk with Pasta. His dreamy pensiveness wondering about just how his mother would react still buzzing in his mind as he approached the flats door, hardly able to keep his enthusiasm hidden arriving back home from his walk with Pasta. As usual Anna having prepared the evening dinner or "Tea" as it was called in England. The two menacing letters nowhere to be seen.

"Buonasera mia amore. Com'è stata la tua giornata? E il dentista?" (Good evening, my love. How was your day? And the dentist?), said Anna. Her voice faint. Portraying a half-heartened smile, like she was preoccupied.

"Oh, Mama, don't ask about the dentist please," said Marco. His voice energetic and excited. Anna hearing her son reply in perfect English sighed, like she'd just been reminded of his otherworldly ability to bump the knowledge of another. Saying after her sigh.

"Oh si, inglese." (Oh yes, English), said Anna.

"Mama. Come and sit down, I've got some fantastic news for you," said Marco, pulling a chair clear from the table and patting its wooden seating area, coaxing his mother to come and sit. Anna obeying pulling free her apron and delicately placing it over the back of the chair nearest to the kitchen. Taking the wait of her feet placing herself upon the designated chair opposite her son.

"Listen, Mama. First, don't get upset. I know about the 'Final Demand' letters. And I know you received two more letters today," said Marco. Anna's suspire accompanied by tear drops, slowly merging the surface of her eyes and dropping silently onto her knees. Her hurt and shame causing Marco to fight back his own sob. Anna's forearms resting upon each of her thighs and her hands interlocked together with her fingers pointing towards her son in a triangular form. Marco going to place his hands upon his mother's palms once again to comfort her. But once again, she detoured his physical touch upon her skin. Their eyes met each other. Both filled with tears.

"Look, Mama. I'm going to go straight to the point. Today. This morning actually. I overheard that horrible nasty neighbour, Ryan Archer from number eighty-one. You know the man who once spat at you. And you stopped Dad from giving him a piece of his mind," said Marco. Anna nodding, as if to say.

"Yes, she knew who Marco meant," said Anna's gesturing response.

"Well Ryan, like many others around here don't know I can understand everything now. And this morning I overheard him giving a racing tip to his mate, Stevie. At first, I didn't make too much of it, but when I heard the name, 'Naples Love' and when I discovered the number of the horse. Number thirteen, your lucky number. Well, I thought of you and dad. I took it as a lucky omen. What's more, the jockey was a guy called Arnold Wish. Anyway, with all these signs of luck and hope. I placed the twenty pounds that you gave me this morning on a 200/1 bet. Naples Love at Cheltenham running this evening at five-thirty. And it won. A total outsider, a complete bowl over as they say in the racing world. We've won four thousand pounds, mama. Four. Thousand. Pounds," said Marco.

"Marco, don't tease Mama like this. It is not joke," said Anna. At the same time shaking her head in disbelief.

"Wait, Mama. Wait," said Marco running into his room. Marco lancing a quick glare at his weird pebble, still wedged between the bedside cabinet and the wall. It seemed to have metamorphosed into a darker green pigment. But his mind too preoccupied on showing the wad of money to his mother.

"Here, Mama. Here. Take it. It's yours," said Marco, adding, to convince his mother and ease her devotional mind.

"I didn't steal it or use my new abilities in an unlawful way. It was your money I bet with. And all I did is take all the signs as a message, maybe from dad. And it worked. We won Mama, we won. You can now pay all those unpleasant bills and even treat yourself to something nice and probably still have enough to put aside for a rainy day," said Marco. At first Anna staring at the bundle of money, Marco having placed it on her lap. Her mind in total nihilism. Then slowly, Marco's reasoning words along with the full impact of what this money implicated, began to project inside her, like a holy spiritual presence entering her physique. Chasing away the pessimistic demon having taken residence within her. Little by little a resplendent colour brimming into her cheeks, her lips curving up to exhibit one of the most beautiful smiles Marco had ever portrayed upon his mother's visage, like a sublime illustration of Da Vinci. The same smile she'd expressed upon her wedding photo and the photograph of Marco's birth. Her earlier suspire now overpowered with relief and joy. That evening they ordered pizza and corked open a bottle of red wine, celebrating their new fortune.

If only every evening could be as joyful as this one. If only mamma would be able to smile like she'd smiled today for the rest of her days. If only every tomorrow could be free from worry, said Marco. Also thinking of his tomorrow. 'Friday'. And his date with Rebecca. The same thought accompanying Marco in his sleep. Things clicking into place perfectly the next day 'Friday'. Anna wasn't working. And after sharing an exquisite breakfast. Marco accompanying his mother to every establishment the vulture's letters had been sent from. By the days end, every worrying bill having been paid. Anna and Marco having even treated themselves to a Mc Donald's lunch. Something Anna found more amusing then actually tasteful. Marco having been allowed. Actually, his mother had more insisted he by some new jeans and T-shirts and a new pair of 'Converse' having explained his strange events with Bill. Mr Richmond and more so his date with Rebecca.

"You make sure you look nice for this girl," said Anna.

CHAPTER TEN

REBECCA

He did. Leaving their apartment dressed in his new blue stone washed jeans. A 'V' necked white T-shirt tightly clinging to his body revealing the shape of his muscular form. Along with his new black Converse and an old 1940s retro style grey Jacket of his father's. Back in mode. Anna gazing at her son with an overwhelming sensation of pride and also a little anxiousness. It was the first time her son having been on a date since their arrival in England. Marco's last girlfriend from his old school back in Naples. But the distance between them, and Marco's lack of access to computers and telephones having brought a rapid end to a short lived romance. Marco making his way into town, the bustling streets rapidly starting to fill with night life. The same avenues, boulevards, lanes and pavements expressing a different ambiance from day to night. Every shop now closed only the muffled sound of music humming from public houses through their thick walls. Loudening for a short outburst as the heavy wooden doors pulled open allowing new clients in and old clients out. Masses of men and women all dressed to please and tease, hustling through the darkening lanes. Streetlight shadows of all different shapes, forms and sizes projecting from curb to curb, climbing walls and lamppost, like spectating outsiders. Marco thinking to himself as he perceived the admiring regards upon him from various women and men.

All these, Johns and Janes. All this intellect and knowledge. All these memories. With one hand shake I could learn anything from anybody. Bump a singer's talents, a musician's, a bar man's, a bouncer, a dancer, or something completely unknown. But just how much forthcoming intelligence would he be able to obtain, said Marco. The darkening pigment of his strange otherworldly pebble, preoccupying a little his thoughts. *What did it mean?*

As he received new data. Did the stone change colour because of this? Or was it a reaction to the earth's atmosphere?

Was it because he'd held it in his palm the other night?

Had it altered its colour because it had extracted some data from Marco?

Or was it transforming, metamorphosing for an entirely different reason Marco ignored? said Marco in his preoccupying questioning mind. Quickly dispersed, as he pushed open the doors of 'JBs' only to fall upon the enchanted smile of Rebecca. Ogling her attire. A very short low cut black dress revealing the full proportion of her busty cleavage. Her almost naked shoulders covered only by the thin straps of her dress. Elegantly covered by a see-through embroidered grey shawl. A pair of grey and black converse on her feet. Marco's entranced ogling causing Rebecca to burst out in laughter.

"Punctual. I like that in a man, as well as other things," said Rebecca.

Her suggestive grin leaving little doubt to her innuendoes. "So, what are you drinking?" asked Rebecca. Turning and squeezing her way through the mass of people blocking a clear access to the bar.

"No, no let me buy," said Marco in an insistent voice.

"Oh, a gentleman and good-looking, nearly all the qualities a girl looks for in a man," said Rebecca, with a little giggle. Marco naively asking.

"What were the other qualities a girl looks for in a man?" said Marco.

"Maybe, I'll just show you some of the others. Some things better done and not said," said Rebecca. At the same time bighting her bottom lip with her front teeth in a sensual manner.

"I'll have a 'Sex on the Beach'," said Rebecca over the rowdy chattering of voices and music.

"What did you say?" said Marco his eyes wide open, half of him unsure he'd actually heard Rebecca right.

"Don't worry. 'Sex on the Beach' is a fruity cocktail. You know Vodka, peach schnapps, cranberry and orange juice all smoothly mingled together. Although actual sex on the beach isn't too bad either," said Rebecca. Still with her provocative expression. Marco giving an embarrassed grin, finally arriving at the bar.

"What will it be, mate," said the bar man in a rapid voice, whilst pulling a pint of lager, at the same time flipping of the caps of two different coloured bottles.

"A 'Sex on the Beach' and a pint of Guinness, please," said Marco. The bar man taking Marco's order with a pitch of salt. No humorous remarks about the Cocktail drink. Within a short period, his ordered drinks placed before him. Marco presenting the bar man with a ten-pound note. The bar man's reaction needed to say no more. Marco clumsily exchanging it for a twenty-pound note. Then scrutinizing the little change dropped into his open hand, by a quickly disappearing barman already taking several other orders.

"Don't get out much do you, Marco," said Rebecca. Having witnessed the whole scene.

"No, not really," said Marco. At the same time calculating in his head just how far his sixty pounds brought with him would last at this rate. Also thinking just how much shopping he could have bought for the price of those two drinks. Even more grateful for his horse winning bet.

"There's two free seats over there, shall we?" said Rebecca stretching her left arm out in a proposing gesture to sit, brushing aside Marco's out of place character. She found his naivety very sweet and an extreme turn-on. They sat and spoke about their respective lives. Marco finding the pleasure to discovers things about somebody without his violating otherworldly powers. Just simple chatting in a language he could now express, even with Yorkshire intonations and better yet understand. It was nice and he felt at great ease with Rebecca. As the evening continued and the bustling bar played various songs and different groups of people entered or left the building. Marco and Rebecca simply smiled and chatted, almost as though they were sat alone oblivious to what was going on around them. Rebecca made the first move, sliding her right hand, across the cushioned couch towards Marco's left hand. Their fingertips embraced. Marco starting to feel the strange tingling throughout his body. Hastily pulling away his hand. Rebecca shocked, hurt and embarrassed, extracted her hand nervously. Moving her had towards her head pushing the hair behind her right ear in an unsure what to do manner. Then clutching her glass taking a little sip from her third cocktail.

"Sorry Rebecca, I didn't mean to offend you. It's just since I came out of hospital, I sometimes get a strange sensation in my hands," said Marco. A little white lie. A half-truth. He did get strange sensations in his fingertips and throughout his whole body. But the whys and wherefores he left out.

"Would you like to come have a drink at home with me? My parents are away with my younger sister and brother this weekend. So, I'm alone until Monday night. We could take a short cut along the beach. I live not too far from Cliffside cove," said Rebecca in a reassured quiet tone.

"I'd love to," said Marco with an admiring smile from his eyes and pardoning words from his mouth. He was also secretly happy to leave the pub. Their respective six drinks. Marco having order the same drinks twice more having nearly cost him all his money. The walk along the beach, blissful Rebecca having honoured Marco's earlier revelation about strange sensations in his fingertips linking onto his right arm, her head tilted upon his muscly shoulder her hands clasped around his bulging biceps. Marco having placed his father's jacket upon her, covering her nearly bare shoulders. As they walked the cool breeze of sea air, transporting the sweet scents odour of Rebecca's perfume to his nostrils. The sands quartz crystals granular, glittering from the growing planets luminescence, like tumbled miniature stars beneath and around their feet. The precedent day half-moon now nearly three quarters. Marco having admired many couples walking in such a way but he'd never thought that one day he himself would have such luck. Especially in a country where people having seemed so hostile at first. Glancing back an instant at the long trail of their footsteps embedded into the dank sandy seashore, like traces of an elderly couples trails of life. The oceans harmonious waves rippling onto the shoreline. The whitecap rumbling wave tips resembling grasping hands trying to seize a gripping hold upon dry land. Amongst the waves a rectangular length of wood washing towards the shore, only to be drag out to sea again.

The repetitive toing and froing of the wooden plank, transporting Marco into the past. The night of his lightning strike. For it was upon that very beach his lifeless body had been washed ashore, certainly his unresponsive physique must have been like that morsel of timber.

How could I have survived? The tide was three times as far out the night of my accident. How long did my body stay in the water?

Why didn't I drown?

It would have taken hours for the tide to wash me ashore?

But I was told the young couple saved me, I'd only seen them an hour or so before.

Even if they'd waiting for the storm to pass, it still would have been a good while before the tide came in. and me with it.

Was I dead? I don't remember seeing a bright light guiding me to the other side. Or the memory of my life flashing before my heaviness of hearts, said Marco. A multitude of silent interrogating questions, racing through his mind. Moments later Marco and Rebecca arriving at the foot of Cliffside cove. Rebecca turning to face Marco, her five foot five body, admiringly peering up to his five foot nine beauty. Marco in return staring down at her sublime natural beauty, tainted with the lightest touch of makeup. Their noses only inches apart, their respiration from the cool night's air, intermingling like waltzing spirits. Rebecca's silver stood earrings twinkling in the moonlight, approaching her lips towards Marco's in an assertive sure of her self-way. The soft moist subtle tenderness of her lips upon his causing Marco's heart to beat twice as fast. Rebecca caressing the tip of her tongue with that of Marco's. His own mouth and tonguing following Rebecca's dominate, passionate actions, like a dancer being taken lead of. Rebecca's hand slowly slipping down from around the back of Marco's neck, across his broad shoulders, down his muscular triceps over his elbows onto his forearms. Stopping a brief moment at his wrists, before moving to take place on his buttocks, having avoided any contact with his hands. Her murmuring canoodling and caressing fondling, causing another sensation and reaction somewhere completely different on Marco's body. Marco's own hands having stayed, like statues around Rebecca's waist, unsure what to do with them, and hesitant what to do next.

"So, you like me then?" said Rebecca, in a raunchy phrase, her lips breaking only an instant away from Marco's mouth her eyes for a split second looking down towards his bulging pleasure.

"Sei bellissima." (You're beautiful), said Marco. Happy that it was night and Rebecca couldn't see his abashed red face.

"What did you say? Only Italian I know is Pizza Peperoni," said Rebecca.

"I said you're beautiful. And to be honest with you, I liked you the very first instant I saw you. It was a Tuesday afternoon the second week in

September, you came down from your office with your friend Kylie, both laughing about something. You were wearing blue dungarees, and the left strap kept falling off your shoulder," said Marco.

"Katie, not Kylie. And you don't remember the actual date that's not good. What was Katie, or Kylie wearing?" said Rebecca, teasing Marco. A peaceful silence, drifting amongst them. Marco unsure if Rebecca was serious or joking with her questions, until she broke the ice again.

"I liked you the first moment I saw you too. In fact, I shouldn't be telling you this, but you're fancied by just about every girl at work, especially the older women. Mrs Alberts said she would devour you like one of her favourite bars of chocolate. So why me and none of the others like Katie? (Kylie)," said Rebecca.

"Some things in life you just feel. Some people shine brighter than others, leaving the others in the shadow. Whenever I saw you, I felt light, that's why you and none of the others," said Marco. Rebecca replying by an even more passionate kiss. Then pulling herself free, turning to run heading through Cliffside cove up towards one of the view scattered houses which dominated the cliffs.

"You felt light. Come and show me how light you felt. That's if you want to?" said Rebecca whilst running up the passageway leading from the seafront to the cliffs. Marco's herculean strength catching up to Rebecca just as she was turning the key in the front door of the first house nearest the cliffs cove. Rebecca letting out a joyful shriek feeling Marco's arms around her waist, turning to kiss him once again. Their passionate embracing causing them to fall into the house. The weight of their lustful bodies pressed against the half-opened door obtaining little resistance. For a long while they laid, passionately fondling in the hallway. Both avoiding all contact to each other's hands, until Rebecca took control again. Her self-assured character leading Marco towards her bedroom. Kicking off her converses whilst walking up the stairs, her grey shawl left hanging over the top barrister. Once inside her bedroom she let her dress fall to the floor, like a towel, her black erotic lingerie leaving little doubt just how perfect her bumps in all the right places were. Turning to face Marco her gorgeous silhouette shimmering from the shaft of moonlight shining a traverse the window, like a faint stage light. Marco gulping then gulping again. If Rebecca had Marco's special abilities to bump another's intellect and clairvoyant memories. She would have learnt he was a virgin and this was the very first time he'd seen or been so close to a half-naked woman. Trying to show some reassurance to an expectant Rebecca. Marco pulling of his T-shirt. But nerves and clumsiness getting the better of him, his head and elbows seemed trapped in a labyrinth of cotton. Rebecca laughing at the same time coming to his rescue. Seconds later his bare muscular torso causing her earlier laughter to halt and her mouth to simply gawp. Marco's belt buckle glittering from the moonbeam, accentuating his rippling six-pack. Rebecca stretching out her left hand, her fingertips rippling over Marco's athletic physique, like a model from one of her girl magazines. Marco trying to make up some confident ground, after his embarrassing T-shirt incident, trying to kick of his converse as easy and elegantly as Rebecca had. Something practically impossible to him. His rigorous attempts causing him to fall on his backside. Rebecca laughing once again. Her own personal timid warrior, half naked in her bedroom, but unable to kick of his trainers. Rebecca kneeling slowly beginning to undo his laces, pulling of each converse and his socks from his feet. Marco staring at Rebecca thinking.

How the bloody hell did she manage to kick off hers so easily? said Marco. Rebecca not revealing the trick was not to tie the laces right to the top. Marco still sat on his arse supporting himself by his hands stretched out behind him. Rebecca leaning towards him, kissing him passionately, erotically tenderly biting his bottom lip. Pushing him easily to the floor, proceeding directly to undoing his belt and slipping off his tight jeans. As she tugged, at the same time his jeans slipping down his burly legs so did his boxer shorts exposing his large, aroused sex to Rebecca. It was the very first time a woman having seen his adult body completely naked. Marco for an instant unsure what to do, and Rebecca too. She unfastened her bra and laid her bare breasts against Marco's chest; he could feel her hard nipples upon his skin. Rebecca could feel Marco's heart racing, pounding. Slipping his right hand down her nude back slowly caressing his fingers in the ditch span of her spinal cord, his hand stopping at the top of her buttocks. His gesturing caressing up her down her back from the back of her neck to the bottom of her spin, continuing for a few moments until a more self-assured gesture. Marco slipping is hand under Rebecca's underwear his hand now tenderly caressing her smooth buttocks. Receiving no resistance Marco slipping of (aided by Rebecca), the last item of Rebecca's attire. Their Adam and Eve bodies entwining in a passionate embrace. Rebecca taking out a condom from the back of her bedside cabinets draw. Placing it with ease over Marco's turned-on manhood. Their four play more sensual and passionate then Marco's ability in love making. His inexperienced knowledge not carrying Rebecca to cloud nine. But it didn't matter so much to Rebecca. She was confident and knew there was defiantly great potential. Finding Marco's celibate purity something rare and special. As they laid huddle close together, Rebecca's body tucked into Marco's. Marco laying behind her, his strong arms wrapped around her, like an eagle's mighty wings around her chick. Rebecca slipping off into a blissful sleep. Marco's mind analysing his poor performance again and again and again. Before finally drifting off to sleep. Woken abruptly by the effulgent light of a new dawn shining directly onto him. The alarm clock indicated 5.52.

"Maledetto! Maledetto!" (Dam! Dam!), said Marco. At the same time gently awaking Rebecca.

"Rebecca it's six in the morning, I've got to go. We fell asleep, I've been out all night. Mama will be worried sick. I didn't call or anything. Sorry but I must go," said Marco.

A wakening mumbling understanding groan coming from under the sheets. Marco collecting his clothes. Trying with great difficulty to slip on his converse. Once fully dressed turning to kiss Rebecca.

"I'll call you later," said Marco. Rebecca suddenly realising he was leaving sitting up as though a bucket of cold water had just been thrown over her.

"Wait you've not got my number," said Rebecca. Pulling out a pen and a block pad from the top draw, the rest of the condom box falling to the floor. Both staring an instant at it. Rebecca turning the attention away slipping Marco her number, scribbled with a little heart at its side.

"Come for tea tonight, I'm a pretty good cook. Make you my speciality 'shepherd's pie'. Five-thirty OK," said Rebecca, her stare hesitant for Marco's reply.

"Better between six-thirty and seven-thirty for me. By the time I've walked Pasta and helped Mama," said Marco.

"That's perfect, meet you here O,." said a very relieved Rebecca. For some strange reason she was half expecting Marco to make all the excuses under the sun, like many men do, not wanting see a girl again, having obtained (even though it was what she desired), sex. But Marco was not like other men. Marco was not like any other being. As Hausbeck and Stanford were secretly due to discover.

CHAPTER ELEVEN

FAST LEARNER

Marco racing along the beach, like an Olympic runner. The tide having drifted in and out again, erasing the traces of his and Rebecca's day before romantic walk footprints. The streets were slowly preparing for the bustling weekend of shoppers. A sign catching Marco's eye outside the newsagent.

'Salon de l'érotisme'. (Comes to Scarborough).

Read the sign. In smaller print was written.

'Top stars of the world's erotic films presenting their talents and more'. Read the smaller printed writing.

Scarborough, thought Marco. *That's only seventeen miles away*, said Marco, carrying on his sprint home. As he creaked open the front door Anna was already up sat gazing out onto the balcony whist sipping on her coffee.

"Mi scusi! Mama." (Pardon me, Mama), said Marco, half expecting his mother to be upset with him. Anna just turning and smiling. "What you think, your mother and father were not young once?" said Anna. Adding, whilst placing a loving palm against her son's cheek, content to see him happy.

"Just call Mama, so I don't worry. Even if late then I sleep good, OK," said Anna.

"OK, promessa." (Promise), said Marco. Nothing else needing to be said, Mother and son respecting each other's changing worlds. Both devoted to each other's wellbeing. Anna a little secretly anxious about Tuesday's hospital appointment and Marco's check-up exams. A motherly sixth sense premonition niggling at her. Anna trying to push aside her worrying vibes, helped a little by her sons juvenile whistling and joyful character.

"Rebecca's invited me for tea and 'shepherd's pie' tonight, she's making it herself. You don't mind, Mama, if I go do you?" said Marco.

"No, I don't mind. Why should Mama mind? You take a nice bottle of wine and have a romantic evening," said Anna.

"Do this girl live alone?" said Anna.

"No Mama, her parents are away with her little brother and sister until Tuesday," said Marco. Tuesday thought Anna, Marco's hospital appointment day. Her anxious gut feeling absorbing her thoughts once again.

"Are you OK, Mama? Don't worry where not having wild parties in her parents' house while their away!" said Marco, seeing his mother in a daydreaming wondering.

"Ehh, no, no I know you don't do bad things in people house, Marco. You are good boy. You have your father's blood," said Anna.

"And yours too. Mama," said Marco.

"Si (Yes), and mine too," said Anna, at the same time unable to stop her curious feeling in her bones wondering.

What else was now inside her son's blood?

"I go do shopping today. Maybe I treat myself to something nice from 'Charity shops' and give something back to those less fortunate then, me and you," said Anna, changing the subject.

"OK, I'll take Pasta, and then we'll go," said Marco.

"No, mia amore. (My love). You do something for you today. You go and make something nice for you. I see you tonight, before you go for 'shepherd's pie' OK," said Anna. Her voice assertive and insistent.

"OK, Mama, if that's what you want," replied Marco, their understanding respected. By the time Marco got back from his walk with Pasta. Anna having already left for town. It was if she was showing him that she was excepting the man grown from the boy. That she could and should adapt to not always doing things with her son. That she knew he should walk his own path, and every now and again join hers. He'd come so close to deaths door saved by a miracle or something unknown to earth. Saved to live every future instant of his life to the fullest. A little note left by his mother causing Marco to giggle.

'Don't forget the *VINO*', said the note. Vino written in capitals; Anna having made three attempts to write wine. 'Vine'. 'Winn'. And 'Vinn'. She'd also left her son a hundred pounds. Marco not hesitating. His night's mediocre performance motivating his latest ambition, like an actor or actress desperate to receive an Oscar. The train ride to Scarborough was faster than he had contemplated. No sooner had he stepped out of the station. A long line of buses waiting readiness. The town having anticipated for the popularity of the 'Salon de l'érotisme'. Sex and anything to do with sex always gathering crowds. They weren't wrong. By the time Marco arrived at the venue hall, a snaking queue of weird and wonderful people. Men with men. Women with women, heterosexual couples too dressed from erotic habiliments to plainer everyday clothes, all stood anxiously waiting to enter the hall. Forty-five minutes later, a gawping inexperienced Marco was walking through the masses of people around a festival of unusual erotic objects from: every sex toy and vibrator imaginable as well as every size and every colour, to harder BDSM clothing, equipment and blow-up dolls. Stalls of sexy, sensual, stimulating, suggestive and kinky items as far as the eye could see. All presented by beautiful and sublime men and women dressed to thrill and turn the eye. Creams, lotions, toys, lingerie subtle and hard. Along with books, DVD's even sensual to hard-core figurines and ornaments. Rapidly being bought by the masses of assertive crowds. Women as much as men knowing exactly what they wanted. Marco's gawping eyes curiosity leading him to a large gathering of individuals circled around something. As he approached the group, his eyes were met by the erotic show of two of the world's best known porn stars. Intermingled in a sexual performance for all to see. The banner at the side of the lit-up stage, where they were exposing their talents read.

'Live performance three times a day'.

'Rocco de Montagna and Jenny Baise'.

'World's number one porn stars'.

Also written upon the sign. Their show just coming to an end. Marco over hearing 'Rocco de Montagna' speak to one of the nearby bodyguards in Italian. A spit second intuition hurtled in his mind. Speaking in his mother's tongue Marco shouting across to Rocco.

"Posso avere un autografo?" (Can I have an autograph?)., said Marco. Rocco answering almost instantly, causing the gathered crowd to turn and stare upon Marco.

"Ma certo." (Of course). said Rocco. Marco pushing his way amidst the aroused huddled people, all seemingly leaving him little space. His body having to closely squeeze through them all. Armed with a piece of paper. The one Rebecca having scribbled her number on.

"Hai una penna?" (Do you have a pen?), said Rocco. Stood naked in front of everybody and Marco, only his draping towel, which'd he'd used to wipe away his sweat covering his sex.

"Scusa no." (Sorry no), said Marco, a little embarrassed. "Non ti preoccupare." (Don't worry), said Rocco's partner Jenny Baise. Taking a pen out of her handbag handing it over to her performing Partner Rocco. Jenny bent over in front of everybody stark naked, as though she was alone in her bathroom. Obviously, she understood Italian, Rocco not having spoken a word to her.

"Per Chi." (For who), said Rocco.

Marco thinking about, saying for himself, but a cheeky consideration changed his mind.

"Per Rebecca." (For Rebecca), said Marco. Rocco scribbling his autograph, handing the piece of paper back to Marco. Turning to leave. Marco staring at his firm nude buttocks.

"Aspetta!" (Wait).

Cried Marco.

Rocco turning asking. "Che cos'è?" (What is it?), said Rocco.

"Volevo solo stringerti la mano." (I just wanted to shake your hand), said Marco. Rocco stretching out his hand in a conceding allowance to a fellow native's request. Marco having babbled on, like a rambling old lady throughout the thirty second transfer. Only having let Rocco walk back to his dressing room when Marco's otherworldly supraliminal sensations coming once again to a sudden stop.

The bus and train drive home, rather awkward for Marco. His recently bumped new intellect, overpowering his sexual emotions. Rocco having slept with over 700 women throughout his long career. The reminiscing knowledge of all his sexual acts and experience making it impossible for Marco's throbbing erection to go limp. Having to discreetly adjust his manhood several times in his jeans. It hadn't calmed once back at home. Marco running into his bedroom to change his T-shirt for a shirt, letting it drape over his groin area.

"Did you have a good day, mia amore?" said Anna.

"Err. Interesting," said Marco. His face expressing a naughty grin. His thoughts thinking how the hell he was going to calm his erection.

"I see Mrs David's in town, she go in Oxfam shop like me. She tell me her husband have only six months to live. Cancer. Life it is so cruel at times," said Anna. Her voice deeply saddened. News like this always bringing back to the surface, the painful memories of Arnaldo. Hearing the sorrowful voice of his mother, had one positive affect for Marco. His hard-on disappearing within seconds.

"If you want Mama, I can tell Rebecca I'll go for tea another night. I'm certain she'll understand," said Marco. His proposition sincere with no remorse.

"No, Marco. You don't let this nice girl down. You make a very special night with memories that staying forever. You make this girl feel special. Life is too short. Life is too short," said Anna. Looking at Arnaldo's photo as she repeated her last two sentences. When Marco came back from his walk with pasta. His mother was sat nibbling crisps while watching a talent show. The appalling act causing the judges to buzz rapidly their disapproving Xs. Their commentaries and that of the performer, making the audience, the judges and Anna burst into laughter. Marco now understanding every word and dialect. It seemed so long ago his word for word translations having nearly caused him to throw up.

'Toad in the hole'. (Rospo nel buco).

It's a good job he now knew what shepherd's pie was. His interpretation would have probably been a pie made from a shepherd. Seeing his mother in an appeased and happier mood. Not feeling any anxiety about leaving her on her own. Even more so seeing Pasta jump onto her lap licking her salty face. Along with his mother's encouraging words.

"You make a very special night with memories that staying forever. You make this girl feel special," said Anna. Marco's accelerated walk through the town and across the beach, leaving little time to admire the dusking sun and its cardinal aura dipping into the ocean. His poetic admiration for nature's sublime magnificence overpowered by the lustful thoughts of Rebecca's curves and bumps. His own personal night before memories merging with the all-powerful bumped knowledge of Rocco de Montagna arousing his inactive sex. Trying as hard as he might to calm his pulsating penis by the time Rebecca opened the door, his turned-on sexual organ even more difficult to conceal from his dangling shirt. Having gone to knock but the door having swung open and a very excited and happy Rebecca dressed with a tight T-shirt and no bra and jean shorts, jumping onto Marco, like a chimpanzee. Her arms supporting herself around his neck, her legs wrapped around his waist, her buttocks pressing just above his waist. A succulent appetising aromatic smell of cooked shepherd's pie gushing out of the door behind her, absorbing into Marco's nostrils causing his stomach to rumble and his mouth to water. Rebecca kissing him all around his face, from his ears to his cheeks to his neck, as though she hadn't seen him for weeks.

"My gentle warrior back from his battles. I missed you so much," said Rebecca in-between her kissing.

"I missed you too. Been thinking of you all day," said Marco. Rebecca notching down just a few centimetres feeling the erected sex of Marco pressing against her backside.

"Humm! Something tells me I believe you," said Rebecca. In a raunchy voice, slipping herself free from Marco, entering the kitchen to turn off the oven and the boiling pan of potatoes. Turning, making her way upstairs slipping off her yellow top and throwing it at Marco's feet. Marco watching her sublime naked back sexily mount the stairs disappearing from his view to the right of the barrister. A very unnerved and sure of himself new Marco, walking through the open bedroom door. Admiring the gorgeous nude silhouette of Rebecca laid on her stomach. Rebecca turning and smiling at Marco with her eyes, stretching out her arms before her, in an inviting and surrendering manner. Seconds later Marco's muscular naked body laid on top of her. The years of experienced knowledge of Rocco de Montagna, synchronically intermingled from Marco's otherworldly bestowed powers. Integrated into his gentle warrior physique, bringing easily the woman out of Rebecca time and time and time again. It was if Marco knew when and where to touch her. When to go faster or slower. When to hold her. Where to caress her. Where not to caress her. His tender and passionate actions stimulating every goosepimply nerve and emotion of her body. Hours later both laying on their backs, once again in a panting orgasmic state. Rebecca catching her breath.

"My God. That's some change from yesterday. They say Italians are the best lovers in the world. I can't doubt that any more. What happened?

Did you swallow a sex journal or something?" said Rebecca in a breathless voice.

"I told you, I'm a fast learner," said Marco laid, staring a brief instant at the ceiling feeling as powerful as a supernatural being. Out of all the knowledge he'd already bumped and obtained. Rocco de Montagna's having without doubt brought him the most pleasure. At the same instant as though, their minds were synchronized Rebecca and Marco turning their sweat drying bodies to each both and synchronically saying.

"I'm starving," said Marco and Rebecca. Cold shepherd's pie having never tasted so good. Marco and Rebecca devouring the totality of the dish, like gluttonous savages, before returning to bed both appeased and blissfully happy, wrapped in each other's arms. Marco laid behind Rebecca once again. As they began to drift to sleep. Rebecca without thinking. A natural loving reaction from her cloud nine mood. Slipping her right palm into Marco's left hand. This time Marco not pulling his hand away as he sensed, de novo, the strange tingling from his toes to his fingertips, conglomerating at his phalange. His palmar crease sensing once again the minor electrical intake. The sensation of pins and needles and charging energetic force, amalgamated with a peculiar humming in his auricles like a faint whale's cry. As the bumped aura of Rebecca united with all of the other intellects Marco having already bumped. Marco learning before falling into a deep and harmonious slumber, that Rebecca was not as confident and secure as she portrayed herself to be. That she'd only ever slept with one other man. Her first and childhood boyfriend. Having spent six years with him before he'd left her in a cruel way for her best so call friend, Emma Richards. But along with the reminiscence and present knowledge he'd obtained. Rebecca's great love from her family, her great suffering for her lost grandmother, her great caring and devoting presence for her grandfather. Her enormous love for the earth's fauna. The attainments which absorbed Marco's mind the most was that, in the words of his mother.

He'd made a very special night with memories that staying forever. He'd made this girl feel special.

And more so she'd fallen in love with him long before he spoke English or had obtained his otherworldly powers. Just simply when he was Marco. Her futuristic visons of them happily together in a beautiful house by the sea. Two children. A girl and a boy, not too far apart age wise. A dog a cat. Rabbits and hedgehogs with the heavenly aura of a harmonious home. Bestowing Marco with one of the happiest smiles and emotions he'd felt in a long time. He too was in love.

CHAPTER TWELVE

ANNA'S CRUEL DESTINY

The Sunday morning awakening was as passionate as the night before. As was the afternoon and most of the day. Marco and Rebecca spending most of diurnal in bed making love. It was, like their lives depended on sex. Complemented by brief siestas and eating. As the daylight hours drew to an end. Their goodbyes were joyful and full of hope, as though a perfect future awaited them both.

"I'll see you Tuesday. Won't be able to see you tomorrow my parents are back, and I'll have to help them with everything. And we always go to see grandpa when their home. But Tuesday after work we could meet in town or, we could walk Pasta together," said Rebecca.

"OK, Tuesday. I'll call you when I'm back from the hospital," said Marco.

"Hospital?" said Rebecca. Her voice sounding concerned.

"Yeah. Don't worry its nothing major, only some minor check-ups the doctors want to do and this guy called Hausbeck from NASA," said Marco.

"NASA! Are you going into space?" said Rebecca with a little laugh.

"Yeah, NASA. This Hausbeck guy thinks what happened to me could help others and make them understand more about coma patients and stuff like that. Anyway, if space is anything, like what I felt this weekend then I have nothing to worry about," said Marco.

"Well, what you did this weekend was defiantly 100% out of this world. Maybe you're an alien amongst us?" said Rebecca.

If only she knew the truth, thought Marco.

"Maybe I am. An Italian alien, with a pizza spaceship," said Marco, clowning around.

"A pizza spaceship, that's no good, when you reach light speed all the cheese and tomatoes will fall out and splatter Earth," said Rebecca. Causing her and Marco to burst out into a united laughter. Whilst they hugged in each other goodbye.

"See you Tuesday, my little alien warrior!" shouted Rebecca as she watched Marco eventually disappear down the steps leading to Cliffside cove. He was still thinking of Rebecca's pizza spaceship remarks when he got home. Anna not having been back long from walking pasta.

"Buonasera mia amore. Do you have a nice weekend with Rebecca?" said Anna while placing some more dog biscuits in Pasta's bowl.

"I think I made her feel very special and gave her memories that will stay forever," said Marco. He didn't think he knew, but he couldn't explain the details to his mother. Even though they had a very open and exceptional relationship.

"She very lucky to find a boy. No, a man like you. She very lucky," said Anna. Followed by, "You hungry. I make some tea for you. I don't make food. Because I don't know if you come home or stay out," said Anna.

"No Mama, I'm fine. Rebecca's shepherd's pie was lovely and it filled me up. I'm just going to rest a while. We talked and talked until the late hours, so I didn't get much sleep. You don't mind, do you?" said Marco.

"You go sleep, I see you later. There is nice 'James Bond' film on tonight," said Anna. Marco knowing his mother adored James Bond films, taking away some of his guilt, for feeling so tired and going to bed after being away for nearly a whole day. Anna knew what Marco meant by talked and talked until the early hours. She was young once too. Smiling to herself. Marco suddenly feeling exhausted, as though all his energy having been drained from him. Walking into his bedroom, his steps heavy like Frankenstein's, like he had steel weights on his feet. Still lodged in the corner between the bedside cabinet and the wall, his alien pebble. Having changed colour yet again, now a tone of light and bright emerald green, with faint bluish cast. Marco thinking to himself whilst staring at the strange, metamorphosed object, before plunging onto his bed, like the last drop of energy leaving him.

"Maybe this is how superman felt next to Kryptonite," said Marco. Waking late Monday morning full of force and energy, like he could compete in a triathlon and still have the force to climb a mountain. The first thing that caught Marco's eye was the pebble. Now a midnight blue pigment.

"Well, it's defiantly not Kryptonite. Otherwise, I wouldn't feel so full of beans being so close to I,." said Marco. Picking up the stone to examine it further. Using an old sock as a glove so that his hand would not come directly into contact with the alien object. Scrutinizing the pebble, like a scientist exploring a strange new find. Noticing tiny pulsating plum purple lines, like a hospitals heart rate monitor, pulsating a travers pebble. Spiralling from the hieroglyphics marks from the outside edges ending every time at the smaller now hollow decagon shape in the centre. Marco still having no idea what the metamorphosing pigments meant.

'Who could he ask? Or not ask. He could simply bump the intelligence of the world's top scientists. Once he found out where they lived and worked,' said Marco. The stone and its mutating colours along with the curious questions and internet research about who, where and how he could obtain access to the world's most intellectual minds, preoccupying most of his Monday, and even the Tuesday morning, in-between the tender and joking text messages between himself and Rebecca. Right up to the point of entering the Royal Duchess Hospital, de novo. The smell and bustling sounds bringing back a flood of memories to Anna and Marco, without any extra-terrestrial energy. Anna speaking for the first time. She'd been as silent as a mouse since back from work and during the bus ride.

"My son, Mr Marco Rosalinni, have appointment at two p.m,." said Anna to the mean looking receptionist. After a rapid click and check on the computer and a push of a button on the telephone. Minutes later a big grinning Hausbeck appearing in front of them.

He couldn't have been far away, said Marco, in a silent wondering thought, little did he know his mother was thinking the same.

"Mrs Rosalinni. Marco. How happy I am to see you both," said Hausbeck. Reaching out his hand in a friendly manner, rapidly shaking Anna's hand. But deferring from shaking Marco's. Simply placing his hand over Marco's shoulder in a farther to son way. Marco thought he'd seen Nurse Brain. A regretful sentiment for not having called him, whirling in his stomach. His pondering contrite thinking, cut short by Hausbeck's questioning.

"So, Marco. How've you been over these last days? How do you feel? Anything strange or abnormal you want to tell me about?" said Hausbeck.

The way Hausbeck placing his questions making Anna and Marco, gaze at each other in a similar curious manner. As if they both doubted the sincerity of Hausbeck. Marco was about to say.

'He felt fine and that he'd felt nothing peculiar pendant his time at home'.

A graceful lie that he was certain his mother would forgive him for. But the beginning of his sentence cut promptly short by the arrival of Dr White and Professors Rama and Cloud, saving grace.

"Lovely to see you again, Mrs Rosalinni. And you to, Marco," said Dr White.

"Yes, wonderful to see you both," said Professor Rama and Cloud, seconds after Dr Whites welcoming.

Their merriment interrupted by Hausbeck. Shortly after leading them all into a large room placed in the basement of the hospital.

"So, Marco like I said before we let you go home, if you remember. NASA are one of the major leading investigators into future technology, we thrive on knew opportunities and unique incidents which in return could help millions amongst us," said Hausbeck. These words Marco hadn't forgotten. Hausbeck carrying on with his repetitive speech.

"In your case, Marco. Like I explained, we feel we could understand more about coma patients and access a way to reach into their minds, maybe even bringing them back from the black hole of solitude themselves and families live through. You've lived through. You Marco, the David who has overpowered Goliath. Are unique and your situation has led me and many of my colleagues down a different road. A road which none of us could have possibly imagined. Unlocking many doors," said Hausbeck. Marco and Anna wondering if he'd learnt his repetitive speech, like an actor learning his lines. Hausbeck continued.

"I understood from you, Mrs Rosalinni, that you didn't want your son to leave England to travel to NASA's Glenn Research Centre in Cleveland, USA. So, for the series of standards and new tests, we'd like to conduct as well as making sure Marco has no side effects. With your permission, of course? I've had a special MRI-A unit shipped here to England from Cleveland," said Hausbeck staring at Anna. Anna staring back at him

"Sorry, what is MRI-A?" said Anna.

"I'm glad you asked. An MRI-A, Mrs Rosalinni, is a unique combination of an MRI and an MRA. A prototype scanning system combining a magnetic resonance imaging testing unit and a magnetic resonance angiography unit. It basically uses powerful magnets and radio waves to generate images of the brain and the surrounding nerve tissues, as well as being able to observe the blood vessels in the brain. This device also has an ERP (Event-related potential scanner), capable of detecting any related neural activity. Both sensory and cognitive, allowing us to observe different waveforms of ERP such as Psychiatric disorders and Neurotransmissions. But don't worry, Mrs Rosalinni. It does not use radiation," said Hausbeck. Not giving Anna or anybody else any time to speak, rapidly continuing with his explanations.

"What's more, the one shipped over from NASA produces up to nearly forty-eight percent higher definition imagery. How it works? We inject a special dye; we call in the medical profession 'Contrast' through a vein in Marco's forearm. The dye used is a gadolinium. Gadolinium is a silvery white, malleable and ductile rare-earth metal which possesses unusual metallurgic properties. It is a very safe substance. Allergic reactions are practically none. Only patients with kidney problems. Which is not Marco's case, could Gadolinium maybe, be harmful. But for Marco there will be no risk. So basically, we use this dye to help us see certain areas more clearly," said Hausbeck catching his breath an instant before continuing.

"What are we looking for? Well, any abnormalities really. Should that be in blood cells, bleeding in the brain, brain abscess, tissue swelling, hydrocephalus, which is fluid around the brain. Any loss of brain tissue any signs of tumours. Even osteomyelitis. Infection of the bones probably easier to understand. Any defects to the brain, any signs of minor strokes even multiple sclerosis. Also, muscle weakness or numbness and tingling. Changes in thinking or behaviour, vision problems, hearing problems, speaking problems. Brain aneurysm. Which is a weak area in the wall of a blood vessel causing it to bulge or balloon out. And more so in Marco's case to see just how his brain and body survived such an unbelievable amount of electrical intake from the lightning bolt, and how his scares self-healed themselves. Errr, I think I've covered just about everything," said Hausbeck. His three colleagues all nodding in agreement to Hausbeck's explanations. Anna not so confident. Her motherly sixth sense stirring inside her again. Even more so after having heard so many unusual medical terms. Marco having understood every word and medical idiom the first time. His knowledge of medicine combining the joint intellect of his two and a half bumped hirelings. Dr White, Professor Rama and a little of Professor Cloud. Using this acquired intelligence to calm his mother's anxiety.

"Don't worry Mama, it's just standard proceedings and I'm not crazy. The person or persons who operates the machine watch you from another room in a close vicinity of the scanner. There is an intercom system which allows me to talk to whoever is there. So, you'll be able to talk with me. The machine produces loud thumping and humming noises when first turned on. So, don't worry its normal. All I have to do is lie very still on a narrow table which slides into a large-shaped tunnel, for around thirty minutes to an hour, or a tiny bit longer. Moving around can blur the images. The only risk there is, is if you're claustrophobic," said Marco. Anna frowning not understanding claustrophobic. Marco having understood instantly his mother's curious facial expression, explaining and continued.

"Claustrophobic or claustrophobia, is a person who's afraid of closed confined spaces. Like Zia Maria (Auntie Marie), scared of going inside elevators," said Marco. Anna smiling at her son with admiration for his intellect and soothing expressive explanations.

"I'll probably have to wear one of those horrible hospital gowns. I've had nothing to eat or drink for the last six hours, so no problems there either. Apart from that you'll have to keep my necklace with my 'Cornicello' (a twisted horn-shaped charm, an amulet of good luck used for protection against the evil-eye curse), as no metal whatsoever can be taken into the MRI, or in this case MRI-A. And once all is over, we'll be able to go home as no recovery time is needed," said Marco, finishing his detailed knowledge of the scanner. Turning to face the four very flabbergasted faces of Hausbeck, White, Rama and Cloud.

"Been reading a lot on the internet, very, very informative," said Marco. Seemingly dissuading the flummoxed expressions of White, Rama and Cloud. But not Hausbeck. All just smiling astutely. At that instant, a joyful nurse Wendy entering the room carrying a turquoise hospital gown and some blankets. Her charming smile and feminine presence bringing an extra reassurance to Anna along with her son's calm and confident mood, that all was going to be OK. Nurse Wendy's presence and Marco's reassuring calm, also appeasing her motherly niggling sixth sense premonition telling herself.

"It was just a mother's deep love for her child," said Anna.

"Lovely to see you Anna and you too Marco," said Nurse Wendy. The use of first names warming Anna.

"Could you change into this gown, Marco? The changing room is the second door to your right. I've brought these blankets from the MRI, sorry MRI-A, can feel a little hard and cold at first. If you'd like I can also bring a pillow," said Nurse Wendy.

"No, I'll be OK. But thank you," said Marco.

"There's a few documents for you to sign also Marco and you too Anna," said Nurse Wendy, handing each of them a clip board and a pen. Holding with a large metal clasp, A4 size papers. Questionnaires and documented information. Moments later Marco walking from the changing room, feeling the cold draft of air, directly on his bare arse and back, the hospital gown not closing completely. Handing his 'Cornicello' necklace to his mother, dropping it into her opened hand without touching her skin, the chain spiralling down slowly into her palm, like a Cobra re-entering his basket.

"Don't worry Mama, all will be OK. OK," said Marco, reassuring his mother yet again.

"Si va bene mia amore." (All right my love), said Anna, at the same time swallowing as though her throat was dry and soar, kissing her son on his cheek. Instants later Marco laid on the cold table length of the MRI-A. The injected gadolinium dye distributed by Nurse Wendy. A familiar voice speaking over the intercom. Hausbeck.

"Everything OK, Marco? Are you comfortable? We're going to start in a few moments. Your mother is right here," said Hausbeck. Marco listening to the muffling sound of voices before hearing the clear voice of his mother.

"I here to mia amore. All is OK? You not Claustra. Claust. Clausy. Clausphob? You not scared in small place?" said Anna.

"I'm fine Mama and no I'm not claustrophobic," said Marco, chuckling to himself hearing his mother's failed attempts to say 'claustrophobic'.

"I'd better stop laughing, the images will be blurred. Don't want to come back here again," said Marco, placing his headset on and holding the emergency cable, like a small plastic ball in his right hand and seconds later the MRI-A scanner's moving the sectioned table he was lying on, transporting him down the tunnel section. Marco staring at the thin blue line which marked the centre of the tunnel section for some reason. Only the bottom part of his legs from his ankles to his feet seemed to be still out in the open. Suddenly even under the headphones he could hear the loud thumping and humming noises beginning, abruptly ceasing his earlier chuckling. The MRI-A Scanner laid in the centre of a bare white room, with no exterior windows, only a thick white door in the far right hand corner and some tainted glass, like a one-way mirror in a police interrogation room stretching across almost the entire wall to Marco's left side. The MRI-A coming to life, like a giant robotic machine from a sci-fi movie. Seconds later the agonising cries of Marco screeching down the intercom, like an animal being slowly and cruelly tortured. Through the one-way mirror Hausbeck, White, Cloud, Rama, Nurse Wendy and Anna. Witnessing in horror the MRI-A scanner sparking. Electrifying bolts of energy projecting from Marco's body like an electro plasma. Red, purple, blue, white and green bolting shafts of electrical energy bouncing of the MRI-A scanner re-entering Marco's body, like a poltergeists unwanted spirit. Marco's body jumping around, like a person receiving unstoppable defibrillator shocks, his veins illuminating as bright as lightning flashes.

"Stop it! Stop it!" screamed Anna. Hausbeck, White, Cloud and Rama all trying to stop the machine in vain. Turning every button switch and knob they could find. The continuous bolts of energy proceeding, even intensify along with Marco's agonizing heart-rending screams. Nurse Wendy holding Anna in her arms, her gesture sincere but bringing no reassurance to Anna. Dr Rama hitting the emergency button, like a crazed game show host, but still the machine continued. Dr White running into the MRI-A room trying to approach Marco, like a rescuer trying to reach a victim in a blazing inferno. Without warning a single bolt of lightning, like a laser beam speared out from under the MRI-A scanner's tunnel, hitting him in the centre of his forehead. White falling instantly to the floor lifeless. The horrifying scene causing Anna and now Nurse Wendy to scream systematically. Minutes later the whole hospital plugged into darkness, the emergency lights and backup systems activating like waiting soldiers. A thick dense fog having filled the MRI-A room. As it slowly dispersed at the same time the bolting shafts of electricity stopping. The hospital main system powering back up. The transporting section of the table activating bringing Marco out of the tunnel. Anna now staring at the plugging lifeless right arm of her beloved son, dangling from the MRI-A table, like a stranded shipwrecked castaway laid unconscious on a makeshift raft.

"Dio buono per favore no?" (Good God, please no?), said Anna, praying in her head, heart and soul for her son not to be dead. Intermingled with the angry sensation why she hadn't listened to her motherly niggling sixth sense premonition. Anna paralysed by the sight, half of her wanting to run to her son, take him in her arms. Half unable to face the sight of her dead boy. If he was dead. Professor Rama, bravely entering the room, firstly checking the pulse of his dear colleague Dr White.

"He's alive, unconscious but alive," shouted Rama. A ray of hope projecting directly onto Anna like a heavenly shaft of light. Dr Rama approaching Marco's motionless body as cautious as lepidopterist moving closer to a rare butterfly. Marco having strangely no apparent scares or burns surprising Professor Rama. After terrifyingly witnessing the electrical shafts of energy relentlessly stabbing into him, bringing great optimism to Rama. The expressive deception and hurt upon Rama's face as he checked Marco's lifeless pulse said it all. His slow shaking of his head from left to right in a no indicating manner, combined with the great sorrow exposed upon his visage as he stared directly at Anna.

"No, no, no Perché? Perché?" (Why? Why?), yelled Anna, her tears and pain inconsolable, her knees weakening her motherly and womanly strength abandoning her, causing her to fall to the floor in a traumatised heap. The eerie silence of the control room, abruptly broken by the internal telephone ringing.

"Hausbeck, MRI, control room," said Hausbeck, in a dry cold voice, having answered the phone after its third ring. Following a short silence, he said only one word to the muffling voice upon the other end of the phone. Who'd asked him if everything was OK?

"No," said Hausbeck. Minutes later a team of medical staff and security filling the MRI-A rooms. Professor White carried instantly away to the emergency ward. Anna carried away to another ward, having been sedated.

Marco taken to the morgue. Instructions given by Hausbeck that no examine in any shape or form was to be conducted upon Marco's corpse without his presence.

CHAPTER THIRTEEN

BACK TO NAPLES

"So, what happened?" said a voice on the other end of Hausbeck's mobile phone.

"I don't know. It was if Marco's body, his blood veins were filled with iron fillings. The contacting metal from within him against the MRI-A scanners giant magnets, causing some strange phenomenal electrical storm. Wait, wait I filmed it. Sending you the video now," said Hausbeck. A silent pause before the other voice speaking again.

"I'll make the arrangements for his body to be shipped to Cleveland. Oh and Martin, next time you have one of your hunches or some information, don't forget who you work for. If NASA can watch the world, then we can watch you too. Remember. See you in Cleveland with a full report. Oh and by the way, don't try to claim your expenses back. Next time go through the right channels and me. Clear?" said the voice.

"Yes sir, clear," said a nervous Hausbeck to his director chief military officer and chief of the O.W.I.Q project, as well as most of NASA's secret programmes. George N. Stanford. A six foot, four inch hulky giant, who'd seen more action and other worldly events then Captain Kirk and his entire crew. Only he was not a fictional character, he was for real. Just as his power and destruction if you ever got on the wrong side of him. The emotion of fear non-existent to him even from his first childhood steps.

"Mrs Rosalinni, Mrs Rosalinni, Anna, Anna," said the quiet tender voice of Nurse Wendy.

Anna stirring in her bed as though exiting a nightmare, repeating the name of her son in her groggy state.

"Marco, Marco, Marco."

Her eyes slowly adjusting to the bright neon lights of the hospital.

"Anna, would you like me to ring anybody for you, can you go somewhere? Or do you want to stay here?" said Nurse Wendy. Her sympathetic benevolence only reminding Anna of the harsh reality. Tears streaming unstoppable down her face, Anna fighting back her snot and weep.

"I have nowhere to go. No one to go too. I only have Marco and Pasta. I am alone here. My family live too far and don't have money to come here," said Anna.

"Listen, Anna. I know it is probably not the right time or place. In situations like this it never is. But you need to know. And I must tell you. Because of what happened today, the hospital is, and will take full responsibility. So, any costs for flights or anything else, even Marco's funeral will be paid for by the hospital. So, you ring whoever you want, I'll personally sort out their flights and even hotel accommodation. If for example you want your entire family here from Naples. The only thing is you'll have to help me with the Italian. I don't speak a word of it," said Nurse Wendy whilst holding Anna's hand. Anna staring at her gripping palm, thinking.

"Maybe she should have let Marco hold her hand and bump her memories and knowledge, even with her womanly secret garden. He would have seen for sure just how much she loved him," said Anna. Suddenly thinking about the word funeral. A parent's worst nightmare to outlive their children.

"What had she done to be hated so much by God?" said Anna. Tears still dripping down her face when she unexpectedly felt a warming sensation. Marco's 'Cornicello' necklace hanging around her neck, heating up by some strange energy. It wasn't burning her just enough warmth to make Anna feel the warming presence and a curious instinct grow within her.

"Can I see my son?" said Anna.

"Are you sure that's wise?" said Nurse Wendy. "Please Wendy, please," said Anna at the same time squeezing Nurse Wendy's hand which was still clutching hers. Nurse Wendy thinking of her own lost child and easily placing herself in Anna's position. She'd wanted to see her child as well, when her second son having died from Leukaemia at the age of seven.

An event pushing Nurse Wendy to leave her poorer home country Romania and study to be a nurse.

"Give me a few minutes I'll see what I can do, OK," said Nurse Wendy.

Minutes later, Nurse Wendy was back in Anna's room, pushing a wheelchair.

"Come on, hop in, I'll take you to see Marco but with what you've experienced today, you're not walking," said Nurse Wendy.

"I can walk. Look," said Anna standing, then sitting back on the bed, holding her dizzy head.

"You see, those sedatives are quite strong. So, no walking OK," said Nurse Wendy in an insistent voice. "OK," said Anna agreeing with ease. Moments later Anna and Nurse Wendy, descending in the cold metal large lift of the hospital. Down towards the morgue. Anna thinking of Marco's earlier words.

'Claustrophobic or claustrophobia, is a person who's afraid of closes on confined spaces. Like Zia Maria (Auntie Marie), scared of going inside elevators'.

"Can you get flight for my sister Maria, she come help me," said Anna just before the lift binged and then opening, presenting a long cold dimly lit corridor. "I'll get a flight for whoever you want. Do you need a hotel also?" said Nurse Wendy.

"No, she stay with me and Pasta. No need to buy hotel," said Anna. Nurse Wendy pushing Anna down the corridor, entering the large double doors at the far end. Once inside the morgue, Marco laying peacefully but motionlessly upon a metal bed. Two other similar metal bed structures to his left, only meticulously clean and empty. A white sheet covering Marco's nude body, his head supported by some strange plastic moulded object. A ticket hanging over his right foots big toe, like an object for sale. An array of large metal cast doors extending the whole length of the wall behind him. Just before them a large metal basin. Peculiar robotic adjustable lights and odd black and yellow dangling boxes suspended from the ceiling above him. The room was as morbid as death. Nurse Wendy stopped pushing the wheelchair a few feet away from Marco. Anna raising to her feet slowly pushing herself up with her arms, like somebody who'd been miraculously cured to walk again. Standing over her beautiful boy. His face appeased, not a wrinkle or strain of life. So young and so much to learn. Her hand softly stroking his face, over and over, her voice soft and gentle, like she was addressing a sleeping baby.

"Mia amore. Mamma ti amera per sembre. Salutami tuo padre. Dormi bene. Aspettami."

(My love. Mamma will love you forever. Say hello to your father for me. Sleep well. Wait for me), said Anna, as she stroked his brow Marco's 'Cornicello' dispersing miniature electrical sparks giving a pins and needles effect upon Anna's chest. Another strange motherly sixth sense premonition telling her.

"Maybe Marco wasn't dead. Maybe his body was here but his spirit somewhere else. Somewhere safer. In hiding until it was safe for him to return," said Anna. The only person having true and accurate knowledge of Marco's extra-terrestrial powers and the other earthly events she'd witnessed in her son complementing a reassuring self-persuading. Inducements most people would say that it was just a grieving mother unable to except the tragic loss of her child. Anna slowly approaching her right hand to that of Marco's. She wanted to see if anything happened. An intuition telling her to hold her son's hand. Her fingertips inches away from Marco's, when she and Nurse Wendy abruptly interrupted by Hausbeck, clacking open the large doors with great force. Staring at Nurse Wendy in a displeased manner.

"How's Professor White?" said Nurse Wendy, hoping her question would calm his seemingly annoyed temperament.

"He's stable, he's in a coma, but his other bodily functions are balanced and steady," said Hausbeck cold and straight to the point but seemingly a little calmer. Nurse Wendy's question chosen well.

"I thought I gave orders for nobody to be down here without my presence," said Hausbeck.

"Orders. This is not a military establishment, Doctor. And Anna. Mrs Rosalinni has every right to see her son," said Nurse Wendy, ready and willing for an argument if that's what Hausbeck was searching for.

"Yes, yes sorry you're right, Wendy. It's just been a long day and I'm concerned for Professor White. I. We was hoping Marco could help us with comatose victims. Now Professor White, is in a coma and the person who could have probably helped him the most, is laid dead on that slab," said Hausbeck.

"Doctor…" said Nurse Wendy gritting her teeth and gazing towards Anna, trying to make Hausbeck realise his cold and hurtful last statement.

"Laid dead on that slab."

Nurse Wendy's facial exasperation working.

"Sorry, sorry Mrs Rosalinni, like I said it's been a bad and stressful day," said Hausbeck, at the same time rubbing his brow, like he was searching for solutions.

Anna not replying only sitting back in her wheelchair and asking Nurse Wendy to take her back to her room. 'How could she accept her child was not of this world?'

'That she'd never hold him again'.

'Talk to him again. See him grow and build a future'.

'How could she accept his death?' said Anna in her puzzled and hurtful mind. By late evening her sister Maria was already on a flight to England and arrangements for her pick up from the airport to Anna's flat organised. Pasta having sensed automatically the distress of his mistress the instant she'd walked through the door. His devoting and loyal presence once again soothing Anna's solitude and pain. Not even pestering her to go out. Anna having stared into Marco's empty bedroom, like she was looking at a bottomless abyss. A strange light glowing from his bedside cabinet's top draw. Her curiosity intrigued, opening the sticking draw. Marco's Maple leaf, a photo of Rebecca, a photo of Marco his mother, father and pasta. Some money and a glowing scarlet strange red pebble, staring back at her. Anna picking up the radiant object cupping it into her palms. It felt warm, as she held its energy bestowing her with a soothing harmonious calm making her feel drowsy. Her eyes heavy and somnolent. All of a sudden Anna brought back from her dozing state, by the loud ringing of the home phone. Thinking maybe it was her sister Marie, Anna answering rapidly.

"Pronto. Maria." (Hello, Maria). "Err, Mrs Rosalinni," said a frail voice.

"Si chi è?" (Yes, who is it?). said Anna.

"Err, Mrs Rosalinni, I'm so sorry. I don't speak Italian. It's Rebecca, Marco's friend. He isn't home by any chance? I've been trying to ring him for hours," said a very concerned Rebecca.

"Orr Rebecca, Rebecca," said Anna. By the time Anna having explained the unexplainable all she heard was, Rebecca's traumatic distraught tears and the thud of the telephone dropping to the floor followed by pips and then silence. Their eyes meeting for the first time at Marco's funeral. Rebecca hadn't eaten in days and her once gorgeous curve and bumps having rapidly abandoned her physique. Her face was thin and drawn, her eyes bloodshot. Just like Anna's and Zia Maria. (Auntie Maria). The small chapel was full. Many members of Anna's and Arnaldo's family having attended Marco's final ceremony. Anna's wish for Marco to be buried in her homeland next to his father and their lost generations of families. Granted. Hausbeck. NASA having paid for everything. Even Anna's desire to leave England and go back to Italy. The distraught memories of a land and failed dreams with so much heartache having needed very little persuasion for her to decide to return to her origins. There she had family. And even though she'd have traded every last penny of compensation for the return of her son. The money assured a secure and troubled free life for her and her family. Even Pasta. NASA having organised his safe transfer from England to Italy, though he found it to hot and spent his days looking for shade. Rebecca having sadly experienced the strength, devotion, faith, love and acceptance of God's will from Marco's family members. In a land where the will of God was briefly questioned. A family she'd for a little while dreamt and wished one day to be part of. Only in very different circumstances. Her dreams, for now buried with Marco. Rebecca having accompanied Anna hand in hand into the back room of the little chapel where Marco's open coffin and blissful sleeping visage sadly greeting them. Her last few days before returning to England to start a new, was in a land, with a population where hope of better days, dreams of faithful new beginnings and a pardon from the heavens, were so intense. Her own sadness having been a little filled with belief. It was certain she and Anna would stay in contact and that she could travel any time to sit and talk to Marco. Which sorrowfully had become Anna's daily ritual. A grieving constantly dressed in black widowed women with only one mysterious unusual, intriguing object, lighting her path of hope every day. An oval shaped mineral around seven by five inches in size, extremely smooth to touch, covered with peculiar hieroglyphics in a sublime sapphire tint, in the middle a smaller decagon shape constantly metamorphosing into different pigments. Marco's otherworldly object now a mahogany red.

Apart from Marco's maple leaf and photos. This was the only other object Anna having brought back with her from England.

CHAPTER FOURTEEN

BACK TO CLEVELAND

Hausbeck arriving back in Cleveland landing with the military (Lockheed Martin C-130J Super Hercules), plane. Having left the Naples US military base only a few hours after attending Marco's funeral. Dr White having been transported back to his hometown New York, still in a coma. Placed in his old hospital only now a patient. Comforted and visited everyday by his family. Professor Cloud, Rama and Nurse Wendy, trying to go on with their everyday lives, jobs and chores. But their stigmata minds would never be free off what they'd all experienced. The bulky mass of military technology touching down with elegance. Its three crew members, captain, co-pilot and a load master along with its minimum payload. One passenger and a closed coffin, presenting no difficulty for its four Rolls Royce AE 2100 D 3 turboprop engines and its nearly forty-one-meter wingspan. As the aircraft came to a slowing noisy halt. Waiting by the rear end of the fuselage for the huge cargo door to open, standing Chief Military Officer George N. Stanford, accompanied by four military personnel and two male doctors and a female nurse. The hydraulic system of the aircrafts door, lowering the opening to its angled loading position. A very exhausted Hausbeck standing staring at his chief in command. His black funeral suit jacket hanging over his left shoulder, held from falling to the ground like a hook, by his left-hand index finger. Stanford taking a small gaze at Hausbeck, rapidly acknowledging his military salute with a similar response salute. Then staring behind Hausbeck at the wooden casket. Marco's coffin attached alone in the humongous nearly thirteen meter long, three meter wide and just short of three-meter-high Cargo hold. Capable of carrying military weaponry. Huge humanitarian pallets and nearly a hundred passengers. Now the voluminous fuselage staring at a tiny six sided, eighty-four inches long and twenty-eight inches wide by twenty-three inches high box. Wider at the top and tapering down towards the feet.

"Any trouble getting him out of Italy?" said Stanford. His powerful Texas accent breaking through.

"No, sir. No trouble at all. Some people in Italy and elsewhere will do almost anything for a few dollars," said Hausbeck.

"How did you exchange the body? And how many people know?" said Stanford.

"We used the false compartment. The identically casket which you see hear is buried only with sand back in Naples. With the help of the funeral parlour owner persuaded by a few thousand dollars, we transferred Marco's body into the specialized refrigerated unit you sent, just after his mother and his girlfriend paid their final respects. His temperature has been stable and no apparent signs of decomposition. I've been monitoring everything and I have the full report which you requested right here," said Hausbeck at the same time waving a red sleeved 'Top secret' folder in front of Stanford.

"So only the funeral parlour owner knows of the transfer and that Marco Soffione Rosalinni is not buried where he was supposed to be?" said Stanford.

"Yes, sir. Nobody but him. And ourselves, of course," said Hausbeck.

"Can we trust him to be silent forever?" said Stanford.

"No need, sir. Those windy roads in the south of Italy are very dangerous. Bad unexpected, unquestioned accidents happen all the time," said Hausbeck.

"Good work, Hausbeck. Now get yourself cleaned up and meet me at the medical morgue, OK," said Stanford.

"Oh, did you recover the data chip you implanted in Marco?" said Stanford.

"No sir, it's still inside him. Just below the back of his neck at the top of his spinal cord. I have the data analysed in my report," said Hausbeck.

"Good. Good. Let's meet at fifteen hundred hours, OK," said Stanford.

"Fifteen hundred hours. Yes, sir," said Hausbeck. Saluting Stanford once again. Then handing him his 'Top secret' report documents. Hausbeck having just a little over and hour to clean himself up and drink as many cups of black coffee as his body could take. The four soldiers carrying Marco's specialised refrigerated unit, disguised as a coffin accompanied by the two doctors and nurse. Placing the box inside a specially designed vehicle. The adapted oxygen and power cables transporting power to the specialised coffin unit. Unplugged from the aircraft and plugged rapidly into the vehicle's generator unit.

15.00 hours exactly. Hausbeck entering the high-tech morgue looking more like a scientific spacecraft's operating theatre. Giant robotically arms and very high technology equipment assembled under a meticulously clean and pale blue lit room. The vast space large enough to place over a hundred people and still have room to move around with ease having only one access in and out. A steel digital coded and biometric handprint security scanning door situated a good two hundred feet away from the digital equipment. Flat screen monitors of every size projecting images of Marco and his dormant status. Transferred by the small internal camera inside his coffin. Smaller monitors displaying numbers, digital data of temperature and other measuring facts, statistics, figures numbers and records. Indicating input such as scan, filter and test. The touch screens all having a menu bar and a video recording, as well as voice analysing capacities. A very long rectangular shaped bed, with a digital endoscopic image of a human body and all its cells and organs. Standing on top of a thick robust rotating hydraulic arm, empty. A huge circular shape like a flying saucer with twelve powerful high intensity lights hovering over the digital endoscopic data bed. Another bed made of stainless steel placed at the digital bed's feet end. Marco's coffin located upon it. An array of medical accessories, equipment apparatus and utensils neatly arranged upon the numerous bordering portable cupboards in the room.

"Are precisely on time we're just making the final preparations. Read your report, very interesting. Very interesting. So, you believe Marco had the power to obtain information from another human being. Like a computer transfer of documents. As you exampled in your findings, from the main computer to a USB stick just by the power of touch," said Stanford.

"Yes sir, as you can see in my report Marco's intellect activity advanced considerably when he came into contact with certain individuals. I don't have any data from where, I believe it started with Dr White. And unfortunately, as you know he's now in a coma," said Hausbeck.

"Yes, yes, I saw the video you sent me, remarkable. Unfortunate but remarkable," said Stanford, interrupting Hausbeck. "Continue," said Stanford after a small awkward silence.

"Well sir, as the data annalistic readings from Marco's microchip, transferred to I.O.W.Q computer analysing system. When Marco came into contact with a list of names, after I secretly implanted the chip. The first being a young nurse working night shift at the Royal Duchess Hospital. Brian love. The second was Professor Rama and Cloud. Another was his old working colleague Bill Sanders, and later the same day his dentist, Dr Denise Dent. Then his trip to a small English coastal resort called Scarborough. Where he came into contact with a porn actor, stage name, Rocco de Montagne. And the last data I have is from his recent girlfriend, Rebecca Brant Jones. I even suspect he obtain information from his dog, but the readings are different. Well apart from Professor Cloud. Because I believe he needs. Sorry needed, a certain amount of time. I calculated thirty seconds for a total transfer. Marco's handshake with Professor Cloud cut short. But in all the other cases his cortex, motor sensory, corpus callosum, different lobes and cerebellum. Especially his hippocampus and entorhinal cortex. Where our memory is stocked in the brain. Well for thirty seconds Marco's brain and body activity intensified by a hundred. To give you a small idea of just how amazing this was. A normal, average body like yours or mine, in thirty seconds will have around twenty-five thoughts. Our eyes will blink around six times, our heart beats thirty-six times our body produces 300 Joules of energy. We take in 0.3g of Carbon Dioxide. We breathe in and out eight times. We produce seventy-two million red blood cells. And our blood travels seven kilometres around the body. Multiply all this data by a hundred and it is no human being data reading any more but something from out of this world," said Hausbeck.

"So, you believe Marco is some sort of alien being? Or some alien being has possessed his body?" said Stanford.

"That I'm not sure about. His body when alive showed no real signs of an alien transformation. The only noticeable physical signs some which have gone others, still are present on him. For example, Marco's occipitofrontal cicatrices has completely vanished and his oculus dexter changed into a cerulean pigment, his oculus sinister to an olive green. As well as the silvery grey streak at the front of his hair," said Hausbeck.

Stanford frowning a little. His background was more military than medical mumbling in an annoyed manner.

"Doctors! Occipitofrontal cicatrices. Oculus dexter. Plain English man, plain English," said Stanford, vexed.

"Yes sorry, sir," said Hausbeck, continuing with his detailed report avoiding any medical jargon and speaking as Stanford had requested in plain English.

"So, like I was saying the only noticeable physical signs, some are gone. Some which are still on Marco. One is his forehead scares self-healed themselves. Two, his right eye colour changed into a turquoise blue and his left eye to an olive green. Three, as his hair has started to grow back, which you can clearly see on the monitor. A silvery grey streak has appeared at the front of his scalp."

"Do we know why that is?" said Stanford.

"Well at first, we. I and my co-workers White, Cloud and Rama thought it had something to do with the huge amount of electricity Marco's body absorbed. But now sir, I'm not so sure," said Hausbeck.

"Well let's open him up, start with his body and organs and then let's go to the brain. Let's see what's inside there. If there is something hidden inside him, here's the place to discover it, no?" said Stanford. At the same time giving a commanding indication from his head to the two doctors and nurse all dressed in green medical suites, plastic gloves and large, transparent, head visors, to commence with Marco's autopsy. Hausbeck slipping into his green medical wear. Only Stanford still dressed in his military attire but placing a mask over his face as Marco's coffin opened. Hausbeck entering the commanding digital code, hidden behind Marco's name plaque on the top of his coffin, activating the catafalque disguised unit to unfasten. The lid of the casket folding down to the bottom. Small rectangular sections automatically lapping over each other like an accordion. The two longer sides and the top and bottom ends folding down slowly like hydraulic panels. The disconnection of the energy source and the oxygen feeding unit to the coffin, causing a loud hissing noise. Marco's naked body covered in a dispersing mist like dry ice. Seconds after his exposed cadaver released from the casket. With a digital input into one of the touch screens from one of the doctors. Six robotic arms activating themselves. Two placed on either side of Marco's corpse near his shoulders and thighs. Another above his head and the last at his feet. The commanded robots lifting Marco's body as delicately as a hand upon a butterfly. Transferring him onto the long rectangular shaped bed, with the digital endoscopic image of a human body and all its cells and organs. No sooner had his anatomy come into contact with the technologized bed, a multitude of lights and digital input displaying 3D images of Marco's skeleton form. Along with his veins, cells and organs in high definition clearly appearing upon the mass of surrounding monitors. Seconds later, a perfect hologram image of Marco projecting itself at his feet, turning constantly 360°. A flashing red light indicating the location of his implanted microchip. Marco's heart monitor flat lined. The green, red and blue lines along with the sensing animated consciousness monitoring indicating data. Displaying no sign of life.

"He doesn't look like an alien, just a young man. Poor bastard didn't have much of a life. Lost his father young. Spent the rest of his time looking out for his mother. Had only one real girlfriend, worked in shitty jobs most of his life. Don't see any superior intellect there, do you?" said Stanford openly, addressing himself to Hausbeck but not acknowledging him with any regard. His stare was laid upon the lifeless athletic physic of Marco.

"Well, looks like he kept himself in good shape. Would have made a good solider. What do you think?" said Stanford, throwing a quick questioning glance at Hausbeck.

"Yes sir, I think he would. I wouldn't say he was a poor bastard though," said Hausbeck.

"Oh, why's that then? I'm all ears," said Stanford. Intrigued by Hausbeck's defending reply.

"Well sir, he was greatly loved. His mother and late father were devoted to him. And he to them. His caring aura touched many," said Hausbeck.

"Love. What is love? It's for the weak. Look where love got him," said Stanford in a cold snapping response.

"Well, let's open him up then see how much love spills out of him eh? said Stanford. At the same time approaching Marco. Closely examining his motionless face. Marco's eyes closed in a dormant manner not an ounce of breath respiring from his lungs.

"So, with a hand shake you could bump the intellect of another? A simple hand shake? Won't be doing much of that now eh, young man," said Stanford mumbling, at the same time slipping his own right hand into that Marco's right palm. The two doctors, the nurse and Hausbeck preparing their medical apparatus.

"Wait," shouted Stanford pulling his hand away from Marco's palm, a good forty-five seconds having passed.

"Start by extracting the microchip. Don't want that thing damaged in any way," said Stanford having seen the doctor preparing to incision Marco from the standard autopsy dissection. Shoulder to shoulder and down the centre of his chest to his umbilicus. Another input into the computer activating the robotic arms again.

"Can't we just bloody turn him ourselves?" shouted Stanford.

"Yes sir, we could. But all this technology has to be justified somehow," said the first doctor in a joking manner.

"Just get on with your job, or you'll be the next cadaver lying on the table," said Stanford. Not at all amused. Marco's body delicately turned over onto his stomach by the robotic arms. The red indicating light and computer data technology guiding the doctor as he made a small incision. Another robotic arm moving closer ready to collect the microchip.

"That's odd," said the first doctor. Having snitched a small scalpel opening in the back of Marco's neck extracting the chip.

"Yes, it is," said Hausbeck, agreeing.

"What? What is odd?" said Stanford. Annoyed, to not have seen for himself what was odd. "He's bleeding, sir," said Hausbeck.

"Well, of course, he's bleeding man. His just been cut. Bodies bleed when they're cut," said Stanford, in an angry astonished way. Hearing such ridiculous talk from qualified doctors.

"Not dead ones, sir. After about ten hours the blood of a deceased coagulates. (Gels if you prefer). In other words the blood thickens in the capillaries (blood vessels), making it unable to travel around the body. Creating a permanent blue staining of the skin called hypostasis. (Poor or stagnant circulation, such as when the heart is not pumping any more). For example," said Hausbeck using his medical terms for his fellow colleagues but simplifying their medical jargon in plainer English for Stanford.

"And he's been dead over a wee,." said Stanford his face perplexed, as though trying to understand what all this recent information meant. Without warning Marco's heart monitor went from flat lined to a sudden display of triangular lines, like a stock change performance chart. The three different square indictors at the right side of the screen suddenly displaying different coloured letters and numbers.

'HR bpm ECG 60'.

'SpO2 / 99 Pulse 60 bpm'.

'NIBP mmhg'.

'120 MANUAL'.

'80 (100) P'.

"My God, he's alive. Quick grab the tranquiliser," screamed Hausbeck. The nurse running as fast as she could to one of the surrounding portable cupboards. No robotic technology capable of moving so quickly or having such rapid spontaneous reflexes as a human being. But she was too late. Marco already stood facing the two doctors and Hausbeck. Stanford and the nurse to the opposite side of him.

"Grab him," said Stanford in a commanding voice. But as the three men tried to overpower Marco's recently roused body, he threw them aside like they were dead sticks. Stanford recognising the use of Marco's defending Wing Chum Kung Fu, Karate. It was what he had mastered over many years. The flashing vision of him shaking Marco's hand pounding into his mind.

"He's bumped my intellect. If Hausbeck's findings are correct, he'll know my every secret and what's more, NASA's too," said Stanford in a crazed panic. At that moment, Marco running to the steel metal door at the opposite end of the immense medical room. Reaching the door within seconds. The groaning agonising cries of the two doctors and Hausbeck, slowly climbing to their feet. Marco punching in the eight digital code as easy as composing a well-known telephone number. At the same time placing his right palm upon the digital biometric handprint scanner. The door opening instantly.

"My God, it's true," said Stanford, watching Marco's naked form disappear through the opened access. His shadow still present for a few seconds before the door closing behind him.

"How could we not have detected with all this million-dollar equipment that he was still alive," screamed Stanford, as though talking to the wind.

"Raise the alarm to code red. All eyes on finding Marco Soffione Rosalinni. That's an order," said Stanford to Hausbeck.

"And get that chip analysed again, see if we've missed something. We need to find this boy," said Stanford now ordering everybody. Marco finding his way to the storage room with ease. Thanks to the recently unexpected bumped absorbed intellect of Stanford. He now knew his way around NASA's Cleveland medical research centre and its grounds as though he'd been there as many times as Stanford. Finding his way discreetly and safely to the stock area. A selection of uniforms and other garments aligned, like a clothes shop, laid out before him. Choosing a dark grey suit, the sentiment this disguise would be more persuasive than a military uniform. The other very useful information Marco had obtained was where the kitchen and food storage area was. Accessing the kitchens cellar with a simple known digital code and a pass discreetly slipped away from one of the kitchens staff. He was starving. Munching away on a cold cooked chicken leg, thinking an instant of Rebecca's cold shepherd's pie, and their passionate evening together. But his main thought was for his mother. Remembering the last horrific scenes from the MRI-A room, but even worse the reminiscing visage of his grieving mother over his supposed dead corpse. It was all there in his mind. The same information Stanford had. Marco had too. How his body was transferred from the false coffin to the specialised unit. How he was brought to Cleveland. How he was coldly about to be dissected, like some frog in a school's biology class. But even more worrying. How a heartless, uncaring Stanford would kill his mother or Rebecca without a bat of an eyelid if Marco didn't come up with a solution very fast.

"We could put out an international APB," (All points Bulletin), said the second doctor to Stanford.

"And how do we explain a very alive Marco's Rosalinni's sudden appearance from Naples Italy to Cleveland USA?" said Stanford adding.

"Do you think the good guys from NASA do this sort of thing? Sneak bodies from one country to another. Dispose of unwanted witnesses. Pay doctors like you two. This is all being financed and covered. Masked is probably a better word, by the O.W.I.Q project. The compensation pay out to Mrs Rosalinni was from another secret offshore account in Panama. Believe me the less the good guys from NASA know about this the better for all of us," said Stanford. The two doctors and nurse abruptly realising they too could soon become unwanted witnesses.

"And what do you think would happen when Rosalinni's family and the south of Italy, where he's supposed to be buried see his picture splattered all over the news. You'll stir the local Mafia. And they'll hunt us all down until the end of the earth. Hausbeck was there. The chapel was overflowing with family members and locals paying their last respects. We can only pray Marco Rosalinni doesn't go to the media. That's why we need to find him, and quickly," said Stanford. A nodding in agreement Hausbeck standing by his side, still rubbing his left arm from his shoulder to his elbow. There where Marco having grabbed him and thrown him aside like a stick. Marco contemplating many scenarios to get him out of his current situation. He now had the information he was part of the O.W.I.Q project (Other Worldly Intelligence quotient). If he had an extra-terrestrial IQ. Marco now wishing he had a spaceship too.

"Maybe I need to find a way of contacting my alien buddies?" said Marco, whilst chumping into another cold cooked chicken leg. Taking a moment to analyse the recently bumped information from Stanford. Discovering Stanford having been with NASA from its very creation in 1958. He'd participated in a large number of other worldly phenomena projects, such as the sighting of the alien satellite, the 'Black Knight. Apollo 11 (eleven's), UFO sightings' and Armstrong and Aldrin's declarations of seeing strange lights and finding alien ruins upon the moon's surface. He'd supervised the Cosmic Radio Bursts "Blitzars" witnessed around the globe. He'd participated with the Russians on the mysterious Alien skull found near one of their nuclear plants next to the Kovashi River. He'd analysed data from as early as 1966 on the double helix, fractals, like nautilus shells crop circles around the world and the USA. He'd worked in Area 51 where various sightings of UFO's had been seen. He'd studied and visited the powerful and unexplained phenomena of the Pyramids, as well as Stonehenge and the unexplained suspension of the laws of physic of the Bermuda Triangle. He'd lectured and investigated the Mayan Mysteries of the earth's position in the Milky Way and their astrological superiority.

Also having visited and reviewed the Nazca Lines in southern Peru and the unusual Hoia Baciu Forest in Romania. Stanford having even learnt about, OBEs (Out of Body Experiences). One of his latest projects was. The Meteorite ALH84001 thought to be from Mars discovered in Allan Hills Antarctica and the Moarki Boulders in New Zealand. But even with all these earthly present strange findings and discoveries. Due to massive NASA and government cutbacks, he needed to find something bigger and more concert. Evidencing without doubt his findings. He'd also participated in his younger years on warfare tests on soldiers. Injecting them with plutonium, exposing them to nerve gases ESP, and various other deadly cocktails. Stanford wanting to build a super solider combing, alien intelligence and genetic DNA with that of a human. The ultimate warrior. Extra-terrestrial proof that would enable the financing of his O.W.I.Q project. Financing NASA like back in its glory days and assuring his obsessional outlandish need to create the first man and alien being. As well as going down in history for being the man who'd proven to the world. Alien intelligence and beings existed among earthlings. United with the risk that they would eliminate mankind if the world. i.e. Stanford and his outrageous idea to create a man-alien soldier to protect earth wasn't taken seriously. NASA's cutbacks on such projects and the harsh abandon of a man who'd devoted his entire life to NASA, now rapidly being pushed out the door towards retirement. Replaced by younger generations of scientist not military. Twisting Stanford's once kind compassionate mind, into a cold-blooded uncaring criminal. His ambitions drugging his irrational intellect, like lost historical crazed leader's ambitions to conquer the planet.

"Moarki Boulders," said Marco thinking back to the night of his lightning strike where'd he believed to have seen one for real on the English coast.

"Moarki Boulders. Maybe in New Zealand I'll find some answers to what's happened to me?" said Marco, now munching on a banana. Thinking of a way how he could contact his mother or Rebecca. Anna's old telephone number in England deactivated when she'd returned to Italy.

"Rebecca's number could possibly be the same." said Marco. Without warning the food storage room door abruptly slamming open. A military personnel pointing a strange looking revolver straight at Marco, three other soldiers covering his side and back.

"Don't shoot," said Marco. But his words were like pissing in the wind, dispersed into the oblivious uncaring mind of military personnel, simply carrying out orders. The powerful tranquilliser slumbering Marco into a paralysed state almost immediately. He'd raised suspicion when the staff badge, he'd stolen having activated along with the security code the opening of the storage room door. Only problem is that the staff member, having reported his missing badge. He'd rapidly returned in a panic to where he'd hung his jacket. Knowing he would obtain a severe warning or even lose his job if found without his security pass clearly visible. The alarm raised to code red by Stanford meant the whole of NASA's Cleveland centre was on high alert. Marco's half munched banana tumbling to the floor, the only remaining evidence of his recent presence in the food storage room.

CHAPTER FIFTEEN

MARCO LEARNS OF STANFORD'S PLAN

"We have him, sir."

"Coast is clear." (There is no visible danger).

"He didn't go to many Klicks." (Kilometres).

"Do you want us to in-ass, sir?" (Leave ones current position). "Or are you sending the meat wagon?" (Ambulance), said the officer who'd shot Marco.

"Meat wagon on its way. What's your current position?" said Stanford.

"40 08 15.60 N, 69 44 21. 72 E," said the military officer. Hausbeck laughing to himself about Stanford's remark for him to explain things in plain English. The shoe now on the other foot.

"Couldn't he just say what their position was? At the food storage room, Northeast Block unit seventy-two. Basically five minutes away for the Meat Wagon (Ambulance), to collect Marco," said Hausbeck in a silent chuckle. Ten minutes later Marco's unconscious body carried back into the lab by the four military officers, placed once again onto the digital endoscopic bed. De novo no sooner his anatomy coming into contact with the technologized bed, a multitude of lights and digital input displaying the 3D images of Marco's skeleton form. Along with his veins, cells and Organs in high definition clearly appearing upon the mass of surrounding monitors. Again, seconds later a perfect hologram image of Marco projecting itself at his feet, turning constantly 360°. Only this time Marco was alive and now strapped down.

"Good work, Corporal Mears. You and your men can stand down. Back here tomorrow at 11.00 hours," said Stanford. At the same time taking the tranquilising gun from the corporal. Corporal Mears and his three colleagues overjoyed with the news that they could have the rest of the day and night off. Only returning back to work at eleven the following morning.

Beer women and more beer awaiting them. As they turned to leave, all having presented their military salute to Stanford. Stanford shouting.

"Wait, Corporal Mears." said Stanford.

"Yes, sir," said Corporal Mears in a military authorised response to Stanford. Corporal Mears and his three colleagues all thinking the same.

"Fuck he's changed his mind, the old bastard."

"One last thing Corporal Mears, before you leave, could you shake the patient's hand for a good thirty seconds?" said Stanford.

"Yes, sir," said Corporal Mears, again in his military yelp. Not questioning an instant Stanford's strange request.

Seconds later, Corporal Mears, standing by Marco's unconscious left side. Placing his right hand into Marco's right palm. The instant their fingers and palms connecting the data on all the screens going haywire. Marco's normal bodily functions multiplying by a hundred and his mind activity, by a thousand. His cortex, motor sensory, corpus callosum and different cerebellum lobes. Especially his hippocampus and entorhinal cortex. Where memory is stocked. The readings were off the grid, irrational and erratic. As though a thousand thoughts and information were being channelled into his brain by some paranormal force. Marco's closed eyes twitching around 600 times, his heart beating 3600 times. His body producing 30,000 Joules of energy. His Carbon Dioxide intake 0.30g. His breathing indication 800 times superior. And his body creating 7200 million red blood cells. Traveling at an increased speed, 700 kilometres around his body. But yet, apart from his closed twitching optics. Which could have passed for someone simply having a nightmare. Marco's other physical intensified readings were only being indicated by the mass of technology analysing his bodies and minds status. His body laid as peaceful and undisturbed as a sleeping baby. Thirty seconds later, Marco's data readings returning back to normal.

"Thank you, Corporal Mears. That will be all," said Stanford.

"Yes, sir. Thank you, sir," said Corporal Mears unsure why he'd been asked to shake the patient's hand for so long. Unsure and unconcerned what all the strange digital numbers and off the grid information, figures and statistics on all the monitors meant. And unsure and even less concerned about the flabbergasted expressions of the two doctors, the nurse and Hausbeck.

"Beer women and more beer were at the top of his mind."

"So, what now?" said Hausbeck.

"Well, we don't need these two doctors and nurse any more for a start," said Stanford, pulling the gun and expertly shooting the two doctors precisely in the neck. Only the nurse hit on her shoulder she'd turned to run. Her reflexes not as rapid as the drugging pellet.

"Make it clean, Hausbeck," said Stanford.

"Yes, sir," said Hausbeck. Almost in a whisper, collecting the three unconscious bodies, placing them inside the ambulance having transported Marco back to the lab. A section of the labs wall opening to reveal a large garage access. Hausbeck driving the ambulance away with his three unwanted witnesses along the tarmacked road. The disguised door closing behind him. Looking as though the road lead only to the buildings wall, like Batman's hidden cave. An ingenious disguised way in and out of the lab. A few hours later, a groggy Marco awakening from his tranquilising pellet.

"Ahh, Mr Rosalinni. Back a second time from the dead. Well, actually a third, no?" said Stanford.

"Where am I?"

"What do you want from me?" said Marco, whilst pulling with all his might trying to break his attached arms and legs free.

"I think you know already. If what Hausbeck believes and now me. Especially having seen your escaping performances. Only one other person has the access code to that door you escaped out off, and only his and my handprint can complementarily activate it," said Hausbeck. Marco staring at the door, then at all the digital equipment surrounding him.

"I'm not an alien. I don't know how or why my mind collects the information?" said Marco.

"Well, it's not how the average human brain works is it now?" said Stanford.

"Your mind and body Macro seemingly having the extra-terrestrial ability to absorb the intelligence and memories of any other being and animal if what I read in Hausbeck's report is true. And I believe it is. In his own words. And I quote. Marco Soffione Rosalinni has possessed an otherworldly power to bump the intellect of any creature which comes into contact with the portion of the upper limb distal to the radiocarpal joint, comprising the writs, palm and fingers," said Stanford, tutting.

"Good, God. What is so difficult about writing 'hand?' portion of the upper limb distal to the radiocarpal joint. Doctors!" said Stanford.

"So, we believe that when your hand. Left or right comes into physical contact of another being. Human or Animal. Then your mind absorbs or bumps this intellect. What's more? As we learnt from your escaping methods today, is that your own DNA seem to chameleon with that of another. Your handprint upon the door, was actually mine. Your own fingerprints metamorphosing into my identifying characteristics," said Stanford pausing looking at his hand as though to double check his fingerprints were still visible, before continuing.

"Can you imagine the possibilities here? We could send you to Libya, infiltrate you into the enemy camps. You could require information on I.S (Islamic State). No need to train you or teach you Arabic. All you have to do is shake the hand of a local to obtain the dialect. Shake the hand of a commando, thirty seconds later you'll know as much as survival and combatting tactics as he or she. We could send you to North Korea. You could shake the hand of Kim Jong-un and discover all he knows on his nuclear tests and the country. No need to teach you Korean you'll learn with a simple handshake. As well as the different dialects. You could obtain all the hidden and secret information of any world leader President Obama. Putin. Merkel. Cameron. May, Trump, Holland, Macron, Giorgia Meloni or Biden. Any world leader and see if they are really telling us the truth. Even the heads of MI5-6, the KGB, Mossad, the limits are endless. Your body and mind could access anywhere and anyone on this planet with a simple thirty second handshake. You could absorb the I.Qs of all the greatest scientists combined on our planet. The I.Q readings measured upon superior earthlings is between 190 and 230 but your capacity could be anything. Alien," said Stanford.

"But that's not what you want from me is it?" said Marco. Sure of himself. "What do you mean, Marco?" said Stanford, smiling like a Cheshire cat.

"I mean you don't want me to go to Libya, or North Korea. Or bump the intellect of the world leaders. At least not yet, do you?" said Marco. Adding.

"You don't care about this world and what's happening to it?"

"You don't care about war and the tyrannising suffering of millions?"

"You don't care if we're destroying ourselves or our planet?" said Marco.

"Well, I'm certain you already know the information I'm about to tell you as you've bumped my intellect. Let's say I like the sound of my own voice, and even though my long career with NASA has been mainly military. I did accompany many of NASA's greatest minds around the world and participated in and on a vast range of mysterious finds. I even gave a lecture on the Mayan Mysteries of the earth's position in the Milky Way and their astrological superiority. Not bad for an old solider," said Stanford, smiling proudly at his reflection from one of the monitoring screens.

"So, as you know, NASA and the world have been investigated UFO's and trying to prove to the earth that the little green men amongst us do exist and have done for many years. NASA and world leaders have been accused by many of hiding alien life and extra-terrestrial presence here on earth. Many great scientists and military leaders along with former astronauts, believe there is abundant evidence that we are not alone. And that alien presence on earth has existed for decades. That they've been trying to make contact with us or even study us. Such belief and facts also indicates that the alien's intellect are far superior to any earthling. Even their capacity of unexplainable technology. Their use of toroid co-rotating magnetic disks with an unknown energy source to propulsion their crafts from different solar systems and penetrate our atmosphere practically undetected," said Stanford staring an instant at the large disc shape object with its twelve powerful lights, seeming hovering over Marco before continued, seemed he did like the sound of his own voice.

"Humans have been estimated to walk upon earth for over 2000,000 years yet Space travel and stories of aliens are quite recent, considering how old our species is. Obviously, a lot of Sci-fi films and TV Shows have opened the public's mind to alien life. But there are a number of very important clues amongst us. For example the Lolladoff Plate the estimated twelve thousand year old stone dish found in Nepal. The flat stone with its sun-like design in the centre with two spiralling arms turning clockwise around 450° from its edge. It has a humanoid figure, with arms and legs and a bald head, resembling the archetypal 'Grey Alien' I've seen it. This stone is not from this world and I believe there are other stones, pebbles or foreign matters with similar characteristics. Or maybe completely different among us," said Stanford Marco instantly thinking about his alien pebble and where it could have come from? More so where it was now?

"And then there's the 'Dogu' the small human like statues crafted in Japan between the 14,000 and 400 BC. These clay 10cm to 30cm forms are rarely found in one piece but it is speculated that 'Dogu's' were used as part of an ancient healing and fertility rituals. The statues appearance resembles humanoids wearing some sort of stylised space suits. The figurines all have helmet like heads and large round eyes. They also have enlarged armoured arms and legs. Many believe these statues were modelled from aliens who visited prehistoric Japan, making contact with the human inhabitants. It is also said that ailments could be transferred from a human to the Dogu and then destroyed," said Stanford, Marco thinking to himself. If in prehistoric Japan, alien intelligence could transfer and destroy ailments, syndromes, conditions from a human to a Dogu. Just how advanced their technology and intellect were today. And what else could they transfer from a human?

Stanford continuing, "And Napoleon Bonaparte's microchip. The French Emperor, King of Italy, Protector of the confederation of the Rhine. Abducted by Aliens. His disappearance in July 1794 when he was just twenty-five years old. Until his return to earth several years later. When Dr Andre Dubois examining Napoleon's skull researching why his cranium was so small in 1997. Discovering the half inch long microchip lodged within his skull. The bone growth around it proving it had been there since Napoleon's early age, giving a greater understanding to the speculations that this extra-terrestrial presence helping him to achieve his rapid rise to power. His intellect being superior supernatural. Maybe he was bumping other's intelligence like you?" said Stanford, his words causing Marco to wonder if he had a microchip implanted inside him.

"And what about the Nazca Lines, still visible today. These series of giant line drawings located in Peru's Nazca desert dated as far back as 500 BC, differing sketches and shapes and sizes. Some are forms of animals, plants or humanoid. Some are simply straight lines. Why would an ancient civilisation incapable of flight create intricate works of art that can only be visible from the skies? Unless they were and are coordinating data and landing strips for alien ships, I've seen them. I'm military it is to me 100%

an alien base landing field," said Stanford pausing an instant, looking at Marco. Marco still attached but no longer struggling to break himself free.

"And the construction of the great pyramid of Giza. The oldest of the seven wonders of the ancient world, and the only one to still be in existence. Believed to have been built in around 2560 BC, over a twenty-year period. A true testament to how advanced the Egyptians were at architecture. The pyramid is perfectly aligned with the points of the compass and the two diagonal lines drawn, north-west and north-east of the pyramids position. Only tools and construction material far superiorly advanced then the ancient Egyptians possessed, indicating the use of technology by extra-terrestrial beings. And the Egyptians hieroglyphics, eh what about that?" said Stanford. Marco thinking instantly of the strange hieroglyphics on his pebble. What did they mean? Stanford not finished with his lecturing data counting.

"And the Sumerian civilisation in Iraq, their existence around 4,500 BC. The Sumerians and their highly advanced farming methods. They also had a unique complexed system of mathematics and writing. Also possessing a knowledge of astronomy and the solar system. How do you explain a species who lived thousands of years before the discovery of Pluto? Possessing an ancient tablet discovered by archaeologists, listing earth as the seventh planet from the edge of the Solar system. This only being possible if Pluto was included in the count," said Stanford looking at Marco, who seemed quite intrigued by his theories. Marco thinking back to the night of his lightning strike laid on the wet sand staring at the Fallstreak Hole widening, revealing the celestial sphere. A travers the opening the multitude of stars glittering their supreme galactic aura, as though another world was levitating above Marco and the rest of mankind. Stanford breaking Marco away from his wondering thoughts.

"And the Aboriginal Wandjina. The mythology telling of spirits coming from the sky to create earth and its habitants. The depictions of these spirits having survived in the form of ancient rock paintings. Exposing the white ghostly visages of the Wandjina and their big dark eyes. Some say their descriptions of alien abductions. Maybe you were abducted Marco and placed back on earth? The aliens advanced technology travelling faster than the speed of light and notion of lost time was erased. Maybe Einstein's theory of relativity and gravity that unites space and time as space-time, curving in the presence of mass or 'wormholes' as he put it. The kind of tunnels a traverse space-time connecting distant parts of the universe," said Stanford taking a short pause for thought before saying.

"Now he would have been a create mind to bump don't you think?" said Stanford. Marco not answering, only wondering if he had been abducted.

"So where was I, oh yes, Aboriginal Wandjina," said Stanford, scratching his head as though trying to recuperate his thoughts.

"As well as the ancient artefacts, ancestral constructions, objects and visible signs upon earth. There are also a number of scrolls, and paintings. For example: the Vimana texts and Sanskrit epics. These ancient Hindu flying crafts which are said to possess lights and powerful weapons. Accounted in the Sanskrit Samarangana Sutradhara. It also specifies the use of light materials and mercury filled engines enabling them to fly," said Stanford seemingly unstoppable with his lecturing data.

"And the unknown authored painting of the sixteenth century AD. The Madonna and child with the infant ST John. The painting residing in Florence Italy depicts the Virgin Mary kneeling over the young St John and baby Jesus praying. On the right hand side of the work of art, you can clearly see a shepherd and his dog staring at something in the heavens. He's pointing to a strange object, which appears to be a flying saucer with a dome shape on top of it. One of many religious art illustrating UFO presence," said Stanford, rolling on like an out of control robot.

"And in Sigiburg France in 776. UFO sightings were seen. Accounted in Annales Laurissenses."

"And on April 14th. 1561 in Nuremberg Germany where strange sightings appeared. Illustrated in the famous 16th century woodcut by Hans Glaser. The Celestial Phenomena over Nuremberg."

"Also, the 1710 Baptism of Christ by Aert de Gelder still hanging in the Fitzwilliam Museum Cambridge England, displaying a flying saucer projecting light," said Stanford, his mind and knowledge of extra-terrestrial findings next to none.

"The list is long and we could talk all day. Even from your native country Italy. The cave painting 'Circa' 10,000 BC from Val Camonica. Artefacts, architecture, paintings, scrolls. Ancient manuscripts like the."

"The strange alien figure found in Kiev 4,000 BC."

"The 700-year-old petroglyph discovered in 1966 Queretaro Mexico."

"The ancient figurines in space suits Ecuador."

"The nearly three billion years old grooved spheres and the rock in South Africa known as Precambrian. The mysterious small metal spheres around one inch in diameter with the three parallel grooves etched around its circumference. Others resemble a bluish metal with alabaster specks. Others are hollowed out with some strange unknown substance," said Stanford. Marco thinking about the bizarre decagon shape with what seemed a miniature brain characteristic embedded inside his stone when he first discovered it. Now also hollow.

"From all four corners of our earth there is still proof of alien life having visited us. Maybe even having forged a part of our history. Some of these artefacts and historical wonders I've seen. Some I've even been even lucky enough to have touched. All I've read upon and studied, but even with these decades of proof and speculation. Nothing has been as real as you."

"Nothing," said Stanford. Silence fell in the room, broken by Marco's questioning.

"I won't be able to discover or collect what you want attached, will I?" said Marco.

"So, you did bump my intellect?" said Stanford smiling yet again.

"Prove to me how much you know. After all there's only the two of us. I tell you what. Detach you, I cannot do as you and I know you have attained all my military and long studied defending Wing Chum Kung Fu, Karate. And you being a much younger physical condition. Well, I think it will give you the unfair advantage. But I could turn off all this technology. Shut it down in a breath and we could talk man to man, if you are still a man? How about that to begin with?" said Stanford. Shutting down the array of digital equipment surrounding Marco.

"Which subject would you prefer me to start element eighty-five or the Antikythera mechanism," said Marco, after a short hesitant pausing thought.

"Surprise me," said Stanford. Marco began to reveal Stanford's plan.

"In the 1900s, a very perplexing artefact was recovered by a group of sponge divers. Found in a shipwrecked vessel off the coast of the small island northwest of Crete. 'Antikythera', found buried under forty-five meters of water. Among various bronze and marble statues, which seemingly was the ship's cargo, there was a chunk of what seemed to be corroded bronze and some sort of inscription on the case indicted it dated from eighty B.C. At first many experts believing it to be an astrolabe, some sort of astronomer's tool. But further examination and an X-ray of the mechanical find discovered it to be far more complex and developed. The Antikythera mechanism has a number of very complex differential high-tech moving parts. Sophisticated meshing gears and cogs structures not known to exist until 1575. It has been named as the very first mechanical analogy computer. Possible designed constructed for foreseeing and calculating astronomical positions even eclipses as well as calendrical astrological reasons. Nothing similar on earth has been discovered. It is still unknown who built it over 2,000 years ago. The device is so accurate its dials and assembled gearing wheels remains. Discovered as eighty-two separate fragments. Only seven contained significant inscriptional mechanism, leaving scientist with their jaws open for explanations. The technology of such a complexing workmanship said to be like an ancient calculator. Some even say it is more valuable than the Mona Lisa. And some say it even comes from a superior species. You believe there's a more advanced mechanism then the one found in Antikythera, left by aliens in Chukotka Tundra Antarctic Russia. Your first clues about this alien object were after the Chelyabinsk meteor, entering the earth's atmosphere over Russia on the 15th of February 2013. The light and energy from the meteor even brighter than the sun. Most people believing the bulk of the metro's energy was absorbed by the earth's atmosphere you believe it was something coming to earth to recuperate or protect the alien computer, and that this extra-terrestrial supercomputer can be activated with the element eighty-five," said Marco.

"Good, very good. No excellent, excellent. And what is element eighty-five?" said Stanford still smiling, like a professor who'd just listened to a grade 'A' lecture from one of his students.

"Element eighty-five is also known as Astatine. Named after the Greek word 'Astatos'. (Unstable). A radioactive chemical with the periodic table chemical symbol 'AT' and the atomic number eighty-five. (Eighty-five protons stuffed into its nucleus). It is the rarest naturel element found in our world. The totality of its Isotopes are short lived. Astatine has a life expectancy of around eight hours, it quickly disintegrates, it materialises on earth as a decay substance of an assortment of heavier elements. It has never been seen under a macroscopic. Its radioactive heating would vaporize it immediately. Even still unknown if this high temperature could ever be overcome by adequate cooling? Even though the quantitative physics of Astatine are uncertain. Estimations based on its periodic chart, place it as a heftier analogy of Iodine and is associated with the Halogens. An ensemble of elements containing fluorine, chlorine and bromine. Even if you scanned the entire earth, you would be as lucky as winning the lottery to find an ounce of the stuff. It has never been directly seen. But you have located pure uncontaminated Astatine on the small Yemen Island in the Indian Ocean 'Socotra', also described as the most alien-looking place on Earth," said Marco, laughing out loud before continuing.

"And you believe because of your discoveries throughout your long NASA career that this element eighty-five will activate the more advanced mechanism than the one found in Antikythera. The one you have located on the Southern Indian Ocean Antarctic Island of Tundra," said Marco.

"And you not?" said Stanford. Marco not given the time to respond, both interrupted by the sound of the hidden doorway into the medical lab opening, the bright lights of the ambulance causing Marco to close his eyes in a squint and Stanford to raise his hand, palm facing outwards in a protecting manner. Hausbeck turning of the contact and shutting of the lights. By the time he'd stepped out of the vehicle, the camouflaged door nearly complete fully and closed behind him.

"Any problems?" said Stanford.

"No sir, all went like clockwork," said Hausbeck, adding, "How long has he been awake?" said Hausbeck, throwing Marco a rapid glance before returning his stare to Stanford.

"Not long. We've actually been having a very interesting conversation. It's good that your back, just in time actually to explain to Mr Rosalinni the rest of what he already knows, having apparently bumped my intellect. That reminds me, can't you simply write 'hand'. Portion of the upper limb distal to the radiocarpal joint, comprising the writs, palm and fingers. Hand man, hand," said Stanford.

Hausbeck not acknowledging Stanford's displeased annoyance of his medical literature. Only asking.

"What does he know?" said Hausbeck.

"He knows about, element eighty-five and the more advanced Antikythera mechanism we believe to have located on the Island of Tundra, and the Chelyabinsk meteor," said Stanford, adding after a short pause.

"And he knows what we want from him," said Stanford.

Hausbeck sighing then pulling a chair next to Marco before beginning to talk.

"I know your father was a great fan of Socrates. I've been studying you and your past for months now. Maybe with your newly gifted otherworldly intellect, you'll understand more about Socrates and many other geniuses of lost time. Socrates said."

"To know, is to know that you know nothing. That is the meaning of true knowledge."

"Well, we earthlings have been given so much knowledge that we did know nothing. But over the last century, the planet earth has ambiguously advanced with scientific breakthroughs of analysed dominant scientific findings and body of knowledge. Modern day science finally starting to find modernistic perceptions that are changing our capacity and opinions about our world and the extra-terrestrial worlds encircling us. Star gates, wormholes and portals having been classed as the factionary imaginary schemes of physical science. As I believe you know now. A wormhole being a hypothetical characteristic of space time. A short-cut through the solar system as sort. Many believe aliens are able to travel as far and so quickly because of their alien ships or as we call them UFO's. But after discovering hidden portals in the earth's magnetic field which we NASA, named X-points. (Electron diffusion regions). These are areas where the Magnetic field of the earth connects to the magnetic field of our brightest star, the sun. Creating an uninterrupted passage leading from mother earth to the sun's atmosphere, ninety-three million miles away. NASA used its Themis spacecraft along with the help of a European Cluster probe to examine the phenomenon. They discovered these portholes, wormholes opened and for some reason closed dozens of times every day. We indomitably believe that these portals help in the transferal of masses of magnetically charged particles that surge from the sun responsible for the southern lights and geomagnetic storms. Like the one which occurred the night of your accident Marco. But we also believe extra-terrestrial life are travelling to earth this way. What, we don't know is why? In 2014 NASA launched a mission called (MMS), Multi Scale Mission. Four spacecraft's that circled the earth locating and studying these portals. That is when we also discovered the location of element eighty-five and the otherworldly Antikythera mechanism we believe we've found and more or less located on the Island of Tundra. We had great unfounded suspicions that extra-terrestrial intelligence were studying and examining us. But we never dreamed in a million years the possibilities and powers like the ones you have been bestowed. The ability to bump the intellect of any being or animal simply by touch. A physical computer download, if you like, from one being to another. You could learn any language even alien if you came into contact with one. You could become a qualified astronaut within seconds you could learn the full mysteries and unanswered questions of our world. Find the truth about Stonehenge, the pyramids, Easter Island, even which came first the chicken or the egg? But what's more important for us is you could prove the true existence of extra-terrestrial beings," said Hausbeck.

"So, you believe when the atomic energy of element eighty-five comes into contact with the other Antikythera mechanism which you believe is on the Island of Tundra," said Marco, hesitating an instant before adding. "Can't you just call it the Tundra mechanism?" said Marco.

"Go on, go on," said Stanford, disregarding Marco's question.

"So, you believe when the atomic energy of element eighty-five comes into contact with the 'Tundra mechanism'. This will activate an energy source indicating all the places on earth that alien life are entering, thus proving the hundred million dollar question. We are not alone," said Marco.

"Something like that," said Hausbeck. Hausbeck's desire to discover the Tundra mechanism and the element eighty-five. Hoping to activate the displaying information of extra-terrestrial quantum wormholes accessing earth from other universal planets, seemingly sincere. Marco having not bumped Hausbeck's intellect and memories only going on his gut feeling. But he knew for certain Stanford's wish was to capture an alien and create his Frankenstein alien-mankind monster solider.

"Well, if you want to prove to the world alien intelligence exists, why don't you just expose me? I could show the whole planet my otherworldly powers," said Marco.

"Nice try to escape Marco. You know why? Because it is the nature of humankind to have concert proof. Gone are the days and thank the heavens too, where the priest or higher authorities could threaten you with hells abominations and the powers of the gods, if you did not believe what was told to you. The rightfulness taught to us by our academic modern world to obtain an honest accurate proof. Many would believe you to be another hoax. You don't look alien and the fact that your extra-terrestrial bumping transfer can only be seen with the use of hi-tech medical data, would only throw speculation on manipulated equipment. Even your ability to obtain the intellect of another, would only be passed as a magical clairvoyant trick. The other more important issue is. If the true authorities or the wrong powers of the world. The so-called bad guys, discover your capability is not a magical clairvoyant trick. Then you will be analysed or even used as a weapon. Do what we're asking and you get to go free? Maybe if you do discover an alien planet and the doorway to get there, your powers to bump another DNA as it were, could possibly even permit you to live anywhere. And your mother too. I'm sure she'll forgive us for faking your death when she sees you alive and well again," said Hausbeck. Stanford agreeing with a nodding head, at the same time rubbing his brow with his left hand and reading another part of Hausbeck's report. Marco thinking about his words. To be analysed or even used as a weapon. The words of his mother hurtling back into his mind.

"Marco, what do you do and say, you talk like you are a medicine man, you must be more saggio, (wiser), you must be intelligente. (Clever). What do you thinka these men and women do too you when they know you have this power, I tell you, I know, I tell you because I am your mamma. They put you in a cage like an animale (animal), a mouse or a maiale (pig), and they torture you with strange machine like those Nazi do in the war. They hurt you, stab you, drain you, and look inside your head, look inside in places not even light can go. You must be more intelligente Marco. I am scared now, no I am terrified. I nearly lose you one time. Please don'ta make me you lose you again, per piacere." (Please),. said Anna, many months back to Marco.

"What makes you believe I won't simply use my powers to escape and vanish, never to be found again?" said Marco.

Stanford smiling diabolically.

"Two things maybe even three. One is, I think you are as curious as we are to discover alien life and find out what happened to you. Even fill in the missing blanks during your months of being in a coma. The second is, Rebecca Brant Jones and the third which I believe is the most important to you is your mother. How will you protect them? We may be slower than you and not possess your physical extra-terrestrial abilities. But if what I read and conclude here to be true," said Stanford holding the top secret report of Hausbeck in his hands.

"Your abilities to bump other beings or animals' intellect. Will only bump the intelligence and memories from their past up until the moment that person or personness came into contact with you. In other words, all that I've done or learnt since you last came into contact with my hand this morning is as mysterious and unknown to you as any normal being," said Stanford staring at Marco for some sort of reaction, before continuing.

"So, let me shine a bit of light on the missing information from your otherworldly being. Whilst you were sleeping from the tranquiliser's pellet you received, I implanted a simple tracking device inside you. No need to explain where. Maybe for security reasons, I implanted a second or even a third. Oh, don't worry its quite simple, you just have to pull the trigger of this gun and the microchip advance NASA technology is implanted into the person you shoot. Although I'm not a doctor, pulling triggers I know a lot about. It works a marvel. Ask Hausbeck here? We or should I say, I followed his every move. That's how I discovered you, Marco," said Stanford. Marco staring at Hausbeck. Then at the strange looking air pressurised gun in Stanford's hand, gazing back at Hausbeck. Hausbeck expressing a sadden expression as if to say.

"It's true," said Hausbeck's expression. Stanford to reinforce his arguments turning on another computer. A 3D imagery of two people like on google earth, appearing next to each other. The location, NASA's Cleveland medical centre. The two flashing 3D displays were Marco and Hausbeck. A map of the world also appearing on another screen and Stanford saying at the same time, demonstrating with the nozzle of his detecting microchip gun.

"Now as you can see, you're here, your mother is here and Rebecca is here. I was always very good at geography and I can safely say these three destinations are quite some kilometres apart. Even if you try to ring or forewarn one of them. The other will be dead before you compose the first three digits of a telephone number. Another thing I did whilst you were sleeping is contact some of my worldwide colleagues, stationed in Naples and in the North of England. If I don't report to them every four hours, or if you should suddenly disappear. Well, I think you have seen of what we are capable here. So, do you want to take the risk? Or is it simply not easier to take the journey to Tundra then Socotra?" said Stanford pointing to the two destinations on the screened map, still with the nozzle of his gun, adding.

"Here's food for thought, Naples Italy is around 1900 km from where Rebecca lives in the North of England. And that's by flight. Cleveland USA is around 5900 kilometres from the North of England and around 7600 kilometres from Naples. Add them all together an all round trip will be about 15'400 kilometres. You may have extra-terrestrial abilities but you're not superman, are you. So, I don't see how you could possibly warn your mother Anna, or Rebecca in time. What you could do is travel the 6566 miles from Cleveland to Chukotka Tundra in Russia. Collect the 'Tundra mechanism' as you've named it. Then travel the 10,000 kilometres from Tundra to Socotra collect the element eighty-five and then return here," said Stanford.

"And how do I stabilise an unstable element eighty-five?" said Marco. Thinking of the risk for Anna and Rebecca, and knowing Stanford's unbalanced ambition. One of his father's deepest desires entering his thoughts.

"Proteggere sempre tua madre." (Always protect your mother).

"Well, we could start by presenting to you all the greatest scientists and physicians known on the planet. Your extra-terrestrial powers have the possibility for the first time to assemble all this intellect into one mind. Maybe with this unique combined intellectual knowledge you will learn how to stabilise element eighty-five. The other is you could maybe bump the Astatine into your body. After all, if you have the capacity to connect with another human and animal there's every chance your body could intermingle with the Astatine. It is after all the rarest 'natural' element found in our world," said Hausbeck, taking over from Stanford. Hausbeck trying to be a little more scientific, then a threatening military.

"And the risk of radiation contamination?" said Marco.

"I'm sure you'll have found a solution by the time you get to Socotra," said Stanford, quickly intercepting Marco's question asked to Hausbeck. Hausbeck secretly relieved of Stanford's rapid intervention. Having no idea how to answer Marco's question.

"And what happens when these two treasures. That's if I find them. What happens when they are eventually combined together? The eighty-five protons stuffed into its nucleus of element eighty-five could active a nuclear bomb. You do know a proton is a subatomic particle, with a positive electric charge. Protons and neutrons, are collectively referred to as 'nucleons'. One or more protons are present in the nucleus of every atom. Protons are a fundamental candidate particle and the building blocks of nitrogen and all other heavier atomic nuclei. God only knows how powerful, these two elements; the 'Tundra mechanism' and the Astatine will be when united. Mankind and the planet earth could be destroyed within minutes. Maybe that's what the alien intelligence are hoping for. To eradicate human existence and recuperate, planet earth for themselves. Have you thought of that?" said Marco.

"We don't believe so. With all the proof we have required from our past history, combined with the major scientific advances of our modern times. Our satellites and probes buzzing around the universe. Nothing indicates that alien superiority wants to destroy us, or earth. Analysts presume, more so that they want to study our species. Maybe to find a way on how to make contact with us. A lot of scientist, medical minds and world leading counterparts, myself included. Believe alien species haven't already made contact with us because they are waiting until we find peace amongst our own species before accepting another. Our planet as you know Marco, for as far back as history has been written has never been free from war. As noted by Mahmadsaid Ubaidulloev." (Member of The National Assembly upper house of Tajikistan).

"War is very dangerous. We know there is life on other planets but we must make peace here first, caveating his knowledge about alien life on other plants by noting. 'We should focus on solving our problems on earth'."

"And that's what all our conclusions come too. The two elements united will not activate a bomb to eradicate human existence. But as we believe indicate the pathways to and from earth from other universes therefore proving without any doubt. We are not alone," said Hausbeck, quoting the words of 'Mahmadsaid Ubaidulloev'. "So, do we detach you?"

"Will you accompany Hausbeck to Chukotka Tundra? Recover the mechanism and travel forth to Socotra?" said Stanford.

Marco closing his eyes for an instant. His mother's loving face appearing in his mind, along with the gentle vision of her tender touch upon his cheek. Followed by the vision of Rebecca wrapped in his arms, like an eagle's mighty wings around her cheek. Her whispering thought penetrating his emotions.

"My gentle warrior back from his battles. I missed you so much." said Rebecca.

Seeing himself complete what Stanford and Hausbeck wanted and returning to be with Rebecca and his mother. The gentle warrior back from his adventures. His eyes still closed and Marco at a snail's pace bowing his head as if to say.

"Yes OK, I'll do what you want just leave my mother and Rebecca alone."

CHAPTER SIXTEEN

MIRNYY AND ZHIZN

"Wise choice," said Stanford.

Understanding instantly Marco's sluggish nod. Untouched by the traumatic choices he'd placed upon him.

"We can detach him. Have him guarded 24/7 and give orders that all personnel must wear gloves. And nobody, unless ordered, should come into contact with him. I'll start with the preparations for your voyage," said Stanford.

"Sir, you gave Corporal Mears and his men the night off, remember," said Hausbeck.

"God yes, I did. Well plan B then," said Stanford at the same instant shooting another tranquilising dart into Marco. Plunging him almost instantly into sleep.

"Shall we meet at 8.00 hours?" said Stanford.

"Yes, sir," said Hausbeck. Stanford leaving by the same digital code and fingerprint Biometric systemised security door, Marco having escaped from. Before vanishing out of the lab, thinking back to Marco's escape, early that morning he shouted.

"We should think of installing an Iris Scan Biometric System too," said Stanford. Hausbeck not having the time to reply, Stanford gone before he could answer. Hausbeck taking off his coat throwing it over the chair he'd been sitting on opposite Marco. Making his way to the lab's basin, staring a long instant at his reflection in the metallic mirror, as though trying to search the good in him. Divide his evil doings looking for the scientific young ambition uncorrupted man he once was. His white blouse and intellectual appearance capable of fooling many. But not his creators. Knowing one day he would pay deeply for his murdering and other sins. Hausbeck not sleeping much. Sitting most of the night near Marco examining his data reading and gazing at his innocent sleeping physic. Wondering why this young adolescent man having been bestowed with such an unbelievable otherworldly capability. He was already up and drinking yet another coffee when Stanford reappeared inside the lab.

"Did he wake?" said Stanford.

"No sir, if my calculations are correct, he should be coming around within the next hour, and no later," said Hausbeck.

"Good. Good," said Stanford.

"Coffee, sir?" said Hausbeck.

"Umh?" said Stanford, his mind seemingly somewhere else.

"I asked if you'd like a coffee, sir," said Hausbeck.

"No. No. Shall we get on, we've got lots to do," said Stanford, carrying straight on with his planed itinerary.

"So, here's how we're going to do it, you and Marco leave in a week from now. Next Friday evening for Moscow. Over the coming week, I've assembled a selection of the world's top scientists. Thirty-three to be exact. From right here in the US to China, Germany, Canada, South Korea, Russia, Australia, France, Israel and Finland. Well, no need to name them all you get the picture. Anyway, they will all shake Marco's hand for thirty seconds and by the week's end he will have the intellectual knowledge of over thirty great nations all bumped into his mind," said Stanford.

"And how do we convince all these great nation's highest intellect to shake the hand of a young man for thirty seconds, without raising some great suspicion?" said Hausbeck.

"Well, you're the scientist. Thought you could work that out quite easily," said Stanford, looking at Hausbeck before continuing, as if to say this challenge should be like a walk in the park.

"So once all thirty-three chosen members have connected with Marco. You and Marco will fly in the Bombardier Global express for the 7,800 kilometres flite to Moscow. Moscow being seven hours ahead will mean after the ten hour flight time, you'll arrive at seven a.m. EDT. (Eastern day time). From Moscow you will be escorted to a private jet which I have arranged. It will fly you both the 6,000 kilometres to Ugolny airport near Anadyr without complication, and there won't be any complications. Once in Ugolny, Marco will have to travel to Chukotka Tundra alone by truck and then the rest by foot. I'll leave it to you to brief him about the local people and land. Or you could simply shake his hand," said Stanford, grinning once again like a Cheshire cat.

"Thirty-three of the world's top scientist. What if my mind capacity won't be able to take in so much data?"

"What if I overload?" said Marco, wakening from his drugged dreams to hear Stanford's crazed idea.

"Nonsense. Look at it on the more positive front. All the information you'll contain and all the different languages and dialects you'll understand," said an uncaring Stanford.

Even with his already bumped intellect. Marco having no idea if his mind and body could absorb such a massive intake of knowledge. He was rapidly soon to discover. The first batch of the thirty-three top world scientists shortly due to arrive. Hausbeck having come up with injudicious idea to present Marco as a young Arabian prince seeking to invest large amounts of money in diverse scientific projects. Instruction were given to each thirty-three members of the world's top scientist to shake the young princes hand and not pull their own palm away until he had done so first. Also, to stare the prince directly into his eyes and bow when leaving. A touch of extra proceedings Hausbeck also thinking of, to reinforce the long thirty second handshake. All financed under the O.W.I.Q project. The thought of millions of dollars that could or would be invested into their own personal or national projects. The shaking of the Arabians prince's hand, staring him directly in the eye and bowing before leaving, having been adopted without any questions or suspicions from every single member who came into physical contact with Marco. Marco's initial worries that his mind would not have the capacity to bump such a massive intake of intellects over a one week period. Unfounded. Hausbeck and Stanford having spread out the visits and contact to no more than five a day. Marco having felt physically exhausted for the entire week, sleeping long periods to recuperate after each bumping contact. But no other apparent signs of change. His skull dimensions still the same, no huge over developed forehead appearing. No massive nose bleeds and no supplementary physical signs or stigmata elsewhere on his body. His mind having obtained the capacity to speak and understand over thirty languages, play chess like a world champion, excel in mathematics and physics, biochemistry. Behaviour and physiology, electronics and interfacing, ecology, biology and genetics, bacteriology, design and analysis of experiments, traditional Chinese medicines, inorganic chemistry, linear algebra, quantum physics, virology and wildlife ecology to name just a few. Marco having travelled a long way since his 'simple' first wish just to be able to speak fluent English. And it was with all this powerful combined intellect that he left NASA's Cleveland Ohio medical base in their private jet. An aerospace, the Bombardier Global express 6000 capable of flying long distances with minimum fuel. Marco sitting, like some sort of guarded rock star in the luxurious cabin. Hausbeck at his side and the transmitting locating devices in his body, direction Moscow. The flight to Moscow mainly silent apart from the rapid irrelevant questions responses, between Hausbeck and Marco. Like.

"Are you comfortable enough?" said Hausbeck

"Yes," said Marco.

"What did you think of the meal?" said Hausbeck.

"Not bad," said Marco. Hausbeck having worn a pair of specialised gloves the whole journey. Dispersing the curious looks from one of the two cabin crew members.

"I have some sort of eczema skin rash and the altitude aggravates it more." said Hausbeck. The cabin crew attendant overjoyed to share the news with his colleague. Hausbeck noticing him secretly whispering to his co-flight attendant behind the curtain. Reading his lips. Hausbeck's mother having been deaf, he'd learned sign languages and lip reading from a very early age. Something which had often helped him in his unlawful practices. Marco thinking a long while about his mother and Rebecca. But then his mind absorbed by the recent acquired amalgamated brainpower. Trying to work out how he could stabilise element eighty-five. His overwhelming scientific intellect almost as eager and ambitious as Stanford and Hausbeck to discover the two treasures. His most powerful organ the heart, eager and ambitious to go home. As the mass of modern technology touched down safely and on time. In a 10° colder wet cloudy Moscow. Marco contemplating if he should shake the captain's hand. To have the knowledge to fly such a mechanical wonder driving his enthusiast. But he never saw the captain, the transfer including their luggage and cargo from the Bombardier Global express aircraft to a smaller 750 Citation jet. The transfer done within less than an hour. Hausbeck still wearing his gloves approaching Marco's seat with a buddle of what seemed like documents and charts. The aircraft having rapidly gained altitude and seemed to already descending. Hausbeck seeing Marco was more alert speaking more in-depth for the first time before they'd departed from Cleveland.

"So, Marco once we arrive in Ugolny, you will leave by truck with a local guide. His name is 'Bacnmek', he will take you to the border of Chukotka Tundra. But then you'll have to travel by foot."

"You speak Russian now, right?" said Hausbeck.

"Da," said Marco smiling.

"Good this will help you along some of the way, even with Bacnmek, although I doubt he'll talk much to you. You must follow the coordinates on this chart. It will take you into the heart of Chukotka Tundra. There you most find a man named 'Ravnaya Zhizn' or more known by his family as 'Zhizn'. Here's the thing Zhizn comes from the nomadic Nenets arctic Russia reindeer herders. But they speak a language unrelated to Russian migrants. They have a unique way of life, cultures and religious beliefs like a tribe. They travel thousands of kilometres through the Arctic Tundra with their mass herds of reindeers. They dress in reindeers-fur, travel by wooden sledges, live in reindeer-hide tents called 'Chums', their diet is raw reindeer meat, organs and warmblood straight from the carcass of a freshly killed reindeer. Sacrificed to the gods of an ancient shamanistic religion that governs every aspect of their daily lives. They are not use to seeing tourist or other cultures either. And although they will not attack you in anyway. Zhizn will only speak to you in their ancient language which you most acquire. Only if he has a total confidence in you will he reveal what he knows. This is another reason why we could never send an expedition team here. He would have fled deep into the Arctic where temperatures of -50° are reached. Not to mention the depth of remoteness land. Exactly where you must go. Here look I've marked it for you," said Hausbeck pointing to the centre of the mapped chart, where he'd scribbled it with an 'X', like a treasure map.

"And how will I know this Ravnaya Zhizn? Any characteristics or even a photo so at least I know who I'm looking for," said Marco.

"No nothing. The only thing I can tell you, which we discovered from the few found documents of a lost colleague, 'Alex Livingston', who went to Russia in 2013 to investigate the Chelyabinsk meteor. His findings took him for an unknown reason over 5000 kilometres from Chelyabinsk to Chukotka Autonomous. He is the only person of which we know who met Ravnaya Zhizn. But he died six months after his visit to Chukotka Autonomous. Cancer. There was a small remark in his notes which stated. I quote.

"Zhizn's aura seems to be one of an ancient spirit. His stare piercing your very soul, as though he can read the traces of your life like Dendrochronology rings from the greatest and oldest (Qercus Stellata bole), Oak tree's trunk. I could not speak his words, and he not mine. But he knew I was of no threat. And I knew his secret I would never obtain," said Hausbeck, reading Livingston's note. Followed by a small pause for thought, for himself and Marco, before he continued.

"The lucky thing is in the vast remoteness of the Antarctic Chukotka Tundra, you're not going to come over crowds of people. The lesser lucky thing is you are looking for a man whose aura is one of an ancient spirit. Whatever that means. And his stare can pierce your soul," said Hausbeck. Hausbeck and Marco's mutual stare at one another, broken by the 750 Citation landing and its airbrakes surging into action. The jet taxing on what seemed a remote airway, too small for the 29.5 meter length and 28.65 meter wingspan of the Global Express 6000. A call came through from Stanford. His words echoing out of the phones speakers as though to remind Marco he was surveying their every move.

"I see you've arrived safely in Ugolny. Have you briefed Marco on Ravnaya Zhizn?" said Stanford.

"Yes, sir. He has all the data we retrieved from Livingston's files," said Hausbeck.

"Good. Maybe he'll be able to find Alex Livingston's lost computer somewhere out there in the wilderness. But the most important thing is finding the mechanism," said Stanford.

"Marco can hear you sir, I've placed you on the loudspeaker," said Hausbeck.

"I know," said Stanford, adding, "Nice scarf, Martin. Bacnmek is waiting, speak to you soon."

The echoing pips on the other end of the phone telling Marco and Hausbeck. Stanford having hung up. The comments about Hausbeck's scarf and the knowledge that Bacnmek was already waiting. Revealing to both of them that Stanford was watching their every move and even surveying them by digital and satellite images. Hausbeck looking around the jet searching for the hidden camera. Marco eager to complete his challenges and assure the safety of his mother and Rebecca. The jets automatic stair doors opening. A gushing icy wind carrying a mass of snowflakes into the cabin, like a ghostly spirit. Hausbeck tightening his scarf around his neck and placing a bonnet upon his head. Marco grabbing his rucksack. Minutes later, his backpack laying on the back seat of the four by four. Bacnmek already having started the engine. Not a word or welcome to Marco or Hausbeck, as though he was following orders. Hausbeck's final words before Marco watched his silhouette shorten and then disappear from the unclean wing mirror were.

"Good luck," said Hausbeck. His last stare deep into Marco's regard was more saying.

"Don't be stupid. Complete the mission and think of your mother and Rebecca," said Hausbeck's stare, something Marco needed not to be reminded of. Even though coming to the end of the April month, where temperatures should have slowly begun to rise. This year was not the case and the small patches of grass, lichens and bushes quickly absorbed into an ocean of snow. Bacnmek driving in silence over the frozen lakes and rivers, chain smoking and only staring at the long stretch of vast whiteness before him, the radio quietly mumbling in the background. Marco understanding the local news and weather report. Temperatures up to -40° being announced and a warning of a snow blizzard. Hours later Bacnmek stopping the truck, pulling Marco's rucksack from the back of the truck throwing it onto the frozen snow. With a simple raising of his left arm horizontally. His index finger extended in a pointing manner.

"*Tam*." (There), said Bacnmek. By the time Marco having collected his pack back Bacnmek, having already turned around the four by four and was quickly distancing himself from Marco. The dirty black outline of the vehicle quickly disappearing only the tyres tracks still a witness of its earlier presence. The air was as thick as ice but the immense Antarctic sallowness seemed to have no end. Marco wrapping his protective clothes tighter inside around his body, distancing himself from the tyre tracks. Heading in the direction of Bacnmek earlier pointing finger. His crisping steps rapid at first but as the night began to fall and the snow deepening his breathing and energy diminuendo with exhaustion. Thinking to himself, he should have bumped the energy and resistance of a polar bear or a penguin. The hallowing wind rising like ethereal echoes. Even though it was still day and the earth's mightiest star invisible from his status. The thoughts of his mother and Rebecca's safety, driving every one of his strenuous footsteps. Even though Marco feeling as lonely and as abandoned as the immeasurable paleness surrounding him.

"He's making excellent progress. Told you he would have made a good soldier," said Stanford.

"Yes sir, I see, but we'll soon lose his signal for over a day, maybe more. There's a massive snow blizzard heading his way, not even Hubble's technology will penetrate," said Hausbeck.

"Have faith man, have faith. I told you his a good solider. I know a survivor when I see one, he'll make it," said Stanford.

"Yes sir, a survivor," said Hausbeck, quietly, wishing he had the same assuring confidence as Stanford. The sun slowly breaking through the fog like sky. It's dominating golden aura staring down at Marco like a heavenly eye. Instantly an effulgent yellowy orange luminous metamorphosing and the humongous white planes into a golden twinkling ocean. The lifting wind transporting masses of snowflakes gushing towards and around his feet like galloping miniature clouds. As the crepuscular light dusked, the golden pigment changing into a pink and mauve. The suns reflection upon the snow highlighting the shadowy mounds of what looked like Miniature Mountains. The firmament metamorphosing yet again from a powerful crimson to amber then mauve and then purple dotted with magnificent Polar Stratospheric Clouds. By nightfall the great clear blue yonder presenting a heavenly display of glistening dancing greenish yellow aurora borealis, as though another worldly energy was hovering above earth. Marco never having seen something so beautiful and powerfully magnificent. But the words of Hausbeck entering his mind and probing his need to succeed the mission.

"These are areas where the magnetic field of the earth connects to the magnetic field of our brightest star, the sun. Creating an uninterrupted passage leading from mother earth to the sun's atmosphere. Ninety-three million miles away," said Hausbeck's reminiscing words. The Tundra mechanism, he needed to find it. By night fall the atmospheric phenomenon sharing the celestial sphere with a multitude of stars as though the earth having stepped into the Milky Way. Without warning, the lifting wind transporting the masses of snowflakes gushing towards and around Marco, intensifying. A zephyr howling glacial airstream encircling him like a cyclone, within seconds his eyebrows frozen the sub-zero temperatures biting at his human physic like polar insects. Within minutes he couldn't breathe, trying with all his energy to grasp bites of oxygen out of the arctic atmosphere. The snow blizzard pounding on him, like a prehistoric dragon from another world. Falling to his knees, scrabbling half blind trying with the squint of his eyes to see some sort of hope and find an exit. The powerful wind howling into is ears even through the thick protective Antarctic clothing and protection. Tumbling to the side the weight of his rucksack seemingly having tripled. His half covered face desperately trying to find a way out. His half frozen mind even with the multitude of recently acquired intellect, as helpless as a snow man in the dessert. Life slowly melting out of him. Through the gale forcing wailing Marco believing to have heard a wolf howling. His body rapidly being covered under the blizzardy snow. Soon he would be hidden under a mountain of bitter cold mounding powdered flakes. His eyes closing as though giving in to accept the hand of the grim reaper guide him into the underworld. A wet presence appearing from nowhere pushing into his forehead, his half dead squinting eyes opening to see what the grim reaper looked like.

"A wolf."

A Canis Lupus Albus staring straight into Marco's eyes. The magnificent grey and white three feet tall. Stretching from its tail to its nose nearly seven feet long, eighty kilo Tundra wolf's adapted Antarctic anatomical physiology. Standing softly breathing over Marco, as though trying to protect him from the blizzard. Again, the wolf nudging at Marco's face with its nose, as if to stop him from falling into death. Its large left paw scratching at his freezing clothes. Through the numbness of cold he could faintly feel the insistent rubbing of its paw upon his right arm and shoulder, as though its fauna's sixth sense, perceiving Marco's ability to bump human and animal's DNA. Its adamant scratching saying.

'Take my paw'.

Marco with this glimmer of unexpected hope, slowly coming to his senses. One of his recently bumped intellect, virology and wildlife ecology, activating in his cerebellum. The Tundra Antarctic wolf anatomical physiology having adapted over centuries too the sub-zero temperatures. Its thick fur coat highly insulating. The inner hair being shorter than the outer hair protecting it from the cold and water. Its ears ratio smaller reducing the surface of heat loss, its large paws covered with fur insulating them from snow. Its paws counter current heat exchange mechanism, like that of a penguin keeping its paws at a lower temperature then its core. Minimizing its heat loss through the extremities which came into contact with the freezing climates. The blood entering its paws warming the blood leaving, preventing its core from losing heat. Marco with a sluggish force pulling down his balaclava, rubbing it against his thick glove. His exposed mouth and cheeks instantly feeling the freezing conditions, with the grit of his teeth pulling free the thick fur glove covering his right hand. Within seconds his bare palm clutched around the paw of the wolf, like an eagle's claw around its prey. Marco instantaneously sensing the strange tingling from his toes to his fingertips, conglomerating at his phalange. Thirty seconds later he was kneeling before the wolf stroking its magnificent body.

"Thank you," said Marco. The Tundra wolf rubbing her head against Marco in a comforting caring gesture. Huddling her body into Marco's. The blizzard bellowing over them through the night and throughout the next day. Their almost hibernating bodies still huddled together as the storm finally passed and the powerful aura of the sun penetrating its shafts of light though the heaps of snow bundled mounds pilled over them. The wolf breaking through the snow shaking its body and the snowflakes from it. Marco stretching at the same time breathing deep into his lungs the clear Antarctic air.

"So, you're Mirnyy. Thank you, for saving me. I didn't think I smelt so bad, but boy I'm glad my out of place odour lead you to me. I'm sorry about what happened to your cubs. I'm sure you'll find the four that went missing. They have your blood in them and look how much you've survived. As for those lost to this world.

I'm certain they're in a happy place looking down at you, waiting until you re-join them. But not yet eh. Not yet," said Marco having bumped the reminiscence of Mirnyy. Mirnyy replying with an understanding howl. "So, you can take me to Zhizn. How far did you say?" said Marco.

Mirnyy barking a numerous of times.

"OK, OK, half a day's walk. You're as bossy as my mother. Must be a women's thing," said Marco.

Mirnyy snarling unhappy with his critic against women. "Sorry," said Marco collecting his rucksack, rubbing away the snow which was clinging to it. The prepared packed food fruit and energy meals no longer appetising him. Marco sharing the carcass of a captured bird with Mirnyy. Rodents, lemmings and fish nowhere to be seen. Marco and Mirnyy walking along together across the vast plains of frozen snow. Mirnyy leading the way, but with every advancing footstep Marco sensing a déja vu.

The sun glimmering upon the freshly fallen whiteness. A carpet of twinkling lights harmonizing alongside their every snow print. The earlier hostile storm having given way to a part of mother earths untouched beauty, where the presence and conflict of man were as distant as peace upon earth. Marco comprehending more and more why such a place having been chosen to hide the otherworldly, 'Tundra mechanism'.

"Any clear signal yet from your end?" said Hausbeck.

"No sir, the storm has passed from where Marco was last seen, but it's still present, and interfering with our satellites and telescopes," said Stanford. Adding, "No news is good news as they say. I told you he's a solider, he'll make it through. If not for our sakes but for his mother and his girlfriend."

Hausbeck not answering only fiddling with the array technology surrounding him, with the hope to get a glimpse of Marco. Bacnmek having returned late the same night collected his envelope of money and disappeared. By mid-afternoon a small rising streak of smoke appearing in the horizon. Marco and Mirnyy approaching, slowly. The outline of a reindeer-hide tent (Chums), becoming clearer, like the vision of a telescope finally coming visible. Behind the tent a heard of around fifty reindeers scratching at the thinner snow looking for vegetation. The smoke coming from the wood splint fire. An old charcoal coloured cooking pot hanging over the flames from a suspended self-made sort of hook. Inside the pot pieces of reindeer meat slowly cooking. Other larger pots sat by the fires edge and a hefty what looked like a tea pot hanging from a branch wedged into the snow, its nozzle steaming from the heated substance inside. Marco now only a few feet away from the tent. Strands of fur scattered across the snow before its entrance, like snipped hair in a barber. Large, wrapped bundles of skinned fur and hide's. Covered by reindeers hide attached with thick ropes to the wooden and reindeer bone made sledges, parked to the right side of the tent. Various tools, pots and bundles of wood scattered untidily next to the sledges. To the left, the blood stained snow and the remains of the sacrificed reindeer. A women dressed in reindeer fur kneeled pounding at the dead carcasses' bones. Her face wrinkled as though she'd walked on earth for hundreds of years. Her stare fixed on her dutiful task, the axe slamming down onto the large pieces of meat and bones, unconcerned and unafraid. Not even the slightest regard towards Marco. Mirnyy instantly welcomed by seven other wolves. Marco gazing at their loving welcome his eyes deviated by a large presence appearing from within the tent. A piercing stare upon Marco, traversing his soul. As though the traces of his different bumped auras were being analysed one by one.

"Ravnaya Zhizn."

Zhizn staring at Mirnyy, saying something to her. His voice deep and powerful as though his vocals were travelling from through a hollow bark. The intonating words as alien to Marco as English had been to him only months before. Only the barking response from Mirnyy permitting Marco to deduct the tone of their exchanging discussion. Mirnyy having replied.

"I'll always wonder off. Never will I cease to search for my four living cubs," said the barking response of Mirnyy. Her reply causing Zhizn, to stutter, before wrenching out a bellowing laugh. Zhizn speaking again to Mirnyy.

Mirnyy replying.

"Stubborn as my mother I may have become. But I am now like she was once, the best wolf in the pack."

Her interpreted woofing, yap's, growls and grunt's response to Zhizn's words, causing a united howling cry from every wolf, as though agreeing to Mirnyy obstinate determination to find her four cups. All also congruent to the fact she was the best wolf in the pack. Zhizn pouring from to left side from his metal battered cup the rest of what looked like black coffee into the snow. The whiteness of the snow turning instantly black as though poisoned. Zhizn staring at Marco once again then turning to Mirnyy, muttering more uncomprehensive words.

"He's come looking for you. He's searching for what you saw and know. He has a profoundly good aura that I know with certitude. He is not searching for his own selfish greed or desire, but for the love of those most important to him. His pain I perceived. He is gifted like the one who came many times to the cave. Take his hand for a short while and he will know what you know and talk what you talk. Have I ever given you reason to doubt me?" said Mirnyy response to Zhizn's question. Mirnyy staring at Marco and not looking at Zhizn, as she spoke her bark like understood words. Her powerful fixed regard, hypnotised into Marco's responsive stare. Her magnificent piercing different coloured eyes. The right a powerful yellowy green, the left a sublime azure blue, showing Marco just how much she understood and felt his pain. Her touching declaration that he had a profoundly good aura, and was there not for his own egoistic reasons, but for those he loved and cherished, causing a multitude of tears to swell in his heaviness of hearts. Zhizn grunting something. Seconds later moving closer to Marco his towering six foot seven colossal body, as wide as three average sized men, now only inches away from Marco. His fur clothing giving Zhizn more the image of some sort of cave man, his poncho mantle attached around him with strips of rope. He wore no hat and his short dark black hair as thick as an animal's mane, bizarrely shiny, like cleanly washed hair. His bulbous face shaven the only hair upon it was his eyebrows, his skin as wrinkled as a new-born and his nose squashed like a boxers. His piercing blue epicanthic fold shaped eyes fixed upon Marco's juvenile features. Zhizn outstretching his left hand towards Marco in a welcoming salute, giving a rapid glance towards Mirnyy. Mirnyy bowing as though to assure him he had nothing to fear. Marco gazing an instant at Zhizn's huge thick hand twice the size as his. Zhizn's stumpy fingers stained with blood and dirt. Even his knuckles encrusted with muck and his dense fingernails black with grime. Hesitating no longer Marco sliding his bare left hand into the palm of Zhizn. Strangely it was Zhizn who pulled his hand away first after the thirty second otherworldly supraliminal sensations having stopped, as though he had detected the same phenomenon. Tapping Marco hard on his left shoulder with his right hand speaking once again in his strange language.

"You'll at least share a meal with us before you leave for the lake crater," said Zhizn. Marco now understanding every word smiling, warmly, replying in the same tongue.

"I'm starving," said Marco, moments later Marco, Zhizn and the old women, Voraste. Zhizn's sister sitting peacefully sharing freshly cooked reindeer, drinking the warm blood in a joyful reunion, like old friends reunited. Their conversation trivial and Marco's challenging forced tasked not spoken about. After a short while Voraste retiring to bed covering her fur dressed body with even more fur. Addressing Marco with a childlike smile exposing her three remaining teeth before drifting off to sleep. The crackling of the fire and its splintering sparks dancing like old spirits come to share the trivial evening. Marco and Zhizn sitting alone staring at the carpet of constellation of stars gazing down at them from millions of kilometres away. They were the only two living human beings who now shared the location of the lake crater and its entrance leading to the mechanism. Mirnyy leaving the pack again in search for her cubs. Stopping, gazing at Marco before softly yapping, as though not wanting to wake the other wolves.

"Never lose faith," said Mirnyy, her body disappearing into the veil of the night. After a few seconds only the trace of her paw prints visible in the snow. Zhizn raising to his feet with a grumbling moan as though his aching bones reminding him of his lost youth. Placing is powerful hand upon Marco's right shoulder squeezing it slightly in a friendly manner saying, before retiring himself to sleep.

"Yes, as stubborn as her mother," said Zhizn. Marco staying a while gazing into the celestial night, wondering where his alien intelligence having come from and if they were watching him too.

"We've found him sir, looks like he's made contact with Zhizn," said Hausbeck.

"Good work, Hausbeck. Any description of this legendary Zhizn?" said Stanford.

"No sir, looks like Marco's alone outside the tent," said Hausbeck.

"Well, keep Hubble directed at those coordinates. Sooner or later, we should get a glimpse of him," said Stanford.

"Yes sir," said Hausbeck.

Marco waking early the next morning alone. Zhizn, Voraste, Mirnyy and the other wolves along with the sleighs, reindeers, the tent and all the equipment vanished. Only the remains of a cindering dimming fire and the odd scattered traces of fur, combined with the marks in the snow, still proof of their day before camped presence.

"Looks like Zhizn only shared a part of his knowledge with me," said Marco, rising to his feet brushing the layers of freshly tumbled snow from him. The new snow having covered any trace of tracks. Marco having no idea where they'd gone and how he hadn't even heard them.

"Drugged me with that green, black substance he called Zhizn's cocktail. That's what he did," said Marco to himself. It was the first time that he'd bumped another's intellect and DNA reminiscence but still couldn't remember or work out what had happened.

CHAPTER SEVENTEEN

THE TUNDRA MECHANISM

An insistent phone ringing tone repeatedly resounding in Stanford's bedroom. "Dam blast, where's the bloody thing," said Stanford, in an angry cursing voice. Eventually finding his portable under a pile of files. Answering in an anger aggressive manner to the voice on the other end.

"What is it?"

"Do you know it's the dam middle of the night?" said Stanford.

"Yes sir, sorry sir, Marco is several hours in front," said a nervous sounding, Hausbeck.

"Well now you've woken me spit it out man. What is it?" said Stanford.

"We've lost them, sir," said Hausbeck.

"Lost them! Lost them! How can millions of dollars of technology lose them?" screamed Stanford.

"We don't know, sir. There was some unexplainable interference with our satellites and Hubble for a period of no longer than an hour. We had to renter all the coordinates back into the main computer, all in all this didn't take longer than a couple of hours. But by then Zhizn's camp had mysteriously vanished along with any trace of him. Marco was last seen arriving at the borders of the El'gygytgyn Crater Lake. But then we lost his signal too." said Hausbeck.

"Wait, wait," said Stanford.

Hausbeck patiently listening to Stanford's fumbling around for a good five minutes before Stanford came back on the phone.

"The transmitting data from his implanted chip still locates him at the Crater Lake of El'gygytgyn. So, let's not panic yet, give him a bit of time. You didn't have much faith on his survival in such extreme conditions, yet he somehow made it through. He'll do the same this time. I told you a soldier, a dam good one he would have made too. I can tell you," said Stanford. Much more awake and reassured.

"Yes sir, a soldier," said Hausbeck. Hanging up annoyed with himself for not having thought about checking Marco's implanted transmitting chip data. Too occupied with searching the data from the eyes in the skies. Hausbeck now fixed on the indicating light communicating Marco's current location. Marco having travelled the short distance from the camp to the hundred and twenty square meter wide and hundred and seventy five meters deep crater Lake of El'gygytgyn in Tchoukotka. Zhizn's partial bumped intelligence having easily guided his way. Despite the sub-zero conditions the unfrozen deep blue lake, locals believed to have been created around three, six million years before. Either by a meteorite collision, or that the lake had formed inside the depths of an ancient inactive volcano. Locals also never approaching the isolated lake, even with its clearly visible aquatic life, believing that rare and otherworldly species lived within the 3° Celsius waters. The El'gygytgyn Lake enveloped in superstitious legends of enormous monsters, giant strange shaded fish and the unexplainable disappearance of many who approach its waters. Those who did returned staying eternally alone. The lake having become as destitute and forgotten as its surrounding landscape. Marco now somewhere with these superstitions and legends.

"Wow it's so beautiful, wait until I explain this place to Mama and Rebecca," said Marco.

Starring awestricken at the hidden tunnel. Zhizn having transmitted to him, how and where to find its entrance.

"You must walk to the west side of the lake. There you will find two large orange and grey looking rocks around ten feet high and three feet wide. One rock slightly taller than the other. Walk into the larger face bedrock as though walking through an open door. The exact positions of the rocks creating an optical illusion that there are simply two large chucks of granite blocks. But in fact, there is a hidden passageway leading deeper into the crater below the lake. Do not fear what is inside your body, will allow you to walk through the rock face as easy as an open door," said the reminiscing guiding words of Zhizn's bumped guiding knowledge and instructions transmitted to Marco. Zhizn not having revealed what he truly meant by "what is inside your body" to Marco. Marco having followed

Zhizn's instruction now staring at the captivated tunnel around him. The passageway resembling something from another world. It's celling and sides looking like mounded piles of snow clumped together suspended in strange curved Mammatus Cloud formations. A refulgent reddish light breaking through at certain points of the ceiling and walls, as though hot lava was pulping behind the icy appearance. Underneath his feet, a crystallised type of floor like clear frozen water. A multitude of strange etchings as though an array of different shapes and forms encapsulated inside. Some inscriptions similar to the Nazca lines, others were different dimensioned. Perfectly circular forms, like different planet formations ingrained under a thick clear ice like substance. The deeper Marco entered the tunnel, the warmer he felt. After around an hour's walk, Marco coming across a modern day instrument poised, like a forgotten artefact on the floor. A computer with the inscriptions A, L and a sticker marked.

"Property of NASA," said the sticker.

"Alex Livingston, he was here."

"How did he find this place?" said Marco, picking up the laptop and opening it. Its battery dead. His eyes quickly deviated from the computer to a green light projecting deeper from the passageway. Replacing the laptop back on the floor, continuing to investigate. His path coming into contact with a forest of what looked like twenty feet tall giant stalactites only they were pointing from the floor upwards like icicle fir trees. In the centre of the stalactite's masses, where the light was energizing. Sliding his way through the robust icicle forms. Warm and extremely smooth when touched. In the heart of the stalactite's plantation an oval shaped form around five feet tall and three feet wide, no thicker than an ancient warriors shield. In the centre a hollowed out one feet square formation, a multitude of strange metallic arms outstretching from its centrum to different circular cogs like shapes. All connecting to triangular, rectangular and smaller square compositional forms. An array of embedded lines leading from every contoured form, all re-joining at different points into a decagon outlined, stepped in a few inches from the exterior perimeter. It was from the decagon form where the light was glowing. The alien object looking extremely heavy like a massive thick armoured shield with weird formations. Each shape penetrating and identically reproduced either side of the strange device. Only the hollowed out form in what seemed like its epicentre presented peculiar inscriptions on its opposite side. The identical peculiar hieroglyphics contouring the shield forms outside edge. Marco approaching the object with caution and wonder. The risk to his mother and Rebecca overpowering his fear. Placing his hands upon the found "Tundra mechanism." Expecting to come into contact with a burdensome hefty weight. Marco's surprised reaction combined with relief and curiosity as the object floated, like a silent hovering craft before him. Hesitating no longer. One of his forced tasks completed. Marco walking with the floating mechanism and the recuperated laptop back out of the tunnel. The reddish lava glow from behind the mounded resembling Mammatus clouds forming the ceiling and walls of the tunnel. Metamorphosing into the same green effulgence as the mechanism, Marco and his Alien find exited the passageway. Marco resurfacing outside of the optical illusion rock face, with the mechanism by his side, and Alex Livingston's computer in his hand. The Tundra mechanism's green glowing light vanishing, as though the contact with the earths outside atmosphere neutralising its energy. Marco's locating signal instantly picked up from Hubble and the now operating satellites. The joyful screams of Hausbeck as he zoomed in clearer on Marco's digital image, echoing into the air, like a hysteric groupie fan seeing his or her idol. Hausbeck now facing the heavens and screaming.

"He did it."

"He did it."

"A soldier. The old bastard was right."

"Unbelievable."

"Un-fucking-believable," said Hausbeck. Marco also staring to the heavens, but not to pray or demand. He knew he was being watched. It wasn't long before a Sikorsky S-92 helicopter, hovering over his head causing a cyclone of snow to torpedo around him. The mechanism still floating by his side but strangely not moving the slightest from the four blades twin engines force. Hausbeck on the ground with a team of six people. Marco unable to see if they were men or women. All the personnel were each dressed like Hausbeck wearing Hazmat suits seemingly made out of silver and gold coloured thermal space blankets. All carrying Dosimeters and Geiger counters. Checking Marco and the 'Alien Mechanism' for radiation or any other toxic substance.

"All clear," said a voice over the walkie talkie, after nearly a good hour. Hausbeck lifting the helmet of his Hazmat suite with a strange hissing coming from the (SCBA), self-contained breathing apparatus. His confident reaction to take of his helmet, spurring the same gesture from his accompanied team. Three men three women, all gazing at the mechanism with stupefaction. Hausbeck staring an instant at Marco. Marco looked strangely older. But Hausbeck's inquisitive stare quickly turned back towards the mechanism. His words said everything.

"My God. It does exist," said Hausbeck. The mechanism rapidly placed into a self-assembling unit container. Various stickers and certificates attached to the outside. Marco staring a moment at the international Pictogram for toxic chemicals. The skull and cross bones an instant warning for delicate handling and transportation. A clever way for the mechanism to leave its current location and arrive at NASA's research centre in Cleveland. There where Stanford was waiting with his team of scientists, to examine in further detail the otherworldly object. There where he and his team would be waiting for Marco to return with the element eighty-five.

CHAPTER EIGHTEEN

HARD LANDING

The helicopter flight back to the private landing strip where the citation 750 refuelled jet was waiting to transport Marco back to Moscow and the Global express to Dubai. Marco sleeping most of the journey his body recuperating its much needed physical force.

"Yes sir, it's indescribable, and unbelievable," said Hausbeck.

"The soldier's fine, he's not muttered a word since we recuperated him outside the tunnel, but he found Livingston's laptop," said Hausbeck, another pause before Hausbeck continued to talk to Stanford.

"No sir, we tried ourselves to enter the tunnel, but where Marco seemed to appear from, there was only solid rock." said Hausbeck. The echoing voice of Stanford speaking again.

"No sir, he looks exhausted and I thought it better he rest. After all, we don't know what will be waiting for him in Socotra. I'll ask him later," said Hausbeck.

"What, yes already downloaded them, you should be receiving the pictures any time now," said Hausbeck.

"ETA thirty minutes, sir," said Hausbeck.

"Yes, as planned. Direct flight to Dubai with all documents already ready, then Prokhor Radoslavic's flight to Socotra," said Hausbeck. Hausbeck finishing his private conversation with Stanford. Marco having heard every word as though his hearing was also of alien intelligence. Staring at Hausbeck like a possessed demon.

"The expedition team he's sending to the Crater Lake of El'gygytgyn, will never find the entrance to the tunnel. Never," said Marco.

"Oh and why's that?" said Hausbeck.

"The deal was to recover the mechanism and element eighty-five and then allow my mother and Rebecca to go free. You get what you want and I get what you promised me. The rest stays as before," said Marco.

"What you've discovered and if element eighty-five as we believe will active it. Then nothing will ever be as before," said Hausbeck staring at the container holding the alien mechanism, attached in the cabin opposite him.

"Sometimes things should be left unturned, Hausbeck," said Marco looking at the speeding growing approaching landscape from the jet's porthole window.

"Nonsense. We must dig, turn and discover what is out there, like archaeologist," said Hausbeck.

"Archaeologist, look into our past and with great respect too. You're trying to look into the future. Discover a world and its population which have chosen for a reason not to reveal themselves to us. We are not ready. Cliché it may be. But we must learn to walk before we can run. You are trying to gallop," said Marco.

"Well with the gift the otherworld gave you, you could shake their hands and then speak to them on behalf of mankind," said Hausbeck.

Marco not replying. The jet already coming to its taxing stop. The flight for Dubai due in five hours' time. "The mechanism and Livingston's computer are on their way, sir. Hopefully we'll be able to retrieve something from the CPU (central processing unit), and its hard disk drive," said Hausbeck, to Stanford.

"He told me that the expedition team would only find rock. I know he won't reveal to us how he recuperated the mechanism. There's something changed about him," said Hausbeck.

"What do you mean changed? Has he transformed into an alien form?" said Stanford.

"No sir, he seems constantly preoccupied. I wouldn't say worried or afraid just elsewhere, and he looks older," said Hausbeck.

"Maybe a side effect of the mechanism, you did check it for toxic substances? And have you checked your own reflection in a mirror?" said Stanford.

"Yes sir. I thought of that too, I feel fine and have no physical change. We analysed the mechanism for any signs of toxicity organism animal, bacterium or plant. Also Metaphorical, chemical, biological, physical and radioactive. Even virus, bacterium. Our specialised hypersensitive Geiger counters and dosimeters picked up absolutely nothing. I wouldn't have exposed myself or the team if there was the minutest sign of danger. I even investigated by touch the unknown material of which it is made before I sent it to you. It doesn't feel organic but more like a mechanical advance engineered structure. Almost like a giant microchip which belongs to some other computerized mechanism. Obviously, I will continue my research with our team when I'm back from Socotra, hopefully with the element eighty-five," said Hausbeck. Throughout the flight to Dubai, Marco slept. Not even eating or drinking anything. Hausbeck observing him sleeping like some hibernating animal. Having no idea of Marco's contact with Mirnyy and how she'd saved his life. The rest of the time Hausbeck checking his notes and zooming in on the digital photos he'd taken of the mechanism.

"Arr, you're back with the living, just in time as we're descending," said Hausbeck, watching Marco stretch his body, like a wakening cat.

"The hostess saved some food for you, but I doubt she'll come now. The captain just announced landing in thirty minutes," said Hausbeck.

"Wouldn't have minded a glass of fresh blood," said Marco.

"You're kidding right? You didn't bump the intellect of a vampire bat or something from the underworld, where you found the mechanism?" said Hausbeck. An expression of deep concern for Marco pasted all over his face.

"No, just kidding." said Marco. Having comprehended Hausbeck's deep concerned visage and questioning.

"Thank God for that, you had me worried for a moment. If you're thirsty or hungry we can get something to eat at the airport, we have to wait a good five hours anyway. We're going to fly into Socotra late evening. A private Cessna 182 is waiting for us, but there's a lot of crosswinds. Strange as the monsoon winds don't normally start until June, but for some reason climate change or something they've started earlier. I'll go over the rest of the details when we've passed the security control." said Hausbeck. Once again Hausbeck's diplomatic papers and Marco's false new documents, passing them through the security control with great ease and without suspicion or questioning. Marco walking towards the VIP longue with Hausbeck by his side. The airport like a city of multicultural populations.

Beings from all four corners of the planet progressing with their own personal duties and challenges. Certain travelling for business, certain for leisure. Some to visit their families and loved ones and a selection for work. But even with this multitude of people, languages, race, colour, religions, profession and earthly intellect. Security officers, police, diplomats, businessmen and women, richer, poorer. Pilots, hostesses, ground staff shop attendants and other. Thousands of intellects with which a simple handshake Marco could know what they knew from their moment of creation to the present day. But none could help Marco or his mother and Rebecca. And all ignorant to his otherworldly powers and recent alien discovery. Marco standing in the VIP lounge with its exquisite luxurious ambience, helping himself to a small portion of the huge selection of free food and drink, lavishly displayed but mostly untouched. In a world where millions upon earth were starving. His words to Hausbeck recalled in his powerful mind.

"You're trying to look into the future. Discover a world and its population which have chosen for a reason not to reveal themselves to us," said Marco's reminiscing words. His intimate thoughts broken by Hausbeck pulling at his clothes, like a child trying to get attention from his mother or father.

"Let's go into the far corner, there's nobody near there and I can go over everything with you before we leave in a few hours, OK," said Hausbeck, at the same time pointing to his far left side. Marco gazing around the humongous lounge dotted with very few people. Not questioning Hausbeck's choice only carrying a few of the rawest pieces of roast beef with him, sitting himself inside one of the luxurious armchairs opposite Hausbeck. Marco coughing a little as though a dry piece of bread was stuck in his throat.

"Are you OK?"

"Do you want some water?" said Hausbeck.

"No, no, I'm fine," said Marco. His right hand clenched in a fist form covering his mouth as though he was coughing into his palm. His left hand stretched out before him, index finger pointed and swaying in front of Hausbeck, like a teacher telling a pupil off. Hausbeck seeing Marco's coughing calming. Began with his explanation.

"So, here's what we're going to do. At 19.00 hours we leave for Socotra. Like I said earlier with a private Cessna 182, the pilot is a retired Russian air force pilot 'Prokhor Radoslavic' who was originally based in Socotra during the 70s and 80s. Socotra was formerly a part of South Yemen which was a close soviet ally at that time. He knows where the isolated old soviet military base and landing strip is located and will land us there. Safely I hope, and hopefully discreetly. We chose by air because there is great speculation that Somali pirates operate around the island's waters, also because of the recent unrest in neighbouring Yemen. From the old disused military base, we will have to make it by foot to the Haghier Mountains, where our findings have led us to believe, is where the Astatine is somewhere at. Our research led us to a close proximity to the mountains base. In 2001, a group of Belgian Speleologists, who were part of the Socotra Karst Project came across a large number of inscriptions, drawings and archaeological finds inside a cave near the mountains. Greek, Palmyrene and Bactrian languages, texts, scripts and drawings, but also descriptions which resemble what was on the mechanism you found. There was also a recent further discovery of a wooden tablet in Palmyrene and another tablet with what seemed like mathematical symbols, not revealed to public knowledge. After years of scientific research and a number of eliminated whys and wherefores. We noted that every mathematical calculation, Algebraic, Polynomials, Linear, Quadratic, Rational, Exponential, Binary, Trigonometric, and believe me dozens more. All without exception came to the same resulting number. 'Eighty-five'. For a long time, we didn't give much thought to the Astatine's atomic number, even though the periodic table, which as you know shows us how the chemical elements are related to one another. The periodic chart, constructed by the Russian chemist Dmitri Mendeleev in the early 1870s. Everything suddenly started coming to light when we analysed every single scrap of evidence, from every know source around the globe into a special programme designed to search Alien presence on earth all under the O.W.I.Q program. We found it quite appropriate and amusing that the most precious and rarest elements within the universe is probably hidden on the most alien looking and also said to be the most magical planet on earth. Socotra considered to be the jewel of biodiversity its unique Flora and Fauna a third part of it which is found nowhere else on earth. It's ironic that in modern times Astatine is named element eighty-five. We believe the mathematical calculations all adding to the same number has more to do with the fact that it is the only element which has eighty-five protons, packed into its nucleus," said Hausbeck.

"Why didn't you go to the proper authorities? Show your evidence and claims and do everything with specialised teams and scientist a joint worldly union? Instead of all this cloak and dagger stuff," said Marco. Still slightly coughing as though a niggling itch was irritating his throat.

"You disappoint me, Marco. I thought you'd obtained. Bumped as you say the intellect of the world's top scientist. I know we did it for you to be able to work out a way to obtain and contain the Astatine. But seriously with all your acquired cerebellum power. Can you image the impact of such a find and if we told the world of its potential. These proper authorities of which you speak. Do you honestly think they would have united as one?" said Hausbeck.

"An honest man is always a child," said Marco, quoting once again, Socrates.

"As said Socrates. We live in a world of dishonesty and mistrusting men and even women. That's why, as you say all the cloak and dagger stuff. You Marco. Sorry to say were an unexpected gift. You are the key to Pandora's Box," said Hausbeck.

"Pandora's box was actually a jar, containing all the evils of the world, and when they flew out after Pandora opened the jar. There was only hope remaining inside," said Marco.

"Hope is an optimistic perspective of mind that is based on an expectation of beneficial outcomes related to trials and circumstances in one's life or as we see the world at large."

"You are our hope of finding element eighty-five and activating the mechanism. You are also your mother and Rebecca's hope that no harm comes to them. Maybe hope should have flown out of the Pandora's box, no?" said Hausbeck expressing a cold cruel grin.

Marco not replying only thinking of the challenging task before him, and that Hausbeck was right he was Anna's and Rebecca's only hope.

"Come on its time to go, we have to meet Prokhor at the west side remote stands at the far south of the terminal," said Hausbeck. Marco following Hausbeck's rapid paces as though he was going to be late. His itchy cough still niggling him. Once at the west side, a very stern old looking man, thin with every expressional joy erased from his face through years of abusive smoking and drinking, standing anxiously pacing up and down. His neck slightly bowed forward as though something was stopping him from straightening his head. Hausbeck and Prokhor's eyes meeting.

"Houusbeck," said Prokhor. His very present strong Russian accent poorly pronouncing Hausbeck name.

"Yes. Prokhor?" said Hausbeck.

"You have ID. You show me ID and show me what I get promised too," said a nervous sounding, Prokhor. Hausbeck showing him his ID and an envelope of American dollars along with two bottles of vodka and a bulk of four hundred cigarettes purchased at the duty free.

"Where is packet you want to transport to Island?" said Prokhor.

"This is the packet," said Hausbeck pulling Marco a little closer.

"These is not packet, these is man. Man weigh more. More weight, less fuel," said Prokhor grabbing the plastic bag of duty-free gifts and the envelope from Hausbeck. Prokhor expressing no real emotion.

"This is the packet OK," said Hausbeck firmly.

"Come, come we go," said Prokhor. Less than half an hour later, after having passed another control. Marco and Hausbeck were following Prokhor to a private hanger. The local temperature even though late evening still in the over 30° Fahrenheit. Worlds apart from the sub-zero climate of the Antarctic. Marco coughing again.

"Are you sure you're OK? You're not coming down with a cold or something else, are you?" said Hausbeck.

"Vodka! Good for all. Vodka that what your packet need," said Prokhor.

"I'm OK. It's probably just the sudden massive change of temperatures," said Marco. Thinking about Prokhor addressing him as a packet and nothing more. Analysing the facility of their transit, once again. His bumped memories of Stanford and the witnessed ease of his world travels piecing together just how long and far Stanford's arm could reach. And how long and far his old and present military worldwide contacts reached. Marco coughing again. Just wanting it all to be over and his mother and Rebecca to be safe and out of the grips of Stanford. Nothing in the knowledge he had of Stanford suggested he would not respect his promise to set them free. But Marco only knowing Stanford's plans from the moment he'd come into contact with his palm. The rest was still in the hands of the unknown heavens.

"Why you keep hand shoes? Gloves is how you say, yes?" said Prokhor, staring at Hausbeck's specialised gloves.

"You're being paid to fly, the rest is on a need to know basis and you don't need to know, OK," said Hausbeck.

"OK," said Prokhor. Taking another big gulp from the vodka bottle whilst snubbing out his cigarette, at the same time scribbling something down on a scrap piece of paper, pulled from a pile of clutter on the desk inside the hanger. Marco listening to his mumbles.

"TAF. METAR, 1800Z 24023KT G46KT 9000 RA SCT025 BKN040 29/34 Q1011 NOSIG."

"MTOW 1406 KG."

"Passenger and *packet* weight."

"What is wrong?" said Hausbeck.

"You don't say *packet* is man. I calculate fuel and weather to Socotra. This small plane fly maximum 1,722 kilometre. Land strip is 1414 kilometres. I fill plane with maximum fuel and inside cabin I store barrel with fuel. Extra weight mean less fuel to carry. Rest fuel I hide on base secret to people but not to Prokhor. I must calculate because only way to land is with crosswind and we need fuel to come back or we stay like pirate on Island. But don't worry we good to fly we have tail wind. So now I calculate like professional I am, and we fly OK," said Prokhor taking another big gulp of Vodka and lighting another cigarette.

Professional. Thought Hausbeck. But he had no choice, the current political turmoil surrounding the magnificent Island limiting Hausbeck and Stanford's resources to transport Marco safely in Socotra. The unknown location of the reserved fuel stored on the island's old soviet base and the difficult landing conditions to approach the old military airstrip, reducing Hausbeck's and Stanford's resources to Prokhor and no other. The only other way was for Marco to bump Prokhor's intellect and fly them himself. But that meant disposing of a body in Dubai. The importance to not raise or provoke arousing suspicions. Killing innocent people and having to dispose of them, would do just that. Even flying around in private jets and helicopters had been avoided to pass Marco and Hausbeck as the millions of everyday world transiting beings. Moments later, Prokhor's load sheet calculations finished. Marco and Hausbeck squashed between different sized barrels of fuel. The smell almost insupportable. Prokhor having been given radio clearance from the tower to taxi to the runway 12R. (R=Right). The anti-collision lights flashing and engine propellers noisily turning at a reduce speed, waiting for the runways lights and the tower to indicate.

"Clear for take-off."

The roaring sound of an Airbus 380 flying over their heads the '*Airboss*' of the sky landing with elegance on the far right side runway. The force of its four Rolls-Royce Trent 970 engines gust, swaying the small Cessna like a rowing boat in stormy waters. The dusking sun hidden behind the ominous-looking Undulatus Asperatus cloud filled sky, as though a heavenly warning of an unknown presence, hovering in wait over the planet earth. Marco not having heard the tower give the 'all clear', only the engines propeller spinning shaft intensifying. Staring at the little planes shadow racing along the runway until what seemed like a very long moment its wings finally lifted from the ground. Its single engine almost struggling to carry its overloaded payload. Marco questioning Prokhor's 'professional' calculations. Eventually the light four-seated aircraft with Hausbeck its packet and barrels of fuel, breaking through the clouds, flying at a cruise speed of 145 knots and an altitude of 10,000 feet, turning at a 120° to its right. Direction Socotra. Not before long the Cessna rapidly dropping altitude as though having entered a massive atmospheric turbulent air pressure.

"There's something wrong," said Hausbeck staring at Marco. Adding. "We shouldn't be descending so fast."

"Prokhor! What are you doing? Why are we descending so fast?" said Hausbeck, at the same time detaching his belt to go see what Prokhor was doing. Squeezing inside the cockpit finding Prokhor holding his left arm with his right hand just above his elbow, leaning forward and desperately trying to breathe.

"It is Prokhor heart not good give me bad pain, I can't hold plane straight," said Prokhor in a painful whispering voice in between strenuous puffs.

"Marco! Come here quick, quick! Prokhor is having a heart attack."

Screamed Hausbeck, at the same time pulling at the aircrafts yoke in the desperate attempt to gain altitude. Within seconds Marco squeezing his head and shoulders unable to access his whole body into the small cockpit already occupied by Hausbeck and Prokhor. Marco placing his left hands index and middle finger against Prokhor's neck to check his pulse.

"He's going into cardiac arrest. He needs urgent medical assistant now. I may be able to resuscitate him but there's no guarantees," said Marco.

"Grab his hand!" screamed Hausbeck.

"What?" said Marco.

"He's going to die and if I'm not mistaken, he's the only one out of all three of us who can fly this plane. And he's the only one who knows where the abandoned soviet military base is located. Now grab his fucking hand and bump into your mind what he knows or there won't be just Prokhor fighting for his life," said Hausbeck.

Marco hesitant for a second until the screaming orders of Hausbeck prompting his actions. "Grab his fucking hand *now*!" said Hausbeck. Marco's placing his right hand inside Prokhor's right palm instantly feeling the otherworldly supraliminal sensations but nineteen seconds later he felt nothing. Prokhor's dead open staring eyes. Closed tenderly by Marco.

"Did you have enough time?"

"Did you bump everything?" said Hausbeck.

"No," said Marco, pulling Prokhor's dead body from the cockpit and laying him down in the cabin, placing his jacket respectively over Prokhor. Hausbeck still holding the yoke, the aircraft flying in a straight line but he had no idea where they were.

"What does *no* mean?" said Hausbeck.

"No, means no I didn't bump all his intellect because he's dead," said Marco. Pointing at Prokhor's covered body.

"Well, what did you download from his intellect?" said Hausbeck.

"Do you want the good news or the bad news?" said Marco.

"I want all the fucking news, my life is at stake here," said Hausbeck, in a hysterical scream.

"It's a different story when your life is at stake," said Marco. Sitting himself in the cockpit and taking control of the yoke. Turing it slightly to the left.

"I didn't want your mother or Rebecca to be in harm's way, but Stanford is a powerful man who always gets what he wants," said Hausbeck.

"Well, if you believe in God, I suggest you start praying. The good news is I know how to get to the landing strip, the other good news is I know how to fly this thing," said Marco.

"Well, that's excellent that's all we need," said a joyful Hausbeck.

"There is one thing I didn't get the 100% information which could come in handy. Especially within the next ten minutes," said Marco, almost blasé.

"What? What?" said Hausbeck expressing a face, like a quiz show host trying to work out the answer to a difficult question.

"Landing," said Marco.

"You mean you don't know how to land this thing?" said Hausbeck.

"I mean, I didn't get all the information needed. Prokhor has landed on the base hundreds of times during his military based career. I'm landing for the first time in cross winds at night on an un-lit abandoned runway with only the help of the reminiscent memories of Prokhor and the moons luminescence. And if I get it wrong those barrels of extra fuel Prokhor loaded to get us back to Dubai will not help our chances of survival. So, I suggest you strap yourself into your seat, and like I said before if you believe in any God. Now's the time to talk to them," said Marco, whispering to himself.

"Why didn't I shake the captain's hand why? Too late now for remorse," said Marco. Hausbeck without haste strapping himself into his seat. Marco descending the Cessna through the carpet of clouds. Socotra already below them. The lower he descended the stronger the cross winds got, oscillating the small plane up and down and side to side, like a small boat in stormy waters.

"It's going to be bumpy so brace yourself!" said Marco in a loud voice to Hausbeck, turning his head rapidly level with is right shoulder before straightening himself up, squinting in search of the runway. The keen nocturnal eyesight of Mirnyy wolfs vision capabilities being able to see at 180 degrees. Bumped and amalgamated into Marco autonomy and mind helping him see clearer. Whispering to himself.

"It can't be far now," said Marco. In the far distance a long rectangular form, with square and circular formations behind it appearing in the centre of what looked like a forest.

"OK, OK. Keep cool, Marco. Think of what you've bumped from Prokhor," said Marco. The plane approaching Marco reducing the throttle speed.

"OK, approach:

Land lights – *as required.*
Taxi lights – *as required.*
Land elev – checked.
Ref data – set.
DH/MDA – set.
FMS arrival – as required.
Signs – as required.
Airspeed indicators X – *checked.*

Altimeters SET/X – *checked.* OK, OK looking good," said Marco. The aircraft abruptly tipping to its left with the force of the monsoon crosswinds, as though an invisible creature, trying to wrench them out of the sky. Hausbeck bent forward in the emergency landing position, hands over his head. Starring at the trickling lines of spilt fuel streaming through the cabin, like water seeping into a sinking vessel. Marco concentrating with all his intellect to land the plane. The concern of his need to accomplish his mission for his mother's and Rebecca's safety. Fuelling his every gesture.

"Fuck that was close, concentrate Marco, concentrate," said Marco, as the light aircraft, abruptly tossed to its left side, like a tulip in a gusting wind nearly flipping the plane completely over. Marco approaching the abandoned unused runway.

"*Final checks.*

Steep Appch – as required.
Landing gear – down.
Flaps – set.
GND *spoil –* as required.
EICAS display – checked.
Parking brake – check off.
NWS tiller – check unobstructed.
Condition levers – max.

GND *spoil* –   Fuck I don't know, it will have to do. It will have to do," said Marco to himself. The Cessna approaching the moonlit runway, like a kite in the wind, unknowingly to Marco or Hausbeck to fast.

"Hold on we're coming in to land, hold on," said Marco. The signal engine light plane hitting the runway way to fast and hard. The retractable hydraulic landing gear almost crushing with the impacting force not helped by the aircrafts overloaded payload. (The packet and the barrels of fuel). The drums of fuel leaping from the ground and bouncing back down spilling more of their contents. Hausbeck holding onto the seat in front of him like a climber gripping the mountains edge with all his might hoping not to fall. The aircraft scrapping along the runway coming to a rapid and spark flying stop. Hausbeck jumping out his seat as though his arse was on fire, projecting the halon gas fire extinguisher almost everywhere in the plane. The gases seeping out of the Cessna like theatrical smoke on a film set. Marco filled with adrenalin, having braced himself for the impact, uninjured saying, as though by some possessed force controlling his action.

"*After landing.*

Flaps –   0°

Landing/Recog lights –   *off.*

Strobe Lights – who gives a fuck we've made it. Hausbeck, Hausbeck are you OK," said Marco in between coughing because of the halon gas.

"Yeah, yeah, I'm good. That was some landing didn't sound too good for the plane though," said Hausbeck. Marco and Hausbeck rapidly exiting the aircraft, gawping at the Cessna's undercarriage and the hydraulic landing gear crushed underneath it.

"Doesn't look like we're flying this thing out of here. Ironic, no," said Hausbeck.

"What's ironic?" said Marco.

"Oh, I was just thinking it's ironic that the owner and his plane should die on the same day. Because that Cessna is fucking dead," said Hausbeck, trying to lighten a little the current situation.

"Well, you stopped me from shaking the Bombardiers pilots' hand," said Marco. Still coughing slightly.

Hausbeck not replying to Marco's allegations, only staring around at the eeric looking abandoned concrete jungle in the middle of nowhere.

"We'll set up camp here tonight and in the morning at sunrise we'll head for the Haghier Mountains, in the meantime I'll contact Stanford to communicate with the satellite phone our current status and position. What time is it? 21.13 p.m. Good, it will be 14.13 p.m. in Cleveland, he'll be at the lab. Maybe he'll be able to send a helicopter in to collect us," said Hausbeck.

CHAPTER NINETEEN

ELEMENT EIGHTY-FIVE

Marco walking around the eerie discarded derelict old soviet military base searching for a place to make camp. Flickering shadows scuttling from every shaft of moonlight, breaking through every now and again out of the ominous Undulatus Asperatus clouds, hauntingly hanging over them. The monsoons winds whistling a ghostly echo through the darkened surrounding unclear landscape. Accompanied by the unnerving snorts, growls, screeches, buzzing, squeaking, chuckles, gobbles, bellows and groans of an invisible fauna.

"Stanford, can you hear me? It's Hausbeck, the lines very crackly. Over," said Hausbeck.

"Yes Martin, you're coming through, it sounds windy. What's your current position? Over," said Stanford.

"It is windy, monsoon, seems to have arrived a good month earlier. Good news is that we've landed on the old Soviet base. Bad news is Prokhor is dead, heart attack. Marco had time to bump his intellect but not all. Would you believe it out of all the intelligence he's acquired, he didn't know how to fly and he didn't learn how to land. The Cessna is AOG (aircraft on ground), big style, its landing gear is crushed. Won't be able to make it out of here by plane. Over," said Hausbeck.

"Not sure I can help you, Martin. You're going to have to find a solution on your own. If we send a military or civilian helicopter or any other craft into the Yemen's airspace due to the current rising political turmoil, we could spark and international uproar. Not to mention alert any Somali pirates operating in the area, raising the risk of you or Marco being kidnapped or killed. That's why we used Prokhor in the first place. Need to keep this, and the fact that you and Marco are actually on Socotra out of the public eye. But don't worry Martin, you're not alone you've have the smartest brain on the planet with you. Certain he'll figure something out. Over," said Stanford, seemingly not over concerned about Hausbeck's and Marco's extreme difficult status quo.

"Loud and clear, sir. Over," said Hausbeck, with sickly feeling of abandon in his stomach.

"Oh Martin, one last thing, we've found some very interesting data on Livingston's computer, and our analyses show that the mechanism is made from an unknown material, contact me when you have element eighty-five and give me your status then. Don't use this satellite communication to much otherwise you'll risk the chances of its signal being picked up. Over," said Stanford.

"Over," said Hausbeck his words already lost in the hollowing monsoon winds. His cry for help to Stanford felt as though he didn't really care if Marco and Hausbeck returned with the element eighty-five or not.

"Maybe he's found another way to activate the mechanism from Livingston's files and he no longer needs us, or the Astatine," said Hausbeck, realising Marco was now not only Anna's and Rebecca's hope of survival but his too. His earlier definition of hope and its significance rapidly changing. Their agitated night passed quickly having wrapped their bodies in thick survival sleeping bags to avoid snake bites or any other creature's bites, near the crashed Cessna. Surrounding themselves like a satanic ritual in a circle of gasoline from the remaining barrels, to warn off any dangerous animal. The monsoon wind still howling at first sunlight. The night had been cool but warm enough to avoid making a fire and attract any unwanted attention. Marco the first to rise. The

Undulatus Asperatus clouds having been dispersed by the monsoon's winds. The clear blue sky and the dawned suns light, highlighting the impact of their crashed landing and just how lucky they'd been, the plane having stopped only feet away from an enormous crater in the runway. Half filled with rust coloured water. The rest of the landing strip dotted with corroded military carcases and tumbled stones, glass and concrete from the eroding destitute buildings surrounding them. The islands plant life having reclaimed its naturel force upon the once dominate Soviet military base. Now just a display of crumbling concrete smashed windows and rampaged interiors peering down at the abandon oxidised skeletons of war.

"We have to head north we should make the mountains by midday," said Hausbeck.

"First we have to burry Prokhor," said Marco.

"He's dead, leave him for the animals, they'll have a feast with him, probably they'll be a little tipsy when they chew through his liver, with the amount of vodka in there. Anyway, why should you care if he gets buried or not, he didn't even know your name? Remember, he called you the packet," said Hausbeck.

"I doesn't matter what he called me or thought of me. He deserves a respectable send off, not just thrown to one side ditched and forgotten like the deserted objects all around us," said Marco.

"OK, but I'm not digging any hole," said Hausbeck.

"No need to, there's one right there," said Marco, pointing to the large hole in the runway. Marco and Hausbeck lowering Prokhor's body in the crater hallow in the landing field, placing a bottle of vodka, a packet of cigarettes and the photo of his dead wife in his hands. Marco now knowing they had no children, his bumped intelligence of Prokhor reassuring him that he was only waiting for the day he could finally join his lost wife again. Placing a mound of stones respectfully over his carcass. His tomb decorated with two sticks joined together with Prokhor's shoelaces in a cruciform. A small pray whispered by Marco alone. Hausbeck gathering the rest of their equipment ready to leave for Haghier mountains.

"Through there. Looks like there's a gap in the trees," said Hausbeck. Marco meticulously following Hausbeck's steps, the hot sun relentlessly beating down on them, only the calmer monsoon wind bringing a cooling breeze. Marco's coughing intensifying.

"Hey, try to control that cough of yours we might be on one of the most blissful places on earth, but it's also one of the most dangerous places on earth. You don't want us to be killed or kidnapped, do you? That would go down great with the US State Department, an official US citizen working as a NASA scientist, and a dead, but now alive Italian man kidnapped by Somali pirates on the island of Socotra. CNN would have a field day. And Stanford a heart attack," said Hausbeck. Marco not answering only trying to control his worsening cough. Gazing at the otherworldly beauty of the island and its jewels of biological diversity gawking in astonishment at the 'Dracaena Cinnabari' aka 'Dragons Blood' trees. Their bizarre umbrella form appearance, like giant green mushrooms or some sort of alien craft, with their outstretching branches, like tree roots growing upside down. Along with the endemic tree species their thick trucks standing on the honey tinted arid earth of the island, a cluster of branches stretching to the skies like the elongated fingers of an Aye Aye, only covered in leaves. Marco and Hausbeck continuing in silence across the rocky out crops, crossing abandoned rock built cattle pens dotted by the cliffs base. Large cliff face rocks to their left, the Indian Ocean in the far distance to their right, a small vessel approaching the island sand dunes to the East. Marco and Hausbeck continuing higher. Stranger trees and plants manifesting their elegance and weird wonder upon their tracks. Dorstenia gigas growing out of bare rock instead of soil. Trees resembling giant cucumbers, (dendrosicyos scotranum), others like elephant feet with flowers blooming at the top (desert rose adenium obesium). The islands immeasurable stupendous Flora, as though another species had planted seeds from their alien world upon planet earth. Watching maybe from near or afar the burgeoning beauty of their Garden of Eden efflorescence elegance cultivate across the 3,796 kilometres of the Islands diversified terra. After a few hours both arriving at the Haghier massif and Diskum plateau. Hausbeck a little out of breath, Marco's tickling throat still irritating. In the near distance reddish covering lichens making some of the rocks appear white. The ancient long lost periods of volcanic activity having created the magnificent granite peak rises, towering nearly 5,000 feet into the midday's firmament. A breathtaking panorama North, South, East and West soaring from the Haghier mountains view. Steep pointed peeks stupendous canyons and gorges. Humongous piles of mounded sand and profound freshwater springs ringed with palm groves in the near distance. Marco and Hausbeck stopping to drink and recharge their energy. A golden Egyptian vulture flying low over their heads, as though circling in wait. It's wrinkled orange and yellow face with its pointed black, orange tipped beak clearly visible. Its peach and cream feathers sparkling from the suns reflection as it soared with a few lethargic flaps of its almighty wings elegantly higher. A Socotra Hermin freshwater crab scuttled sideways away from them as though fearing it would become lunch. A Chamaeleo monachus with its dark green and white scaled prehistoric reptile presence clinging to a rock like a spider. Unconcerned about Marco's and Hausbeck's close proximity presence.

Two colourful Beetle endemic, pita patted by Marco's left side. An analysing thought whirring in his all-powerful thirty-three combined world scientific bumped intellects mind.

"Insects," said Marco.

"Not far now Marco, I hope all that bumped intelligence has discovered a way to obtain and contain the Astatine and also get us of this island safely," said Hausbeck. Marco sipping more water scooped up into his two palms, his eyes fixed onto the two beetles happy and go lucky scuttling along. Another stare into his wet palms and then at his what seemed like his aging reflection rippling from the water drops dripping from his hands in the clear waters pool.

If I can bump the intelligence and DNA of an animal like I did with Pasta and Mirnyy. And I can bump the intelligence of and reminiscing auras of mankind, even the most powerful minds. Then in hindsight nothing is stopping me bumping the brain power of an insect. Even the tiniest of them have a brain. Some can even live several days without a head, providing they don't lose too much Hemolymph, when decapitated. Animals and insects have survived and adapted to more climate change and the constant evaluation of the planet better than any human. said Marco with his pondering thoughts, before coughing again.

"A penny,"said Hausbeck.

"What?" said Marco.

"A penny for your thoughts," said Hausbeck.

"Insects brains," said Marco.

"What's brain?"

"Did I hear you right?" said Hausbeck.

"Here's the thing. We need, or should I say I need to find a way to obtain and contain the radioactive eighty-five protons stuffed nucleus chemical Astatine. It is the rarest naturel element found in our world, right?" said Marco.

"Right," said Hausbeck

"The totality of its isotopes is short lived, Astatine having a life expectancy of around eight hours. Way too short for getting off this Island, getting back to Dubai and then back to Cleveland right," said Marco.

"You're telling me things I already know and dam well don't need to be reminded of," said Hausbeck, looking at Marco in an inpatient manner to get to the point. Adding. "And where do insects brains come in?"

"An insect's brain is located dorsally inside its head. They have three pair of lobes. Fused ganglia, clusters of neurons which process sensory information. Every lobe controlling different functions and activities. The first protocerebrum connecting via nerves to the eyes and the ocelli controlling sight. The middle deutoccrebrum innervates its antennae from neural impulses transmitted via the antennae, allowing it to collect odour sense taste cues, even tactile sensations as well as analysing environmental information such as temperature and humidity. The third lobe. Tritocerebrum has several functions. Connecting the labrum (insect's movable upper lip), along with its integrated sensory information coming from the other two lobes. Tritocerebrum also connects the brain to the stomodaeal nervous system. A system that functions independently to innervate most of its organs, allowing other ganglia in its body to control most of the overt behaviours. Like the thoracic ganglia controlling locomotion, movement kinetic energy as sort. The stomodaeal nervous system and other ganglia have the capacity to control a majority of its bodily functions independently of the brain. An insect like an ant is so strong it can carry up to fifty-two times its weight. That would be like an average man carrying four tons. The other thing is an insect's blood does not carry oxygen it pours out over the brain and then flows back through the body. Its digestive system is a hallow tube that leads from the mouth to an opening at the tip of its abdomen. Its saliva glands chemical 'enzyme' is what digest the food. It is probably the most complex creature apart from microbes on planet earth. In 1919, Dr W.P Davey proceeded with one of the first tests of insect- radiation survivability. He sprayed a flour beetle with small doses of X-rays. His astonishing findings showed that the sixty rads that the beetle had been exposed to made it live longer. The experiment repeated by Dr J.M "Cork in 1957 showed the same results and further experiments after the two atom bombs drooped on Japan in the Second World War. These findings revealing that insects were much more resistant to radiation then mankind. For example: wood-boring insects and their eggs were able to survive doses of 48,000 to 68,000 rads with no apparent ill effect. Astatine quickly disintegrates. It materialises on Earth as a decay substance of an assortment of heavier elements. If I can bump the intellect and DNA factures of an insect, then I believe I'll be able to carry the Astatine in my body and bring it safely back to Cleveland," said Marco.

"How will we or you extract it from your body?" said Hausbeck.

"Either by my blood or a more natural passageway," said Marco.

"You're kidding right, you're going to shit element eighty-five out of you." said Hausbeck.

"It is the rarest natural element found in our world nothing more natural than human waste," said Marco. Adding, "Better not fart, it would be some atomic blast."

"Maybe you should and the blast will launch us both of this island," said Hausbeck, whist laughing. The two men laughing almost like good friends, only the insistent presence of Hausbeck's gloves expressing his cautious suspicions towards Marco.

"What insect do you plan to bump?" said Hausbeck.

"A beetle is as good as any," replied Marco.

"A beetle!" said Hausbeck, as though Marco having told him, he was going to bump the intelligence and DNA of an irrelevant housefly.

"Most modern beetles have been around since the time of dinosaurs, diversifying ever since. Some scientists even believe they've been around longer. Beetles having an exceptional ability to seize, ever developing ecological opportunities. Their ecological diversity adaptability having triumphed the changing phases of our world for nearly 300 million years. They are peaceful creatures that are not inclined to bite humans. And there's a whole bundle of them over there," said Marco, pointing to the cluster of colourful beetles gathered near the base of a rock only a few feet away from him and Hausbeck.

"Maybe Hollywood will make a film about you. *Beetle man, vs Spider and Ant man*," said Hausbeck, in a joking manner.

"Yeah, maybe," said Marco raising to his feet walking towards the cluster of beetles. "No time like the present," said Marco, his cupping hands isolating one beetle out of the bunch inside his palms, closing his grip around it, like a child having just captured a butterfly. Feeling nothing but the hard coleopteran form scuttling around in search of light and an exit. A disappointed expression portraying from his face. His thirty-three combined world's best intellects seemingly wrong when suddenly Marco sensing the strange tingling from his toes to his fingertips, conglomerating at his phalange. His palmar crease sensing the minor electrical intake, amalgamated with a peculiar humming faint whale's cry, in his ears, simultaneously with a powerful throbbing in his brains motor sensory cortex. Thirty seconds later, his otherworldly supraliminal sensations coming once again to a sudden stop. Marco freeing the beetle from its prison cell inside his clutched united palms. The beetle having bitten him three times whilst trying to escape, spreading its wings and flying in a buzzing circle around Marco and Hausbeck as though stating its displeased anger, before re-joining its colleagues.

"Did it work?"

"Did you feel the strange sensations again?" said Hausbeck.

Marco pretending to try and scuttle under a rock like a beetle, Hausbeck's terrified expression, thinking Marco had metamorphosed into a beetle causing Marco to burst into tears of laughter, calmed by his continuous and worsening cough.

"Ha, ha. Very fucking amusing," said Hausbeck. Adding. "Let's hope your intellectual findings and conclusions are correct. Stanford said the element eighty-five is located deep inside the Halah cave, far deeper than any man has ever been."

"But maybe not an insect?" said Marco.

"Only a probe was sent down, its analysing data revealed a strong presence of Astatine in the atmosphere and soil. A NASA team of scientist, myself included, planned to return and abstract more samples, and try to contain it. But the political turmoil changed everything, and funding and priorities were focused on other areas, such as Mars explorations and returning to the moon. Let's go see if you're right eh, Marco," said Hausbeck, rising to his feet, wiping the dust from his trousers and collecting his rucksack.

"The entrance to the cave is situated behind the second peak, we'll have to climb a little down the rocks façade to access the trail leading into the cave," said Hausbeck. Marco de novo following Hausbeck's steps like two co-working expeditioners continuing the next stage of their adventure. Just over forty minutes later Marco and Hausbeck arriving at a shallow cliffs edge around ten feet steep. An arch of jagged edge bluish, greyish, greenish and faint orange pigment rocks, dropping down like a giant step standing before them. The different angled cliff forms projecting out, allowing them easy access to the strange trail below. The limestone plateau passage heading towards the cave dotted with circular shape forms, filled with water like salt pools. Different coloured pebbles and rocks all as bizarre and outlandish as Marco's find, so many months before. But none seemingly having a peculiar hieroglyphic encapsulated or a decagon shape in their centre. Both men walking silently along the trail, eventually coming to a large crevasse opening, like a giant reptile's eye staring into the heavens. Scuttling their way deeper into the fissure, sliding their feet on the slippery rocky sandy surface, as though they were walking on unsteady ice, their hands stretched out behind them supporting their stance. Now only a few feet away from them, the opening to the cave. Hausbeck pulling out his torch from his pack back, handing a second to Marco.

"No, I can see well in the dark and the rest I'll feel my way through," said Marco.

"As you want it," said Hausbeck, not questioning why. Marcos combined bumped and absorbed DNA of a wolf and its powerful nocturnal vison united with the Beetles special organs sensing antennae receptors, making it able for Marco to see and feel his way around the darkening cave without hindrance. Hausbeck and Marco commencing their descent further into the dark, after a short while having inched their way around obstacles and puddles of shallow water. Both moving cautiously slow, entering deeper and deeper into the hot but very humid cave. Sweat pouring of Hausbeck like he'd plugged his body under a shower. Marco's otherworldly anatomy adapting to the conditional metamorphosing world around them and its atmospheric conditions, only his cough still very present.

"You OK, Marco? That cough of yours doesn't seem to be getting better," said Hausbeck, in-between wiping the sweat from his forehead.

"I'm OK, don't worry about me. You'll get your element eighty-five," said Marco. Hausbeck could hardly be annoyed from Marco's blunt response, after all, he and Stanford were threatening to kill his mother and Rebecca. A few steps deeper in silence leading them to an unexpected wonder. Marco and Hausbeck staring at the gigantic Stalagmites and Stalactites raising from the caves floor, like tree trunks erupting from the underworld. Others hanging from the caves ceiling, like giant spike form suspended like bats. The gigantic Stalagmites and Stalactites staring at

Marco and Hausbeck, like warning warriors not to continue. But the stakes were too high, both squeezing their way past the cautioning giants, entering what seemed another chamber inside the cave. Hausbeck's torch light flickering over an un-estimated number of unique millions of years old drawings, etched into the walls and ceiling around. Human, animal. Geometric patterns and other unknown forms. Marco looking at the same etchings he'd seen at El'gygytgyn Crater Lakes tunnel but revealing nothing to Hausbeck. Hausbeck's torch beginning to fade. Hausbeck banging it over and over as though this gesture would give more power to the weakening batteries.

"Go back, Hausbeck. Wait for me at the caves entrance, I can continue on my own much quicker. But if I have to guide you or carry you in the dark because of injury or other, then you're not making it any easier for us. I got the message the element eighty-five is deeper within the cave, I'll know when I've discovered it and I'll bring it out with me, OK. Don't worry, you have my word I won't leave you abandoned on this Island, I'm not you," said Marco. Hausbeck recognizing, Marco was right and knowing Marco was far from the cruel uncaring selfish person he'd become. Remembering his caring gesture and private religious ceremony to allow Prokhor a final respectful funeral, and his corpse not left exposed to be savaged by the Islands Fauna, like Hausbeck had wanted. Marco would recuperate the element eighty-five, like he'd recuperated the Tundra mechanism. But not for him or Stanford, not even for Marco. But for his mother and Rebecca. Hausbeck back tracking his trail to the caves entrance. Marco now alone staring into the cavernous profundity of the cavern. His nocturnal vision and extra sensory touch perceiving a large decagon form, as he approached a larger fissure descending even deeper into the cavernous sub terrane. Walking deeper and deeper until a passageway revealing itself before him. Again, it's ceiling and sides looking like mounded piles of snow clumped together suspended in strange curved Mammatus cloud formations. A refulgent reddish light breaking through at certain points behind the icy appearance. The identical forms and crystallised type floor underneath his feet. Along with the same multitude of strange etchings of different shapes and forms encapsulated inside. Some inscriptions similar to the Nazca lines, others were different dimensioned perfectly circular forms, like different planet formations ingrained under a thick clear ice like substance. Marco entering a large space once again with a forest of what looked, like twenty feet tall giant stalactites pointing from the floor upwards like icicle fir trees. In the centre of the stalactite's masses, just like the cave where he'd recuperated the Tundra mechanism, was where the light was energizing. Sliding his way, like before past the robust icicle's forms. Seeing the light projecting from the centre of the room coming from what looked out of the earth, only this time it was Aegean colour. Marco approaching his eyes fixing his stare upon a smaller decagon shape encrusted in the centre of the rooms base, around one foot wide in diameter, a channel with floating fulgurating particles levitating and gradually rotating from an unforeseen force. Diminutive electrical discharges, surging from the decagon tube shaped form.

Instinct and his highly adapted otherworldly intellect telling Marco each floating particle was a combined pellet form of pour Astatine. All Marco hand to do was reach his hand inside and extract the small sphere forms and swallow them inside his alien gifted anatomy. The question Marco and his otherworldly intellect didn't know was.

"How many do I ingest?" said Marco whispering to himself. Moments later, kneeling like a worshiping servant before a statue or God, Marco hovering his bare right hand and arm, over the decagon tube form. Watching an instant the small sphere forms floating like miniature planets within the galaxy, his skin tainted a shade of Aegean, from the irradiating energizing glow. Coughing yet again, breathing deeply in to ease his still present irritating tickle in his throat. Closing his eyes for a second, his mother's angelic apparition followed by Rebecca's beautiful loving smile penetrating his thoughts and once again overpowering his fears. Hesitating no longer, plunging his hand and forearm deep into to tunnel form, right up to his shoulders. A tingling sensation prickling against his bare skin like nettles, his fingertips touching one of the sphere forms, pulling it away. A small retainable force, like a miniature magnet holding the sphere back, but with a light tug it broke free into Marco's grasp. Marco still kneeling staring at the small circular form of a greyish stone colour extracted from the tube, clutched in- between his Index, middle finger and thumb like a peg. Minute phosphorescent alabaster and a yellowish green spots coruscating from its form. Marco approaching the sphere to his mouth. The moment of truth only instants away. Placing the sphere form inside his mouth its taste bitter and coarse like eroded mud. The contact upon Marco's wet tongue causing the pellet form to gradually melt, only the phosphorescent alabaster and a yellowish green small particles was hard and not dissolving, as though he'd placed a small ball of quartz filled sand in his mouth. Marco sticking his tongue out like a child in front of a doctor staring at the oozed goo substance. After a few minutes, swallowing the rest of the solid particles along with its melted outer shell, waiting a while to see any reaction upon or within his body. Nothing. No sickening feeling or painful digesting cramps. No ailing effects on his strength, no diseased or feverish apparitions upon his skin, no nauseating migraine, no trembling or shaking, no poisonous convulsions. Nothing. Marco pulling off his T-shirt followed by taking off his shoes, socks and trousers. Stood only in his shorts observing his bare skin from every angle that his twisting body's stance would allow him. Nothing out of the ordinary apart from his tingling cough.

"Is one going to be enough to activate the mechanism?" said Marco, scrutinizing his mind for an answer, not even his all-powerful intellect and otherworldly powers could answer.

"Two to be on the safe side." said Marco to himself. Kneeling yet again before the tunnel form and plugging his arm inside to collect another sphere form pellet. Rapidly swallowing it, not even waiting for the totality of its substance to dissolve in his mouth. Waiting yet again and observing his anatomy for any change. Nothing, nil, zilch.

"Three times lucky and then I'm out of here." said Marco, reaching for a third sphere, like he was collecting precious truffles, managing just to abstract the third with his fingertips, the magnetic force pulling the Astatine pellet ball always back into place, as though they'd realised that they were being eaten. Marco adjusting his body just enough to give him the leeway and strength to pull the sphere form free. After a small struggle extracting the sphere free from the retaining force, swallowing the third pellet almost whole.

"Well even if I wanted or needed another, looks like three's going to have to do, " said Marco to himself. The remaining floating spheres too far down for his stretching human arm form flexibilities to grasp.

Whatever placed the rest of the spheres inside the Aegean irradiating energizing tunnel, had a reach far longer than any human, said Marco in his pondering thoughts, at the same time collecting his clothes and dressing himself. His cough suddenly intensifies and his breathing beginning to wheeze, his muscular energy rapidly weakening, causing him to fall upon one knee.

"I don't feel good."

"Something's not right," said Marco, faintly, now laying on the floor, like a paralysed being. His eyes softly closing as though his body slipping into slumber.

"I can't die here."

"Not here."

"Rebecca, Mama, they need me."

"Not here, please."

"If you're there. Anywhere. Give me the strength to make it back to Cleveland. I beg you," said Marco, addressing words talking to all his beliefs and disbeliefs. God's, soul's, spirits, aliens or other to help him. Slowly with some sort of reserved energy, rising to his knees and then his feet. Pacing small steps, like a hundred year old man, leading him out of the alien room. With every languish wearying step, as though his once youthful might was bit by bit dripping from his body. Even his great intellect slowing down, like a computer reaching the limit capacity of its totality of bytes. His every thought sluggish. Fumbling his way out of the cavern his hands scarping across every surface like a blind man in an unknown environment. After what seemed like hours, a faint light finally appearing at the end of the tunnel. Hausbeck pacing up and down in a hemming and hawing status. Earlier he'd watched a bunch of scuttling beetles climb the rock face walls of the caverns entrance before disappearing out of sight. His first thought was.

Beetles, they've really been around that long and can survive so much radiation intak,. said Hausbeck silent thought. His second thought, as he watched them pitter-patter over the straight steep bedrock surface, like miniature mountain climbers was.

Why don't they just fly? said Hausbeck. But having seen the hours tick by, his uncertainty, mistrust and scepticism slowly getting the better of him. His reluctant decision not to re-enter the cave due to the fact that he had no other choice but to wait. His torch completely dead, the second torch he'd left in Marco's rucksack. Visibility deeper inside the cave, to Hausbeck, was none. With Stanford's unwilling motivation to come to their help, concretising his only option was to stay and wait, and hope Marco had not discovered and alternative way out of the cavern. Hausbeck relieved yet horrified when Marco's appearance finally breaking out of the cavern's dark shadows.

"Hausbeck, Hausbeck," said Marco in a faint mumble, holding on to the side of the cave, as though he felt he was about to faint.

"My God Marco, what did you do?"

"Look at you you're grey with illness, and I mean literately grey," said Hausbeck. Marco's skin, a sickening cyanosis greyish pallor, like a cardiac patient's physical signs of bluish discolouration of the skin and mucous membranes, as though not enough oxygen was reaching Marco's blood.

"What happened?" said Hausbeck, rushing to Marco's aid.

Marco wheezing like a dying lung cancer patient. Hausbeck placing his right arm under Marco's left arm pit and around his back and right shoulder in a supporting hold.

"Can you walk further?" said Hausbeck.

"I don't feel too good." said Marco.

"That I guessed," said Hausbeck, helping Marco closer to the tunnels opening. Marco's limp muscular mass as heavy as dried cement bags.

"Prokhor was right you really are a packet, and a heavy one too," said Hausbeck trying to lighten the current situation.

"Somali pirates," said Marco.

"What!" said Hausbeck, lifting his head straight, Marco's lameness and his supporting help causing Hausbeck only to look at their feet. Hausbeck staring direct out of the cave. Marco's declaration about Somali Pirates causing his heart to almost jump into his mouth. Expecting to see a group of pirates pointing armed weapons towards the two helpless men.

"There's nobody there, Marco."

"You're not hallucinating, are you?" said Hausbeck, at the same time wondering what the Astatine was doing to Marco's body and mind.

"Somali pirates have boats." said Marco in a whispering faint voice in between his wheezing.

"Yes, I know, normally stolen ones too," said Hausbeck.

"You said before we entered the cave. I hope all that bumped intelligence, has discovered a way to obtain and contain the Astatine and also, get us of this island safely," said Marco, in between his short breaths.

"Yes, I did Marco, keep your strength try not to talk too much," said Hausbeck, sitting Marco up against a rock, like a wounded solider.

"I have the element eighty-five."

"It's right here," said Marco still wheezing and pointing to the centre of his chest with his limp left arm, his fingers cupped like he was suffering from arthritis. Adding.

"And Somali pirates have boats. Boats will get us off the Island, and I saw one approaching the island sand dunes to the East, before we entered the cave," said Marco.

"So, what you're suggesting is we sneak back down the mountain which took our healthy bodies how long to climb up? Steal a boat from heavily armed and heavily numbered Somali pirates, who may I add. Will not hesitate for an instant to shoot or kidnap an American and European citizen who have unlawfully entered their island," said Hausbeck.

"Boats float on water and boats will get us off the Island," said Marco in a delirious state.

"Stay with me, Marco. Stay with me," said Hausbeck, making his way out of the tunnel, to get a better reception and call Stanford. Now nearly 19.00 hours, the dawning cardinal orb already half plugged into the Indian Ocean like a giant melting blazing aura. Its rapidly evanescent effulgent rays, metamorphosing Socotra's Indian Ocean into a greyish blue pigment. The sky quickly transforming into an apricot and mauve splendour. The mountains dark shadows outstretching across the arid terra. Soon nightfall would be upon them.

"Stanford its Hausbeck."

"Can you hear me clearly? Over," said Hausbeck.

"Yes, Martin. Loud and Clear. Over," said Stanford.

"What's your current status? Over," said a very cheerful sounding Stanford, on his way to lunch.

"Not good, sir. Marco found the element eighty-five, he's absorbed it into his body using help from a beetles DNA. But…" said Hausbeck abruptly interrupted by Stanford.

"Did I hear you right, DNA from a beetle?" said Stanford, adding to his sentence.

"Well, if Marco's found the element and he's come up with a way to transport the Astatine within his body. What's not good? Over." said Stanford.

"Marco, sir. Marco's not good. I think he's dying. The Astatine radioactivity is slowly killing him. Need to send air rescue to get us out of here. Urgent. Our current location is. 51°18'30''N 119°13'30''W. Over," said Hausbeck.

"No can do, Martin. It's nearly night fall where you are, by the time I get a rescue team organised it will be hours. We're not talking about locations to Miami beach, but Socotra's Haghier mountains region. No helicopter will venture there, more so overnight. Your best bet is to get to the main town of Hadibu. From there it will be easier to send in the sky rescue and bring you back to the jet stationed in Dubai safely. Not unless you have a better solution. Over," said Stanford.

"And Marco. The element eighty-five. Me. Are these things not important enough to shake up, and wake up every possible person or solution available? Over," said Hausbeck sounding desperate.

"Martin, if there was another solution I'd have proposed it to you. You're on your own. Make it through the night and morning then you'll be home. Over," said Stanford.

"Over," said Hausbeck feeling abandoned, but deep down inside knowing Stanford was right. The missions were dangerous and built of scrabbled bits of facts and clues. Never would they have ventured so far without Marco. Never would Hausbeck or Stanford have found the Tundra mechanism alone. Reading between Stanford's words. Hausbeck having given him all the information he needed.

One:

Marco had found a way to obtain and contain the element eighty-five.

Two:

Stanford knew Hausbeck was with Marco.

Three:

He knew their location and that Hausbeck would do all he could to get himself and Marco off the Island.

Four:

And most important. Element eighty-five was contained inside Marco's body. Dead or alive, Stanford believed he could get access to the

Astatine. Another element Hausbeck having no idea about. The decrypted files of Livingston revealing just how big the mechanism was. Hausbeck rushing back to Marco.

"Do you think you can walk?" said Hausbeck.

"Boats, Somali pirates have boats, boats float and can of the island get us," said Marco, his grammar jungled, like he couldn't think straight any more.

"Come on Marco, you gotta help me here. *Come on Marco, stand*! Stay with me, stay with me," said Hausbeck, whilst helping Marco to his weary feet. Helping his weak body out of the cave's entrance. "We've got to make it to Hadibu, you've gotta find the strength, Marco," said Hausbeck. The monsoon winds intensifying, swirling mounds of sand around them, like they'd stepped into a dust storm. It's echoing haunting howl and their current situation. Alone, illegal castaways, high in Socotra's mountainous zone, miles from the nearest town. A sick man hardly able to walk, nightfall at their doorstep and no other form of transport to get to Hadibu quickly and safely, causing Hausbeck to seriously worry. The only man knowing their dire straits was happily munching on his side salad, sipping his glass of red wine back in a sunny warm Cleveland.

"Marco, wrap this scarf around your head and mouth, it will protect you from the dust," said Hausbeck helping Marco like a caring father, coiling the woven cotton cloth Shemagh scarf around his head, nose and mouth. Only his eyes visible like a dessert storm solider. Repeating the same gesture for himself, mumbling under the protection garment.

"We can't stay here. We gotta keep moving," said Hausbeck. Marco and Hausbeck walking slowly for a good hour like two destitute souls fighting for their survival, Hausbeck following the compass's indicating directions, and using Marco's flashlight to guide them through the dry and dusty land. The last traces of the sun having cindered into the Indian Ocean like the last flames of a fire, giving way to its celestial brother. The three quarter moons glint rippling an elongated shaft of light upon the water's waves, like a secret passageway.

"Maybe it would be easier to scrabble to the coast and steal a boat. Somali pirates or not. Maybe they'll be sleeping. Somali pirates have to sleep too, no?" said Hausbeck questioning himself. His analysing thoughts quickly dispersed seeing Marco crumble to his knees.

"Marco. Marco, stay with me," said Hausbeck tapping at Marco's face to bring him around.

"We can't stay here, we've got to keep moving," said Hausbeck, his voice concerned and insistent.

"Nanoarchitectronis, neologism, magnetron, mendelevium, nous sommes, pääruoka, w nocy, appen, eck, beck, FPM, KIAS," said Marco in an uncomprehensive rambling of words, as though all his heterogeneous intellects, languages, scientific knowledge, slang, dialects professional terminologies and other were spilling unorderly from his brain and his vocal linguistics trying to place some directive in his confused jumbled mind. Marco laid upon the hard rough ground, like a tumble tree the wind having quietened further down from the mountainous zone. Only Marco's delirious rambling echoing into the night and intensifying Hausbeck's already deep concerns. Hausbeck lifting Marco over his shoulder, like a fireman or woman evacuating a victim from a blazing building descending the fire engines steep ladders. Marco's continuous mumbling assuring Hausbeck he was still alive. After a strenuous half hour walk. From behind them, came the sound of a snapping dry branch ricochet into hours of darkness. Hausbeck turning sharply, his agitated gesture nearly causing Marco to fall from his shoulders, shining his flashlight to where the noise had come from. Stood in front of him staring at them with eyes as big as an owl, a young Arab man. His shadowy figure looking thin and malnourished.

"He needs help."

"He's sick."

"Do you speak English?" said Hausbeck the young man still gawking at them, his left hand raised over his eyes to protect them from the powerful torches beam. Hausbeck lowering the flashlight, quickly analysing the juvenile looking presence. He was alone and carrying no weapon, Hausbeck's intuition telling him this boyish man was no Somali Pirate.

"I have American dollars."

"Can you get us to Hadibu?"

"Do you have transport?" said Hausbeck. The juvenile man looking at Hausbeck's mouth as he spoke as though he was trying to read his lips. Without words the boy raising his right arm and extending it and his index finger in a pointing manner. Hausbeck staring at what the young man was indicating. A donkey. Its shabby frail build already overloaded with huge sacks, standing obediently waiting its master.

"What! You want that thing to carry this guy to Hadibu, looks like we should be carrying it," said Hausbeck.

The young man looking at him confused as if to say.

'Do you want help or not?' said the young man's stare. Hausbeck having understood his regard, placing Marco upon the donkeys back, like a saddle. The donkey moving a few steps to its right, but after a few seconds excepting its extra load with no further manifestation.

"What's your name?" said Hausbeck.

The young man speaking for the first time. "Abu."

"Nice to meet you Abu."

"We need to get to Hadibu."

"Can you take us there?" said Hausbeck.

"Yes, Abu take you to Hadibu for American dollars."

"Yes, yes of course, here's 200 dollars. 300 more when we get to Hadibu," said Hausbeck.

Abu taking the two hundred dollars and slipping them inside his ragged Thoub's front pocket, walking barefooted through the rocky surface making his way across the trail as clear as if it was day, leaving his goats to graze alone. Knowing he would find them again, and that his father would forgive him for straying from their livestock, when he saw the five hundred dollars. Hausbeck, and Abu's donkey with its extra packet straddle across its weary back following Abu's strides. Marco still mumbling. Hausbeck, Abu and the donkey even with its heavy charge, walking the whole night, without a pause. Just before dawn Abu coming to a sudden stop and kneeling, placing his body southeast towards the direction of the Kaaba (Salat). Fajr (pre-dawn), the first of his five prayers, to be constantly reminded of God and be given the opportunity to seek his guidance and forgiveness. Hausbeck watching Abu in a confused and somewhat ignorant understanding. The half-starved barefooted ragged dressed young man, having walked through the entire night to help two complete strangers, for an amount of money Hausbeck could spend on a bottle of wine. This trail boy taking his first prayer with the remembrance of God. Hausbeck envying Abu's faithful trust and simplicity. Given so little but thankful for the minutest of earths gift. Fresh water, a piece of bread, a place to rest his weary head, a family and good health. Things million upon earth expect without a blink of an eye, never giving a single thought or prayer for those who had to salvage often with great difficulty such gifts. Abu standing and continuing his steps still in silence.

CHAPTER TWENTY

MARCO'S BLOOD

As the first signs of dawn rose from the east side of the island. The earth's all-powerful mightiest star irradiating the entire vault of heaven into a magnificent golden aura. In the near distance arising like an ancient city; the coastal town of Hadibu guarded like a mighty presence from mount Jabal al-jahir. Moments later Abu, Hausbeck and the donkey carrying Marco entering the town, resembling a cluster of rock houses construction's, surrounded by giant piles of plastic garbage by the ocean. Abu running into the centre with excitement, disappearing into a half crumbled building leaving his donkey Marco and Hausbeck alone. Hausbeck agitated expecting to see a whole mob of Arab men come out and attack him. His ignorance and stigmata caricatures of a whole population and religion placed to shame. Abu rapidly returning to Hausbeck Marco and his Donkey, an older man by his side. Abu rambling on in Socotra Arabic. Hausbeck having no idea Abu was explaining their dilemma.

"Papa, this man is injured, sick. He's been mumbling strange words all thorough the night, like he's been poisoned. We must help," said Abu, to his father.

"Quick we must take him inside out of the rising sun, maybe your friend has been bitten by a snake," said Abu's father, in a broken English. Hausbeck staring at the dark skinned man with magnificent blue eyes dressed in a cleaner Thoub, and a light white Shumagg scarf upon his head, like he'd not understood his words.

"My name is, Hasan. I am Abu's father, he tells me your friend has been deliriously rambling through the night. We must take him inside and see where he has been bitten."

Hausbeck quickly realising Hasan and Abu believing Marco had been bitten by a snake or a spider or even some other creature upon the island.

Making things a little easier for Hausbeck, having no idea how he could explain about Marco's otherworldly gift and the element eighty-five, following Hasan and Abu into their humble home, entering a large room made of rock piles, with concrete grout and cinderblock corners. A bright neon orange tarp, held together with more rocks, for a roof. Two small holes allowing shafts of light for windows. Dust particles dancing it the sunlight beams like swarming insects. A few pots assembled near a pile of dried sticks. The black form of a Chador dressed women scuttling quickly out of sight upon hearing strange voices. Hausbeck extending his left hand in a thankful hand shaken gesture. His right hand supporting Marco, having lifted him of the Donkey. Hasan only staring expressing a half-hearted smiled. Hausbeck not knowing to use a left hand was considered rude in Socotra, also ignoring women did not share living quarters with men and women did not to come out and greet guests or visitors unless they were women.

"Run to the Wadis (Fresh water source in the village), and bring some fresh water," said Hasan to Abu, in English for Hausbeck and Marco to understand, adding.

"And fetch Mohamed too," said Hasan. Hausbeck only wanting to call Stanford but knowing if he suddenly told them he had a satellite phone. Suspicions and doubt, unable for him to explain why he hadn't simply used the phone to call for help and travelled through the night with a seriously injured man on the back of a donkey. Also, the seven hours difference between Socotra and Cleveland meant it was the middle of the night, and the helicopter rescue having not been summoned. If Hasan could make Marco in any way better, then Hausbeck's and Marco's journey home would be easier. Getting back to Cleveland at that precise moment seemingly as easy as getting back to earth from the moon, with no space craft. Marco laid upon the hard dried earth floor, Hasan lifting off Marco's T-shirt and cloth Shemagh scarf, checking his upper body for any signs of bites. Nothing. Stripping off his boots, socks and trousers, examining Marco's legs and feet too. No signs of bite wounds. Small drops of blood beginning to drip form Marco's ear lobes and nostrils. Abu appearing holding his pot of fresh water another taller dark skinned man behind him. Haman warmly welcoming him with an open nose-touching moving gesture and right hand handshake.

"Mohamed, I speak to you in English so that these men can understand. I found no traces of bite wounds, but he is delirious and now there is blood slowly seeping from his nose and ears." said Hasan. Mohamed greeting Hausbeck with a gestural nod, before kneeling by Marco, dripping fresh water across his lips and tenderly wiping the blood from his nose and ears.

"Maybe something is inside, like a moth or other insect, they crawl deep inside the ear and make home there," said Mohamed, adding.

"This man needs to get to the mainland hospital there is nothing we can do," said Mohamed. Hausbeck seeing his cue, steeping in.

"I have a satellite phone I can call for help," said Hausbeck.

"Call," said Hasan and Mohamed at exactly the same time, after having simultaneously stared upon one another and then at Hausbeck. Both wondering why Hausbeck he hadn't just done that in the first place. Hausbeck picking up on their confused expressions saying.

"I tried to use the phone in the mountains but the monsoon winds were to strong, blocking the signal," said Hausbeck. His story telling working, both men looking more understanding. Telling Hausbeck to try by the oceans coast where phone signals were always better. The phones dialling tone only ringing twice.

"Stanford. Its Hausbeck, are you receiving me? Over," said Hausbeck.

"Martin, we've been waiting for your call. Everybody is on standby, just need your coordinates. Over," said Stanford, awake and apparently anxious to receive Hausbeck's call.

"We've made it into the Hadibu the coordinates are…." said Hausbeck, interrupted by Stanford before he could finish.

"I have the coordinates Martin, they'll be a helicopter with you within the hour. There is a specialised medical team already waiting on the jet. How is Marco?" said Stanford.

"Not good, sir. He's seems to be haemorrhaging, but I can't say from where. He has blood loss from his auricle and proboscis openings. Sorry sir, from his ears and his nose. said Hausbeck.

OK Martin, hold on we'll be there soon. Oh and good work Martin, good work. Over," said Stanford. A sense of great relief that help was finally on its way, merged with fear for Marco absorbing Hausbeck's feelings. Hausbeck having discovered a side of Marco. A side he would never have, a young man scarifying all for another because of love. Within less than an hour the four powerful blades of an EC145/H145, hovering over Hadibu's coastline. Hausbeck, Mohamed, Hasan and Abu all standing in wait. The air ambulance descending to land, the three men and boy carrying Marco's comatose body towards the landed craft watched by a group of curious locales, placing Marco on the stretcher inside. The helicopter ready to take off immediately, only waiting for Hausbeck, who'd ran towards Abu handing him the 300 dollars more. Then shaking Abu's, Hasan and Mohamed's right hand. Expressing only two words.

"Thank you," said Hausbeck. The three men caught in a tornado of sand as the helicopter whirled into flight, rapidly gaining altitude into the scorching clear blue sky. Minutes later, the spectacle over, only the oceans waves washing upon the shores, along with the chatter of the town's population returning to their daily tasks, resonating in and around the town. Abu proudly handing the rest of the money over to his father. His screaming joy could be heard high into the mountains and low into the valleys, as his father gave him twenty dollars for himself. The rest to be spent on more livestock and food. Marco, Hausbeck and the helicopters passage along with its rapidly distancing view, already passed history upon Socotra. The air ambulance landing near NASA's Bombardier Global express 6000. Five neatly dressed white coat medical staff all ready and waiting to assist Marco, like he was some sort of injured celebrity or president.

"He's gone into a coma," said Hausbeck in a loud voice, shouting over the resounding thrust of the helicopters twin engine rotating blades. Marco rapidly installed inside the aircraft's readymade intensive care unit mounted by the team of doctors and the aircraft's on-board engineer.

"He was haemorrhaging from his auricle and proboscis openings. But his blood seems to be thickening maybe even clotting. We need to thin his blood otherwise he could have a heart attack, stroke even pulmonary embolism. Start with 10mg of 'Apixaban'," said Hausbeck in a quieter voice, the EC145 / H145 ambulance now long gone. The Luxurious Bombardier Global express 6000 with half of its pressurized cabin transformed into a temporary intensive care unit, already taxing to the runway. Having requested (ready to go), urgent take-off clearance.

"10mg!" said one doctor, adding.

"The average dose is 5mg, and that's for patients who've been operated or suffering from an accelerated heartbeat."

"*Ten fucking mg, now*. And get me some blood samples under the microscope. I'm not asking, I'm telling. If you need to know more, Marco is not an ordinary patient OK. So, we need to be doing the extra *fucking* ordinary to keep his arse alive. Understood?" said a very exhausted Hausbeck. His screaming words followed seconds after by the fasten seat belt sign light and ding manifesting themselves.

"Understood, sir," said the doctor, expressing no emotional reaction to Hausbeck's anger. His four colleagues also briefly observing Hausbeck's angry outburst before returning to help Marco. Doctor's professionalism over power personal vendettas and upset emotions. One injecting Marco with 10mg Apixaban, another slowly abstracting a few trickling blood samples, another taking his temperature and blood pressure, the other examining his eye pupils. The last recording data. Hausbeck slumping in his chair, he'd been awake and on the move for over forty hours. Staring out of the aircrafts window at the cloud filled carpet sky. The jet having rapidly rocketed to cursing altitude, his slumbering eyes and body giving in to sleep.

"Sir, sir, we've found something inside Marco's blood." said a voice whilst at the same time shaking Hausbeck's left shoulder.

"What. What time is it?" said Hausbeck, rubbing his eyes and exiting his slumber.

"Its 13.10 US time, we've been flying for a couple of hours not estimated to arrive for a good twelve hours though, sir," said the doctor.

"How's Marco?" said Hausbeck, swivelling his chair around to check on his patient.

"His haemorrhaging has stopped. His body signs are stable, heart pulse, temperature, even his respiratory passageways have eased, his breathing without wheezing like he's sleeping," said the doctor.

"What's with his blood?"

"You said something about Marco's blood," said Hausbeck.

"Yes sir, we've done a series of tests on Marco's circulatory system and we've analysed the small drops we extracted. His blood is still thicker than normal but is circulating, only slower. We found abnormal traces of Erythrocytes, (red cells), Leukocytes (white cells), and Thrombocytes (platelets), as though Marco's blood has been mixed with other human blood, of different Homo-sapiens. We even found traces of Erythrocyte

Antigen DEA 4 which is canine blood. And there's more. We've discovered, the metamorphosing traces of Endopterygota found in certain insects like butterflies, bees and even beetles. There are also traces iodine, chlorine and even bromine. But there's another element even more unexplainable and unknown to us, mutating inside his cells."

"Has Marco been exposed to some radioactive material?" asked the first doctor.

"Or bitten by some strange creature on Socotra." said the second doctor.

"Has he been to another planet?" said the third doctor.

"Because frankly with what is flowing through his cells, pumping around his body and mind is unexplainable," said the fourth doctor.

"We don't even understand how he is still alive with such a cocktail hemodynamic mutating foreign substances circulating around his body," said the fifth doctor.

"It's our annalistic belief that these aliens' entities are blocking the way for Marco's nutrients and hormones O2 and CO2 to maintain his cell-level metabolism and pH osmotic pressure. Preventing his cardiovascular system to be able to protect him from microbial and mechanical harms," said the second doctor.

"He's going to die, sir," said the first doctor, with a small pause looking at his fellow colleagues, then at Marco, then back to Hausbeck, adding, "Maybe even before we land in Cleveland," said the doctor whom Hausbeck had screamed at.

"Thank you, doctor…" said Hausbeck, with a questioning pause.

"Dr Aramis, sir. Endocrinologist from the National Technical University of Athens. These are my worldly colleagues. Dr Nosnoraa, Dr Fnora, Dr Dilahk Debba and Dr Tobba. All specialising in…" said Dr Aramis also about to explain his worldly co-worker's credentials.

"You're Greek?" interrupted Hausbeck.

"My mother is Greek and my father American, sir." said Dr Aramis.

"Marco would have loved to talk to you, he and his father were great fans of Socrates," said Hausbeck, staring at Marco in his comatose state.

"My father too, sir."

"Is there anybody, family member or other you can inform for Marco?" said Dr Aramis.

"What, eh no."

"Marco was orphaned at a young age," said Hausbeck.

"We'll keep checking for any progress and keep you informed. Try and get some rest sir, if there is the slightest change in Marco's status, you'll be the first to know," said Dr Aramis, with a sympathetic expression for Hausbeck.

"Let's leave him to rest." Staring at his colleague.

Hausbeck slumping back into his chair, wondering if Marco would make the journey. Pondering about what Marco had been put through and questioning if. As Dr Aramis had said.

"There's another element even more unexplainable and unknown to us muting inside his cells," said Dr Aramis.

"The element eighty-five would and could activate the mechanism. Along with what would happen?" said Hausbeck in his head, the only one on the plane to know the whole truth. The Bombardier Global express after a long thirteen hours and forty-five minutes shortened flight time, due to tail winds and a quicker route. Making its final approach towards NASA's Cleveland Research Centre's private airstrip. Marco miraculously still alive, and still in a coma. The aircraft swooping down with elegance, like an eagle in flight before touching down with ease at 3.33 a.m. Outside temperature 7° cloudy with light rain. Stanford. Corporal Mears and his three men waiting at the runways side. The long nose of the plane pointing towards them, slowly moving closer, until coming to a total stop, its engines shutting down but the stentorian sound of its APU (Auxiliary power unit), at the aircrafts tail end, blaring into the still night. Seconds later the pressurised air stair cabin door opening. Hausbeck already stood waiting.

"Welcome home, Martin," said Stanford.

"Good to be home," said Hausbeck.

"How's our boy?" said Stanford.

"No significant changes," said Hausbeck.

"Let's get him inside."

"Corporal Mears, have your men carry the subject inside. Transfer him onto laboratories endoscopic bed," said Stanford.

"Yes, sir," said Corporal Mears, gesturing to his men Stanford's orders.

"Oh and confiscate all telephones and personal possessions from the aircrafts medical team and crew. Bring all the data to me. This is top secret for NASA's eyes only. That's and order, understood?" said Stanford.

"Loud and clear, sir," said Corporal Mears

"No more suspicious accidents or disappearances, Stanford," said Hausbeck.

"Don't worry Martin, they'll live. Just being precautious OK," said Stanford. Corporal Mears, entering the aircraft, following his orders to the letter. The five doctors and five crew members placed under house arrest. All astonished but none manifesting their misunderstanding towards Corporal Mears, his men and their guns. Their personal belongings and portable phones confiscated. Marco's digital and papered documented files and data handed over to Stanford. His unresponsive body transferred and placed upon the long rectangular digital endoscopic bed. Instantly images of his human anatomy, cells and organs displaying themselves once again on the multitude of digital monitors. The technologized bed array of lights and digital input displaying once again the 3D images of Marco's Skelton form. Seconds later the perfect hologram image of Marco projecting itself at his feet, turning constantly 360°. The flashing red light indicating the location of his implanted microchip. Marco's heart monitors different coloured lines, indicating he was still alive. Hausbeck surveying Marco, staring at the flashing red light from Marco's locating transmitter. Quickly realising why Stanford had not needed his locating coordinates for Hadibu.

"So, you followed us all the way," said Hausbeck.

"All the way," said Stanford, adding.

"Don't take it to heart, Marty boy. You made it."

"Couldn't you have sent in help earlier?"

"I walked all fucking night behind a donkey," said Hausbeck.

"So did Joseph to get to Bethlehem and he didn't complain," said Stanford.

"Marco is not the son of God," said Hausbeck.

"No, no he's not. But what's inside his mind and body is not from our world."

"This is going to change all religion, all ways we look at the heavens and all ways we look at each other," said Stanford.

"What do you mean?" said Hausbeck.

"Look Martin, I'm sorry I didn't send in a rescue team sooner. Things got complicated. There was speculation of a violation of Yemen air space by an unidentified American craft only hours before we picked up your images from Hubble outside the caves entrance. Russia blamed America and vice a versa. The world's eyes were on Yemen. If they'd have found you and Marco there, an American and European civilian. Well, you can imagine the political international uproar. That donkey, the boy and his family saved your arses more than you can imagine. Maybe your prayers were answered," said Stanford.

"OK, apology accepted. But that's not what you were getting at when you said."

"This is going to change all religion, all ways we look at the heavens and all ways we look at each other," said Hausbeck.

"No, Martin. Its Livingston's files, we decrypted them," said Stanford.

"What have you discovered?" asked Hausbeck.

"Livingston died in six months from cancer right," said Stanford.

"What does that have to do with Marco and the mechanism and his files?" said Hausbeck.

"Well, if you let me explain, without interrupting you'll understand," said an annoyed Stanford.

"So here's what we found..." said Stanford, his words cut short.

"Sir, all personal data and phones indicating nothing has been secretly monitored or downloaded, concerning the subject. What would you like us to do with the detainee's, sir?" said an, uneasy interrupting Corporal Mears.

"Good work, corporal. Release the pilots and cabin crew along with the mechanic, have them transferred to the living quarters, it's been a long haul for them."

"Yes, sir," said Corporal Mears.

"And the medical team?" said Corporal Mears.

"Bring them here to monitor Marco's condition," said Hausbeck. Stanford agreeing with an acknowledging nod.

"At your orders, sir," said Corporal Mears, minutes later Doctors, Nosnoraa, Fnora, Dilahk Debba and Tobba, all having forgotten their house arrest incident, rapidly jumping back into their medical roles, hovering around Marco checking his vital signs and status.

"So, here's what we found. The mechanism is only a piece of a bigger, unit, computer, ship, another mechanism whatever, like a computer chip, if you prefer. Its data should indicate the hypothetical characteristic existence of the wormholes. The short-cut through the solar system as we believed. It should indicate the hidden "electron diffusion regions portals in the earth's magnetic field which we named X-points. And also show us the uninterrupted passages leading from mother earth to the sun's atmosphere. Ninety-three million miles away. But not only in the universe Marty. Also, right here on earth. The phenomenon, the portholes, wormholes. Exist! And according to Livingston's files he discovered when they open and close throughout our planets days hours. He travelled through one and back, but he didn't predict the massive radiation intake his human body would acquire. It's astonishing he lived as long as six months," said Hausbeck.

"So, what you're saying is we will know where the wormhole doors open and close. When they open and close. And where their passages lead too in the universe," said Hausbeck.

"Not only that, Marty boy."

"Apart from being capable to prove, beyond all reasonable doubt and other that we are not alone."

"This is almost secondary now."

"We will be able to go to different worlds, planets without space travel, just a simple passage through."

"We can monitor these openings with military surveillance."

"Anticipate and prepare any alien invasion."

"Capture an alien form alive and study it, even clone it into our DNA."

"But even better, we will have the capability to travel anywhere around our planet, unseen, undetected and unlimited."

"Explore earth and its population, like never before."

"No country or border will stand in our path."

"We will be a superpower," said Stanford.

"My God," said Hausbeck.

"Told you, Marty. This is going to change all religions, all ways we look at the heavens and all ways we look at each other," said Stanford, looking like a man who'd just won the world lottery. Adding, "Unseen, undetected and unlimited. A superpower"

"And how did Livingston activate the mechanism without the element eighty-five?" said Hausbeck.

"That we don't know. His files are a little vague at the end."

"Either he found another source of Astatine, or…" said Stanford.

"Or what?" said Hausbeck.

"Or something, or someone activated the mechanism for him," said Stanford.

"And how do we activate the mechanism?" said Hausbeck.

"In the centre of its hollowed square formation."

"It's centrum." said Stanford.

"What we just switch it on?" said Hausbeck.

"In retrospect, something of that sort," said Stanford, adding.

"According to Livingston's data, the mechanism is activated from the hollowed square centrum."

"Even though the mechanism is part of another or other unknown mechanism."

"All mechanism have an independent sort of central processing unit."

"We simply drop the element eighty-five into its centrum and…"

"And what?" said Hausbeck.

"And we abstract the Astatine from Marco's blood, bring it into contact with the mechanism centrum and watch," said Stanford.

"Watch!" said Hausbeck.

"And wait," said Stanford. Looking a little more perplexed.

"Dr Aramis." said Hausbeck.

"Yes, Dr Hausbeck," said Dr Aramis.

"Sorry for the unpleasant welcoming earlier," said Hausbeck.

"Already forgotten," said Dr Aramis.

"Do you still have some blood samples extracted from Marco earlier?" said Hausbeck.

"No sir, they seem to have desiccated from the contact with the atmosphere, as though oxidizing from our oxygen," said Dr Aramis.

"Extract some more. Five to 10mg, if possible," said Hausbeck.

"We can't find his veins, Dr Hausbeck." said Dr Dilahk Debba, adding.

"His skin seems to be crystallising, solidifying like some sort of protective crust," said Dr Fnora.

"His veins are no longer visible," said Dr Nosnoraa.

Hausbeck approaching Marco closer, glaring at his hardening skin, whilst at the same time tapping data onto some of the touch screen monitors. Mumbling to himself.

"Elytra," said Hausbeck.

"Did you say Elytra?" said Dr Dilahk Debba, standing close to Hausbeck's right side.

"What does it mean?" said Stanford.

"It means Marco's skin is modifying, hardening, like certain insects, notably beetles," said Dr Dilahk Debba.

"For Marco's anatomy, I don't know what it means," said Dr Dilahk Debba.

"For us, we may soon not be able to abstract his blood," said Hausbeck, Stanford looking even more confused.

"Human skin is the outer cover of a human body, the largest organ of the integumentary system. Its multiples layers of ectodermal tissues, underlying muscles, bones, ligaments and internal organs. If his skin is solidifying, there's every possibility his other organs are solidifying too. And his blood," said Hausbeck to Stanford.

"They are, Dr Hausbeck," said Dr Tobba.

"Are What?" said Stanford.

"His organs are solidifying too. Look at the data." Hausbeck tapping more input onto other screens.

"My God, she's right," said Hausbeck. More activated commands from Hausbeck, displaying Marco's crystallising organs. Extra computer input and responsive data, also highlighting Marco's languish gradual decelerating of his circulating blood.

"There between his left foots great toe and second toe, just before the tarsometatarsal joint. His circulatory readings indicate his blood his thinner."

"Quick pass me a syringe," said Hausbeck.

Hausbeck at a snail's pace extracting tiny drops of Marco's green pigment blood. The simple transparent needle with its black plunger tightly squeezed into its hollow tube, syringed between Marco's big and second toes like a druggy. It's indicating cc/mL numbers and lines stagnating just before the 1 ml stripe.

"One millilitre."

"Will that be enough?" said Hausbeck.

"There's only one way to find out," said Stanford. Hausbeck carrying the syringe with his two hands containing Marco's one ml of contaminated element eighty-five blood, over to the opposite side of the room, as though he was carrying a deadly explosion. With an indicating gesture from his head to Corporal Mears and his men. Corporal Mears and his men quickly wheeling aside the square formation, light blue movable panels, revealing the 'mechanism' poised on a specialised fabricated stand. The Mechanism staring back at them like an otherworldly artefact.

"Enough for what?"

"And what is that?" asked Dr Fnora, staring befuddled at the magnificence of the mechanism.

"That is history in the making."

"And you are the gifted few," said Stanford.

Dr Aramis, Dr Nosnoraa, Dr Fnora, Dr Dilahk Debba and Dr Tobba. All gawking at each other in a bewildered manner. Hausbeck, Stanford, Corporal Mears and his men seemingly disconcerted for Marco's metamorphosing illness and the fact he was slowly dying. They were more involved with Marco's tiny blood drops and the strange artefact.

"Do you think I'll need protective clothing?" said Hausbeck.

"Hausbeck. We don't have any more time," said Stanford, adding, "Didn't I hear someone say Marco's blood was desiccated from the contact with the atmosphere, as though oxidizing from our oxygen?"

"How long do you think that tiny plastic plunger will prevent our atmosphere entering the syringe?"

"Place the blood into the mechanism centrum now," said Stanford. Hausbeck approaching the mechanism, standing at arm's length, the plastic syringe gripped in his left hand. Hausbeck holding his breath as though he was about to dive from a high cliff face into deep water, with an unstrenuous push with his right thumb, upon the syringe's plunger tube. Squeezing the one ml drops of Marco's modified sanguine fluid direct into the mechanisms controlling centrum. Within seconds the multitude of strange metallic arms outstretching from its centrum to different circular cogs like shapes, all connecting to triangular, rectangular and smaller square compositional forms. The array of embedded lines leading from every contoured form, joining at different points into a decagon outlined, stepped in a few inches from the exterior perimeter.

Activating.

CHAPTER TWENTY ONE

WE ARE NOT ALONE

From the decagon moulded engraved contour a powerful ultraviolet Verdigris cosmic glowing light energising. The mechanism levitating with an unforeseen energy source from its stand and turning horizontally, floating shoulder high to Hausbeck. Seconds after streams of highly intensified sapphire phosphorescent beams projecting from the triangular shape forms. Followed by more coruscating cardinal coloured laser beams jutting from the square formation contours. The three bright effulgent lights energizing from the mechanism like a film projectors image. Its powerful beams stretching as high as the laboratory's elevated ceiling. The outpouring mass of different coloured glowing lines looking, like a tower's aircraft flight path tracker.

"The pathways to the wormholes," said Stanford in an over excited mumble, approaching closer to the mechanism. Hausbeck gawking almost paralysed. Corporal Mears and his men all standing in a confusing wonder. And the five doctors staring with uncomprehensive bewilderment. Suddenly the mechanism gradually rotating clockwise, like a watches second hand at the same time an alabaster glow slowly spiralling, like sparkling dust particles from the rectangular forms, intermingling with the other effulgent lights. Planet constellations vividly appearing within the energizing beams. Floating and rotating like the earth orbiting upon its axe. Like 3D images of the solar system. The celestial forms all different sizes but none bigger than a tennis ball. Each magnificently detailed in appearance. The vivid green and orange draught lands of the earth combined with its oceans blue, even the cloud forming formations floating above the earth atmosphere. Along with the moon's creators and mountains, the suns erupting blazes. Jupiter's orange, brown, white and light bluish swirling lines. Mars's orange red vibrant pigment. The powerful beams stretching as high as the laboratory's ceiling, looking like a tower's aircraft flight path tracker suddenly precipitously projecting into every spherical planet form at different degrees and angles. Bright lines all perfectly straight stretching horizontal, vertical, perpendicular, parallel, acute, obtuse, angled intersecting and gradient. Like some sort of symmetrical and geometrical gif.

"It's the universe, our universe."

"It's amazing, look."

"Earth, the Sun, Mars, Phobos and Deimos. Jupiter. There's even Ganymede, Callisto, Lo, and Europa," said Hausbeck.

"There's even the dwarf planets, Ceres, Makemake, Haumea, Sadena, Eris and Eros," said Dr Aramis having approached Hausbecks side. Hausbeck staring at him perplexed.

"Greeks were and still are great astrologers. My father is a great passionate, taught me everything he knows about the universe," said Dr Aramis, adding.

"Look there you can even see the smaller moons around Neptune. Proteus. Triton and Larissa. There is Saturn and its neighbouring planets, Titan, Tethys, Enceladus and Mimas. And if I'm not mistaken those are satellites," said Dr Aramis.

"Good God, he's right," said Stanford, adding.

"There is ISS. And there Aqua, Erbs, and Envisat. Jesus, there's even Hubble and the James Webb telescope," said Stanford, his words along with everybody else abruptly silenced. The different circular cogs shapes rotating into a united mechanism command, interlocking with each other. Seconds' later a radiant bright white and pinkish spot forms around the size of a white seed dandelion head, appearing around the planets. Each dispersing glimmering angelic rays. The same perfectly straight horizontal, vertical, perpendicular, parallel, acute, obtuse, angled intersecting and gradient lines also projecting into radiant bright white and pinkish spot forms.

"What the hell are those?" said Stanford, leaning his head closer like a person suffering from short vision.

"Stars," said Dr Aramis.

"What did you say?" said Stanford. Dr Aramis and Hausbeck looking at Stanford like he was dumb.

"Stars," said Dr Aramis. Adding.

"There are not only planets, satellites and telescopes floating around up there, light years away above our heads. But millions of stars too."

"There look that is Rigel Kentaurus, there Wolf 359, there Etamin, there Alpha Coronae Borealis, to name but a few."

"Stars," said Dr Aramis, pointing his pen towards a selection of his named objects. Adding. "And if I'm not mistaken, which I'm certain, I'm not mistaken."

"Those are comets, Borrelly, Hale-Bopp, Haylley's and Ikeya-Zhang."

"Doctors," said Stanford.

"But there are planets and stars we've not discovered yet. Look," said Hausbeck.

"Oh my God, your right,." said Dr Aramis, counting the unidentified spherical forms.

"One, two, three, four, five, six, seven, eight. Nine…"

An unexpected array of erupting cosmic lights, like miniature firework explosions. Immediately stopping Dr Aramis's counting. Cerulean blue spiralling whirl winding formations suddenly appearing, projecting a powerful white tube form beam from their centres.

"Quantum loopholes."

"Those are Quantum loopholes, wormholes. Passageways through the universe. They're, they're, they're real," said Dr Aramis, in a befuddled and excited stutter.

"I did say…"

"That its history in the making."

"And you are the gifted few," said Stanford. Looking less dumb. The cerulean blue spiralling whirl winding shapes central holes opening and closing at different times and moments. When one unlocked, causing the projecting powerful white tube beam to erupt from its central formation. This action causing another to seemingly seal. Instantaneously one of the straight geometrical lines gleaming brighter every time one of the cerulean blue spiralling whirl shapes unlocked, like an indicating road on a map.

"It's the wormholes Quantum loops passage times. It has to be," said Hausbeck out loud. Everybody mystified by the otherworldly phenomenon.

"Look, there and there and over there." Hausbeck pointed to different Quantum wormholes opening and then closing.

"Wait, wait. There's more. The same phenomenon is producing not only in the different galaxies but also upon the planets. Look at Earth," said Dr Aramis, excitedly. All five doctors, Corporal Mears and his men, along with Hausbeck and Stanford, staring at the orbiting spherical replica of planet Earth. The identical projecting powerful white tube beam erupting from different areas across the Earth.

"There in Egypt. There, Italy, there Canada, there Asia," said Dr Aramis.

"The phenomenon happening around all four corners of the globe. But also, within planet Earth's seven seas. The same thing is happening on every other planet," said Dr Tobba. Pointing to Venus and then Pluto. All eyes instantly turning from mother earth to the surrounding planets spheres observing the identical erupting light beams.

"Livingston's findings were correct the opening and closing data of the Quantum wormholes and their passages throughout our universes planets, stars and even within the planets cores."

"My God. You were right, Stanford."

"Apart from being capable to prove, beyond all reasonable doubt and other that we are not alone."

"We will be able to go to different worlds, planets without space travel, just a simple passage through."

"Anticipate and prepare any alien invasion."

"Capture an alien form alive and study it, even clone it into our DNA."

"But even better, we will have the capability to travel anywhere around our planet, unseen, undetected and unlimited."

"Explore earth and its population, like never before."

"No country or border will stand in our path."

"We will be a superpower," said Hausbeck, repeating Stanford's earlier declaration. Hausbeck approaching the mechanisms projecting beam. Scrutinizing the Quantum wormholes phenomenon. His presence so close that the diverse bright lights and geometrical lines reflecting upon him, metamorphosing his pallid skin, like a chameleon. His near presence and exhaling air without warning, activating a digital display of hieroglyphics shapes. At their side, the illustration of every planet, star and wormhole along with the Tundra mechanism and similar looking devices. Hausbeck stretching his hand towards the image of the Tundra mechanism his right hands index fingers only millimetres away from the illustration shape.

"Martin. No," said Stanford, expressing deep concern.

"We've come this far," said Hausbeck, at the same instant touching the Tundra mechanism replica illustrated shape. His finger piercing through the image like it was made of fog. His action causing a 4D replica of the Tundra mechanism to project from the orbiting sphere of earth, like a computer's popup. Hausbeck recognising its pinpointing location. The El'gygytgyn Crater Lake.

"It's indicting where the mechanisms are."

"Look the deep crater lake of El'gygytgyn in Tchoukotka," said Hausbeck excited, quickly pressing another mechanism image, causing the 4D image in Tchoukotka to vanish and a different 4D image to popup, only its location was the coming from the Krubera Cave in Abkhazia Georgia.

"It's phenomenal, come look."

Hausbeck pressing another image, like a child playing with a new game. The Krubera Cave 4D image vanishing and another displaying from the Moon's Webb Crater. His crazed enthusiast touching more images, now with his right and left index fingers. Every time the old images vanishing, new ones appearing.

"There's one on Jupiter and Mars and even Mercury," said Hausbeck, like a kid discovering new features to a game.

"They're everywhere."

"What does it mean?" said Dr Tobba, gawking like her fellow co-workers, as well as Corporal Mears and his men.

"It means we're not alone," said Stanford. In a deep concerned voice. Everybody turning to look at why he seemed so distressed. Stanford being the only one out of all of them to have noticed another presence enter the laboratory, without a key, or a biometric palm scan. Neither with the help of the new recently instated retinal scan.

"We are no longer alone," said Stanford repeating his sentence.

"Yes, we know, sir."

"That's what you've been wanting to prove all along. Isn't it?" said Hausbeck.

"Martin. We are no longer alone in this laboratory," said Stanford, his voice almost as quiet as a whisper. Hausbeck turning around rapidly, having felt a ghostly presence shimmer past him, like a light breeze coming from behind, causing his skin to goose pimple and the hair on the back of his neck to stand on end. A transparent alien presence, at first looking like the rippling scorching hot spell of a heat wave. But quickly coming more into focus, standing only inches away from Hausbeck. Its eight foot lucid transparent skeletal form sharpening in appearance. A translucent glass figure as though made from ice, towering over Hausbeck. Its oval shaped head, like a rugby ball sideways twice the size of a human skull. Two large white tube forms for its eyes around ten inches in diameter with a black pigment retina, submerged around five inches inside the bluish glass form skull. The alien's presences eyes located at the bottom of its oval head around fifteen inches apart. In-between a cluster of translucent tentacle forms around twenty inches long and two inches in diameter. Its mouth opening seemingly hidden under the resembling Cranciidae squid (Glass squid), head. In the centre of its cranium a smaller decagon shape with what seemed a miniature brain characteristic embedded, clearly visible. Diminutive electrical discharges, like fulgurations surging from the alien shaped brain. Like from within the stone Marco had discovered. The extra-terrestrial long and thin diaphanous arms with seven elongated fingers, like an Aye Aye stretching over seventy inches long. Its long legs and feet anatomy resembling the hind legs and the four digit claw form of a T-rex. The alien levitating inches from the laboratory floor by some gravitating force. Fulgent energy sources vividly visible circuiting around the semi-transparent alien anatomical form. The alien extending its long arm and one elongated finger towards Hausbeck in a pointing status. Its face expressing what seems to be anger. Hausbeck running in a frightful panic to the other side of the laboratory, his sweating hand and tear feared eyes hindering the biometric palm scan and the Retinal scan to unlock the door.

"Come on, come on open you fucking piece of modern technology," said Hausbeck in a stressful anger.

The alien floating towards him like a phantom.

"Open, open."

Hausbeck, in a screaming panic. The alien presence abruptly stopping just feet away from Hausbeck. Turning to face the opposite direction. An identical alien form levitating by Marco's side, like an angelic aura, having communicated by telepathy to its partner.

"His human form is suffering, I can ease his anthropological physical pain but the radioactivity, his body has absorbed may be impossible to eradicate."

Communicated the first alien.

"And his miniature brain?" telepathically transmitted the second alien, having let Hausbeck to flee.

"It seems to still be functioning even helping him stay alive," mind communicated the first alien.

"Do what you can to help him he, he…" sadly, transmitted the second alien. Seemingly not able to finish her sentence

"I know, we'll make it right."

Positively telecommunicated the first alien. The second alien turning back to where Hausbeck having run too. Hausbeck having taken full advantage of the aliens' unknown distraction, calming himself down and successfully activating the biometric palm scan and the retinal system he had recently installed. Squeezing through the half open door and fleeing, leaving his colleagues behind like a coward. Corporal Mears and his men having gone to draw their weapons, but the physical functions blocked by an unforeseen force. Only their eyes and mind absorbing the images and actions of the two alien forms. The same invisible energising paralysing momentum, having blocked Stanford and the five doctors too. All observing the two levitating alien forms movements and behaviour. Like half alive medusa statues. The aliens identical in every way accept the shape of their eyes. A transparent body, with a translucent glass skull. Two arms and two legs almost human, but no joint forms like elbows or knees apparent. The different characteristics to mankind being the extra fingers and strangely formed feet. The first alien with an upturned eye shape, extending its long fingers over the whole of Marco's body like a physical healer, causing strange rainbow coloured auras to ooze from Marco's body and absorb into the alien's seven fingertip forms. Causing an osmose shimmer to appear around the alien's form, as though it was extracting something from Marco. Soaking it inside itself and then re-disperse it into the atmosphere. When the alien's hands approached the vicinity of Marco's crown diminutive electrical discharges fulgurations surging, like miniature sparks into its transparent palms. Its tube form eyes adjusting like lenses on a microscope as it observed scrutinized, seemingly every inch of Marco's unconscious anatomy. The second alien with round shape eyes, having gravitated over to the mechanism its translucent fourteen finger forms and eight translucent tentacle forms swiftly gliding over the bizarre hieroglyphic's shapes and forms, like a pianist over a keyboard. The aliens inputting actions causing the mechanism to activate different wormhole openings and an asymmetrical assortment of lines to differential points (countries), upon planet Earth.

"There, open, we can begin," communicated the second alien operating the mechanism. Adding, "How is he?"

"His mind is better, he should wake from the human traumatic sleep status, but his body is not responding," telepathically transmitted, the alien trying to heal Marco.

"Will he make the journey to Htraenus?" transmitted the second Alien.

"Yes," telecommunicated the first alien.

"Then let us begin."

Communicated the second alien. Seconds after activating some final input into the mechanism. The two aliens floating over to where the five doctors four military personal and Stanford were grouped together. With a communicating telepathic command the ten human bodies floating a few inches off the ground, all their eyes expressing the same terrified fear. The two aliens placing themselves around the ten human bodies their extra-terrestrial force having placed them in a circular form like Stonehenge. Marco transported by a gravitating force from the digital endoscopic bed into the centre of the circle, poised in a foetus stance. Stanford, Corporal Mears and his three men. Dr Aramis and Doctors Nosnoraa, Fnora, Dilahk Debba and Tobba all still conscious and observing with their eyes and mind, but all still physically paralysed. The aliens in position outside the circle of mankind their elongated arms outstretching around the ten in place floating bodies with Marco levitating in the middle. The aliens combining their twenty eight fingers joining together like electrical plugs into a socket. A cerulean blue spiralling whirl winding energy, like an otherworldly gyratory tornado, spiralling around them, picking up momentum, causing the humans hairs and clothes to flap and flutter, like they'd been caught in a storm. Five of each of the two aliens cluster of translucent tentacle forms also outstretching the outer perimeter of the circle. A single tentacle arm stopping behind the back of the head of every human. All except Marco.

The tentacle acicular form, piercing through the skin and into the brain stem. The rotating momentum energy intensifying causing the laboratories equipment to plunge into darkness, only the energetic lucent of the mechanism flickering its aurora phenomenon upon the laboratory's human built architecture. Within seconds, one by one of the ten encircled humans starting with Stanford, vanished, as though by magic. After Stanford, Corporal Mears, followed, one by one by his three men. Then Dr Aramis, Nosnoraa, Fnora, Dilahk Debba and Tobba. All gone, leaving only Marco and the two aliens. The mechanism moving from its position, hovering over them. The Tundra mechanism indicating planets, pathways, Quantum wormholes, stars, other mechanisms and other displaying information no longer visible. The mechanism positioning itself over Marco like a floating UFO, projecting an effulgent white light penetrating from its decagon outlined, stepped in a few inches from the exterior perimeter. Beaming down on and around Marco, like the sunrays' heavenly glow breaking through the clouds. The effulgent light shining only within the permitted circle, formed by the alien's joining arms and linked together fingers. The transparent centres of the alien's cranium with the smaller decagon shape embedded miniature brain characteristic. Fulgurating powerful electrical discharges, like a lightning storm. Minutes later the laboratory lights and equipment powering back into action. A prolonging continuous bleep from the digital endoscopic beds heart monitor, indicating flat lined, breaking the eerie silence of the unoccupied laboratory. Stanford. Corporal Mears, his three men, Dr Aramis Nosnoraa, Fnora,

Dilahk Debba and Tobba, the mechanism, the two aliens along with Marco, vanished, evaporated into thin air. Only the trace of Marco's locating transmitting microchip poised on the floor, like a fallen penny from where Marco was last seen. A silent witness to the extra-terrestrial visit.

CHAPTER TWENTY TWO

EPOH AND ECAEP

A door silently creaked open at the far end of the laboratory. Hausbeck having witnessed the whole scene. Having seen nothing follow him, he'd secretly returned. Curiosity overpowering his cowering abscond. Hausbeck peeping like a jealous spying husband through the cracked open door. Watching in stupefaction what had happened.

"Where have they gone?"

"How am I going to explain the disappearance of one of NASA's senior officers four military personnel and five of the world's top doctors?" said Hausbeck, to himself in a totally befuddled mumble, whilst slowly and cautiously, walking deeper into the laboratory, his left foot, crunching on Marco's locating transmitting microchip. Hausbeck bending down collecting the damaged piece of technology, holding it between his right thumb and index finger.

"There was more than one?" said Hausbeck. Rapidly walking over the laboratory's array of digital screens and computers. Tapping like a crazed computer programming different commands onto the keyboard.

"Transmit, transmit."

"Give me something," said Hausbeck, trying desperately to recuperate the slightest of proof. But his efforts in vain, video recorded data, documents, concerning the mechanism and Marco. Their secret voyages to deep crater Lake of El'gygytgyn in Tchoukotka and Socotra. All red sleeved top secret files and Livingston's documented data. Everything on Marco's alien bumping intellect. Vanished. Evaporated like Stanford and the others. The sound of a phone humming turning Hausbeck's attention away from his befuddled mind. Hausbeck stood scratching his head as though he was trying to scratch into his brain.

"That's my phone."

"It has recorded data on it," said Hausbeck in a joyful relief, scrummaging through the piles of documents in search of his portable phone. The phone humming again. Hausbeck pushing aside a pile of files seeing his jacket slumped over one of the portable cabinets, scrambling into his pocket, his joy and relief, as though he'd just recovered a winning lottery ticket. Holding his portable phone in his hand. Three missed calls two from his new on and off girlfriend Liz. One from Stanford.

"Stanford?"

Hausbeck going to messages.

"You have two new messages."

"Today at 3.27 a.m.," said the sweet telephone recorded voice. A very drunk and pissed off Liz on the other end.

"You treat me like shit."

"Twenty one days no frigging news."

"Yes, I'm pissed and pissed."

"Château Margaux 2011 first Cru Classé from your private collection."

"Still got your keys."

"Call me you bastard, all I'll be ex-wife number four."

"Even though you don't want to marry."

"Call. Or your Petrus, Cépage Merlot will die too!" said a very pissed off and pissed Liz. The message ending with the distinctive clinging of bottles.

"Next message."

"Today at 10.11 a.m."

"That was seven minutes ago?" said Hausbeck, looking at his phone then looking around the laboratory as though he was in some strange place. Approaching the phone to listen to the second message.

"Hi Marty boy, it's Stanford, you were supposed to get back to me."

"Your message said something about taking some time off for a personal voyage."

"Are you back?" said Stanford's voice. Hausbeck realising it was what he had found for a pretext to give to Stanford, after Dr Whites call and before leaving for England to see Marco.

"What the hell is going on?" said Hausbeck, pressing the redial button. After two rings Stanford answering. Hausbeck listening to him saying goodbye to a fellow colleague in the distance.

"Don't forget our golfing date Billy boy, it's about time we got out of the stuffy office and stretched our legs a bit." said Stanford.

"Next Thursday 9.30.," said the voice of Billy Boy.

"You're on," said Stanford, approaching the phone closer to his mouth and ear his voice rapidly becoming sharper.

"Marty boy. Where are you?" said Stanford.

"Where are you?" said Hausbeck.

"What do you mean where am I?"

"I'm where I'm always at, cooped up in this stuffy office."

"Those bureaucrats from NASA, always whining about how much money we spend on the O.W.I.Q Project."

"They won't whine any more when an alien climbs up their arse."

"Got to keep fighting Marty, their talking about shutting us down."

"So, what's new?" said Stanford.

Silence prevailed.

"Marty boy, are you there?" said Stanford.

"Yes, yes sir, I'm here. Listen sir can I get back to you, another call just came up and it's rather urgent," said Hausbeck.

"Make it quick Marty, you were supposed to ring me two days ago."

"Those bureaucrats want answers."

"Ah Marty, what I wouldn't give to be able to prove the second Antikythera mechanism exists."

"Soldiers we need better soldiers," said Stanford.

"Me too, sir. Me too," said Hausbeck. His mind flashing back to the moment he'd seen the tentacle arms stopping behind the back of the head of every human. All except Marco. The tentacle acicular form, piercing through the skin and into the brain stem.

"They've erased his memory."

"And the others?" said Hausbeck making his way hastily outside of the laboratory, heading towards the military controlled barrier entrance. A familiar voice and face standing next to the controlling cabin's station box, talking to an annoyed well dressed women sat in her convertible luxurious car.

"I can't let you through without a visitor's pass mam, you need to turn around head back to point C."

"Go into the ground floor offices."

"There my colleagues will take your details and issue you with the right pass."

"Sorry mam, procedures and orders."

"Can't be too careful these days." aid the familiar voice.

The women angrily reversing her car away from the barrier. Her car wheels spinning and screeching for an instant on the tarmacked surface, before she disappeared direction, point C.

"Morning, sir."

"It's indicated everywhere what the visitors have got to do."

"You would think these intellectual super brains would understand such simple procedures."

"Anyway, not too bad, lovely pair of legs, leading all the way to paradise, if you know what I mean."

"Slept in the lab again, sir?"

"Didn't see you arrive this morning," said Corporal Mears.

"Are your men with you, corporal?" said Hausbeck, trying to keep cool and calm.

"Yes sir, Jonesy and Whistle on perimeter duty, they should be back at any moment."

"Bulk, is on the Jon."

"Why do you need us sir?" said Corporal Mears.

"What time have you been working since?" said Hausbeck

"Six till six today, like every day this week."

"Are you sure you're all right, sir?" said Corporal Mears, looking deeply concerned for Hausbeck.

"Yes, yes I'm fine, just need a good night's sleep," said Hausbeck.

"Don't we all, sir. Don't we all," said Corporal Mears. Placing his index finger and thumb inside his mouth spaced apart left to right, blasting out a couple of loud belts from a whistling cry. 'Bulk' back from the Jon, turning to acknowledge Corporal Mears call. Giving him a hand signal requesting a cigarette. Their leisurely carefree attitude given no signs that only minutes before they'd witnessed one of the most modern day discoveries. If not the signal most. That of alien intelligence. Hausbeck making his way back to the laboratory, as he walked checking the data on his phone. Vanished too. Nothing. Hausbeck, checking the Bombardiers crew quarters too. But the aircraft along with pilot co-pilot the steward, hostess and mechanic also gone. Hausbeck collecting his jacket containing his car keys. Driving home, his mind buzzing with questions. Moments later, pulling into his driveway. His villa half ransacked, a half-naked, Liz sprawled in a drunken stance half on the coach half on the floor. The Château Margaux 2011 first Cru Classé from his private collection, empty. The Petrus, Cépage Merlot, laid unopened on the floor. Hausbeck searching a corkscrew from his kitchen draw. Sitting himself down at his breakfast table, pouring himself a very large glass of Petrus. With some further inquiries from his NASA, FBI and CIA contacts, discovering that the Bombardier crew still stationed in Washington. Also quickly learning Dr Aramis was back in Greece. Doctor's Nosnoraa, back in Amsterdam. Dr Fnora back in Barcelona. Dilahk Debba back in Japan and Dr Tobba back in Argentina. Hausbeck's contacts also informing him that none of them having left their respective counties within the last six months.

"The Quantum loopholes, wormholes. Passageways through the universe and within the Earth's core were real. They'd been transported back to their lands through them. That's what the alien was programming with the hieroglyphic's symbols and images. Activating the passageways capable of bringing everybody back, with no memory of their trip to Dubai or Cleveland's laboratory. Marco, the mechanism, Stanford, Corporal Mears and his men and the aircraft crew. All those having witnessed the same thing as me. Having parts of their memories erased. The mechanism gone and no traces of element eighty-five. I have nothing. I have nothing." said Hausbeck repeating his words, his whole body language expressing his deception and defeat.

But the most important question Hausbeck, asking himself as he poured himself, yet another glass of wine was. "Where was Marco?" said Hausbeck. A cruel reminder of his vivid painful memories as though to rub salt into his deep wounds suddenly appearing. His tipsy clumsiness spilling some his Petrus, Cépage Merlot wine over the remote control, a sharper reflex reaction, wiping away the red liquid with a tea towel, causing the television to switch on. Just at that precise moment a documentary about donkeys the small flat screen TV in the kitchen flashing images back at Hausbeck.

"Where are you, Marco?" said Hausbeck in a drunken slurring manner, after his third big glass of wine.

^^ooo///))/ (```" "oo: ==β

Decrypted an alien voice.

"You need to speak to him in a language he can understand, like what earthlings call English." said an alien melodious voice.

Seconds after, another voice talking softly in English. "Marco. Marco, can you hear me?"

"Ummhh, errrrh," groaned Marco, as though waking from a nightmarish sleep, gawping around what resembled a large square space mysteriously carved out of the sea, rippling greenish walls ten feet high, stretching in length as far as his eyes could see, his body levitating inches from the floor. Marco extending his finger curiously touching the strange texture. It rippled like a stone thrown into water but it was dry and warm against his fingertips touch. Marco then standing to face the aliens. His crystalizing body now strangely in a healthier stance.

"Where I am?"

"Who are you?"

"What are you?" said Marco in a faint voice. Starring at the extra-terrestrial presence, but strangely feeling no fear.

"I am, Epoh."

"And this is, Ecaep," said Epoh.

Ecaep, floating by the mechanism Marco had recuperated.

"We are Ynomrah's."

"And you are on our planet Htraenus," said Epoh. Her upturned eyes smiling at Marco.

"You're aliens?" said Marco, his vital signs rapidly becoming more alert.

"To your world, yes."

"But to many neighbouring planets and what you call the universe, we are one of the longest existing species."

"Like, if you're dinosaurs were still around."

"We saw them die," said Epoh, her eyes expressing sadness.

"Our technology was not as advanced in those times."

"Not like today," said Ecaep.

"Did you do this to me?" said Marco.

Epoh and Ecaep gazing at each other. Ecaep wide round eyes diminishing in diameter as though he was expressing sadness. Epoh's eyes turning even further downwards in a similar saddened expression.

"Yes," said Epoh, her voice full of remorse.

"We intercepted what you humans call a wish," said Ecaep.

Marco looking confused. Asking, "My wish?" said Marco.

"Maybe we should explain," said Epoh.

"We Ynomrah's have been exploring what humans call the universe, for what your years would calculate around ten million years. Our calculation of time are shorter. What you call a million years is one year to an Ynomrah. We explored time evolution in definition $f(x)\#(Og(z))=\S$," said Epoh.

"Epoh, he doesn't need an Ynomrah maths lesson," said Ecaep.

Yes, yes, you're right, said Epoh.

Marco thinking to himself.

"What. Aliens disagree and argue too?"

"Sorry, Marco," said Epoh, before continuing.

"We are exploring scientists if you like. Over time all times we have evolutionally progressed like human's evolution and adaptations only more. We faced the same adaptive challenges as all organisms have. Even though humans are the unique species to have most of their adaptations transmitted culturally, biologically, basically, imitativeness, sociability, inventively just incrementally over your earth years. Our evolution was more intellectually and quicker. Our anatomy is now capable of living on every planet. Like different human's genetic adaptations of the earth's climate. For example. Tropical Homo-sapiens tall and lean to lose heat. Antarctic and mountain mankind short and wide to conserve heat, certain of mankind's' epicanthic eye folds to protect their eyes from extreme sunlight or cold climates. Along with the epidermis, glutathione, melanosomes, stratum corneum bestowing homo-sapiens across planet earth with different skin pigments, cohesion and thickness. And other visible characteristics, like your hair or your blood. Our eyes profile indicates our sex. My upturned profile indicates the XX chromosomes of my feminine gender, the round form of Ecaep shows his XY chromosome masculine gender. Our body's evolution has a great resistance against diseases our diet is ninety-five percent intellectual and five percent nutritional. So, finding food has never been a problem. The translucent physic you see is capable of withstanding intense heat and cold. We breathe through these tentacles, each having a different genetic system allowing the diverse atmospheric vapours or gasses to filter and be fed into our brain. Like the composed nitrogen and carbon dioxide most organisms respire on earth. Or the atomic and molecular particles of the lunar atmosphere, even the metallic, liquid hydrogen along with the liquid helium of Saturn's atmosphere. We can even breathe underwater at very deep levels. Like a humble earths frog who can breathe in or out of water even in the earth's thick mud or frozen water. The earth's frog can breathe through their lungs, mouth and skin and some can stop breathing altogether. Our tentacles operate in a similar way as a frog and other amphibians absorbing the atmospheric gasses through them and through our blood vessels, which project around our body. The ones you can see now, resembling electric fulgent dischargers. We have no ribs and diaphragm like human's, so we have no pressure in our lungs. We can slow our metabolism down, our blood contains specific proteins to prevent any damaging affect to any of our organs which are there, only a human retina reflects our image like a transparent cloud. We can even stop our hearts from beating for long periods of time, like a sort of hibernation. Even our eyes have a transparent membrane to protect them from damage. Our brain capacity is currently operating at 93% of its ability. Not like a human brain which averages at 10%. And one of our goals is to reach 100%. Our advanced intellect allows us to levitate so our bodies can travel upon different planets surfaces and diverse gravities. Our exolingustics, xenolinguistics and astrolingusitics as you say on earth. Are capable to communicate and understand not only every species upon your planet. But also, within are neighbouring universal galaxies. Why am I telling you everything about our anatomy Marco, is because your human body, organs and cells are badly damaged. If it wasn't for the miniature brain that we implanted inside your brain. Your body would have already withered, failed and eventually deceased. We can save you, but you will no longer resemble a human being. But one of us. An Ynomrah," said Epoh.

"I don't understand."

"What has all that do with my wish?" said Marco, having taken great attention to listen to Epoh's explanations, but still befuddled what all that had to do with a simple wish.

"We explore planets, Marco. We saw earth being created, it was and still is the most universal planet in the entire galaxy. We have travelled too nearly all of them. Even though some smaller planets resemble earth's atmosphere and capability of evolution. None are as beautiful as earth. We've been studying your planet and its population for your millions of years, we even helped certain of your cultures develop. But then—" said Ecaep, with a hesitant pause.

"Then what," said Marco.

"War," said Epoh. Adding.

"Not just one war, but many wars. We used and have been using the entire ninety-three percent of our intellect to understand why? That's why we are aiming so high to reach our maximum capacity of one hundred percent. We have never seen a species, not even within the planet Earth's own fauna or sea life. Not upon any other planet, or the population. The ssenmalac, ytineres, msimitpo, htiaf, eveileb, ecneconni to name but a few. Tyrannise and kill so many of their own. We disagree and present logical arguments but we never hurt, abuse, damage, torture, or kill our own or any other. Like earthlings do," said Ecaep.

"So, we studied you and the human race. Not only to try and understand but help. Our populations, all the other planets and civilisations like ourselves, the Ynomrah's. Are free from war. And have never been at war. We've helped each other and other planets develop and advance. We wanted to help earthlings too, but our intellectual findings and analysing studies always came back the same readings and annalistic response.

"If you cannot even except and live with your own species."

"How could, would you accept other planets' species."

"You would call us aliens, and we would never be Ynomrah's to you."

"Our superior intellect would be considered a threat and you would attack us."

"We would be seen like certain of your animals are seen."

"You would shoot to kill then ask questions."

"Not all of you. But earthlings would not help us. That we know," said Epoh.

Marco thinking of his tyrannising past. The simple fact that he spoke with a different accent and came from a different country having brought so much racial abuse from his equal mankind species, listening further to the Ecaep's and Epoh's whys and wherefores.

"So, we studied you in secret. At first, we could travel to your planet via the galaxies. Our vessels which you on Earth call UFOs were undetected carrying many of us and our equipment. But as your technology advanced, your eyes in the sky were more prone to detect these vessels, and therefore see us as a threat upon your civilisation. So, we created the wormholes. A quantum leap from one point in the universe billions of lights years away from your earth and another planet connecting different universes only to a shortened distance.

"Like earth's measuring feet or centimetres. We quickly understood if we revealed ourselves because of mankind's diverse beliefs and faiths."

"Our presence would have only created more war," said Epoh.

"Now having the capacity to travel into Earth and around Earth through internal wormholes. Easily activated by the mechanism you took from the deep Crater Lake of El'gygytgyn in Tchoukotka. Only a small number of us still travel and are interested in Earth. Many feel you are programmed to destroy yourself and your planet. And if we brought earthlings back to other civilisations you would eventually try to destroy them too. To present our arguments and prove the sceptics wrong we developed a miniature brain, the size of your microchips. You earthlings still operate with small memory size chips you call bytes. Kilobytes, megabytes, gigabytes, terabytes and petabytes. We knew an average human brain has the ability to store around 2.5 of what you call petabytes of memories. We also knew, that until your brains did not develop in a way. To naturally use more of its capacity, like ours. An overdose of data, would kill you. But we needed to get into your minds. Understand what was happening in your brains, to understand your constant need for war. So, we invented a brain with a microchips capacity if you like, which began with a trillion bytes then quadrillion bytes. We chose certain earthlings over many of earth's decades. Installing the chip, and analysing their data, but we only got individual information back, so we invented another micro brain chip, like the one we implanted in you, Marco. It has the capacity of stellabytes. Capable of bumping information from one human to another.

"When your palm came into contact with another human or animal or even insect. The synchronous gesture causing the chip to activate sending electrical impulses through your body and mind into theirs and bumping their collective data and memories and storing it inside your mind. The new chips technology, if you like. Was experimental. Its draw back meant it took thirty seconds of earth time to transfer the totality of information from one mind back into yours and back into the chip, but for the first time we have been able to amalgamate different human intellects into a combined data. But we never anticipated your courage and love to save those you carry most precious in your mind and your organ the heart. The atom molecules of the element eighty-five have absorbed into your human body. Normally the micro brain implantation would have prevented your anatomy's organs and even your own mind from being affected or damaged, but the massive radiation intake that entered your blood stream, pumping around your brain and body. A part of the chip's capacity leaking into your blood stream, along with all your bumped intellect. That is why your body has abnormal traces of erythrocytes, leukocytes and thrombocytes because your blood was mixed with other human blood data from different Homo-sapiens, along with traces of Erythrocyte Antigen DEA 4 from Mirnyy the wolf. But the worse for you was the metamorphosing traces of Endopterygotes, seeping into your human skin and internal organs. Solidifying your human anatomy and blood. The microchip is helping you live but was not designed for such massive radioactivity. We can purify your body. But if we take the chip out now before we heal you, you will die. The only way our intellectual data is telling us is for you to bump our intellect and DNA. Our advance evolution deoxyribonucleic acids, molecules and genetic reproducing organisms will absorb into your body and over time metamorphosing you into an Ynomrah," said Ecaep.

"So, I'll be like you?" said Marco.

"Yes and no," said Epoh, adding.

"Your physical appearance will be like ours, but your mind will still be human, you will constantly have to have a micro brain chip implanted alongside your brain. Like certain humans have assisting medical devices to help them live with their genetic disorders. Until in time your brain develops like ours and is able to use its maximum capacity on its own."

"How long will it take for my body to fully heal?" said Marco.

"A fraction of a Sraey," said Epoh.

"What does that mean, a fraction of a Sraey?"

"One hundred of your Earth years," said Ecaep.

A tear rolling down Marco's cheek. Epoh and Ecaep looking at him in a fascinated manner. Marco wiping his tears from his face.

"And Mama and Rebecca?" said Marco.

"We cannot bring them here, Marco, we need another two of the same chips that we implanted in your brain. Which takes us five Sraey to finalise," said Epoh.

Marco quickly working out the maths. If a fraction of a Sraey was one hundred Earth years. By five Sraey. His mother Anna, and Rebecca would be long gone.

"You said you intercepted my wish and that's why you chose me right?" said Marco.

"We can show you, Marco. Fill in those missing blanks if you wish?" said Epoh. Ecaep agreeing with his eyes. Marco's expression more powerful than words, his countenance almost screaming.

"Yes, show me. Please!" said Marco's facial expression. Epoh moving to Marco's rear. Her towering eight foot presence standing, like a statue behind him. Her fourteen fingers pressing against Marco's heads like the cables from his electroencephalogram bonnet wiring when he was in hospital. Marco's breathing softly calming, seconds later Marco and Epoh floating like spirits, her alien fingers connected to his head, an instant later one of her translucent tentacle forms outstretching. Stopping behind the back of Marco's head. The tentacle acicular form piercing through Marco's skin and into his brain stem. Like it had done with Stanford and the others. All of a sudden, a flash of memories flooding into Marco's mind. A mixture of things he could remember and things seemingly blanked from his consciousness. Starting with the vivid memory of him and Pasta persisting towards the seashores, walking through the large public park, dominated by a magnanimous quantity of sublime saplings, bushes, shrubs, flowers, herbs, plants and trees. Marco seeing the recollection of Pasta ruffling through the diversified perishing foliages. Then the reminiscing sentiment about his father's lost presence and devoted love also coming back to him. The bunch of tumbling leaves gliding in different directions and speeding towards the ground. His father's superstitious and family inherited beliefs, telling Marco.

"If you manage to catch a falling leaf you can make a wish, and maybe your wish will come true."

The vision of himself running under the Maples trees trying to catch a drifting tumbling leaf. His wish clear again in his mind.

"I wish I could speak fluent English."

The sudden zephyr from seemingly nowhere, Marco seeing it was created by Epoh camouflaged presence energising force to make a mass of leaves float past Marco like plummeting stones, causing him to turn and face this strange unexpected phenome. Witnessing his great surprise as what he thought a heavenly breeze detaching a multitude of differential foliage from different trees, all gliding at a deviating pace and height towards him. The relived image of him ceasing his chance to grasp a leaf. Watching again the unpredicted swarm of leaves whiz, twirl, fly, spin, and float past him. Along with the poignant memory of his right hand clasping a small Maple leaf. The reminiscing visions, smell and sensations feeling and seeing the air mild and still, and him taking off his shoes and socks, rolling up the bottom off his jeans and promenading across the sands. His powerful sensation as though it was real and his feet were squishing into the sodden earthen, bequeathing him with a strange sentiment once again. Then seeing himself approach the oceans tide line, the seas ebb quite some distance from the main shores. The wild blue yonder metamorphosed into a sumptuous azure, without a cloud or star in the sky, not even the North Stellar visible, only the waxing beginning of a new moon in the far radius. Visioning himself and Pasta alone with no other soul to be seen or heard for what seemed miles around and the past images of the distanced street, shops and house lights of his town illuminated. The reassuring sentiment that he hadn't wandered too far floating back into his emotions. Then the calm waves washing gently over his feet. The ice cold sensation and warmer sensation, like his body heat adapting to the changing atmospheric temperature. Pasta splashing through the water, like a happy child on a summer's beach. And the mass of migrating geese breaking the oceans harmonious melody, chattering with their loud honking like nagging old men and ladies. His wondering thoughts also present.

"Where were they heading?"

"Which lands and cultures would they cross throughout their journey?"

"What would the see?"

"Would all of them make it?"

And his questioning daydreaming thoughts distracted by the large piece of drifting wood now seeing it was placed there to entice Marco by Epoh and Ecaep. The driftwood drawing nearer in his memories along with the ebbs, repeating teasing gesture toing and froing the wood back and forth. The image of him holding the driftwood in his hands, having lost his patients and waded further into the sea to grab it. Then the flashing vision of a scintillating light in the far distance. And his words.

"Tesoro." (Treasure).

His heart racing twice as fast, from his burst of adrenalin. The vision of him and Pasta running towards the glittering unknown object. The vastness coming back to him and the sight of earth's brightest star having earlier dusked. Along with the accumulation of rumbling clouds, uprising in the atmosphere, forming an image of a mountainous panorama. The flashes of the magnitude of manifesting nebulosi's rising from the ocean rather than forming in the earth's atmosphere. And the remembrance of the enormous spherical object, resembling a giant boulder, only a few feet away from the tides line. The flashback of his powerful flashlight against the round object and his excited words.

"Moeraki Massi." (Moeraki Boulders). Along with his past curious thoughts.

"The unusual large mudstone spherical boulders, found between Moeraki and Hampden in New Zealand."

"How in God's name had one of them arrived on the north English coast?"

His befuddled expression. Epoh's showing Marco the clouds having magnitude resembling a frothing gigantic monster from another world, with the immense flashes of light, illuminating the obscurity of the hours of darkness. Marco now seeing what had really caused the storm. Epoh and Ecaep energizing force spiralling their joint arms and fingers together.

Marco also seeing the powerful flash, causing Pasta to look at him as if to say.

"Oh, can't you see there's a storm brewing let's get out of here."

And then another almighty shimmer, followed by the horrifying rumbling and the powerful gigantic cracking of thunder. And the memory of his intrigued thoughts seeing the glittering light at the bottom of the strange sphere-shaped boulder, the object twinkling again in the lightening's flash backs of his mind. He saw himself grasping the curious oval shaped mineral raising it to his eyes. Its magnificent olive green, extremely smooth to touch pebble form, penetrating once again his emotions, along with its peculiar hieroglyphics in a sublime sapphire tint encapsulated within the stone. His past and present memory now knowing what it was. The miniature brain microchip. The visible smaller decagon shape with the miniature brain characteristic that was shortly to be embedded into him. Seeing his captivated curiosity once again. Epoh showing Marco what caused the gigantic mass of Undulatus Asperatus clouds having moulded above him, hoovering like a menacing presence with the multitudes of lightning flashes fulgurated from all around him, causing the electrical shimmering's to expulse from the encapsulated cerebrum. He saw himself placing the stone object in his left jean pocket, stuffing his socks into his right jean pocket, and swiftly going to place his sneakers over his bare feet. The memory of the Undulatus Asperatus clouds, and a Fallstreak Hole, having mystifyingly appeared directly over where Marco had stood. It was a wormhole activated by Epoh and Ecaep. Epoh showing Marco how they arrived near him, seeing his panicking stumble having tried to place his sneakers on. And the vison of him laid upon the dewy sand, staring up at the petrifying yet majestic sight. Marco relieving the vison of the Fallstreak Hole widening, revealing the celestial sphere and the multitude of stars glittering their supreme galactic aura, as though another world was levitating above him. It was another universe the other side of the wormhole he had seen. He felt again the warm sensation from his left pocket, and saw himself reaching his left hand to pull out his weird and wonderful discovered object. Sensing his touch coming into contact with the smooth rock like substance. And then seeing the sudden single bolt of lightning propelled by Ecaep and Epoh, united energy. Striking him at his forehead. Epoh now showing Marco what happened next. The vision of his arms flopped to his side in a motionless state. When he thought darkness and silence were now his world. Epoh and Ecaep. Placing the stone over Marco's left ear, within earth's seconds the miniature brain having travelled through his earlobe and connected into his corpus callosum (centre of the brain), its alien technology connecting into every part of Marco's human brain. His entorhinal cortex, amygdala, hypothalamus, lateral orbitofrontal, olfactory bulb, dorsolateral prefrontal, frontal lobe, anterior cingulate, motor sensory. His parietal, occipital and temporal lobes, his cerebellum, hippocampus and brain stem all intermingling with his genetic molecules. Marco seeing Epoh and Ecaep carry his body with their gravitating force over to the Moeraki Boulder. With a strange input from Ecaep fourteen fingers the boulder opening and revealing its hollow capsule. Marco placed inside the life support capsule as the tide was too far for his body to survive the rapidly rising waters and his intellect having not yet bumped another. The capsule hidden under the sea's waters, carrying Marco back to the shore so he didn't drown. Its molecules then liquidating deep into the seabed like sand, waiting to be activated again when needed. Marco seeing how he'd been saved by the young couple. And shown the reasons why Epoh and Ecaep having chosen that moment. Their near proximity to Marco having intercepted his wish. His kind and caring aura and his profound love for his mother and nature, having taken no further hesitation that their highly developed experimental alien technology should be placed into Marco's brain and not another human who could use the advanced technology and unlimited data powers to harm others. His isolation from other civilisation as he'd ventured far out onto the see's bed alone and the presence of the energised storm assuring no other human risking to walk so far out to on the tide like Marco, making it the perfect opportunity and destined moment for Epoh and Ecaep to act upon, without further haste. A perfect chance an idealistic subject for them to test their new experimental microchip brain. Marco also being shown the reason for his four months comatose sleep. Caused due to the rapid time Epoh and Ecaep having travelled back to their planet. Marco also being shown what when wrong. Epoh retracting her tentacle needle from his brain stem and bringing Marco back from his reminiscing memories with now nearly all the blanks having been filled in.

"So, your trip back took four months of earth time?" said Marco.

"Yes. Even though that is faster than we have done before. Sometimes earthlings have stayed in comas for many of planet Earth's years. We saw the sadness and distress that is brought upon their loved ones, so we modernised arc quantum wormhole. Placing mechanism on and around different planets. The mechanism you found is one of seven positioned in hidden locations on earth. We knew human technology and intellect would never be able to find them recuperated them or even activate them. But your intellect is not human," said Epoh.

"And normally these miniature brains microchip implants are not detected by human technology?" said Marco.

"No, we had an interference slowing us down only a split second as earthlings would say, of your time. But this split second of 'Sraey' which registers our time. Was enough for your brain readings from human equipment to be detected and alert human suspicion." said Ecaep.

"What went wrong?" said Marco.

"You have an association on Earth called NASA with some of the greatest minds on your planet working for them. We've been monitoring their advancements and progress for quite some time. In planet Earth's year 2009 NASA Launched a spacecraft, they named Kepler. Designed to survey a portion of our Milky Way and search Earth-size exoplanets orbiting around other stars. Something we did a long, long time ago. But this progress of your human technology can also detect Stellar, Flares star spots and dusty planetary rings. These are our galaxies natural phenomena. But when we open the quantum wormholes, we harness the energy of the nearest star. Using such Stella energy has never been a problem as there are hundreds of thousands of millions of stars in the different universes. Even ourselves have not been able to calculate how many. NASA's craft, Kepler, has travelled father then we expected. We open wormholes in galaxies normally too far for your technology to detect. But Kepler can. Having already detected certain of our friendly planets millions of light years from planet Earth. Earthlings not having the capability to travel too. For now. Even though this was something new to earthlings, the physics of planetary formation mass governed by hydrostatic equilibrium is round. A wormhole curves and bends. And these unnatural irregular shapes, aperiodic dips and fluxes would have been detected by Kepler's instrumental readings, sending the signal of artificial intelligence phenomenon back to earth. The other thing we have had to avoid is colliding with Earth sent crafts. When we travelled back to Htraenus after having implanted your micro brain chip. The space craft Kepler was in a close proximity to detect our presence, so we deviated at the last moment to another universe and then back to

Htraenus. Earthlings are not ready to except another intelligence. They must focus on their own species and your gifted planet. Throughout mankind and planets earth's history you have been plagued with wars. You're desire to not only rule your surroundings but other humans, other civilisations and other planets. Revealing our presence to you we must not do. Not yet. You are simply not ready. By the time we'd deviated and back, your extra ordinary brain activity had been noticed. We wanted to intervene but watching this new experimental miniature microchip brain technology, Bump, so many intellects animals and insects was so fascinating and exciting for us all. Until you absorbed the element eighty-five. The Astatine which we stored into sphere shapes; we call 'Ygrene' are our reserve power. A backup system if you like, as stars are sometimes too far away from earths axe to harness their energy. We located the mechanisms and our reserved Ygrene power sources in different areas upon earth, where we calculated humans could never access. The Ygrene spheres always placed within the energetic tubes, preventing any of earths Fauna to access or be harmed. A human arm would have been too short to ever reach the Ygrene. But the seismic quakes around earth causing three of the spherical Ygrene energy pellets to surface. The three you swallowed. When your blood containing the Ygrene's power source activated the mechanism we knew we had to intervene quickly. The only way to limit our chances of being detected was to wait for all of you to be grouped together like you was in the laboratory. Many humans are selfish and keep their findings to themselves until they can draw some sort of earthly financial profit. We knew the mechanism would be hidden from the outside world under one place, allowing us to recuperate the mechanism, bring your body back to Htraenus and erase the memories of all who'd witnessed our advanced technology and presence," said Epoh, seemingly finished with her explanations. Epoh and Ecaep not telling Marco that Hausbeck had got away.

"My wis,." said Marco, in a soft whisper.

"We find this a fascinating culture that earthlings have to wish. For we see you need not to wish, you have the genetic blueprints to do so much good for your planet and your species. But also, so much bad. You are capable of so much hate. But also, so much love," said Ecaep.

You are the perfect example of this love," said Epoh.

263

Marco looking at her curiously, having not understood her point of view.

"For there is no greater action and love than the willingness to lay down your own life for another. That is true love," said Epoh.

"Many upon your planet have done this, but sadly, mainly due to war, such as the millions sacrificed in World War Two. There is so much suffering and hate on your unique planet. The saddest this is that all of your species are capable of this love. We Ynomrah's and our neighbouring planets other species. Do not have this love, which captivates us all. But we do not have your hate either," said Ecaep.

"My wish," mumbled Marco again. Adding in a stronger voice, whilst staring at Epoh and Ecaep, levitating side by side.

"I have another wish now."

"What is your wish, Marco?" said Epoh.

"I wish to go home. Be with Mama and Rebecca," said Marco.

"But you will die, Marco," said Epoh.

"When your body leaves this special chamber which has slowed down your solidification of your human anatomy and blood. Earth's atmosphere will reactivate the process and you will only have a little of earth's time to stay alive. That is why we brought you back to our planet Htraenus. This room, like Earths hospital life support units is the only thing that can heal you and save you. Not even the capsules disguised as boulders upon earth have this healing technology. The strange ripples you see in the walls ceiling and floor are ultra-high energy electromagnetic waves travelling through your body like infrared terahertz, healing your damaged cells and Organs. On Earth you were in a coma, here you are standing and talking. You are also the first ever human to enter Htraenus," said Ecaep.

"But here I am an alien," said Marco.

Epoh and Ecaep. Looking at each other realising Marco was right.

"You said Ynomrah's and our neighbouring planets other species. Do not have love?" said Marco.

"Yes, it is true, we do not feel love like humans. Maybe when our brain capacity is operating at one hundred percent we will feel what you feel. And understand why earthlings are like the way they are," said Epoh.

"There is a quicker way to understand a human's love," said Marco.

"What do you mean?" said Ecaep.

"Take me home back to Rebecca and Mama, and you will see our love," said Marco.

"But you will die," said Epoh, her eyes turning downwards again, expressing her deep sadness.

"My father who gave me all his love until his life was taken told me many times."

"Death may be the greatest of all human blessings," said Marco.

Epoh and Ecaep talking to each other in their alien tongue, Marco not understanding their words. His memory going back to this very sentiment of not being able to understand another species, having sparked his wishful desire to speak fluent English, get a better job and uphold his father's request.

"Proteggere sempre tua madre." (Always protect your mother).

"We cannot take you to see Rebecca…" said Epoh. Her words abruptly interrupted by Marco.

"Why not?"

"Are you going to keep me locked here like a prisoner?"

"If you let me finish," said Epoh, her eyes opened to their widest capacity, as though she'd been shocked by Marco's outburst.

"Yes, sorry," said Marco.

"We cannot take you to see Rebecca, because the radiation seeping from your body will damage her human foetus," said Epoh.

"Rebecca's pregnant?" said Marco looking excited and sad. Whispering.

"Who's the father?"

"You are, Marco," said Ecaep. Marco's memory flashing back to the moment he'd slipped his hand inside Rebecca's, bumping her intellect. Learning, he'd made a very special night with memories that stay forever. That he'd made her feel special, and that she'd fallen in love with him long before he spoke English or obtained his otherworldly powers. Just simply when he was Marco. And that he'd fallen in love with her. The tender vision of their love making without protection plugging back into his mind.

"I'm going to be a father," said Marco.

"Yes but you will not see you son grow," said Ecaep.

"It's a boy?" said Marco, seemingly ignoring the part about he wouldn't see his child grow.

"By the time we have healed you. Your son will be old or deceased. Things are different on Earth," said Ecaep.

Marco standing in silence, deep in his thoughts.

"Mama is going to be a grandma," said Marco.

"Yes, it is a human custom to give yourself such names, father, mother, uncle, aunts, grandfather, grandmother and so forth," said Ecaep.

"You Ynomrah's don't have this custom?" said Marco.

"No. We are all equals," said Epoh.

Marco going back deep into his thoughts again.

"You said you surveyed earthlings with vessels before?" said Marco.

"Yes, we sometimes still do. For wormholes can transport our beings undetected, but it's more difficult to transport large giant vessels and apparatus undetectably," said Ecaep.

"Can you take me nearer to Rebecca, so at least I can see her and my unborn son?" said Marco.

"As you wish," said Epoh, rapidly, as though having understood Marco's deep thoughts. Ecaep, activating the mechanism and Epoh and Ecaep circling their arms once again around Marco. Marco Placed once again in the centre of their orbicular formation. Within what seemed like earths seconds, his body transported to another place. Marco standing in what seemed like a spherical giant alabaster room, like he'd been tele-transported inside of a gigantic golf ball made up of triangular formations all symmetrically joined together. Epoh and Ecaep brushing their fingertips over an array of different hieroglyphics symbols. Activating a mass of triangular forms to telescope towards them, seconds later an image began to clearly appear. Like a video projected image onto a screen. Rebecca, laid on her bed stroking her enormous round belly, her tender right hand slowly caressing her bare stomach, stopping at certain points, causing her to smile. It was the baby acknowledging her caress and presence, her dark hair a little longer, shining with good health and nutrients, her skin bestowing her with a radiant aura, her eyes smiling, but a tear trickling down her left cheek. In her left hand, a photo of Marco. Her words joyful but painful at the same time.

"Your daddy was a lovely man. A handsome man. A good man. He would have loved you as much as Mummy, and certainly spoiled you far too much. I know he's never far because he's always in my heart and I know he'll always look down on us both and protect us," said Rebecca. Marco watching, like some sort of guardian angel possessed with the angelic powers to peer down at their loved ones and be there in a harmonious silence. Rebecca with an affectional kiss upon his photo, before placing it near her heart, her appeased body drifting into a blissful sleep, her hands poised on her stomach and Marco's photo. His unborn sons manifesting bumps, pushing out of his Rebecca's belly, easing too, as though mother and child having joined together in their dreaming world. There where Marco was always present.

"Have I been away so long?" said Marco, wiping his tears.

"Htraenus measure of time is different from Earth," said Ecaep, with no emotion. Marco beginning to cough. Epoh and Ecaep, looking at each other, their different shaped eyes both expressing the same deep concern.

"We don't have much time Marco," said Epoh.

"Yes, I know," said Marco, wheezing. Ecaep as though in a frenzy drifting his fingertips over more hieroglyphics symbols, before he and Epoh encircling Marco yet again. Marco's wheezing intensifying.

CHAPTER TWENTY THREE

MARCO'S AND ANNA'S LOVE

"I know that smell." said Marco in between his wheezing. The mouth-watering smell of his mother's fresh baked bread, absorbing into Marco's lungs. Overpowering his ill health symptoms and transporting his mind back in time, when he was a small boy back home in the South of Italy. The sound of a scooter's engine racketing through the nearby streets before fading in the distance, the distant chattering of women sat in the town's piazza, huddled together talking about all and nothing, along with the manifesting groans of men losing their card games. Marco standing on his mother's balcony outstretching the miniature forest land, where he used to play when he was a small boy. In the corner his father's old pottery filled with the lemon tree they'd planted together. The old wicker chair that his grandfather used to sit and watch the world go by whilst absorbing the succulent odours from the neighbouring kitchen waiting to be called to the table, by Marco's grandmother now poised empty and bare. Marco slowly steeping into the hall alone, Epoh and Ecaep nowhere to be seen. His mother, Anna, preparing more bread, to bring to the church and share with those less fortunate. The old TV set poised in the far corner Anna half watching the diffusing evening film, whilst kneading her dough. Her motherly sixth sense abruptly stopping her physical actions. A strange premonition telling her to turn around. Anna slowly spiralling her body in the opposite direction. Her recompense, both frightful and joyful. Marco standing only feet away from her, bent slightly forward like he was suffering from stomach cramp.

"Marco, Mia amore!" shouted Anna running to embrace her son, kissing him all over his face like a mother welcoming home her son after many years away.

"I know you not dead. I know because mother know all. And I know because your magic stone. It changed colour like a rainbow. Sometimes slowly, but sometimes it changed like Christmas lights, one colour after another. I know you just go somewhere to hide and come back to Mama. Mia amore. I miss you so much," said Anna, fighting her tears and holding her son in her arms. Marco falling into his mother's embrace, his force rapidly leaving his body. Anna crumpling onto the floor with the weight of her son. Marco laid across her thighs, looking up at her and smiling. Anna staring down at her son, her tears dripping none stop, her right arm supporting his back, her left hand caressing her sons beautiful face.

"What is wrong, Marco?"

"Tell Mama what she can do," said Anna.

"You're going to be a grandmother," whispered Marco, smiling.

"I know. Rebecca has come to live here Marco, she wants your son to be near where you were when you were a baby," said Anna, wiping her tears and then Marco's tears.

"I am going to be a dad," said Marco softly, his wheezing breathing intensifying.

"Si Mia amore," said Anna.

"Teach my son to speak English, Mama," mumbled Marco.

"Promessa." (Promise).

"We teach together," said Anna, gazing at her dying son at the same time feeling another strange presence.

"Don't take him from me. He have so much to live for," said Anna, staring directly towards her as though looking at the grim reaper coming to take Marco. Her eyes adjusting to the clearing vision coming more and more into focus. Anna feeling no fear looking at Marco then at the otherworldly presence towering before her.

"Save my son. Take me to where you want go. But don't let him die."

Epoh and Ecaep gawping at each other. Their ninety-three percent of alien intelligence seeing and trying to understand the sacred love and sacrifice of one human being having for another. One of the greatest loves in the universe. That of a mother and her child.

"We cannot save him."

"His wish was to be with you," said Epoh.

"Mia amore perché?" (Why), sobbed Anna.

"Perchè ti amo, Mama." (Because I love you, Mama), whispered Marco. His bodily functions rapidly weakening.

"We are sorry Anna, or intention was never to harm anybody. We wanted to understand your species to help you, help each other." said Epoh.

"We must take Marco away from you. His body is sick and your own body is at risk of becoming harmed," said Ecaep.

"There is no risk, if my son dies. Then he dies in my arms." said Anna.

"We implanted something inside your son, we must take it from him before his human body deceases or all the data will be lost," said Epoh.

"It is a thing that makes Marco's finger feel a strange sensation when he puts his hand into another. And why he learned so much about other men and women?"

"It is thing that make this stone change like rainbow?" said Anna, holding out Marco's strange pebble towards them. An object she'd constantly carried in her pocket since Marco's fictional death.

"Yes. It changes colour when Marco's mind bumped and absorbed information from another being. The times its pigment transformed so much in such a little space of Earth's time. Is when Marco received a numerous influx of data within short periods of time. (Thirty three top world scientists and other)," said Ecaep. His alien emotion explaining technical information Anna was not concerned with.

"And it still works?" said Anna, unconcerned about whom Marco had bumped intellectual, reminiscing data from.

"We only have a little of your Earth's time," said Ecaep.

Anna understanding Marco was going to die. Her left hand softly caressing his angelic face with all her love once again, then gently sliding her left palm into Marco's right hand. Marco sensing the strange tingling from his toes to his fingertips, conglomerating at his phalange. And the peculiar humming in his auricles like a faint whale's cry. Thirty seconds later his lifeless arm slipping from his mother's grip. Epoh, placing the alien pebble over Marco's earlobe, the stone shape object perfectly moulding around his external ear. A few Earth seconds later, Epoh extraditing the alien object from Marco's lobe. In the smaller decagon shape a miniature brain characteristic embedded.

Diminutive electrical discharges, like fulgurations surging from it. The alien objects colour metamorphosing back to its olive green pigment.

Marco's head slumping without life to its right side. His last bumped memories were that of his mother's and father's love and how they'd wished simplistic things for him. That he should be constantly happy and in good health. Marry and have children. Do the things he wished to do and not what others forced him to do. Live his life peacefully without hate or selfishness, surrounded by love and harmony. Marco's last visions before his human body and mind deceased, was his magnificent few days with his mother and Rebecca after having come home from hospital. Followed by that of Rebecca rubbing her belly and talking about him to their son. And finally by the touching image of him taking his first steps. His mother's and father's arms outstretched before him, encouraging him to walk towards them. Their faces overwhelmed with, pride, joy, love and happiness. This poignant image bestowing Marco's face with an ultimate radiant smile. Anna sobbing from her soul, holding her dead son in her arms, Epoh's alien arms wrapped around her in a human comforting manner and for the first time causing a tear to spill from her eyes. Epoh and Ecaep never having witnessed the force of human love and forgiveness.

"We know it is your custom to bury your dead in a place where you can visit and remember them. We can help you to do that," said Ecaep. Anna wiping her sob and nodding in agreement. Moments later Anna, Epoh and Ecaep standing over the spot Marco was supposed to be buried, with a simple gesture from Ecaep's hands, a block of solid earth the shape and form of the earth piled over Marco's coffin. Rising like a solid piece of block, followed seconds after by Marco's coffin hovering from the hole in the earth. The sandbags having replaced Marco's weight by Hausbeck sent into a wormhole and dispersed into the ocean at the very spot Marco having discovered the pebble. Marco's peaceful body levitated into the coffin.

"Wait," said Anna.

Epoh and Ecaep, eyes expressing incomprehension. Anna unclipping Marco's 'Cornicello' necklace and pendant from her around her neck placing the twisted horn-shaped charm, an amulet of good luck used for protection against the evil-eye curse, around Marco's neck.

"Mamma come soon."

"Buonanotte mia amore." (Good night my love), whispered Anna kissing her son on his forehead, there where he'd been struck by the lightning bolt. Ecaep going to close the coffin's lid.

"Wait," said Epoh.

Placing a small, dried maple leave upon Marco's chest. She'd found Marco's superstitious desire so powerful. She'd captured a leaf having caused the zephyr wind to manifest so many dried Earth's foliage that autumn evening.

"My wish is that all mankind become like you and Marco. Full of love, peace and forgiveness," said Epoh, in a soft loving whisper. Anna half-heartedly smiling at the alien form. An extra-terrestrial being, with so much intelligence but still so much yet to learn. In hindsight there wasn't that much difference between an alien's mind and that of a human. All searching for knowledge and wisdom. But few understanding one another.

"Your son chose to be with you."

"Chose death over life, to be able to hold you one last time in his arms."

"If we can harness this love and bump it into the minds of all mankind. Your Earth would be free from war. Free from suffering and hate," said Epoh.

"We are already free. It is just a human's choice to love or hate another," said Anna.

Epoh and Ecaep, just like humanity, trying to understand.

"Why mankind would choose, hate and war?"

"When they had the choice of love and peace?"

Epoh and Ecaeps are still asking themselves this very question five of Earth's years later.

CHAPTER TWENTY FOUR

FIVE YEARS LATER

Certain of the planet Earth's wars and conflicts having ended, others having begun. Some of humanity's population, still doing all in their physical and mental power to protect their planet. Others to destroy it. The Ynomrah intellectual capacity now at ninety-five percent. Marco's miniature brain microchips data, having advanced their findings about humankind leaps and bounds.

Five years having passed.

Anna sat on her father's old wicker chair a woollen shawl she'd made herself when she was first married wrapped around her shoulders. Her hair thinned and her face weak from illness. The beauteous garden staring back at her on a magnificent autumn day. Arnaldo's and Marco preferred season. A festival of contrasting glorious colours, harmonization displaying one more time the eternal repetition of Mother Earth's force. Mother Nature and Father Time, once again in a perfect balance, resting together like a midsummer siesta, recuperating some much needed force and energies before the harsh winter months and the challenging springs workload. Marco Soffione junior, giggling with glee as he ran through the masses of tumbled foliage, trying with all his might to catch the falling leaves. Rebecca by Anna's side. Anna letting out a last sigh and mumbling the words.

"Sapevo che stavi aspettando per me." (I knew you were waiting for me).

Her eyes and mouth having smiled with peace. Rebecca having understood every word. She'd learnt Italian and Marco Soffione junior English too. Anna having lasted just over five years, her body contaminated by the radioactivity from the astatine waves seeping out from Marco's body. Epoh and Ecaep having warned her. But nothing would have stopped her from holding her son one last time. Her sacrifice was total. Anna buried next to Marco and Arnaldo. When the ceremony was over, Marco junior having turned to his mother and said, "Is Nana with Papa and Grandpapa now?" said Marco junior.

"Yes. But they'll always be right here and here," said Rebecca pointing to her son's heart and the centre of his forehead. Marco junior laying his wreath of flowers.

"Look, Mama," said Marco junior holding in his tiny palm, a magnificent smooth olive green pebble with a smaller hollow decagon shape in the centre, found placed near Anna's tomb stone. As Rebecca was staring at its outstanding beauty. A rainbow appearing, as if from nowhere, its colours so vivid and intense, as though another worldly force having knocked over a tin of the universes aura and spilt it into the earths celestial sphere. Rebecca's motherly sixth sense telling her, that she and her son would always be safe. Marco Soffione junior running back to the house to place his 'Tesoro' (Treasure), in his secret old wooden chest, filled with pictures and objects of his father. A wobbly old Pasta trying to keep up with his youthful sprinting energy.

Nurse Brian had made it all the way to Broadway, his acting skills having landed him a roll in a new Shakespeare film, Romeo and Juliet. And his fame helping gay rights all over the world.

Bill now married with two twin boys. Having left the printers' firm and becoming a social worker. Working alongside deprived and depraved families, especially children suffering from racial abuse and bullying.

Dr Denise Dent having sold her dental practice and travelled the world. Stopping in India to help the poor and destitute.

Dr Cloud still working as a neurosurgeon only in London. He'd become the chief of the HGP (Human Genome Project), one of his team's breakthroughs was to discover genetic illness before they became too harmful for patients.

Dr Rama having left the hospital, shortly after Marco's and Dr White's tragic accidents. Having entered Syria. Helping the tyrannised children and victims of war.

Rocco de Montagna. Donating all his fortune to diverse charitable organisations around the globe. His sanctified gestures having permitted him to meet the pope. The pope having asked what his former profession had been. Rocco having answered, "I touched people."

"Much like faith."

Luckily one of the Pope's council of cardinals having whispered in his ear, Rocco's true profession. The pope stared at Rocco from tip to toe and simply said, "God bless you, my child."

At the same gesturing the shape of a cross sign upon his body with his right hand.

Mirnyy. Playing with her four cups. She'd never lost hope and found them deep inside the Antarctic Circle a whole year after having saved Marco.

Zhizin and his sister, Voraste, still peacefully travelling undetected across the Antarctic Plains, with their herd of reindeer. Alone with the surrounding fauna and mysteries. Their harmonious simple life far from mankind's hate and conflict. The nightly display of the resplendent celestial Aurora Borealis, a constant reminder that they were not alone.

The thirty-three top world scientists, having united their intellect, force and discoveries, creating a world respected association named 'Thirty-three and you'. Their aim to help the planet. Diminish, global warming, droughts, water and food shortage, alternative safer energies, diseases, medicines, poverty, floods, earthquakes, child abuse, animal torture and slaughter, to name but a few. Within five years the planet Earth's universal helping minds, religions and world leaders. Authorities, governments, private enterprises as well as the everyday man and woman. Sharing their inventions and engineering technology advancements, hand in hand. Like a simple handshake.

Corporal Mears having left NASA and become a priest helping underprivileged children and adults in his old neighbourhood in Detroit.

And the Socotra beetle, still alive after five years. The oldest living beetle on Earth. Spending most of its time rapidly flying from place to place. Instead of sluggishly scuttling.

"Martin, your phone keeps ringing," said Liz trying to get herself ready for their evening invitation.

"Then answer it," said Hausbeck, looking for his cufflinks his voice raised and annoyed. Hausbecks phone ringing again.

"Hello," said Liz, having answered the phone.

"Hi Martin, long time no hear," said a quiet voice on the other end of the line.

"Wait, wait it's not Marty. It's his wife Liz. Who shall I say's calling?" said Liz in a jealous manner.

"Tell Martin it's Emma White on the phone," said Emma. A long silence prevailed.

"Emma. My God how are you? How are Katie and Wendy? And how is, Jonny boy?"

"It's been how long now?" said Hausbeck.

"Five years and four months," said Emma, adding. "The girls are fine, all grown up, with new boyfriends and a new iPhone on their minds," said Emma.

"How's Jonathan, Emma?" said Hausbeck after a long pause.

Emma sighing expiring all the air from her lungs. "We're switching the life support off. Jonathan wouldn't want this. He'd want his organs to go to another and help them enjoy the joys of life. I've discussed it with the girls and his family and we all agree," said Emma her voice, bursting with emotion.

"When?" said Hausbeck.

"In two days. Friday at ten a.m. time for everybody to arrive," said Emma.

"I'll be there tomorrow," said Hausbeck.

By the time he'd arrived from Cleveland at the New York Neuro Hope Clinic. All the others having already gathered. An array of reminiscent memories haunted Hausbeck as he made his way through the déjà vu corridors. Emma, welcoming him in a warm embrace.

"Thank you for coming, Martin," said Emma. Hausbeck only holding her, without replying. Quickly hugging her twin girls Katie and Wendy, followed by a formal warmly handshake with Dr White's parents, older sister and brother. Seconds after, Professor Cloud and Rama along with Nurse Wendy appearing. All having thinned and aged slightly but all having made every effort to be present.

"Good to see you, Martin. Heard you're a bureaucrat now, working in Stanford's old office. Also heard that you may soon be going to the Pentagon. What was it, heart attack?" said Professor Cloud.

"Yes, two years ago this November. He was sat on the Jon one minute. The next gone," said Hausbeck.

"So, what ever happened to those so called secret files, about proving we are not alone?"

"What was the organisation called O.W.I.Q or something of that sort," said Professor Cloud.

"It was shut down just after Stanford's death, apparently he'd been misusing certain of NASA's funds," said Hausbeck.

"And you, Professor Cloud, I heard, you moved to the great city of London working at the national hospital. Even a leading role figure in the HGP. (Human Genome Project)," said Hausbeck.

"Yes," said Professor Cloud, with no further explanations to his scientific research or findings.

"And you were in Syria Dr Rama?" said Hausbeck.

"Yes, that's correct. I will be based there for a good few years, God willing, even though the war is over," said Dr Rama.

"And you, Wendy?" said Hausbeck.

"I look after my grandson most days. Do some freelance nursing, but after what happened at the Royal Duchess Hospital, I couldn't stay in the profession any longer," said Nurse Wendy, her eyes gliding towards Cloud and Rama, as though to quickly cut the conversation short.

"I understand," said Hausbeck. An eerie silence entering the hospital corridor, broken by Emma.

"They're going to begin," said Emma before placing herself by her husband's left side holding his hand, her two girls behind her. Jonathan's parents, sister and brother stood to his right side. Hausbeck, Professor, Cloud, Rama and Nurse Wendy standing at the end of his bed, behind the priest reading Professor White his last rites. Two doctors and a nurse by the life support machine. One doctor staring at Emma. Emma acknowledging him with an assuring nod, as if to say, "Yes, we are ready."

Seconds after the diverse switches and cables upon the machine, attached to Professor White, disconnected and turned to off. The rapidly silencing pumping, beeping, monitoring and registering equipment distancing, like passing crowds from the room's atmosphere. An array of eyes fixed open Dr White, in wait for his last breath. But instead of his body slumbering into death, his pupils twitching, like irritated creatures trapped under his closed eyelids. Minutes later they were opened. Dr White's dry and croaky voice asking where he was. His wife Emma their girls and the entire family, even the priest overwhelmed with miraculous joy. No medical explanation to how he'd returned from darkness back to light. As the days followed Professor White's phenomenal healing, spreading throughout the hospital and the world. The local and international news, Headlines blurting.

'Doctor comes back from death coma after five years'.

Hausbeck deciding to stay over in New York a little longer than previously planned. On his last visit to his old friend and colleague, before heading back to Cleveland, Ohio. Hausbeck noticing Professor White's occipitofrontal cicatrices had completely vanished and his oculus dexter having changed into a cerulean pigment his oculus sinister an olive green, along with a silvery whiter streak appearing in his receding but growing back hair. Professor White warmly shaking the hand of his dear colleague Dr Rama, who was heading back to Syria.

"Still so much to do there. The war may have ended, but not the suffering," said Dr Rama.

"Come back and see us soon, please," said Professor White. Only in Dr Rama's native Andhra Pradesh tongue. Hausbecks mind instantly flashing back to the moment a single bolt having shot out from the MRI-A scanner having placed Professor White into his long coma.

It's mutated, cloned, Marco's brain activity transferred by the harnessing electrostatic discharge of a thunderbolt caused by the metal in Marco's cells, like a disease spreading, pathology. A mutational virus. Marco's DNA cerebrum cells, neurons genetic gene have absorbed into Professor Whites intellect.

Evolution!

But of course, said Hausbeck in his whispering mind. Two other thoughts joining his bestowed revelations.

One:

Socotra and the location of element eight-five.

Two:

The 4D image of the popup, he'd seen when the mechanism having been activated. And the location he'd remembered of the replica mechanism located in the Krubera Cave in Abkhazia Georgia.

Dr Rama, leaving. Hausbeck and Professor White alone. Their eyes meeting in a bizarre stance, as though each one was trying to read the mind of the other.

"Emma tells me you're leaving today, Martin," said Professor White.

"Yes. Liz gets jealous when I'm away too long," said Hausbeck, jokingly trying to break the tension in the air. Both men staring once again at each other, as though a mutual respect needed to be shown. But a profound mistrust overpowering their joint emotions.

"Good to see you safe and well again," said Hausbeck, adding, "Do you remember anything?"

"Only patches, a lot of blanks, but five years is a long time to miss. The others told me what happened and what happened to Marco. Terrible," said Professor White.

"Yes, it was terrible," said Hausbeck.

"Did you ever discover what was causing his brain activity to give out such extra-terrestrial readings?" said Professor White, staring deep into Hausbecks eyes, as though he was staring into his soul.

"No, unfortunately we didn't and now the O.W.I.Q project was shut down by NASA and Marco being buried in the south of Italy. We will never know, another one of life's unsolved mysteries," said Hausbeck, trying to keep his thoughts and secrets to himself, hoping Professor White's mind hadn't the power to read minds.

An awkward silence entering the room once again, Hausbeck thinking about the element eighty-five and the second mechanism he knew was located in Krubera Cave in Abkhazia Georgia. His intelligence already planning an expedition and thinking of a way how he could analyse the data in Professor Whites mind. So much to do and he had to be quick, smart and discreet, lucking discreetness something Hausbeck was an expert on.

"Well, Jonny boy, like I said, it's great to see you back from the darkness, back in the light and back among the living. I better be going though don't want to miss my plane back to Cleveland, we could maybe catch up in a few days, maybe when you're back home?" said Hausbeck, getting ready to leave.

Professor White watching Hausbeck collect his briefcase and turning to exit his hospital room, speaking once again. "Well Marty boy, aren't you at least going to shake my hand before you leave?"